Praise for Anna
Moriarty Meets H

"Sherlock Holmes fans will find *Moriart*
well-done: true to the nature and characters of both men, but adding extra dimensions to Professor Moriarty's character that greatly enhance the entire Holmes scenario. Very highly recommended as a 'must' for Sherlock enthusiasts and anyone who relishes a good whodunit mystery." — D. Donovan, Senior Reviewer, Midwest Book Review

"Fans of both Sherlock Holmes and the man he dubbed the 'Napoleon of Crime' will absolutely love Castle's fidelity to the details and atmosphere of the canon, and newcomers who have never read Arthur Conan Doyle (or, for that matter, John Gardner's great Moriarty novels) will also find themselves eagerly reading along, thanks to Castle's great skill as a storyteller. Enthusiastically recommended." — Steve Donoghue, Historical Novel Society Reviews

Praise for *Moriarty Takes His Medicine*

"A captured wife, a clever and devious doctor, and women in disguise ... all the trappings of a Holmes case are embellished and enhanced throughout, contributing to a mystery whose tension is well-drawn and whose plot is satisfyingly unpredictable and complex... Especially recommended for fans of Sherlock Holmes, this addition to a growing series continues to add nuances and details that grow characters and present plots that are engaging, fun, and complex." — D. Donovan, Senior Reviewer, Midwest Book Review.

"The rollicking story is satisfyingly predictable, and this easy read entices us to pick up Book 1 and to also look forward to the next in the series." — Cindy Rinnamon-Marsh, Discovering Diamonds.

Praise for *Murder by Misrule*

Murder by Misrule was selected as one of Kirkus Review's Best Indie Books of 2014.

"Castle's characters brim with zest and real feeling... Though the plot keeps the pages turning, the characters, major and minor, and the well-wrought historical details will make readers want to linger in the 16th century. A laugh-out loud mystery that will delight fans of the genre." — Kirkus, starred review

"*Murder by Misrule* is a delightful debut with characters that leap off the page, especially the brilliant if unwilling detective Francis Bacon and his street smart man Tom Clarady. Elizabeth Tudor rules, but Anna Castle triumphs." — Karen Harper, NY Times best-selling author of *The Queen's Governess*

"Well-researched... *Murder by Misrule* is also enormously entertaining; a mystery shot through with a series of misadventures, misunderstandings, and mendacity worthy of a Shakespearian comedy." — M. Louisa Locke, author of the Victorian San Francisco Mystery Series

"Castle's period research is thorough but unobtrusive, and her delight in the clashing personalities of her crime-fighting duo is palpable: this is the winning fictional odd couple of the year, with Bacon's near-omniscience being effectively grounded by Clarady's street smarts. An extremely promising debut." — Steve Donoghue, Historical Novel Society

Praise for *Death by Disputation*

Death by Disputation won the 2015 Chaucer Awards First In Category Award for the Elizabethan/Tudor period.

"Accurate historical details, page turning plot, bodacious, lovable and believable characters, gorgeous depictions and bewitching use of language will transfer you through time and space back to Elizabethan England." — Edi's Book Lighthouse

"This second book in the Francis Bacon mystery series is as strong as the first. At times bawdy and rowdy, at times thought-provoking … Castle weaves religious-political intrigue, murder mystery, and Tom's colorful friendships and love life into a tightly-paced plot." — Amber Foxx, Indies Who Publish Everywhere

Praise for *The Widows Guild*

The Widows Guild was longlisted for the 2017 Historical Novel Society's Indie Award.

"As in Castle's earlier book, *Murder by Misrule*, she brings the Elizabethan world wonderfully to life, and if Francis Bacon himself seems a bit overshadowed at times, it's because the great, fun creation of the Widow's Guild itself easily steals the spotlight. Strongly Recommended." — Editor's Choice, Historical Novel Society.

Also by Anna Castle

The Francis Bacon Mystery Series

Murder by Misrule
Death by Disputation
The Widow's Guild
Publish and Perish

The Professor & Mrs. Moriarty Mystery Series

Moriarty Meets His Match
Moriarty Takes His Medicine
Moriarty Brings Down the House

The Lost Hat, Texas Mystery Series

Black & White & Dead All Over
Flash Memory

MORIARTY BRINGS DOWN THE HOUSE

A Professor & Mrs. Moriarty Mystery – Book 3

ANNA CASTLE

Moriarty Brings Down the House
A Professor & Mrs. Moriarty Mystery — #3

Print Edition | January 2018
Discover more works by Anna Castle at www.annacastle.com

Cover design by Jennifer Quinlan
Editorial services by Jennifer Quinlan, Historical Editorial
Chapter ornaments created by Alvaro_cabrera at Freepik.com.

ISBN-10: 1-945382-13-9
ISBN-13: 978-1-945382-13-0
LCCN: 2017919778
Produced in the United States of America

ONE

London, December, 1886

James Moriarty peered through his drawing room window at the man emerging from the coach in front of his stoop. "A gentleman, by his choice of vehicle and outer garments. With a taste for dramatic effects. Who else would wear a cloak in the middle of the afternoon? A shade over sixty, by the silver in his moustache, and a lover of the creature comforts, by the circumference of his waistcoat." He turned to render his judgment. "One of your theater friends, my dear. But a manager rather than an actor. He's the very model of an impresario in a *Punch* cartoon."

Angelina treated his exercise in deduction to a tolerant smile. "That would be more impressive, darling, if you hadn't met the man at a party two weeks ago."

"Did I? Well, I don't remember, so it doesn't count."

"Then I read his letter requesting this appointment to you over breakfast yesterday."

Moriarty grunted. He did remember that. "It didn't mention his age."

She laughed, that musical trill that never failed to lift his heart and make him glad to be alive, with her. "How do I look?" She held out her hands to display a gown composed of lavender-striped silk with drapes in front and flounces aft. Her mahogany-colored hair was piled atop her head in a mound of artful curls.

"Lovely." He turned back to the window in time to see the front door close. He noted the coach bore the insignia of a hire company. Their visitor might not be as successful as the cape and ebony walking stick would imply.

"James, you barely even looked at me!"

"I don't need to, my dear. You're always lovely." He smiled at her with a suggestive twitch of the eyebrows, but voices on the stairs curtailed any further show of appreciation.

Their young footman opened the drawing room door, announced the visitor in his ineradicable Cockney accent, and returned to his post. The moment the door closed, Angelina flew toward her friend with a cry of joy, grasping his shoulders with both hands and planting a kiss on each cheek. "Lionel, *darling*! What a pleasure it is to welcome you into our home at last!"

He chuckled, shooting a wink at Moriarty. "I would have called on you sooner, my dear, but the press of business . . . you understand."

"It's been pressing you since we first met, though it doesn't seem to have made you any thinner." They both laughed, beaming at one another with genuine affection. This was a real friend, then, not one of the acquaintances she pretended to like so they would pretend to like her. Moriarty had trouble keeping the nuances of his wife's theatrical relationships straight.

Angelina released her friend's shoulders and grasped his arm with both hands. "You've met my wonderful husband, Professor James Moriarty. James, this is one of my oldest and dearest friends, Lionel Hatcliff."

Moriarty reached out to shake the man's hand. "Welcome to our home. I understand you need our help with a peculiar sort of problem. Won't you have a seat and tell us about it?" He ushered the guest to the seat of honor in the center of the half-circle facing the hearth. He and Angelina took their customary chairs on either side.

Angelina perched on the edge of her chair as if ready to spring right up again. "I've been positively on *tenterhooks*, Lionel, wondering what it's all about." Her amber eyes shone with excitement.

Ah. Now all the primping and eager pacing made sense. She was hoping her old friend, the impresario, had come to offer her a part in a play. She'd been edging her way back onto the stage, party by party, for the past year.

Moriarty had mixed feelings about it. They'd been married for a year and a half and had settled into a harmonious routine, spending most of their time together under the roof of their South Kensington home. They hadn't grown tired of one another — for his part, a sheer impossibility — but there had been signs of increasing restlessness on both sides. They needed new challenges. He just wasn't sure he was ready to share her with the rest of London.

Hatcliff smiled at her fondly, but then his expression sobered. "As a matter of fact, it's your husband I've come to see. I hear he has a knack for solving certain kinds of problems — the kind one can't bring to the authorities."

Angelina's bubbling excitement went flat, like a glass of stale champagne. But she mastered her disappointment with characteristic grace. "Well, you've come to the right place. My husband is an absolute *genius* at investigation. We'll do everything we can for you, won't we, James?"

"We'll certainly try," Moriarty said. "What is the nature of your problem, Mr. Hatcliff?"

Hatcliff sighed. "There's no way to tell it without sounding like a perfect fool. Either my theater is haunted by angry ghosts or someone's trying to drive me out!"

"Angry!" Angelina cried.

"Ghosts?" Moriarty raised a questioning brow at his wife.

"All theaters have ghosts," she explained. "Usually they just float across the gallery or flicker a few lights now and then. Nothing harmful. I've never heard of one being malicious."

"What's happening at the Galaxy goes far beyond the ordinary run," Hatcliff said. "Everyone believes the show is cursed."

"Oh dear. That is serious." Angelina turned to Moriarty. "When people lose faith in the production, everything starts to go sour."

"What sort of problems are we talking about?" Moriarty asked.

"It started last spring with things like spilled paint or a tool gone missing. Common enough accidents, but more than usual and always managing to cause a delay or extra expense. Traps failed to open, ropes broke. Props moved themselves overnight, forcing everyone to waste time searching for them. That went on right through the spring burlesques and the autumn melodrama, costing me a pretty penny, I don't mind saying."

"It sounds like a disgruntled employee," Moriarty said.

Hatcliff shook his head doubtfully. "I've always had a happy crew."

"Lionel is famous for his fairness," Angelina added. "He respects his people, and everyone knows it."

"You're too kind." The portly impresario smiled at her. "When we started working on the Christmas pantomime, things got worse. Then came the cold drafts and dancers' skirts being lifted on the stairs. Several hats for the men's chorus were crushed beyond repair and one of the dancers' costumes was shredded. Now people are hearing eerie voices in empty corridors and everyone's jumping out of their skin at the slightest bump."

"What play are you doing this year?" Angelina asked, as though that were the most important question.

"Jack and the Beanstalk," Hatcliff said. "With an exciting new script."

"Oh, I *adore* that story! Who's playing Jack?"

Hatcliff licked his lips again. "That's one of the problems."

"Let the man tell us in his own way, my dear," Moriarty said. "Apart from the drafts and the voices, it sounds like a malicious prankster to me."

"It's the malice that's troubling me," Hatcliff said. "Last week, someone added weights to the star trap, so the poor fairy flew up too fast and stumbled onto the stage. She wasn't badly hurt, but she was furious with the cellar men. They claimed innocence, and I believe them."

Angelina added for Moriarty's benefit, "The star trap is a mechanism for raising an actor up through the stage floor, sometimes very quickly, to surprise the audience. Demons, fairies, that sort of thing. Lots of fun for the audience and usually safe enough."

Moriarty nodded, imagining how such a thing must be constructed. "I presume the hats were spoiled and the trap altered after hours. Don't you have a night watchman?"

"Of course," Hatcliff said, "but he can't be everywhere at once. The Galaxy's a big place, Professor. I seat more than a thousand people."

"And the drafts and the voices must happen when people are there," Angelina said. "That must be maddening! Once people start thinking a show is cursed, things start falling apart on their own.

People get jumpy, bicker over nothing. Ill feelings suck the life out of every scene."

"I knew you'd understand," Hatcliff said. "It's not just the sour mood. Many of these pranks, if that's what they are, cost me money in properties, costumes, and lost time. After a year of it, I'm at the end of my rope. At this moment, I'm not sure how I'll scrape together this quarter's rent and it's due on the fifteenth."

"Surely old Pennyman will give you more time," Angelina said. "He knows pantos are expensive, but they pay the investment back tenfold."

"Pennyman sold the building in February. Now it belongs to one of those beastly faceless syndicates. Could be Chinamen, for all I know. I mail a cheque to a solicitor's office." Hatcliff frowned, drawing down the ends of his walrus moustache. "I used to call round to Pennyman's house every quarter for a cigar and a long chat. The world is changing, my dear friends, and not always for the better."

"Not always," Moriarty said, although his interest had been piqued. A tenfold return? He'd been looking for investments a little more exciting than the three percents. Perhaps he could please his wife and earn a few pounds in one stroke here.

"I managed to get a one-week reprieve," Hatcliff said, "but that's it. After a year of bad luck, my usual sources have dried up. I need a thousand pounds by the week before Christmas or my goose is cooked. I'll have to fold up my tents and retire to a cottage by the sea."

"Never!" Angelina scooted her chair forward to clasp both his hands. "We'll put a stop to this mischief, whoever or whatever is causing it." She let that promise sink in, then asked softly, "Who's playing Jack?"

Hatcliff nodded as if he'd expected the question. "Eleanor Verney."

Moriarty frowned. "Isn't Eleanor a girl's name?"

Angelina trilled a laugh, sitting back in her chair, letting Hatcliff explain. "The Principal Boy in a pantomime is always played by a woman." He shrugged his plump shoulders. "It's tradition; don't ask me why. Dame Trott, Jack's mother, is always played by a man." He smiled at the question on Angelina's face. "Timothy Tweedy."

"Oh my stars! I utterly *adore* him!"

"So does everyone else in England. I'm lucky to have him."

"Do they get on well, Mrs. Verney and Tim Tweedy?" Angelina's bland question carried a particular undertone. She was hoping for an answer in the negative.

"Better than you'd think," Hatcliff said, "but it's moot now. Nora sprained an ankle climbing up the beanstalk. She says a rung was greased, making her slip and fall about five feet. Naturally, everyone blames the ghost."

"Ouch!" Angelina said with a minimal effort at conviction. "You'll be needing another Jack, then. It'll be hard to find an actress with a ticket-selling name at this late date."

"Nearly impossible," Hatcliff said, grinning, "if I didn't have an old friend who once held every heart in London in the palm of her hand. And could again, if she were willing to sacrifice her life of leisure for four months of hard work."

Four months? For a *Christmas* play? Well, if women could play boys and men play mothers, Moriarty supposed Christmas might as well drag on through April.

"Whoever could you mean?" Angelina tittered. "Not — not *me*! Oh, you're too kind, Lionel. I would never *dream* of trying to fill Eleanor Verney's — Well, if you really are *that* desperate, I'd be the most ungrateful . . ."

The men waited patiently for her to work her way around to the inevitable *Yes.* Moriarty tuned out the subsequent animated discussion of the part, the script, and the other actors. He'd known since the words "Who's playing Jack?" had fallen from his wife's lips and lit that sparkle in her eyes that whatever was going on at the Galaxy Theater of Varieties had now become his problem.

TWO

"Are you really thinking about putting money into the show?" Angelina asked her husband's reflection in the mirror over her dressing table. He was combing the shrinking fringe of hair around the bald dome of his head. His slight frown might mean he was estimating the weekly hair loss or possibly calculating the compounding interest on a thousand pounds invested at various rates of return.

"If you want to play the Principal Boy, I'll at least have to pay that quarterly rent, but I want to learn more about theatrical investments before promising more." He switched to his small moustache comb, smoothing the brushy fringe above his lip and his short beard.

They had separate calls to pay this morning in pursuit of confirmation of Lionel's complaints, and each wanted to make a good impression. James preened as much as she did, though he would never admit it. For her part, she adored his little vanities. They leavened his intimidating brilliance, making him more human. Not reducing him or pulling him down, just bringing him into her realm a bit.

He cocked his head at her reflection. "Do you really want to play a boy? I thought you were looking for a grander role, where you stroll about in a gorgeous gown singing."

"There's lots of singing in a pantomime. And the costumes can be quite imaginative." Angelina tweaked the curls arranged across her forehead to make them slightly more natural. Then she stopped mid-tweak. "Haven't you ever seen one?"

He shrugged off the shock in her tone. "You forget that I grew up in a very small town with a very strict father. Vicar Moriarty would never allow such nonsense to be performed in his church. His idea of an appropriate Christmas treat for a growing boy was a brand-new copy of Sidgwick's *The Methods of Ethics*."

She shuddered in sympathy. Her father hadn't been a model of paternal love and kindness either, but at least she'd had London to grow up in. "Well then, you are in for a treat, my darling. Pantomimes are the funnest things in all the world." She poked through her jewelry box for a pair of diamond earrings, holding them up to see the effect.

"Diamonds, for lunch with a girlfriend?" James asked. "Isn't that a bit much?"

"This particular girl was my greatest rival back in the day. It was Adorable Nora at the Alhambra versus Lovely Lina at the Galaxy. You could stand in the middle of Leicester Square and hear us both belting it up to the gods." She chuckled at the memory, though she felt a tightness in the pit of her stomach. She hadn't sung any place bigger than a drawing room for two years. Did she still have what it took to fill a major West End theater?

"When are you meeting Sebastian?" she asked. James was having lunch with her younger brother, another successful actor. More successful than she was, truth be told, since he'd been rising steadily during her years of wandering abroad.

"Noon on the dot." James nodded at her reflection. "I know — he'll be late. But I can never predict how late, so it's simpler for me to be on time."

"I'm not sure how much he knows about theater finance."

"More than I do, and I can trust him to keep the Galaxy situation under his hat." James adjusted his tie. "Does this look all right?"

"It's perfect." It should be. She'd chosen his clothes herself this morning, as she always did when he ventured beyond the Royal Society of Badly Dressed Scientists.

"Will you have lunch with this girlhood rival of yours?"

"She won't offer. I'll skip lunch today and go straight to the Galaxy. I'll have to drop a few pounds to play a boy, I'm afraid. I've gotten a little hippy in recent years."

"I like your hips," James said firmly. His brown eyes darkened as he bent to reach for her waist.

She grabbed his hand to stop him disarranging her carefully draped lace cravat. "You'll get used to the new me soon enough."

She had more faith in his adaptability than in the kindness of London's critics. She could see the headline now on the reviews of her opening night: "Lina Lardington breaks the Beanstalk in her come-back — or should we say fall-down — performance!"

* * *

Eleanor Verney, known to most of the world as Adorable Nora, occupied the first-floor flat in a terrace on one of the less fashionable streets in Regent's Park. Angelina expected lots of pink and lace with wallpaper full of smirking cherubs, but the uniformed maid admitted her to a room more business than boudoir. The wallpaper was a sedate dark rose color that did wonders for a woman's complexion, and the adornments were quietly classical — short columns bearing shapely urns and chairs sturdy enough for substantial gentlemen. It smelled like jasmine with an undertone of cigar smoke.

Nora had dressed the part of the injured damsel. She lay frail and pale on a velvet chaise, her shoulders wrapped in a lacy bed jacket. A silk shawl failed to conceal the thick white bandage wrapping her slender ankle.

"Darling!" she cried as Angelina entered. "Do forgive me for not getting up."

"Nonsense." Angelina swooped down to plant a kiss two inches from the offered cheek. They batted their lashes at one another.

"Sit, sit, sit!" Nora waved at an upholstered stool near her feet.

Angelina spotted an empire chair and pulled it to a spot where Nora would have to turn her head to speak to her. "You look marvelous, darling, in spite of your *ghastly* disfigurement. It's as though time has stood still for you."

Nora's pert little nose wrinkled at the faux compliment. "Not for you though, has it? All those *marvelous* adventures and worldly experiences. It really shows!"

"There's nothing like a change of scene to keep a woman young." Angelina smiled. "That, and true love. Someday perhaps you'll be as lucky as I am."

"I *heard* you married last year. Who was it now . . . some sort of clerk, isn't he?"

Angelina trilled a laugh. "Darling! Where *do* you get your news? James was a mathematics professor. Absolutely brilliant and *very* famous on the Continent." She leaned forward and murmured, "And *so* clever with money. He gives me everything I want."

"And jots it all down in a neat little account book for you, I'm sure. Between you and me, I'm holding out for a title next time around." Nora had married a music hall owner years ago, before Angelina ran off to Italy. It had been something of a scandal at the time. She'd been barely seventeen and he'd been over fifty — an unsavory arrangement on both sides.

"What happened to old What's His Name?" And his two small but popular halls.

"He died. He wasn't young when I married him, if you recall." Nora's mouth pursed as if remembering a sour taste. "This time I want it all: looks, title, and money."

"Three things seldom found together in the English male. Besides, if you married a lord, you'd have to leave the theater. Lady Eleanor can't strut the boards every night."

"I've had enough of those creaky old boards to last a lifetime," Nora said. "I wanted to go out on a high note rather than like this" — she waved at her ankle — "but I'm taking it as a sign the time has come. I'm ready for a new act."

Angelina didn't believe it. The theater was all Nora knew. She'd been bred to it from childhood, just like Angelina and her younger siblings. What would she do with her time? How would she support herself? Unless she already had an heir waiting in the wings . . .

Nora flicked her fingers at the maid, who brought a silver tray with two glasses of pale sherry and a plate of ginger biscuits. Angelina sipped the drink but declined the sweets. Her hostess noticed, picked one up, and savored it as if it were the most delicious tidbit on earth.

"I can't believe you'd really quit," Angelina said. "You've been in the business as long as I have, almost."

"Longer. I didn't take ten years off to play the housewife on some dusty ranch."

"I was the lead soprano in the San Francisco Opera!" Angelina cried, genuinely insulted.

Nora lifted one languid shoulder, her eyes glittering at having struck her mark. "Some rustic village in Outer Colorado, I suppose. It can't compare to the London stage."

"What can?" Angelina sighed. "I miss it. Wouldn't you miss it? The lights! The costumes!"

"The freezing dressing rooms and the roasting stage."

"The exhilaration of playing a fabulous role!"

"The exhaustion of working on your feet for hours every night."

"The camaraderie among the actors on the stage!"

"And the backstabbing behind the curtain."

Angelina's tongue clicked. "The adoring fans! The applause!"

"Mmm . . ." Nora waggled her head from side to side. "No," she decided. "I can live without those too."

"I can't." They sipped their drinks in silence for a moment, each wrapped in her own memories of performances past. Then Angelina asked, "What's going on at the Galaxy, Nora? Do you really believe in those ghosts?"

"I'm sure there *are* ghosts," Nora answered. "There always are, though I've never heard of a spirit greasing a ladder. And there's been a lot of tension even without the accidents. Little spats sparking up between actors and among the crew."

"Because of the incidents?"

"There were bad feelings from the start. People not being helpful. That Tweedy, for one. He's nothing like as nice as you'd think from his act."

"I love him," Angelina said. "I always have. He was so kind to me once. I must have been about ten. My father had done something horrible — you know how he was."

Nora hummed. "I did feel sorry for you sometimes."

Angelina smiled at the honest confession. "I ran off and sneaked into a dressing room on the men's side and hid behind a big trunk. Tweedy came in and heard me snuffling there in the corner. He took me out and bought me a raspberry sherbet. He told me funny stories about some silly dog he once had and made me laugh till I snorted sherbet."

"What a charming tale," Nora said with that sour twist to her mouth. "You obviously don't know the man today. He's as greedy as they come, for money and the limelight."

"I'm sure we'll muddle along." Angelina suspected it was more the other way around, with Nora upstaging the other actors at every turn. "But what about poor Lionel? He seemed positively distraught yesterday."

Nora raised a single arched eyebrow in a calculating look, as if deciding whether to speak freely or not. "If you want the truth, I think old Hattie's behind the troubles himself."

"Impossible! He's the one suffering the most harm, or will be if the show fails."

"You don't know him anymore either, Lina. He's turned into *such* a martinet. Always grumbling about the cost of this and the price of that. He's an absolute *Scrooge*, strangling the production with his cheapness. The crew resents not having what they need to do their jobs, and frankly, we actors are frustrated by being unable to offer even the *tiniest* suggestions."

"Hmm. That does sound frustrating." Angelina nodded as if revising her opinions while weighing the words against Nora's reputation. She'd always been a fussy star, demanding extras like tips for her dresser and a coach to collect her on opening night. But if Hatcliff was so short of funds he had to scrimp on supplies, safety measures might well be thrown out the window.

Nora sniffed. "You've forgotten how hard it is. The long hours, the foul smells, the sheer, hard physical work. Jack climbs that beanstalk four times a night, you know, and it's every inch of twenty feet tall. You've been playing house with your maths professor for the past year. You must be horribly out of condition. If you want my advice, don't do it. Find another play."

Angelina bit her lip, wishing for the perfect retort. She had none. True, she'd been taking dancing and singing lessons for months now, but that was nothing compared to a Christmas pantomime. Six hours on opening night, with her onstage for most of them. "I'll be ready."

"You'd do better to cut your hair. It's easier to wear a long wig over a short cut than the other way around." Nora's forehead bore curls as tightly coiled as steel springs. They looked as if they'd been sewn on, which Angelina now realized they must have been. "Is your husband prepared for that?"

He was not. In fact, poor James hadn't the remotest idea how his life was about to change. Wigs were the least of it.

"And don't forget the pink tights," Nora said, "which is all you'll be wearing from the hips down. You're what now — about thirty-seven?"

"*Darling!* Barely twenty-eight." She'd turned thirty-one in October, but neither of them cared about the actual dates. They'd been eleven or thereabouts when they'd first met, both pretending to be older back then.

Nora smirked as her eyes flicked over Angelina's hips, which did rather fill the brocade seat. "You've been gone so long no one will remember you. You'll be a complete unknown jumping into the title role. There's already friction backstage."

"That doesn't worry me one bit," Angelina said truthfully. "I haven't been playing house for that long. I've sung on every stage in Europe. I've played New York, Philadelphia, and Chicago, as well as *Outer Colorado.* I've filled in for sopranos more beloved than the queen. I can get along with any cast on earth, and the crew always loves me."

Nora rolled her eyes, rounding her lips in a dramatic O. "I stand corrected, or I would if I could stand. You may think you're ready, but this is not a normal show. Somebody wants to put a stop to it. Before you take that first bow, you'd better watch your back."

THREE

The Garrick Club looked much like Moriarty's regular club — all polished woods and plush carpets — but it didn't sound the same. A roar of laughter startled him as he entered the foyer, earning a disdainful curl of the lip from the butler. One should expect a club catering to members of the theater world — actors, managers, and owners — to be livelier than the Pythagoras, his usual club — a place where mathematicians and other scientific gentlemen could find a quiet place to think.

"I'm meeting Sebastian Archer," Moriarty told the butler. "Though I believe I'm a trifle early."

The supercilious expression vanished, replaced by affability. "He won't keep you waiting long. Mr. Archer is always *so* considerate."

He ushered Moriarty to a small waiting room, where a couple of other gentlemen sat reading newspapers. He picked up a copy of *The Stage,* which appeared to be a journal wholly devoted to the theater business. Settling back in the leather armchair, he skimmed the pages, searching for financial matters. His attention was caught by a headline with the word "fire" in bold print. A medium-sized theater in Islington called the Laycock had burned to the ground over the weekend. No one was hurt, but the owners, a private investment house, lost six thousand pounds' worth of properties. Fortunately, they carried insurance and had already filed their claim.

Six thousand pounds! Could that be typical? It seemed a staggering sum for a splash of paint and a few yards of fancy stuff. Add that to an annual rent of four thousand pounds, plus the crew's wages and the actors' salaries, and this theater racket was a far richer business than Moriarty had imagined.

He had been keeping half an eye on the foyer, where well-dressed men came and went in a steady trickle. Now a palpable shift in the atmosphere attracted his attention to the man who had just entered: his brother-in-law, Sebastian Archer.

He didn't do anything unusual that Moriarty could detect, other than stroll with that extra touch of grace and greet people with that extra quality of focus that made you feel like the only person in the room. Sebastian's eyes followed the butler's gesturing hand. He waved at Moriarty, who put aside his paper and rose to go meet him.

"Good to see you, James," Sebastian said as they shook hands. "I'm glad for a chance to offer you lunch for a change, though the cooks at the Garrick can't compare with yours." He wore a dove gray suit and a dark blue tie, which highlighted his fair complexion and his bright blue eyes. His appearance was impeccable, as always, right down to the break in his trousers.

A burst of song in three-part harmony smothered Moriarty's conventional response.

Sebastian pretended to frown at the interruption. "What a frightful row these fellows make. Theater people! No sense of decorum. Are you sure you want to get involved with this tribe?"

"That is the question of the day."

They entered the bar for a short drink while waiting for their table. As they moved through the crowded room, Sebastian nodded at friends, spoke a word here and there, and paused once or twice to listen to something and laugh. Everyone he passed touched him in some small way: a pat on the shoulder, a grip of the elbow, a stroke on the sleeve. He seemed oblivious to the touches, always meeting the eyes of his interlocutor.

A tall, gangly fellow in a checked suit walked past them toward the front door, then noticed Sebastian and turned right around. He gave him a light punch in the shoulder, saying, "Sebastian Archer! Funny meeting you here."

"I thought I'd become quite a fixture in the place. How are you, Mr. Sparrow?"

"Right as rain and looking sunnier. A little bird told me a certain once-famous actress, known to you as 'Sister,' will be taking Adorable Nora's place as Jack in the Galaxy's panto."

"Don't be daft, man," Sebastian said. "My sister just had a baby. She isn't up to any giant-slaying this year."

"Not your twin," Sparrow said dryly. "The other one."

"Oh, *Lina*! Well, well. They'd be lucky to get her, wouldn't they, Professor?" Sebastian winked at Moriarty.

"Have it your way," Sparrow said. He touched the side of his long nose with a long finger, making a droll face. "But it looks like *Beanstalk* is on the rise." He shot one curious glance at Moriarty and left.

"There's the cat let out of that bag," Sebastian said. "You can't keep secrets for long in this business."

"How did that fellow find out so quickly?" Moriarty asked. "We only agreed to help Hatcliff yesterday."

"That was one of your principals — Frank Sparrow, popular comic actor and gossip extraordinaire. Hatcliff probably started the rumor himself to counteract the negative reports circulating about the Galaxy."

The maître d'hôtel arrived to lead them to their table in the dining room, which was equally full, but with a more restrained level of conversation. A waiter appeared as they seated themselves.

"They do a superior roast lamb here," Sebastian said, shaking his napkin into his lap. "And let's have a nice cabernet, Phillip. What do you think? The Mouton?"

"An excellent choice, Mr. Archer." The waiter paused, giving Moriarty a chance to confirm those selections, and left.

Sebastian said, "Your note said you wanted to learn about the business side of the theater. I must know all sorts of odds and ends, but I'm not sure where to start."

Before Moriarty could ask his first question, a couple of gentlemen rose from a nearby table, dropping their napkins onto their chairs. One of them merely nodded at Sebastian as he passed, but the other one, a jowly, middle-aged man, stopped and laid his bejeweled hand on the young star's shoulder, leaning down to speak in a confidential rumble. "I'm installing electricity over at the Paramount this summer, Mr. Archer. Twice the light with half the heat. I'd love to see your name at the top of my bill."

"No business in the club, Morrison," Sebastian said. "You know the rules." He smiled toothily, holding the pose. The man got the message and left.

"You do get a lot of attention," Moriarty said, wondering if this was how dinners out with Angelina would be henceforward. "Everyone touches you, I've noticed."

"The price of stardom. You're not entirely your own, not in public." Sebastian shrugged. "At least they can't pull me into their laps anymore. When I was a kid, I pretended I had a coat of invisible armor that protected me from head to toe. It magically appeared the moment I left the stage and put itself away when I got home."

"I don't think I could stand it."

"You get used to it. Oh, you're thinking about Lina. Well, you needn't worry. Actresses learn to cope early on. They wear padded jackets and carry little dogs or fans to swat at people who get too close." His blue eyes sparkled. "Or you could stand beside her with that exact expression on your face. That ought to do the trick admirably."

Moriarty grinned sheepishly. "It's just that I've gotten used to things the way they are. But if this is what she wants —"

"She'll have it. She's a force of nature, my sister. I'm afraid this was always in the cards, old bean. But I shouldn't worry. You're the One. You know that, don't you?"

"Which one?"

Sebastian treated that pathetic begging to a wry smile. "The Only One; the one she loves. She wants a theater full of applauding admirers, but she doesn't want them following her home — or meeting her for lunch in out-of-the-way hotels, if that's what you're afraid of. She was never that kind of actress, for one thing, and for another, she loves you. Case closed."

Moriarty nodded, relieved. He trusted his wife. Someday — not soon — he might even be able to watch her stroll through a gauntlet of grabby admirers without grinding his teeth.

The first course was served and their wine was poured. Moriarty took a spoonful of the tomato soup and judged it above average for a club kitchen. "Has there been a lot of bad news going around about the Galaxy?"

"*Beanstalk*'s not a happy show, I've heard that much. Though now that Nora Verney's out, that may turn around."

"Is she difficult to work with?"

Sebastian laughed. "She's quite the prima donna. Not above throwing things when she doesn't get her way, and can that woman shriek?" He shuddered as if receiving an electric shock. "I worked with her once. We're all a little fussy, I confess it. Acting is hard work. But there are ways and ways. Take my sisters, for example. They cajole, they hint, they sigh, they flatter. And then they're surprised and so deeply, deeply touched when they get the bigger dressing room and the later starting time." He clasped his hands together in mock delight.

"Hmm," Moriarty said, "I've noticed that myself."

"But you don't mind it, do you? Or not much?"

"Not at all. Angelina gives far more than she takes, from my perspective."

Sebastian raised his blond eyebrows skeptically. "If you're happy, why complain? Adorable Nora never acquired that knack. She expects everyone to jump when she snaps her fingers, as if she owns the place. In fact, what she really wants *is* to own the place. She dreams of becoming an actor-manager, like Marie Wilton, but she doesn't have the depth or the stamina for that much responsibility." His eyes gleamed as if he had similar aspirations.

"I've seen that kind of trouble," Moriarty said. "Academia has its share of prima donnas, or rather, dons. Men who expect their students to worship them and the university to pay homage, along with more tangible benefits." He sipped his soup. Too much bay leaf. "What about the rest of the cast? That fellow out there seemed cheery enough."

Sebastian thought for a moment, then shook his head. "I don't know everyone over there, but they're mostly old hands, like us Archers. Hatcliff has the Delaney sisters, for example. An old theater family. They can take anything in stride. Timothy Tweedy, your Dame, is another old pro. You could cut his head off in the middle of a scene and he wouldn't drop his line. He's an old friend, especially of Lina's. He was nice to her once, and she never forgets a kindness."

He pointed his spoon at Moriarty. "There's another difference. Adorable Nora never forgets a slight."

"Old grudges seem far more plausible to me than old ghosts."

"Oh, there are ghosts, never you fear!" He winked at the waiter, who had come to replace their soup plates with the main course. "Aren't there, Philip?"

"Certainly, sir. The Garrick is honored with the ghost of its founder." The waiter served their lamb and roasted potatoes, refilled their wine glasses, and walked away.

The lamb truly was superior, more than making up for the soup. Moriarty noticed faces of other diners turning toward them now and then, or rather, toward Sebastian. It had been going on since they sat down, but the beautiful young star seemed oblivious to that as well, giving his full attention to his luncheon companion and their shared meal.

All the Archers possessed that gift, of making one feel as if nothing else in the world existed when they conversed with you. It was the foundation of their charm, along with their good looks, though not altogether benign. They'd been bred to larceny as well as acting to fill in the gaps between bookings. They shone their angelic gazes on their marks, winning their confidence before eliciting whatever it was they wanted: trinkets, favors, money. Love.

Moriarty had long ceased minding. It was as natural as breathing for the gifted clan, and both sisters had chosen men with strong moral compasses to keep them on the right path. Success was the best cure for larceny anyway. Today Moriarty wondered if that special focus wasn't protective as well as manipulative, a way of drawing an invisible shield around an intimate circle into which the curious gazes of their admirers could never penetrate.

Sebastian savored a sip of wine, then asked, "How deeply are you thinking of getting involved at the Galaxy, if you don't mind my asking?"

"I'll lend him enough to pay the rent this quarter, which appears to be the minimum required. Angelina would be so disappointed if the show folded before she got her chance."

"It's less likely with her in it. Sparrow wasn't wrong about the sun coming out. You may not fully appreciate what a big star she was before she left. People will buy tickets just to get a look at her after all this time. A couple of good weeks should plug some of the holes in Hatcliff's pocketbook."

"What kind of numbers are we talking about?"

"Well, I make seventy a week during the run of a play," Sebastian said, grinning. "All told, for a Christmas panto, you'll be looking at tens of thousands, I should think."

"For a play!"

"A panto's not a play, old chap. It's a spectacle. You've got to build a twenty-foot beanstalk, to say nothing of Cloudland and whatever else is in the script. I love pantos! I've been a fairy swinging from a star, a soldier in a troop of a hundred other boys, and one of Ali Baba's forty thieves crowded into a huge cave filled with glittering treasure. The effects can be breathtaking and they're all built right there, by your crew of a hundred-plus men and women."

Moriarty struggled to imagine a painted beanstalk worth a couple of thousand pounds. "That sounds like a tremendous outlay for something so ephemeral."

"Things get re-used. Scenery, costumes. Kings tend to dress alike from show to show, and a beautiful forest scene can be lit in different ways for different plays. Besides, you'll send the whole thing out to the provinces once you've finished your London run and get another three or four months' revenue from them."

"Who owns all this finery?" Moriarty asked. "Hatcliff has a lease; he doesn't own the building himself."

"No, but he owns his properties and his scripts — and his reputation. The manager's taste defines the theater. You think of Gilbert and Sullivan at the Savoy, though D'Oyly Carte owns the place." Sebastian reconsidered. "Though he also manages the company, so that's a bit different. Hatcliff is famous for high-quality spectacles and rollicking burlesques."

Moriarty had been to the Savoy with Angelina. They'd heard some sprightly nonsense purportedly representative of Japanese culture, though he found that hard to believe. "That sounds like it would appeal to a large audience."

Sebastian laughed again at his innocence. "He packs them in when he's up to snuff. And don't forget the music hall stars coming in to do their bits between acts. Viola and I used to do a song-and-dance version of "Deck the Halls" that was so popular we'd play three houses in one night." He sighed at the memory. His twin sister had retired from the stage several years ago when Lord Brockaway had offered her his permanent protection. She'd borne him a son earlier this year and transformed herself into a plump matron at the ripe old age of twenty-five.

"You make it sound like great good fun."

Sebastian flashed a grin. "It's the only life for me. If I had money, I'd put it into Lina's show in a blink, especially with Lionel at the helm. She'll bring in the crowds, never fear. A successful panto will pay for the whole year and put a healthy profit back in your pocket." He leaned forward to murmur, "Rumor has it Squire Bancroft and Marie Wilton retired a few years ago with 180,000 pounds!"

Moriarty blinked at him, stricken mute with astonishment. He could never reach that level by investing in the three percents.

The waiter appeared bearing a silver salver. "Professor Moriarty?"

"That's me." He took the envelope from the tray, slit it open, and scanned the short lines written in Angelina's sprawling hand. *There's been an accident at the Galaxy. I'm fine, but you must come at once. Act normally. Raise no alarm!*

He folded the letter again and passed it to Sebastian with a smile. The younger man read it and handed it back with a chuckle. "Utter nonsense, of course. Shall you bother to answer?"

"No answer." Moriarty smiled blandly at the waiter. "But let's go back to my house for pudding, if you have the time. Our cook promised me a jam tart today, and Antoine's tarts are not to be missed."

FOUR

Angelina paced back and forth in front of the stage door at the Galaxy. Old Sampson, the guard, followed her with his eyes, turning his head left and right as if watching a tennis match. She'd sent boys running with notes to both James and Lionel. A boy could run the three or four blocks from Leicester Square to the Garrick in five minutes, but gentlemen's clubs were so sedate, it could take another five for the note to reach her husband. If he was fool enough to take a cab, he could be stuck in traffic for who knew how long.

She'd begged the lighting men to touch nothing and close the door on the accident until James could turn his eagle eyes upon the scene. She hoped — no, she prayed, begging any deity who ever loved a play — that this wouldn't force Hatcliff to shut down the production. From the moment Sampson had let her in that morning, she'd felt a thrill welling up from the core of her being. A longing, a kinship for the Galaxy itself, like nothing she'd ever experienced. She wanted this play, in this theater, at this time more than she'd ever wanted anything! Nora's spitefulness only added fuel to her desire.

But now a man was dead, and her ambition must do battle with her conscience.

The door opened at last, admitting James. He'd brought Sebastian. Good! Old Sampson recognized her brother and accepted his identification of the newcomer. Angelina ran toward them and took both of James's hands. "Oh, darlings, it's just awful! The stage manager's been killed."

"What happened?" James asked.

"I don't know. One of the light men found him in the room where they make the limelight. He came tearing down shouting his head off. I made them keep everyone out of the corridor until the authorities came." James quirked a brow and she shrugged. "It sounded more convincing than asking them to wait for my husband."

"Where's this room?" Sebastian asked, heading toward the stairs to the right of the door.

"All the way at the top."

As they wound up the stairs, people asked, "What's happened? Is it the ghost? Are the police coming?"

Angelina gave the same answer on every floor. "There's been an accident. Mr. Hatcliff's on his way. The professor here is going to have a look before we call the police." That seemed to relieve people's minds, if not satisfy their curiosity. No one wanted blockheaded constables poking about in their dressing rooms.

When they reached the top floor, they found a short man with a ruddy beard and an air of authority barring the way. He blinked at Sebastian, frowned at Angelina, and finally fixed his glare on James. "No one's to enter this hall until Mr. Hatcliff arrives."

"I'm Professor James Moriarty. Mr. Hatcliff engaged me to investigate the rash of accidents you've been experiencing here, Mr. —"

"Ben MacDonald. I'm the lighting chief."

"I understand the victim is your stage manager."

"That's right. John Fowler."

"Are you the one who found him?"

"No, that was one of my crew, Tom Williams." He jerked his thumb over his shoulder at a man standing at the shadowy end of the corridor with his arms wrapped around his thin frame. "I sent him up to fetch some red filters. Miz Lovington said the police would want to talk to him."

James blinked at her stage name, but his inner dignity stood him in good stead. "Quite correct. But first I'd like to inspect the scene."

MacDonald grunted and led them down the hall. Their figures made the shadows darker as they blocked the light from the lamp at the top of the stairs. Thin wisps of sweet-smelling smoke floated in the air.

"What's this smoke?" James said. "Do people cook up here?"

"That's from the smoke powder." MacDonald stopped to meet James's blank look with a scornful twitch of his brushy moustache. "For smoke on the stage. You know, for sorcerers and demons and suchlike. We store it up here along with the rest of our stock. Williams said he saw a cloud of it when he first came up."

"I see," James said in the tone that meant he didn't.

"Thick as purple fog, it was," the crewman said. "I knew at once it meant trouble."

MacDonald laid his hand on the knob of a door labeled *Lighting Crew Only* and waved the others back. He opened the door the merest crack and paused. Nothing happened. Angelina let out the breath she'd been holding as he swung it fully outward, his right foot sweeping across his left in an odd dance-like motion. "Where's the wedge, Williams?"

"It was outside, pushed under. Meant to trap the poor bloke, I reckon." Williams stuck to his patch of wall as if glued to it. "If it's our ghost, he's a nasty one."

MacDonald shot him a dark look, then said to James, "We keep the door open when we're working in here. Get a bit of air going."

"Isn't that door normally kept locked?" James asked.

"No need," MacDonald said. "Nothing but storerooms up here. Ours and the scenery crew. They keep ropes and paint and such." He entered the room.

James paused on the threshold. Angelina snugged in behind him, peering past his shoulder. Sebastian's hand landed on her back as she felt his smooth cheek near hers.

A worktable, its surface mottled with stains, spanned the rear wall underneath a skylight set into the sloping ceiling. Shelves with clay jars, leather bags, and a variety of glass vessels lined the other walls. A tall stool had been overturned beside the table. Beside it lay a man in a vest and shirtsleeves, crumpled into a curled position, as if he'd simply dropped where he stood. A small round stick lay near his slack fingers.

"That's Fowler, all right," MacDonald said.

"He looks like he just fell asleep," Angelina said.

Sebastian said, "He almost looks like —"

"Shhh!" MacDonald held up a finger, cocking his head. "Quiet!"

James thrust his ear forward to listen. Angelina held her breath again, straining to catch a faint hissing sound rising from one of the shelves.

"Gas!" James cried. He thrust her back. "Out, out, out!"

Sebastian's arms wrapped around her as he pulled her into the corridor. She cried, "James!" but the mad fool stayed inside the room.

"Get that window open!" MacDonald stooped to grab the little stick while James leaned across the table to press the sash up. The lighting chief fixed the stick into position, holding the window open a good four inches.

The two men stood under it, noses up. A cold, wet breeze smote Angelina's cheeks, making her shiver, but clearing away the last shreds of purple smoke.

"Where's that leaking jet?" James asked, his eyes darting around the room.

"No jets up here," MacDonald answered. "Strictly natural light. I know my business. I chose this room for the window."

"Then what's leaking?" James asked, the sharpness in his tone revealing the depth of his recent fright.

"Must be oxygen or hydrogen," Macdonald said. "We make both."

"What on earth for?"

His peremptory tone was ruffling the chief's feathers. "To make the limelight, man. What do you think we do with it? Fill up balloons?"

Sebastian, who had released Angelina as soon as the window went up, went back into the room, a genial smile on his face. "Limelight's the magic that turns a play into a dream world, Professor. These men here are the magicians. They perch way up at the top of the theater to shine brilliant circles of light onto the stage. Correct me if I'm wrong, Mr. MacDonald, but you use Drummond lamps, don't you? They mix oxygen and hydrogen to make a fine flame that burns a little piece of lime. We'd be nothing without it, would we, Lina?"

She shook her head. "Nothing at all."

"I've heard of limelight," James muttered, feeling ruffled in his turn. Really, these scientific men! More competitive than actresses at a gala.

But MacDonald seemed mollified. "Very good, Mr. Archer. Of course I know who *you* are. I'm impressed. Most actors don't trouble themselves with the whys and wherefores."

James rolled his eyes. "Oxygen wouldn't kill a man."

"Not unless you get too much of it," MacDonald said. "But it's more likely the hydro." He turned to the shelves and examined the leather bags, which looked like fat bellows lying on their sides. "Yep. This is it. Looks like the bag's cracked." He reached past James to grab a towel from a stack on a lower shelf, which he wrapped around the bag. It didn't look terribly effective.

"Cracked or been cut?" James asked.

"I said cracked, didn't I?" MacDonald scowled at him. He checked the other bags. "I knew these needed replacing. I told Fowler as much, but no, the fancy new props came first."

"How toxic is hydrogen?" James asked. "I'm not familiar with its properties."

MacDonald shrugged. "It can make you dizzy if you get your nose into it. Like drowning, they say, only painless. It's lighter than air. It'd rise. Fowler must have breathed in too much before he could get the window open."

"No doubt that's what happened," James said. "He felt dizzy. Then when he reached over the table here to open the window, he fell and hit his head." He looked down at the pitiful figure on the floor, scratched his beard while steeling himself, then knelt to run his hand under the man's head. "Well, the coroner will be able to tell for sure, but I think I can feel a soft spot here." He rose to his feet and dusted off his trouser knees with a cough.

"Can't we at least cover the poor chap?" Sebastian said. "One of those drop cloths would do."

"Och, aye." MacDonald unfolded a table-sized square of canvas and draped it over the curled body. "We may have had our differences, John Fowler, but I never wished such a fate as this on you."

Angelina asked, "What sort of differences?"

MacDonald shrugged. "Thought he knew everything, did our Mr. Fowler. And pinched the pennies where he thought it wouldn't show. Well, it's come back to haunt him now." Then his eyes widened as the words he'd chosen struck home.

"Nonsense," James said. "No ghost stuffed that wedge under the door. Now would you please go back out into the corridor and stop moving things until I have a chance to inspect the scene?"

Sebastian nipped out to stand beside Angelina, but MacDonald held his ground, crossing his arms over his chest. James glowered at him, then pointedly ignored him while he turned his head slowly, his gaze traveling up and down as he studied every shelf and corner, storing each detail in his capacious memory.

"What's that?" He pointed at a shallow pan topped with a folded cloth on the floor near the door.

"The cause of this tragedy, I suspect." MacDonald picked it up, setting the cloth on the table. He held the pan toward James, who gave the contents a tentative sniff. "Sweet, like the hall. Is this that smoking powder, then?"

"That's the stuff," MacDonald said. "We're lucky it didn't ignite the hydrogen. The merest spark can set it off. But it rises, and this was on the floor."

"How hard is it to light the powder?"

"Och, not hard at all. It'd be no good otherwise. We use fuses, as a rule." MacDonald poked his finger into the pan. "Aye, here's a bit of fuse left unburnt. I suppose that's how the fellow did it."

James peered into the pan, then studied at the floor again, his gaze moving across the threshold and into the hall. He shook his head. "Any traces of burnt fuse have been scuffed to nothing by all the feet. I should've come ahead by myself."

MacDonald raised his bushy eyebrows at that. "It mightn't have been a long fuse. We've got all lengths, ready-cut there next to the powder." He jerked his chin at another shelf where small boxes stood next to an array of jars. Each container had a neat white label. "That pan must've been billowing smoke when Fowler opened the door. He'd have dropped that rag on top to smother it."

"He's lucky the rag didn't catch fire! I must say, I don't believe I've ever seen any workplace more unsafe."

"James, darling," Angelina said in a warning tone. They'd just lost the stage manager. The last thing they needed was to antagonize the lighting chief.

He ignored her. "You've got flammable gases leaking right and left alongside boxes of fuses, with matches, no doubt, and God knows what other hazardous materials." He picked up a jar and barked a horrified laugh. "Sulfuric acid! Good lord, man! These things ought to be strictly segregated. In fact, you should be making these compounds off the premises or purchasing them from a reputable manufacturer."

"Now, James," Sebastian said, casting a glance at the mottled fury rising in MacDonald's freckled cheeks. "This really isn't the time —"

"The place is filthy," James ranted on. "And that door ought to be kept locked at all times. You've created a death trap and left it wide open for everyone to help themselves."

"That's it!" MacDonald cried. "I've been running the lights at the Galaxy for nigh on fifteen years, and I'll be damned if I'll stand here and be insulted by you, Mr. — whoever you think you are! I quit!"

He thrust pan of ashes into James's hands and stalked off, followed by his man.

FIVE

"What did I say?" Moriarty set the pan on the table and met his wife's exasperated gaze with outstretched arms. "Surely a man senior enough to call himself a chief can tolerate a little constructive criticism."

"Oh, James!" Angelina rolled her eyes to heaven. "How *could* you? Raving on about safety regulations with that poor man lying right there —"

"Which only serves to underscore the validity of my observations."

She shook herself with a little cry of frustration, then gave up and turned to her brother. "We can't lose the chief too. We simply can't!"

"I'll talk to him," Sebastian said. "I'll take him out for a drink and explain that my brother-in-law is a bit of a pompous ass, but his heart's in the right place." He shot a wink at Moriarty to take the sting out of his remark and hurried off after the outraged Scotsman.

"We may as well go down too," Angelina said. "Lionel should be here by now."

"One more minute, if you don't mind." Moriarty had been stung by his wife's unreasonable objection to his perfectly justified critique, but he was man enough to let it go. "Now that it's quiet, I'd like to make sure I've seen what I can before the police take over."

Moriarty went back inside the little room with its doleful occupant and stood for a moment scratching his beard, repeating his earlier survey of the wedged door, the stool, the jumble on the table, and the crowded — yet admittedly tidy — shelves. He went to the one holding the bladders of gas and unwrapped the towel from the leaking hydrogen bag. "It's cracked, all right. Good lord! This bag's an antique! Look at it!"

He held it out to show his wife, who stood leaning in the doorway with her arms crossed. "I'll take your word for it."

"It's no wonder the thing is leaking. I don't know the specific properties of hydrogen, but if it's anything as explosive as natural gas, the merest spark could have blown up the whole room. They ought to use metal canisters to store this stuff. They're much more secure."

"And probably ten times as expensive. Theater crews have their traditions, James. Methods that have served them through the years, handed down from father to son as often as not."

"Amateurs." Moriarty scowled. "Making and mixing gases is a science. It ought to be done in a laboratory. A controlled environment. But I see your point about the cost." He held the leaking bag to his nose and took a tentative whiff. "Ho!" He hastily wrapped the towel around it again and set it back on the shelf.

"James!"

"Just curious. It's quite an odd sensation. It goes straight to the head." He picked up the pan of burnt smoke powder and poked a finger in the coarse ashes. "I should get a sample of this stuff and have it analyzed."

"Not by Holmes, I beg you. Let's leave him out of this one."

"He wouldn't help me anyway. He hasn't forgiven me for hanging out my own shingle. As if there weren't dozens of private investigators in London! He doesn't have a patent on the term 'consulting detective,' after all."

"That man has a monumental drive to make himself distinctive. He doesn't care about the dozens of ordinary types. You're the only one who can give him any real competition."

Moriarty smiled at her partisanship. "I don't need Holmes anyway. I know a chemist in the Royal Society who might do me a favor."

"You could ask the theater's lighting chief, who probably mixed it himself." Angelina snapped her fingers. "Oh, but you've just sent the man off with a burr in his beard!"

"I'm sure he can be replaced."

"I'm not. These men are specialists, James. Artists, in their own way, just as much as the scene painters. And they know their theaters inside out. Most of his crew will go with him out of loyalty."

Moriarty blew out an exasperated breath. "I concede that my comments were ill-considered. I clearly do not understand the intricacies of theatrical production. The question may be moot, in any case. I'm afraid this show is doomed, my dear. Ruined hats are one thing, but now a man has died." He saw the bleakness in her eyes, and his heart melted. "Never fear, we'll find you another show. A better one."

"But not this Christmas." Her shapely lips turned down in a sad pout.

He could never withstand that look. "We'll see what can be done. Shall we go down? I'm finished here."

They descended into a milling throng around the stage door. Sebastian stood under the stairs, leaning against the wall with his arms folded and his head bent, nodding as he listened to MacDonald grumbling in a low burr. A group of men and women in a motley array of outfits surrounded Lionel Hatcliff, distinctive in his black cloak and gleaming top hat. He drew his entourage slowly in the direction indicated by a sign reading *To the Stage*.

Another gentleman in a top hat strode through the stage door, followed by two men in bowler hats bearing a stretcher. This must be the coroner, come to collect the body. The doorkeeper pointed toward MacDonald, and the coroner stopped to speak with him as the others started up the stairs. MacDonald shook Sebastian's hand and led the coroner up as well.

Moriarty followed his wife toward the stage, letting himself fall behind as she wove through the crowd, calling, "Lionel!" Her voice rose easily above the general chatter. Heads turned and murmurs rose. "Lina Lovington! We may not be dead yet!"

Hatcliff walked out onto the open stage and raised his hands for silence. Moriarty stopped at the edge behind a great red curtain. He wasn't part of this.

Hatcliff grasped one of Angelina's hands and held it up. "Lina Lovington, everyone! Our new Jack!"

A round of applause greeted this announcement. Someone shouted, "Thank God!" and everyone laughed. "What's happening?" someone else called, and the clamor started up again.

"I hope she's up to it," Sebastian said softly, coming up behind him. "She'll be wonderful, don't get me wrong, but she's never been Principal Boy. Pantos take stamina."

"She's champing at the bit," Moriarty said loyally, but he had his doubts. The backstage of a theater was much bigger than he'd imagined, like a vertical labyrinth. If they kept storerooms filled with volatile chemicals at the top, who knew what hazards lay hidden below? How could he protect her in a place like this?

He wouldn't say it, but part of him hoped the stage manager's death would effect the demise of this whole perilous production. They'd find something safer, like the light comedies Sebastian excelled in or a charming operetta.

Hatcliff bent his head to listen as Angelina spoke in his ear. Then he told the assembly that John Fowler had met with an accident and died. "That's all we know at present. Why don't you all take the rest of the day off? My treat!"

Another round of applause met that offer. Sebastian said, "Generous of him! That means he's paying for the lost time. Chalk up another delay and more losses to your prankster."

People straggled off the stage, some of them pausing to pat Angelina on the shoulder or give her a quick embrace. When all had left, Hatcliff took her arm and walked over to Moriarty and Sebastian. "I told the coroner I'd wait for his initial determination. Won't you keep me company?"

"Of course we will," Angelina said.

He led them down into the stalls, choosing a section where they would be easily spotted. Angelina sat next to him. Moriarty took the seat on her other side, while Sebastian sat in the next row with his legs slung over the armrest. Hatcliff said, "You three got here ahead of me. What happened up there?"

Moriarty answered, "We don't know exactly, but we have a fair idea. Someone lit a pan of smoke powder and set it inside the door of the storeroom where the lighting men keep their chemicals. It was probably lit with a fuse running under the door. The window in the room was shut, so the smoke had nowhere to go but into the corridor. It must have billowed down the stairs, where your stage manager noticed it. When he entered the storeroom to locate the source of the smoke, the prankster, who must have been hiding in the murk at the end of that dark hall, swung the door closed and wedged it with a block of wood, trapping Mr. Fowler inside. The prankster presumably ran away at that point."

"Horrible." Hatcliff shook his head, his long moustache drooping.

"You know," Angelina said, "if that prankster hid in that smoke, his clothes would smell like sugar." She sniffed at her own sleeve.

Sebastian tested his as well. "Barely, but yes, I can smell it. If we ran back and nosed about, perhaps we could sniff out our villain straightaway."

"I just sent them all home!" Hatcliff wailed.

Moriarty said, "He probably walked straight out of the building. A tour around the block in this drizzle would have him smelling like nothing more sinister than wet wool and sooty streets."

"How did Fowler die?" Hatcliff asked.

"Painlessly, I think," Moriarty said, "for what comfort that might bring us. He smothered the smoke pot with a folded towel. Unfortunately, an old leather bag had cracked and was leaking hydrogen gas into that small room. The merest whiff makes you dizzy. Fowler must have been overcome as he reached to open the window and fell, hitting his head on the worktable. I doubt he felt it much."

"Poor old chap," Hatcliff said.

They gave Fowler a moment of silence, though three of them had never known the man. Then Hatcliff said, "You're sure it was an accident, then, Professor? I mean, you don't think it could have been" — he dropped his voice to a hoarse whisper — *"murder."*

"No, I don't. I doubt the prankster knew about the leaking gas. If that's what he wanted, he could've sliced open another bag or two. Without the gas, Fowler would have sorted the smoke problem in short order. He'd have pounded on the door and shouted until someone came along to let him out."

"I don't like that wedge," Sebastian said. "That's quite a different level of meanness than crushing hats."

"Also, not something a ghost could do," Moriarty said dryly. "Which answers one of your questions, Mr. Hatcliff. You're not going mad."

"I suppose that's something," Hatcliff said, smiling weakly.

Angelina said, "I think it's more horrible to think of one of our own doing these vicious things."

The coroner appeared on the stage, looking frustrated. He spotted them in the stalls, waved as if stopping traffic, and started casting about for a way down to them. Sebastian leapt up and bounded down the aisle to guide him toward the steps. He remained standing as the coroner addressed the theater owner.

"It won't be official until I've made my examination of the body," the man said in a nasal drone, "but I'm prepared to recommend a ruling of death by misadventure."

"Very good," Hatcliff said. "Are we free, then, to go on about our business here?"

"Certainly. Though I'd advise you to get that door fixed straightaway. Your lighting chief said it was prone to blowing itself shut. That's unacceptable in my book."

"I'll see to it first thing in the morning."

The coroner left, going off the way he'd come. "One disaster averted." Sebastian swung himself into his former seat and grinned. "Looks like Old MacDonald came through in the end."

"Thanks to you," Angelina said. "Did you persuade him to stay on?"

"On condition that James apologizes." Sebastian flashed his dazzling smile. "I'm afraid I rather promised you would."

Moriarty sighed as if accepting an onerous chore, though it was only fair if he truly had insulted the man. "Will a whiskey at his local do, or must I abase myself in accordance with some ancient ritual?"

"Nothing too dire," Sebastian said. "You only have to crawl across the bridge up there" — he pointed up to the cavernous space high above the stage — "wearing a pirate costume with a pasteboard knife between your teeth."

"Sebastian!" Angelina said. "You should allow Mr. MacDonald, as the injured party, to select the costume."

Moriarty looked from wife to brother-in-law, uncertain for a moment if they were joking. The twitching of Hatcliff's white moustache gave them away. He barked a laugh, and they all joined in.

"Whiskey will do admirably," Sebastian said. "I'll join you." He turned toward Hatcliff. "He also wants a rise in pay."

"I haven't got it!" Hatcliff moaned, sinking into the plush seat. "But what difference does it make? The show will have to close anyway. I'll never replace Fowler at such late notice. Every man who knows how to stage a pantomime is already up to his eyebrows in one. Boxing Night is only two and a half weeks away."

"What does the stage manager do?" Moriarty asked.

"Easier to tell you what he doesn't do," Angelina said. "He manages everything from the proscenium back: cast, crew, props, lights . . ."

"He coordinates the choreographers," Sebastian added, "and hires specialists as needed, like fencing masters."

"He conducts the technical rehearsals and the dress parade too." Hatcliff shook his head. "This is a Christmas pantomime, not some kitchen-table drama by Henrik-bloody-Ibsen." He caught himself. "Pardon my language, Professor."

Moriarty waved his hand, wondering why he should draw the apology and not the lady present, but Angelina didn't seem to have noticed.

"It's a huge job," Hatcliff went on. "We're doing *Jack and the Beanstalk* this year. Sounds simple, eh? But people expect a lot more than a cow and a sack of beans. They want spectacle, and that's what we give 'em! I've got a giant in Cloudland with two hundred dancing children playing his troop of guards. I've got a twenty-five-foot beanstalk that can support two adults climbing in different directions. I've got a dozen of Shakespeare's most famous characters descending from the giant's prison on a bank of clouds. Then I've got a giantess with a secret recipe for flying potion. I daresay you can imagine what happens when Jack gets his hands on that!"

Angelina would be swung over the stage on a slender rope. Moriarty could imagine it all too easily, and he didn't like the idea one bit. He kept himself in good condition, taking near-daily exercise at the London Athletic Club, but he doubted his heart could withstand that level of sustained terror.

"Flying potion," Sebastian breathed, his eyes dancing.

"Who've you got for the Shakespeares?" Angelina asked.

"I understand the difficulty," Moriarty said as gravely as he could, given his rising sense of gratitude that Fowler's death would put a stop to this lunacy. "It sounds like a job demanding an exceptional range of skills. The man would practically have had to grow up in a theater. Let's put our heads together about the financial situation, Mr. Hatcliff, and see if we can't sort something out. Then we can all enjoy a quiet holiday and look forward to finding something more manageable in the new year."

He smiled brightly at his wife, who looked at him as if he'd just shot the family dog. He started listing consolatory gifts in his mind. Roses, to start. Breakfast in bed, delivered by him. A few weeks in the south of France. She'd get past this disappointment soon enough and be safe and sound and able to enjoy whatever came along next.

Sebastian cleared his throat. "What you said just now, Professor. About the chap we want growing up in the theater."

A spark lit in Angelina's eyes. "Sebastian!"

"Oh, my boy," Hatcliff said. "Well, I don't know! Do you really think you could?"

Moriarty looked from one to the other, left in the dust again — a position it would seem he had better get used to. "What are you suggesting? You can't mean for Sebastian to take on the job. You made it clear that it required an experienced man."

"There aren't any," Sebastian said. "Not at this late date. And I did grow up in a theater, James, as you suggested."

Moriarty frowned at him. He hadn't meant *this.*

Sebastian shifted limberly onto to his knees, the better to plead his case. "You know me, Lionel. You know I've clambered every inch of every big theater in London, including this one, pestering the crews about their work. What keeps the sets up in the air? How do you make sure they come down the right way? I know how to mix smoke powder, and I've watched them making the hydrogen gas. I know how everything works! More, I've played every part in a pantomime except the Dame and the Principal Boy. I've danced in the children's troupes and carried a spear. I've swung from the rafters dressed like an angel and popped up from the cellar in a sorcerer's gown. I can do it, if you'll give me the chance." He clasped his hands in supplication.

Hatcliff tugged on his moustache, doubtful. "Are you sure you want it, my boy? It's a hell of job, even without a curse."

"I know. But I want it. I didn't know how much until this very moment. Hugh and I were going hiking in Greece, but we did that last year." He turned pleading eyes toward his sister. "I need new challenges or I'll grow stale. *You* know I can do it, Lina. You of all people."

"Yes, I do." Angelina turned to take both of Hatcliff's hands in hers. "Say yes, Lionel. Between the three of us, we'll make this show the biggest success in London!"

Moriarty's heart sank. No one could resist *two* Archers bent on persuasion. He let their excited babble about bold new plans fade into the background as his mind filled with a vision of his wife dangling twenty feet in the air from a slender rope while a faceless villain lurked above, snapping a long pair of scissors.

Then an even darker thought crowded out that vision. Could it be a coincidence that the prankster's tricks turned lethal on the very day rumors started about Lina Lovington stepping in to save the show?

SIX

"I'm not ready," Angelina told her reflection as she tilted her hat and stuck in a pin.

"Not like that, ducky." Peg pulled out the pin, straightened the hat, and stuck the pin into a thicker portion of coiled hair. Peg Barwick was Angelina's dresser and oldest friend. She'd joined the Archer family at age thirteen to make costumes for Lovely Little Lina, a rising child star in the East End. Angelina had been six. When Mrs. Archer died giving birth to the twins, Peg added baby-minding to her duties. She'd been with Angelina ever since, through all the travels and travails, from Stockholm to San Francisco and home again.

Angelina studied her costume in the tall mirror. She'd gone all out for her first day in her new job. Hatcliff had closed the theater over the weekend, promising everyone half pay for the lost hours. Another frightful expense, but what else could he do? He had a new stage manager *and* a new star. They both needed a little time to get their bearings.

She'd gotten a partial script with her lines and cues and spent the better part of the weekend pacing the length of the drawing room learning her part. She wanted to be word-perfect before the first rehearsal so she could lend Sebastian her full support. She'd leapt at his offer as the only chance to save the show, but she had doubts. The boy was barely twenty-five and had no experience managing people. He'd need her at his side every step of the way.

She fluffed the pile of ostrich feathers at the top of her dark gray hat, which was styled like a man's top hat with the brim curving down over her hair. Feminine yet businesslike. The hat matched her walking suit, whose open collar framed a white shirtfront with a row of jet buttons.

"I want to look like Success Incarnate. It gives people confidence. What do you think?" She turned from side to side, testing the effect.

Peg sniffed at the air. "I can almost smell the boodle. But you won't be able to sit in the stalls with the rest of us with that much flounce over that bustle."

"I don't plan to sit down. I'll stand next to Sebastian to add my experience to his enthusiasm."

Peg snorted.

Angelina ignored that. She knew her brother better than anyone. He'd be grateful. She picked up her rouge pot, leaning forward to smudge a little on her lips, and shot a sidelong look at her friend. "Tweedy will be there."

"Who?"

She clucked her tongue. "You know who. Timothy Tweedy, your old flame. He's playing Dame Trott."

"Oh, him!" Peg flapped her hand in disdain, but dipped a pinkie into the rouge pot to dab at her own lips. "I haven't thought about that old rascal for years. He must be fat as a hog by now."

"He was never thin." Angelina suppressed a grin. "Is that a new hat?"

"It's my return to the West End too, you know." Peg's hat sported a whole stuffed bird spread across its crown. Its blue feathers matched the blue of her eyes, but her thick, dark hair was already freeing itself from the coil at the base of her neck.

The footman knocked on the door. "Cab's 'ere, Missus!"

Angelina caught her old friend's eyes in the mirror. "Are we ready?"

Peg shrugged, too much the Cockney to display the slightest hint of unwarranted optimism. "We'll find out soon enough, won't we, ducky?"

The cab dropped them at the stage door. They lifted their skirts and trotted up the stairs, where they were greeted by the watchman. "Good morning, Miss Lovington. Mr. Archer said to go straight in, if you please. The cast is in the stalls."

"Have they started already?"

"Mr. Archer said ten o'clock sharp."

Angelina widened her eyes at Peg in mock dismay. "Then I guess we'd better hurry, hadn't we?"

She heard Sebastian talking as she walked through the wings. He stood center front, his low topper tilted back on his gleaming blond hair. His fashionably short jacket was unbuttoned to reveal a striped silk waistcoat. He had his hands in the pockets of his loose trousers. He spoke in a conversational tone, but his well-modulated voice would carry clearly to the last row.

He seemed to be talking about schedules or some such. She waited for a pause, then strode across the stage. "Here I am," she sang as she took her brother's hand and swung it gaily.

"Case in point," he said, throwing a broad wink to the cast members ranged throughout the stalls.

She hesitated as she caught his meaning, then recovered. "I'm here to help, dear boy, if only by serving as a cautionary example." She mugged for the audience and won a laugh.

He dropped a kiss on her cheek and smiled, holding up their joined hands. "My sister, ladies and gentlemen. Our new Jack!"

She liked it that he didn't bother to call her by name, even if half the people out there must be too young to remember her. But he spoiled the moment by adding, "Do try to be on time in future, Lina. We were just talking about how important it is for us all to pull together."

"I'll be punctuality itself henceforward." She beamed at him. "What's next on the agenda?"

"Why don't you take a seat, dear?" He moved his hand to the small of her back and walked her toward the steps going down from the apron. "See? We've saved the best one for you." He pointed at a pair of seats in the center. She'd have to climb over half a dozen people to reach those!

"Not in this dress, darling." She was trapped. She couldn't very well stalk back onto the stage and had no intention of slinking off to the benches under the dress circle. "I'll just perch here on the stairs."

Peg had already gone down to stand in the aisle. "I'll take that seat, if I can get into it."

People chuckled and shifted to make room for her. Angelina wondered at her forwardness until she saw the last man rise to lower Peg's seat for her with a flourish. Timothy Tweedy, the now-famous comedian who had once been the light of Peg's young heart. The way she batted her lashes as she allowed him to assist her suggested a few embers still smoldered.

"All settled?" Sebastian asked. No doubt he'd noticed the sparks as well. Peg was the only mother he'd ever known. He'd indulge her beyond anyone else — especially his sister.

"Sorry, darling," Angelina said. "It really won't happen again."

"I don't want to play the tyrant," he said, pitching his answer to the group, "but we've lost so much time already, what with one thing or another. We're all going to have to put our shoulders to the wheel and our noses to the grindstone." He mimed that impossible position, taking the sting out of the admonishment. He let the laughter fade and added, "Let's come ready to work each day, shall we? Let's learn those parts inside and out: lines, songs, steps, stunts. And let's make a point of helping the crew when they need us to weigh a fairy or measure a prop."

Angelina hitched up the back of her skirt a subtle inch or two and perched on the steps. Not up front at Sebastian's side, where she'd imagined her place would be, but not down among the *hoi polloi* either. It would have to do. Besides, it allowed her to watch people's faces as they listened to their new manager.

And she loved this view; she'd forgotten how much. The house lights were half-up, the yellow glow picking out the gilt fretwork trimming the rows of box seats and the dress circle. The stalls were half-full, with many familiar faces sending welcoming smiles her way. The Delaney sisters, a troupe of five nearly identical ballet dancers, occupied second row center. They waggled five sets of fingers at her in unison.

A dark-haired woman sat near, but not with, the women's chorus, glaring daggers at Angelina every now and then. She didn't look familiar. Then Angelina realized she must be Jack's understudy. The poor thing had been the star for one whole week, but now she was pushed back into her closet. Oh well, that was life. They needed a name that sold tickets, especially now.

"We're all simply stunned by John Fowler's death," Sebastian said. "I didn't know the man, but I've gained respect for him in the past couple of days, studying the meticulous notes he made in the prompt book."

A few soft murmurs rose, but not many. Some faces hardened; others looked down, unreadable. Only the dancers lifted watery eyes toward Sebastian. Fowler had not been universally liked, it would seem. Well, the stage manager had an impossible job, worse than herding cats. It wasn't his job to be liked.

"I've got big shoes to fill," Sebastian said, lifting a foot and frowning at it doubtfully. That raised a chuckle. "But I'm excited too! What a show!" He clapped his hands together, rubbing them eagerly. "We're going to give people something to talk about this year, by golly!"

"What happened to Mr. Fowler?" one of the Delaneys asked. "The papers said it was an accident."

"That's right," Sebastian said, turning appropriately somber. "A terrible, tragic accident. No less, and no *more.* As far as we can determine, Mr. Fowler went up to the lighting storeroom to fetch something. The door stuck, trapping him inside with a leaking bag of hydrogen gas. The bag was old and the door was sticky; that's all. Those things have been remedied. It won't happen again."

"But what about the gho —"

Sebastian stopped her protest with a flat palm. "I know there have been other losses, less tragic, but not trivial for those who suffered them. Your hats will be replaced." He addressed that to the men's chorus, who grinned, surprised and gratified. Sebastian had won their goodwill.

"What about my makeup?" The deep voice issued from a man whose shoulders began where his neighbors' heads left off. That must be the Giant. Angelina eyed him with interest. The bigger he was, the slenderer she would look in their scenes together.

"That too, Mr. Easton," Sebastian said. "Fair's fair. We don't want anyone to be out of pocket because of these mishaps, which are going to stop right now. We don't have time for any more nonsense!"

Many people nodded and murmured agreement. But not all.

Timothy Tweedy was among the latter class. "There are other matters of a pecuniary nature that have yet to be addressed, Mr. Archer." He used his stage voice, rich and resonant.

Sebastian walked to the brink of the stage and met Tweedy's stubborn glare straight on. "There will be no salary increases, I'm afraid. Not until Lady Day at the soonest." He took a step back, turning away from the disgruntled comic to address his remarks to whole assembly. "Money is tight, ladies and gents, as you know. I'm not taking a cent for my turns on the boards. I'm just picking up Fowler's salary where he left off."

That got 'em. Eyes popped and mouths gaped, if only for a moment. Then the murmurs began in earnest as everyone shared their estimates of how many pounds per week Sebastian Archer might otherwise have commanded.

When he looked her way, Angelina mouthed, *Well played.* He shot her a grimace of relief.

Then a terrible thought struck her: Would she be expected to follow suit? Verney had been making eighty pounds a week. It would be a come-down to accept less. Your standing in this business was measured by your salary as much as by your position on the bill.

Tweedy must have been making a similar calculation. "That's all very well for you, Mr. Archer. But I've heard Mr. Hatcliff has found a new partner. That's why he's loosening the strings to buy hats. Why can't he loosen them a bit more, eh?"

Sebastian met the challenge with a light laugh. "There truly are no secrets in this theater! Well, now that you mention it, Lina's husband will be pitching in to smooth out some of the roughest patches. Nothing's firm yet, and as far as I know, it'll all go toward safety measures, like new hydrogen bags. That benefits everyone; I think you'll all agree."

Tweedy plainly didn't, but one detail buried the main message. "Husband?" many voices cried. "Who's the lucky gent?"

One plaintive tenor sang out above the rest. "Ah, Lina, me darlin'! How could you? I thought ye'd wait for me!"

Angelina trilled a laugh. "Why, Frank Sparrow! I never knew you cared!" She blew him a kiss, which he caught like an arrow to his heart, collapsing melodramatically in his seat.

Everyone laughed. Sebastian gave them a moment, then raised his hands to gather them back in. "I knew I could count on you, Mr. Sparrow, to keep us all in good humor."

The lanky comedian touched the brim of his hat. "Yes, sir! You crack the whips and I'll make the quips!"

Everyone laughed again, but Sebastian's lips tightened. Sparrow had just neatly undercut his *we're-all-in-this-together* theme. Comedians! Always willing to sacrifice the scene to get in one more joke. Angelina had little experience with rapid patter, but most of her lines were in scenes with Tweedy or Sparrow. She'd have to learn how to hold her ground.

Tweedy had not laughed at his partner's foolery. He ignored it, frowning and whispering something in Peg's ear while she nodded and patted his hand. Angelina watched the byplay with interest. He certainly seemed to be the sourest grape in this bunch. Luckily, Peg could do a little diplomatic service between comforting pats and squeezes and find out what the trouble was.

"But what about the ghost, Mr. Archer?" The quavering query rose from someone in the women's chorus.

"Ah," Sebastian said, breaking off whatever he'd been saying to the Delaneys. "What about that ghost?"

He sat down between two footlights at the edge of the stage, letting his legs dangle into the orchestra pit. Then he took off his hat, set it beside him, and ran a hand through his hair. He looked toward the women's chorus. "I believe in ghosts. I really do. I've never seen one myself, even though I've worked in half the theaters in this city."

"More than half, darling," Angelina said, winning a chuckle from the old hands.

"I don't know if the Galaxy is haunted, but I do know all theaters have souls. Lord knows they have moods. I know that for a fact because I've spent most of my life inside a theater. I wasn't born in a trunk, like Lina here." He tilted his head in her direction. "Though they say Viola and I were born between acts."

"My stars, what a night!" Peg said, winning an even warmer chuckle.

Sebastian smiled at her fondly. "Lina's dressing room was our nursery and the theater was our school. Other boys roam the countryside, chasing squirrels and hunting fish or whatever it is they do out there."

Several men laughed out loud. The Delaney sisters hummed together. The youngest of many generations of performers, their childhoods had been much the same as his.

Sebastian acknowledged the kinship with a flick of his eyebrows. "Theaters were my playground, from the fly tower to the cellar depths." His accent subtly shifted from West End to East as his tale unfolded. "They've also been my sanctuary. Whenever I got in trouble — a rare event, I assure you."

"Ha!" Peg cried.

Sebastian raised his eyes to heaven, pressing his palms together like the little angel he was not. "I'd escape punishment by running off and hiding. I've spent many a night curled up in Cinderella's coach or the Old Lady's shoe. Sometimes I'd wake up when everyone else had gone and sneak onto the stage, the one place with a light left on, apart from the lamp beside the gently snoring watchman. I'd sit dead center, close my eyes, and listen."

He closed his eyes now and tilted his face up as if listening to some faint voice high up above. Angelina smiled as half the cast closed their eyes too. No one broke the silence — not a cough, not a rustle.

Then Sebastian stirred and drew in a long, audible breath. He spoke in a wondering voice. "I could feel her heart beating, the spirit of the theater. They all have one, you know. Some are old, some are young. Some are easy to please, some are next to impossible. They have to be placated. They have to be wooed."

Now he tossed them one of his patented saucy grins and leapt lithely to his feet. "And where's there's a will, there's a woo." Everyone laughed, as much in relief that the ghost story had ended as at that feeble bit of wit.

Sebastian set his fists on his slim hips. "Something's put Lady Galaxy's nose out of joint. My job from here out is to make her smile again. I'll devote my every waking minute to making her happy. Then she'll make you happy and you'll make the audience happy. By Boxing Day, this house will be so filled with light and laughter, all of London will queue up to get inside and join the fun!"

"Hooray!" Cheers rose from every throat. Even Timothy Tweedy managed a smile.

Sebastian had them, heart and soul. They'd do anything for him now. Pride welled in Angelina's chest, warring with the envy that had been simmering in her belly. She'd meant to be up there with him, getting her share of the glory.

Well, there'd be time for that. She was the star, after all. Once the show actually started, she'd be the one getting the cheers, night after exhilarating night.

In the meantime, she could help by keeping spirits up backstage. Sebastian would have his hands full with the crew, but she'd have time to get to know everyone in the cast. With a pinch of sympathy here and a dollop of praise there, she might tease out a few confidences to help identify the prankster.

Feeling the nip of the green-eyed serpent in her own breast made her wonder if envy might not be the venom poisoning this show. Maybe Lady Galaxy wasn't the only one whose nose had been put out of joint?

SEVEN

Moriarty spent the latter half of Monday afternoon in a most instructive conversation with a chemist at the University of London, a fellow member of the Royal Society. He brought his sample of smoke powder, expecting to leave it for a later analysis, but the chemist simply gave it a sniff, tasted a few grains, and laughed.

"No mystery here, my friend. This is a mixture of potassium chlorate and sugar, meant to smolder rather than flame. Undergraduates love the stuff. Your theater man probably guards his recipe as if it were a state secret, but this looks like standard issue to me. Some add a touch of potassium nitrate — saltpeter — for a bit of flash. A dash of indigo and auramine will give you green smoke instead of purple. Otherwise, it's all pretty much of a muchness."

He confirmed Moriarty's hypothesis about the nitrogen gas causing dizziness. "We call them inert gases, but they can be quite hazardous. You don't want to be making hydrogen in an unventilated laboratory. These theater men make the stuff themselves to save money, which means your man kept supplies of sulfuric acid on hand as well. They follow traditions handed down from one lighting chief to the next. They're deuced clever and pretty careful most of the time. But you're right to be concerned. If they're cutting corners on essentials like gas bags, there could be worse trouble lurking in those storerooms. An explosion wouldn't just start a fire, it would release deadly amounts of poisonous compounds into the air."

Moriarty jotted the information into his notebook. Lacking a Watson to follow him about with pencil and paper, he had to serve as his own amanuensis. Lacking Holmes's thirst for notoriety, he had no intention of turning his notes into stories for the popular press.

One family member in the limelight was enough. However, he was learning many curious facts in the course of his new profession — one of things he liked best about it — and thus considered it wise to write up reports of each case for future reference.

Moriarty walked out of Somerset House into full darkness and an icy rain. The sun set at four o'clock on these dreary December days. He hailed a cab and snugged his arms under the cape of his ulster coat, grateful for the good British wool. He pondered the chemist's warnings as his cab clopped down the Strand toward South Kensington and home.

He was in no particular hurry, apart from a natural desire to reach the shelter of his own house. Angelina would doubtless still be at the theater. She'd expected to lunch with Sebastian after their meeting with the assembled cast and then take possession of her dressing room, whatever that entailed. Moriarty had authorized Sebastian to issue funds to the lighting chief to replace his faulty equipment and put a lock on that storeroom door, and also reimburse any actors who had suffered losses. Angelina assured him the gesture would go a long way toward restoring morale. Anything that improved her safety won his approval.

In fact, he intended to do more. The idea that he might put down his husbandly foot and insist she stay home barely skimmed across the surface of his mind. He had courted and won a paragon, a woman of rare beauty, intelligence, and talent. Naturally, such a woman had her own ambitions; she would be infinitely less fascinating without them. He hadn't risked the tattered shreds of his reputation — not to mention his life — last year in order to place her under a glass jar on his mantelpiece.

No, if Angelina wanted a Christmas pantomime, he would move heaven and earth to give her one. But Sebastian had suggested costs in the tens of thousands. Moriarty didn't have that kind of money, even for a sure bet, which Hatcliff's predicament indicated it was not. He didn't mind a gamble — that was how he made his living — but he wanted a better estimate of the hazards and returns before sinking any more of his savings into the show.

He paid the cabman and jogged up the steps to his own front door, which opened before he could place a hand on the knocker.

Rolly, their young footman, hustled him inside with more haste than grace, eager to shut the door on the bitter night. Moriarty noticed Angelina's wet cloak on the rack as the boy helped him out of his own coat and hat. "She's home. That's a pleasant surprise."

"Just come in and going out again after dinner."

"What are we having?"

"You'll find out soon enough, Perfessor," came the pert response.

Antoine Leclercq, their French chef, expected each meal to be perceived as a special event, even on an ordinary Monday night. All artists had their little ways, and he was well worth their tolerance. The man was a genius in his chosen field.

Moriarty jogged upstairs to freshen up, then joined his wife in the drawing room. She had come back at some point during the day to change into the small-bustled, brown wool dress she wore when she didn't care who saw her. The warm color accentuated the bronze highlights in her hair and the simple contours made her look more like a woman than a showpiece. He liked it.

He kissed her on the cheek and accepted the glass of whiskey she'd poured for him. "How did the meeting go? Will the cast accept Sebastian as their new manager?"

"He has them in his palm." She held out a cupped hand to illustrate. "He has more charm than Viola and me put together. Let's hope the glow lasts long enough to pull everyone together until opening night."

"I have every confidence." Moriarty raised his glass to toast her. Then he told her what he'd learned from the chemist. She was less impressed by the potential dangers than he would have liked.

"Theaters are full of hazards, darling. Accidents happen all the time." She spoke as if pointing out a commonplace, but, on noticing his pursed lips, hastily added, "Although I feel much, much happier knowing you're looking after us."

He wasn't mollified; in fact, her complacency restarted his earlier train of thought. His happiness would be best served by the pantomime's collapse, and the sooner the better. But as he followed her downstairs to the dining room, he abandoned that futile wish once and for all. Angelina was nothing if not persistent. Once she conceived a goal, she pursued it to the end, full steam ahead, with a total disregard for her own safety. It was her nature. He couldn't admire her for it and seek to prevent it at the same time.

He seated her and then took his own chair. Rolly served a fragrant onion soup, just the ticket on a nasty night. He listened to Angelina chatter about the people she had recognized at the assembly this morning and her speculations about the ones she hadn't, murmuring platitudes at the appropriate intervals.

The soup was removed and the main course served. Moriarty took a moment to appreciate the rich aromas rising from his plate: a thick broiled pork chop, rubbed with sage and pepper, accompanied by Antoine's incomparable roast potatoes, oozing with herbed butter. Then he noticed Angelina's woebegone expression and observed that her plate held something different. "What've you got there?"

"Grilled fish and steamed vegetables." She poked at a green-and-orange mass. "Isn't there any butter in this at all?" she asked Rolly.

"You told Hantoine you was slimmin', Missus. 'E says that means no butter, not even if you begs me."

"I would never stoop so low." She sniffed at a forkful of fish.

Moriarty took up his own utensils without a shred of guilt. She'd asked for the special meal, and Antoine could make anything delicious, even steamed celery. He hummed with pleasure as the savory pork melted on his tongue and got a sharp glare from his wife. "Sorry." He hadn't meant to gloat.

She picked at her fish until Rolly finished pouring the wine and went back down to the kitchen, then lunged at Moriarty's plate to stab a potato, popping it straight into her mouth. She shot a glance at the door and stabbed up another one.

"I really shouldn't," she mumbled through a mouthful of potato, "but I'm so hungry!"

Moriarty let her have them, contenting himself with crusty bread. She'd polished off his potatoes in addition to her dietary meal by the time Rolly came back to collect the plates. If he noticed the trail of butter leading across the tablecloth, he wisely kept the observation to himself.

"There's treacle tart for pudding, Perfessor. Shall I bring you a nice big piece?"

"No pudding for me." Angelina rose and smoothed her dress over her tummy. "I've got to get back to the theater, James. That vile Nora Verney left my dressing room in a shambles!" She kissed him on the cheek. "Will you mind terribly, spending the evening alone?"

"I suppose I'd better get used to it." Then he had a better idea. "On second thought, I think I'll drop around to my club to see if Sir Julian's there. I'd like to get some expert advice before plunging more deeply into this production."

Her eyes sparkled at the promise implied by that cautious remark. "Give Sir Julian my love, won't you? We really ought to have him for dinner sometime soon." She started toward the door and then turned back. "Well, not *soon.* Sometime after things get settled into a new routine."

Moriarty strove to maintain a casual tone. "When do you imagine that might be?"

She hummed a doubtful note. "It depends on how well we do. But don't worry, darling. I'll have every Monday night off."

* * *

Sir Julian Kidwelly was an economist who analyzed business trends, both foreign and domestic. Ostensibly employed by his father's global import-export business, Sir Julian wrote articles for the *National Review* and *The Economist,* as well as serving as an unofficial advisor to several government offices. He and Moriarty met once or twice a week at the Pythagoras Club for brandy and a game of chess.

Moriarty found his friend in their favorite corner of the game room, in which low-voiced conversations were not deprecated. The portly baronet occupied a leather chair placed at the optimal distance from the crackling fire. He'd opened his jacket to reveal a figured silk waistcoat with a gleaming gold chain rounding his ample midsection. Sir Julian had passed the age of forty, but his Savile Row tailor kept him *au courant.*

He glanced up from his newspaper at Moriarty's entrance, smiled a welcome, and set the paper aside. "I didn't expect to see you this evening, Professor. What could drive you from your domestic comforts on such a dismal night?"

"Your wise counsel. I have a new case which raises questions of a financial nature."

A waiter shimmered up to receive their requests for refreshment. When he left, Sir Julian rubbed his plump hands together. "Tell me all. Begin at the beginning."

Moriarty obliged him, giving him a full account of events since Lionel Hatcliff's first visit, pausing when the waiter brought their snifters and lit their cigars. Sir Julian listened in silence, his head slightly tilted, making no comments and asking no questions. His area of expertise was economics, which he interpreted as encompassing the whole of human experience, so his interests ranged widely. He especially loved obtaining advance news and inside information. He could join one odd fact with a seemingly unrelated incident and discover a hitherto unnoticed and potentially explosive trend.

Moriarty concluded with his question. "I've been looking for something more interesting than the three percents. And I wouldn't mind something requiring my active involvement. But I don't want to throw money out the window. How risky is it to invest in a single play, or pantomime, since they seem to be different?"

"Pantomimes are far more profitable than most plays, unless they fail from the start. Always a risk. But I would say you're guaranteed at least a limited success. Lina Lovington's return to the London stage after so many years abroad will be an irresistible draw that should fill seats for at least a few weeks. You'll need more than that to pay back the full cost, however. The ultimate success depends on many factors. Your wife has been a woman of leisure for several years now. Do you think she has the strength to sustain a long-running production?"

"She's in the very peak of condition," Moriarty said with a touch of indignation.

"I meant no disrespect." Sir Julian chuckled. "But if she falters, the play will suffer. That's one factor. Next, a pantomime is mostly spectacle, which means elaborate stage effects. The success in that arena rests on the shoulders of your stage manager. Do you believe Sebastian Archer has what it takes?"

Moriarty drew on his cigar, savoring the smoke before releasing it. "As far as I can tell, that job largely consists of prodding other people into doing theirs. The Archer children have a natural talent for getting people to do what they want and they don't like to fail. Sebastian may play the idle young toff, but he's no fool. I doubt he would take a job he couldn't excel at."

"You sound as though you've already made up your mind."

"I do, don't I?" Sometimes a man just had to hear the truth spoken by a trusted friend. "I have committed a thousand pounds already to pay the quarterly rent. The question is whether I want to go further. Hatcliff hasn't said it in so many words, but I suspect he would welcome a full partner. That could be a major investment. My brother-in-law said pantomimes run into the tens of thousands."

"He's probably right. Some of those scenery paintings are works of art, you know. They're signed by the painter, whose name appears prominently in the program. The true aficionado will find that of greater interest than the man who plays the Dame." Sir Julian pursed his lips in a droll expression to indicate his membership in that select society.

"To be candid with you," Moriarty said, "I don't have tens of thousands to invest. Five thousand would scrape as close to the bottom of my barrel as I care to go."

"I don't believe that much is spent on every show. A good theater manager like Lionel Hatcliff commissions the more expensive works with an eye to the future. *Jack and the Beanstalk* may be valued at twenty thousand pounds, but half of that would have been spent in earlier years. Hatcliff must have quite an accumulation of properties squirreled away at the Galaxy." Sir Julian paused to take a draw on his cigar. He tapped the ash in the silver tray and said, "You'd get a steadier return if you bought the building. Pay that four thousand a year to yourself, risk-free. If you remodeled, replacing the gas with electricity, you'd reduce your operating costs and lower your risk of fire."

A jolt of surprise dropped ash from the end of Moriarty's cigar. "The thought of *buying* a theater never crossed my mind."

"That's the best route to the largest profit. If you electrify, you can offset some expenses by putting an engine in that enormous cellar and selling the excess to your neighbors."

Moriarty blinked at the baronet, his cigar forgotten. "My own generator?" He found the new means of energy production fascinating, not only for the power they produced. Some of them were truly works of mechanical art.

Sir Julian tilted back his head and laughed, one hand holding his shaking belly. When his mirth passed, he wiped the corner of one eye. "The look on your face, my dear Moriarty. Priceless! Most men contemplating an investment in the theater are captivated by the magic of the stage or the beauty of an actress — or an actor. Only you would be enraptured at the prospect of a great, oily electrical generator."

"We all have our weaknesses." Moriarty grinned. "You've given me something to think about. But to return to the mundane reality of hard numbers. I would like to get a sense of the average costs and returns for these Christmas pantomimes before I sit down with Lionel Hatcliff to work out a deal."

"You don't trust him to give you an accurate accounting?"

"Trust is a variable word." Moriarty gave the baronet a wry smile. "Hatcliff is an old friend of my wife's from her music hall days, which recommends him as a dinner companion, but not necessarily as a business partner."

"I understand." Sir Julian knew something of Angelina's history, including her flexible views regarding one's individual responsibility toward the law. "I don't know your Mr. Hatcliff, though I have known a few theater managers. They tend to bounce from one extreme to the other, crying imminent disaster one moment and boasting about the hit of the century the next. You're wise to seek independent corroboration."

"I was hoping you might provide some insight."

"Only in general terms. You need specifics. Luckily, I know the very man you ought to consult." Luck had little to do with that. Sir Julian knew everyone who mattered in London society, along with many who only thought they did. He summoned the waiter to ask for paper and pen, then scrawled a note and folded it into the envelope provided. "Please have this delivered to the Honorable Charles Cudlow." He consulted his pocket watch, snapping it closed with a nod. "I believe you'll find him at White's."

"Charles Cudlow?" Moriarty asked after the waiter left.

"He's the leader of a group of young bucks who used to gamble in the usual way until Cudlow got them into investing in theatrical and sporting events. They're younger sons of peers who've taken jobs at banks or investment firms as a sort of window dressing. You know the type I mean. Young men with polished manners and excellent clothes whose sole task is to give prospective clients a chance to rub elbows with the upper class."

Moriarty nodded. "I've met many of that type at the gaming tables in the better spas and holiday resorts. They place their bets according to the whim of the moment."

"Cudlow's more focused than the average. As far as I can tell, his group is thriving. He'll give you the insider's perspective. I've asked him to invite you to White's tomorrow. That's where he spends his evenings when he's not at the theater."

"I appreciate the introduction." Moriarty checked his watch. "No point going home to an empty house. Mrs. Moriarty won't be back till after ten. Would you care for a game of chess?"

They moved to a table already supplied with a board and absorbed themselves in the calculation of branching ramifications for each possible move. When Sir Julian pronounced, "Checkmate," Moriarty tipped over his dead king with a grunt of defeat.

"Next game will be mine," he promised. He leaned back in his chair and checked his watch again: fifteen minutes past ten. "I should be going." He drained his brandy, rose, and grinned at his friend. "Last week I lunched at the Garrick Club with a major star. Tomorrow I'll have drinks with a group of young aristos at White's. I'm becoming quite the *bon vivant*!"

Sir Julian smiled indulgently. "Don't forget to reserve me a box for opening night. I prefer the ones closest to the dress circle. Privacy, with a decent view of the stage."

Box reservations? Moriarty hadn't yet thought farther than reaching opening night without another death or a major conflagration. Somehow the thought of rotund Sir Julian beaming down at the stage from a gilded box brought the reality of his new circumstances home in a way that nothing else had thus far.

EIGHT

Angelina slept like a rock, exhausted after only one day's work. But when she smelled the tea James waved under her nose to wake her, she hauled herself out of bed without complaint. She'd get used to it again. If all went well and they settled into a nice long run, she'd allow herself to sleep until half past ten. Until that happy day arrived, it was all hands on deck.

She left James buried in his newspaper after lowering it far enough to plant a sound kiss on his upturned lips. He seemed his usual self — calm, silent, absorbed in the daily news — not unduly concerned or in any way miffed about her dashing off first thing in the morning. He wouldn't admit it if she asked; she had to read the subtle signs — the creases on his forehead, the pace at which he stirred his tea — to determine how he felt.

She wanted to play Jack at the Galaxy on Boxing Day more than she wanted anything — except James. She'd drop it all in a heartbeat if he truly wanted her to. She *thought* he knew that, but she'd keep a weather eye on him to be sure. So far, he seemed to be enjoying the opportunity to learn all sorts of new things.

She shivered as she stepped out onto the stoop. The rain had stopped during the night, blown off by a bracing east wind. She and Peg climbed gratefully into the waiting cab and then hustled into the shelter of the Galaxy, though it wasn't much warmer inside. They wouldn't waste money heating the vast hall until absolutely necessary, so it sucked warmth from the heated spaces backstage.

They shed their outer garments in her dressing room, but didn't linger. They had a mission this morning to explore the wardrobe. Angelina had piously offered to help Peg do a rough inventory of the Galaxy's costumes.

As Peg unpinned her hat, she asked, "Do you remember when Sebby played a grenadier in *Ali Baba*? He must have been nine or ten years old."

Angelina laughed at the memory. "He loved that uniform so much, he wanted to run off and join the French Foreign Legion. He was *so* disappointed when he found out you had to be a grown-up."

"That's when I first met Mr. Tweedy, as I recall." Peg's tone was matter-of-fact, but Angelina caught the meaningful glance tossed her way.

"Was it?"

"He's put on a few stone since then, hasn't he?"

Angelina hesitated, not sure how to answer. Had the bloom faded from the rose so quickly? "Perhaps a pound or two . . ."

Peg nodded with satisfaction. "It suits him. I like a man with meat on his bones. Shows he loves life and knows how to live it."

Roses blooming nicely, then. Good. Peg was long overdue for a spot of romance. Angelina began thinking about ways to help things along, put the two into each other's company . . . Perhaps Peg could take charge of Tweedy's costumes too? Then she'd have to measure him — more than once.

They wrapped shawls around their shoulders and left, locking the door. As they climbed the stairs to the second floor, Angelina asked, as if only mildly interested, "Did you see a great deal of Mr. Tweedy back then?"

"A fair bit," Peg said slyly. "You and he played the same houses so often back then, and you were on stage so much of the time . . ."

"Oh, so that's what was going on in my dressing room! Selfish me, I never even noticed."

Peg clucked her tongue. "Your Pa didn't give you time to turn around in those days. You were doing trouser roles as Lionel Lockwood in between Lina's routines, keeping a roof over all our heads, with help from the twins. I've never seen children work so hard! Even the Delaney sisters got time off now and then."

"We've all landed on our feet." Angelina never saw much point in grumbling over the past. The present was ever so much more interesting. "Did you ever —" She searched for a delicate way to ask the most indelicate of questions. "Did you and Mr. Tweedy ever . . . ?"

"Ha! That's none of your business, Miss Pry." Peg smirked like a cat with a mouthful of canary.

"I'm just glad someone was having fun back then. Did you ever think of marrying him?"

"Never asked me, did he? Then we ran off to Italy, and that was that."

"I'm sorry if my little drama ruined your chance." Angelina had left England and her domineering father the day she turned eighteen.

"Don't know if there was any chance, ducky, nor if I'd've said yes if he'd asked. I've no regrets."

"Well, now you two will have time to get reacquainted." Angelina remembered his complaints at the meeting. "What was he going on about yesterday anyway? Pestering Sebastian about salaries like that. And on his first day, in front of everyone."

"How would I know?" Peg's face took on a mulish quality.

"Didn't he tell you? I saw him whispering in your ear."

"I have no idea what you could possibly mean." She stopped at a double door. "Here we are: *Wardrobe*."

Peg was the world's worst liar; always had been. Angelina contemplated her stiff back with a hollow feeling in the pit of her stomach. When had her old friend started keeping secrets from her?

Peg opened the door and they went in, gasping in unison at the riches displayed before them. The room occupied the space of three dressing rooms, extending to their left. Whitewashed bricks marked the back wall, or what could be seen of it behind the ceiling-high shelves of hats, masks, weapons, and other accessories.

Angelina thrust her nose forward to inhale that indefinable mix of dust, wool, sweat, and makeup. "Oh, how I've missed this smell!"

"No skimping in here anyway. Look at this stuff!" Peg put her hands on her hips as she surveyed the room, her head bobbing as she counted racks of clothes. Men's and women's costumes — kings, queens, soldiers, villagers — all neatly hung and ordered by size. She moved to a rack of fairy dresses and pulled one out, holding it up to show Angelina. "I remember the last time you played a fairy."

"Don't remind me of how much I've grown! I'm dreading the sight of myself in a Jack suit."

Peg examined the gauzy dress, fingering the fabric and inspecting the stitch work with narrowed eyes. Then she smoothed it deftly back into place in the rack. "That's real chiffon, ducky, and the stitching is neater than neat."

They forgot their not-quite spat and moved forward with *oohs* and *ahs,* hands outstretched to stroke and fondle the marvelous clothes. A low whistle rose from the closely packed aisle between racks Peg had drifted into. "They've got a fortune in here, Lina! I couldn't begin to add it all up."

"Come look at these," Angelina said. "I think they're for Shakespeare because they seem to be historically accurate. I'm no expert, but look at the details on this doublet! Right down to the silk-wrapped buttons." She turned toward the wall holding an array of ruffs and cuffs from every period in England's history. "Oh, look at *this!*" She pointed at one of those fantastic wire-and-lace confections Queen Elizabeth wore in her famous portraits. "I would *love* to play a role that let me wear one of these."

"I thought you hated Shakespeare." Peg appeared at her side.

"Hate the bard? *Moi?*" Angelina pantomimed a melodramatic faint. "I just don't like memorizing long speeches. And don't tell me Nora Verney ever stumbled through a rendition of *Romeo and Juliet.*"

"I'd pay to see that, I would. I like a good laugh."

"Romeo, O Romeo!" Angelina crooned in Nora's girlish soprano. They strolled on between the racks, occasionally pulling out an exceptional garment to exclaim over, happy as a pair of butterflies in a field of daisies.

"Lord, love a duck!" Peg cried. "Would you look at all this fur!" She pulled out a cloak decorated with lush trim. She fondled the stuff, then buried her nose in it. "Dyed rabbit, but nicely done. Who's this lovely thing for, then? Not Romeo."

"No, we seem to have passed into the Middle Ages." Angelina explored the other side of the same rack and found an ebony gown shot through with silver threads that would shimmer under the limelight. Lust burbled in her breast. "I know what these are for! But what could Lionel have been thinking, spending so much on that play? This is a variety house. He doesn't do real Shakespeare. And who on earth would pay to see a burlesque of Macbe —"

A shriek cut her off, making both of them jump clear off the floor. The sound had arisen from a heap of clothes a few feet in front of them. They'd reached the far end of the long room, where the racks ended and the workshop began. The heap shifted to reveal a short, squat woman draped in layers of shawls with a tall pile of unnaturally glossy black curls atop her head. Her lap was full of gauzy fabric she'd been sewing while listening to Peg and Angelina chatter on.

Her small black eyes glared malevolently at Angelina, making her shrink back a step. "*Never* utter the name of the Scottish play!" The creature's voice had a raspy, childlike quality. "You call yourself an actress? Do you want to call down more bad luck upon this unhappy theater?"

"I'm sorry," Angelina said, shrugging questioningly at Peg. "A slip of the tongue. I'm Lina Lovington, and this is my dresser, Margaret Bar —"

"I know who *you* are," the woman said, turning her baleful glare toward Peg. "But you've forgotten *me*, haven't you, with your famous travels and your fancy friends."

Peg leaned forward for a closer look, then reeled back in surprise. "Why, it's Annie Draper, as I live and breathe! Fancy meeting you here. Are you one of the dressers?"

"I am Madame Noisette now, the mistress of the Galaxy's wardrobe."

Noisette? Angelina had to bite her lip to keep from laughing. Didn't she know it meant "little nut" in French?

"Wardrobe mistress?" Peg echoed. "My, my! Haven't we come up in the world!"

"Draper, Draper . . ." Angelina mused. "Why does that name sound familiar?"

Peg leaned on the end of a tall rack, folding her arms and regarding the little woman with a challenging air. "Annie — Madame Noisette, *excuse* me — gave me my first job, Lina. Before your father hired me to do for you."

"Really!" This was a day for memories. Angelina had been six and just making a name for herself in the East End music halls when her mother died giving birth to the twins. Her father, not wanting to miss a single booking, had hired thirteen-year-old Peg to stitch costumes and mind the babies. He'd chosen her because she was cheap; the children had loved her because she was warm and kind and cared about their well-being, unlike dear old Dad.

"I taught her everything she knows," Noisette squeaked, sounding as if someone were squeezing her around the middle.

Peg snorted. "You taught me to thread a needle and which end to poke into the cloth. That's about it. Oh, and how to stitch hems for twelve hours a day by an open window in all weathers, for ha'penny a dress." She shot Angelina a wry look. "Your dad thought himself a shrewd dealer, but I'm the one got the best of that bargain."

"No, darling. The twins and I did. We knew it from the start."

"Isn't that sweet!" Noisette sneered. "Like treacle on cake. What're you doing in here anyway, pawing through my racks, getting your grimy hands all over my beautiful gowns?"

"My brother, Sebastian Archer, asked Miss Barwick to make an assessment of the costume inventory. He wants to be sure we're ready for a busy new year."

Noisette's black eyes narrowed. "Why not ask me? Does he expect me to lie to him? Why else would he send spies to prowl around looking for evidence against me?"

What sort of evidence would they find if they looked? Angelina wouldn't have thought any such thing if this little nut hadn't brought it up. Still, she had to work with the woman. Best try to get on her good side — if she had one. "We were distracted by your extraordinary craftsmanship. And we wanted to see my Jack costume. Actually, we'll need to take it with us. It's bound to need a little alteration."

"A *little?* Ha! It will never fit you. I'll have to let it out" — she leaned forward to survey Angelina's figure — "four inches, maybe five. What've you been doing during your retirement, Miss Lovington? Selling pastries?" She burst into a cackling laugh, shaking the pile of curls.

No good side, then.

Peg stepped forward, hand on hip. "No one dresses Lina Lovington but me. I've been with her nigh on twenty-five years. I know how she moves. She's a dancer, is my Lina, as much as an actress. Not like your Nora Verney. I've seen that one. Like an old cow lumbering around the stage."

"How dare you!" Madame Noisette hopped to her feet and drew herself up to her full height. The top of her head barely reached Angelina's chin. She folded the gauze onto her chair and pushed past Angelina to replace Lady Macbeth's gown with exaggerated care. "I made this dress myself, every stitch. Miss Nora chose the play. She was *brilliant*." The black eyes flashed.

Nora Verney in the Scottish play? Even in a burlesque version, it boggled the mind. Nora was adorable twirling a parasol and singing "Buy Me Some Almond Rock" while a funny man lolloped around her, slipping and falling at her feet. But standing alone in the spotlight, intoning, "All the perfumes of Arabia will not sweeten this little hand?" In Nora's chirpy voice, it would sound like an advertisement for Pears Soap.

The critics would have heaped scorn upon it, killing the play inside a week. No wonder Lionel had been losing money!

"It was the curse," Noisette said, turning her basilisk eyes on Peg. "The Scottish play should never have been attempted in this unhappy house. Not with that odious John Fowler living up to his name. We had nothing but trouble from the start."

"These costumes are truly beautiful," Angelina said, wondering about Fowler. It didn't look like he'd pinched any pennies in this department. "It's a shame hardly anyone got to see them. Can't we work some of them into the panto?"

Noisette didn't answer. She turned her back on Angelina and walked slowly down the aisle between the tall racks, tucking a sleeve in here and straightening a collar there. She spoke in a raspy monotone, as if telling her story to the clothes. "Miss Nora found another play, a musical retelling of *King Lear*. I added a silver veil to that gown, an ethereal effect, for her Cordelia. I remade a harlequin costume for her Fool."

"Did Sparrow play the Fool?" Angelina asked, following her.

"The odious Frank Sparrow played Goneril," Noisette said, as if that should have been obvious. "Mr. Tweedy played Regan. He was *brilliant.*"

"That must have been frightfully funny," Angelina said, meaning it.

Noisette stopped to give her a measuring look from under her thick black brows. "No one appreciates Mr. Tweedy as I do. No one *understands* him. He relies on me. I'm the only one he could trust in his hour of need."

"What did he need?" Angelina asked.

"That's none of your concern." Noisette raised her nose in the air.

Money would be the obvious answer, but why ask the wardrobe mistress? She must be the least-well paid department chief; that was always the way of things.

Angelina returned to the spring plays. "How did your musical *Lear* do?"

"The curse killed it in the first week," Noisette said. "By means of that odious John Fowler. Everything went wrong. Lights went out when Miss Nora began to sing. Traps stuck. Sets fell down in the middle of a scene."

"How was that Mr. Fowler's fault?"

"It was his job to make sure everything went right. Now it's Mr. Archer's job." Noisette tilted her head to gaze obliquely at Angelina. "What will he want, I wonder?"

She came to the end of one aisle and turned back toward the work area, where a single rack of costumes hung ready for something. She held up one for Angela's inspection. "This is Jack. You'll wear your own tights. They should be pink."

"Oh my stars." The blood drained from Angelina's cheeks. She took the proffered outfit and held it against her body, turning to show Peg. The thing had started out in someone's mind as the ordinary garb of a lad from sometime back in the days of Good Queen Bess. The rounded pants might cover Angelina's bloomin' arse if she stood perfectly still and never raised her arms. The shirt was a filmy confection of transparent linen with full sleeves and a wide collar open to the top of a corset-like vest, which might cover two-thirds of Angelina's breasts if she rounded her shoulders and kept her chin tucked.

"Oh, ducky," Peg said in a quavering voice. "The professor ain't going to like that outfit. Not one bit."

"We can make it a little bigger, can't we?"

"We'll have to. There'll be children out there watching you gallivanting up and down that beanstalk."

Stark fear raced up Angelina's spine as she met her dresser's eyes. She barely heard the wardrobe mistress snickering behind her. "No more potatoes," she told Peg, making it a solemn vow. "Not until our one hundredth night. And then only a small one."

NINE

The butler at White's had been informed about Moriarty's invitation. He bowed politely and summoned a footman to guide him upstairs. They traversed a span of thick Oriental carpet to a double door with a hunting scene painted above the header. The footman knocked once, then admitted Moriarty to a long room dominated by a billiard table, twelve feet of carved mahogany topped with an expanse of smooth green felt with a chandelier hanging over the center. Other lamps glowed warmly on small tables flanked by deep leather chairs. A sideboard held bottles and glasses, and a fire crackled in the hearth.

"You must be Professor Moriarty." A young man with dark blond hair and a pencil moustache came forward. "I'm Charles Cudlow."

Moriarty shook his hand. "Thank you for giving me some of your time. I'll try not to take too much of it."

"Always happy to oblige Sir Julian." Cudlow introduced the other two men, who were standing by the table with cue sticks in their hands. "This is Louis Peckham" — he nodded toward a slender man in round spectacles — "and that one's Peter Deering. Don't let his diminutive size fool you. He's has the devil's own luck at billiards."

"It ain't luck, old man, I assure you."

All three men wore the new sack suits with the shorter jackets. Cudlow's brown one had a fine pink stripe while the other two wore checks in muted hues. Moriarty possessed one such suit, though it left the cupboard only when Angelina insisted. The jacket exposed more of his backside than he found comfortable, especially in activities that required a forward bend like billiards.

The two players stared at Moriarty with quizzical half-smiles, as if trying to identify his species. He had no idea how to respond and it was becoming a trifle offensive.

Cudlow laughed. "Forgive these buffoons, Professor. They're trying to discover your secret."

"What secret?"

"Well, on the surface, you appear to be an ordinary mortal like the rest of us. Yet somehow you managed to win the hand of the incomparable Lina Lovington."

That broke the spell. The two players came forward to pump his hand, bubbling over with admiration for his wife. They had been among her most devoted aficionados as adolescents, stealing every possible hour during school holidays to spend in her exalted presence. They spouted songs and sketches, topping each other's memories.

"That's enough, you chowderheads." Cudlow gave Moriarty a curious look. "You don't know any of those old favorites, do you? Weren't you among her legion of admirers?"

Moriarty only smiled and shook his head. "We met socially a little more than a year ago." A simple explanation for the most exciting month of his life.

He wasn't altogether discommoded by their enthusiasm. He preferred it to the disapproving glances Angelina attracted at the few Royal Society events she'd attended. Those stuffy men of science and their stuffier middle-class wives thought he'd lowered himself by marrying an actress. These men, in contrast, recognized his achievement and applauded him for it. He might wish for more decorum, but he couldn't dispute the fundamental axiom.

Cudlow gestured at the sideboard. "What can I offer you, Professor? A spot of whiskey, perhaps?"

At those words, his friends shot Moriarty a last grin and returned to their game. Moriarty accepted a glass and allowed himself to be led to a pair of comfortable chairs near the fire. "Very pleasant," he said, waving his glass to indicate the room in general.

"It beats rattling about alone in my flat on a cold winter night." Cudlow sipped his drink, allowed a polite interval to elapse, then moved on to the main theme. "Sir Julian's note said you wanted advice about investing in a play. Dare I hazard a guess as to which one?"

"My wife's, of course. *Jack in the Beanstalk* at the Galaxy."

"She's playing Jack, I presume." At the nod of confirmation, Cudlow asked, "Will she be taking any of the variety turns?"

"I believe so. She spent the weekend at the piano learning new songs."

"Pay up," Deering said, snapping his fingers. The players must have been listening. Peckham groaned and fished a bill out of his notecase, handing it to his friend.

Cudlow smiled. "There's one answer for you, Professor. These men would pay any sum you care to name to hear Lina Lovington sing again. Hatcliff may have been having a run of bad luck, but her name on the bill will have changed that already."

"It seems a lot to hang on one woman's shoulders," Moriarty said. "I don't think this is at all likely, mind you, but what if she finds she doesn't care for the part? Or, God forbid, she loses her voice or sprains an ankle?"

"Ah yes, Adorable Nora!" Cudlow's eyes flashed. "She has talent, but not much grit. Most actresses would have their costume altered to accommodate a bandage and keep right on going."

"Wouldn't the understudy take the part if it happened while the show was running?"

"The audience doesn't pay to see understudies, Professor. But you're right; the success of a pantomime doesn't depend solely on the star. They're mostly spectacle, lavishly built up around a thin story. The actors matter, but far less than they would in a play."

"Spectacle provided by big props, painted backcloths, and fancy lighting effects, I understand."

"All that and more. Lavish costumes covered with spangles. Fairies and angels swinging overhead, devils and frightening beasts popping up from below, endless processions of adorable children dressed up as bees or soldiers or whatever the writer cooked up this year." Cudlow winked. "It can be quite thrilling, especially the first time you see it. Many people go back more than once to savor the details. That's one of the ways you make your money."

"I'm getting the impression the sets and so forth are a greater expense than the actors' salaries."

"Far greater!" Cudlow laughed. "And mostly before opening night, I might add. That's one of the hazards of investing in pantos. Most of the money is spent in advance. You can't be certain when you start building your sets that you'll open with your first-choice cast."

"I've heard numbers in the tens of thousands," Moriarty said, "but I can't bring myself to believe in such enormous sums."

"Brace yourself, Professor." Cudlow raised his glass and took a sip. "I have it on good authority that last year's production of *Sindbad the Sailor* at Drury Lane cost upwards of thirty thousand pounds."

"Great Scott!" Moriarty cried, louder than he intended.

The billiards players' heads turned toward him. "Don't frighten the man off, Cuddy. We're panting to watch Lovely Lina climb that beanstalk." Moriarty shot him a dark look, and he grimaced an apology. "Sorry, old man. I keep forgetting you're the husband."

"It does boggle the mind," the other one said. "Lina Lovington, married — and not to me. Another boyhood dream shattered. It's your play, Peckham."

Cudlow said, "You wanted numbers, Professor. But remember, most of that went into the creation of tangible properties that can be used again and again. Judging by what I've seen from the audience, I would estimate Hatcliff's properties are worth something on the order of twenty-five thousand pounds."

Moriarty gave a low whistle, followed by a large swallow of the excellent whiskey. "I had no idea."

"In my judgment," Cudlow said, "he's spent too much. He's made some bad choices and had a series of flops this past year. He must be about at the bottom of his purse by now."

"Which is where I come in — if I decide in favor of the venture."

Cudlow pointed at his glass. "Care for another?" He rose and fetched the bottle. "The profits can be equally astounding, mind you," he said, refilling their glasses. He offered Moriarty a cigarette from a silver case, took one himself, lit them both with an ivory-plated lighter, and resumed his seat.

"They'd have to be," Moriarty said. "Else who would risk it?"

Cudlow grinned. "Theater-lovers always believe the next one will pay for all. But a successful panto should yield a threefold return."

"Threefold." That made more sense than Sebastian's optimistic estimate of tenfold. But it was still a tremendous rate of return. "You're saying Drury's *Sindbad* earned ninety thousand pounds. For a fairy tale?"

"A tale with flying fairies and hundreds of supernumeraries." Cudlow chuckled. "*Sindbad* had everything but a real ocean. If your show really tickles the public's fancy, it will run every night in London for four months, plus Sunday afternoons. Then it will go on tour and play in every mid-sized borough in England. They'll toddle back to the capital just in time to start building the next one."

Moriarty frowned. "The cast is away from London for the better part of the year?"

"Don't worry, old chap. Your wife won't be on that train. They hire a new cast to play the provinces."

"That's a relief. I do have a lot to learn. But I'm beginning to understand why Hatcliff is coming up short at this point in the season."

"You're getting it backward," Cudlow said. "He should be fairly flush. Not being among his confidantes, I couldn't tell you where the summer touring profits went. Presumably on the spring and autumn flops. But even with an infusion of cash, I'm afraid Hatcliff is doomed. I understand his stage manager was killed in an accident last week. The competition for experienced theater crews is intense at this time of year. I doubt you'll be able to replace him."

"Sebastian Archer is stepping in. Hatcliff and my wife seem to think he's qualified, and I'm inclined to agree."

"Sebastian Archer?" Cudlow tucked his chin, taken aback. "I hadn't heard that and I keep my ear pretty close to the ground."

"He started yesterday. His last play ended a few weeks ago and he's giving up his holiday in Greece. I have every confidence he'll put an end to this rash of accidents."

"Do you? Well, here's luck to you!" Cudlow raised his glass. "You'll need it."

A loud groan and a victorious cackle arose from the players, signaling the end of their game. The one with the spectacles went to pour a couple of drinks while the short one called, "Care for a game, Professor?"

"No, thanks," Moriarty said. "I'm not much good at billiards."

"How's that?" Cudlow asked, shooting a wink at his friend. "Haven't I heard that you're a mathematician? Billiards is pure geometry."

"With a dose of physics," Moriarty agreed. "But statistics is my area of specialization." At their blank looks, he added, "Probability. Measures of chance."

"Like knowing which little hole the ball will fall into when the wheel stops spinning?" Deering asked.

"I'm not fond of roulette," Moriarty said. "The tables are so easily rigged. I prefer cards, especially whist or poker. You've a one-in-fifty-two chance that any given card will turn up."

"How does that help you?" Peckham asked, handing his friend a snifter.

"It's pretty good odds to start with," Moriarty said. "Then you can quickly narrow it down further. Think of it this way. You have a one in — what? Four or five million chance of meeting a given individual when you walk down a London street."

"Depends where you're walking," Deering said.

"That's right," Moriarty said, ignoring the jocular tone. "You can improve your odds by walking in the neighborhood where the individual lives, for example."

"Card suits," Peckham said, snapping his fingers. "There are only four of those."

"Precisely," Moriarty said. "And each card that's revealed eliminates whole branches of possibilities. It's rather a lot of calculation to be done under pressure. I won't say it isn't challenging, but that's a large part of the appeal for me."

Deering wrinkled his nose. "Too bloodless for my taste. I prefer to clasp my hands and pray to the gods of luck."

"I like craps myself," Peckham said, "with a pretty girl to blow on the dice before they roll."

Cudlow had been shaking his head through these declarations. "Casinos are a waste of time and money. How long does it take that little ball to find its way into a pocket? A minute? And your odds don't change if you get to know the croupier or spend quality time watching the wheel. It may take months for your theatrical investment to pay off, but you have a fair degree of control over results, depending on your manager and how hands-on you want to be."

"Very hands-on," Peckham said, "if we're talking about the ballet dancers." Deering laughed with him.

"They're idiots," Cudlow confided to Moriarty. "I only keep them around for comic relief."

"And for our money." Deering didn't seem the least offended.

"And for their money." Cudlow shrugged. "Although I'll confess to a weakness for pretty actresses. But that's not an attraction for you, Professor. You've won your prize. And it doesn't sound like you gamble for the thrill of the game."

"Thrill doesn't enter into it." Apart from watching Angelina circulate through a glittering casino in a low-cut evening gown. "Gambling is simply the most expedient method, given my particular skills, of supplying the funds that became necessary after I married. My wife, you see, has rather expensive tastes."

"The only kind of wife worth having." Cudlow gave his guest a measuring look. "You came to me for advice about investing in Hatcliff's pantomime. I would recommend caution. Plays of all kinds are always risky. Sometimes the public just don't like 'em."

Moriarty shot a meaningful glance toward the billiard players. "But I've got both Lina Lovington and Sebastian Archer on the bill."

"True, and that does alter the equation in your favor." Cudlow nodded, weighing his words. "I had intended to advise you to stay out of the Galaxy, Professor. That theater is cursed. But now that your family's in it, your decision's been made. And if you're going in, then I say go all in. Give it everything you've got. I will recommend one thing."

"What's that?"

"Make sure you have plenty of fire insurance. That place is a tinderbox."

TEN

Angelina had toast and tea while dressing the next morning to save time. She left with Peg before James was halfway through his eggs and bacon. Just as well since she'd ruled out bacon for the time being, along with potatoes and puddings. Once the show started and she was spending four or five hours every night singing and dancing — and climbing up and down that beastly beanstalk — she could indulge in principal player's hours and richer meals.

But she would never be late again, not with Sebastian stalking the wings.

As they entered through the stage door, she greeted Old Sampson, asking him to let everyone knew she could be found, ready to work, in her dressing room. Then she and Peg tackled that skimpy scrap of a Jack costume.

"These puffy pants are easy enough," Peg said, holding them up. "I just open the top and bottom bands and add a few more strips on each side. This dark red is good for you. You've got a linen shirt with the right sort of sleeves. Might need another gusset or two . . ."

Her voice became muffled as she plunged her top half into a deep trunk. She rummaged around, muttering to herself in the gruff way that said she was as happy as a hog in a wallow, then emerged victorious with a big white shirt. She shook it out and held it to Angelina's shoulders, cocking her head.

"Don't tell me," Angelina said. "I've grown on top as well as on the bottom."

"All right, I won't tell you."

"I blame Antoine."

"He's not the one holding the fork, ducky." Peg tossed the shirt to Angelina. "Try that on for me, won't you?"

Angelina grabbed a pair of pink tights and went behind her carved teak screen, a gift from an admirer in her salad days.

She'd retrieved the cherished object from Viola's flat last week, along with the rest of her dressing room furnishings. These consisted mostly of silk scarves, mostly in shades of purple, which looked good with most colors — even the bilious greens that covered the walls backstage in this theater. She had a fainting couch with thick shawls for naps and a cushioned armchair with a low footstool for Peg to sit in and sew. They'd spent the better part of an hour unpacking cards and publicity photographs of herself and the twins from bygone days — Angelina and Her Little Angels, Lionel Lockwood, La Perichole . . . so many memories! Adding all this stuff to the dressing table with its big mirror and the long table where they put tea fixings crowded the room enough to feel cozy. It felt like coming home again.

She stripped to her combinations, shivering. This room was never warm enough. "Be a lamb and toss me my boy's corset, won't you?" This one flattened her breasts without squeezing her waist, exactly what she needed for this active role. She sat on the stool to pull on the warm tights, then pulled on the linen shirt, plucking out the puffy tops of the sleeves. "Shall I try those pants on for laughs?"

Peg handed them over. "Let me see how much to add."

Angelina got the miniscule bottom half of her costume more or less around her hips and came around to look in the tall mirror over the dressing table. "Lord help me, Peg! I'm a moose!"

"What do you know about mooses?" Peg took out her tape and her little notebook.

Three raps sounded on the door. Angelina sang, "Enter if you dare!"

The door opened and Sebastian appeared with his trusty prompt book. He broke into a wide grin as he took in Angelina's costume. "It's a shade on the small side, don't you think?"

She gave him a level look. "Peg will fix it."

"I'm not sure even Peg can work that miracle." Sebastian chuckled. "Has James seen it?"

"I've decided to let it be a surprise on opening night."

Peg and Sebastian burst into laughter. "A *fait accompli,* you mean." Sebastian shook his head. "But no, you're right. There's no other way. He wouldn't let anyone buy tickets to see you, and we need the money."

Angelina clucked her tongue at him and went behind the screen to change back into her dress. "What can we do for you, brother dear?"

"It's Peg I want this time," Sebastian said. He sat down at her dressing table and started poking around in her makeup boxes. He picked up a stick of Ruddy Rouge and gave a little laugh.

"What's wrong with that?" Angelina demanded.

He shrugged and put it back. "Nothing, if you're used to it."

"I'll change to the new kinds as I use things up."

"Thrifty! I approve." He chuckled at the change of heart. "Funny how different things look from the other side of the fence."

"What can I do for you, ducky?" Peg asked.

"More alterations." Sebastian swung around and leaned his elbows on the table behind him. "The dress parade is scheduled for next Wednesday, one week from today, including the music hall people doing the Shakespeare turns. They're using the costumes from the spring burlesques. They're bound to need a lot of alterations, and Madame Noisette is already up to her eyebrows."

"A small emergency, then," Peg said.

Angelina smiled at the wounded look on Sebastian's face. "She doesn't mean you, darling." She buttoned the neck of her dress and came out from behind her screen. "Did you know the little nut gave Peg her first job?"

"No." Sebastian chuckled. "Do you think she knows what *noisette* means?"

Angelina shrugged, surveying herself in the mirror. A well-flounced bustle covered a multitude of sins — and potatoes. "Maybe it's a nickname given by some long-ago admirer."

Peg snorted. Sebastian went to kneel beside her chair, gazing up at her with a winsome look. "Won't you help me, dearest Peg? If I say pretty please and promise to love you till I die?"

She rolled her eyes and shook her head, as if surrendering against her will. Peg had never been able to resist the twins' wheedling. Not many could. "I won't work for Annie Draper, mind you. Not for love nor money. How many Shakespeares are there?"

"Let's go up and look." Sebastian took both of her hands to pull her out of the chair, kissing her on the cheek as she rose.

Peg snatched up the puffy pants on the way out. "Might as well see what they've got in the way of fabric up there."

They followed Sebastian up the stairs to the wardrobe, finding the door wide open. "I wonder if there's anything in here I can wear for my variety turns," Angelina said.

"Don't you have your own dress?" Sebastian asked.

"It depends on what I do. I'm thinking of the tipsy song from *La Périchole,* if I can put together a nice gypsy outfit."

The wardrobe mistress materialized in front of them, already talking. "Mr. Archer has condescended to visit me in my workplace, isn't that surprising. To what do I owe the honor? Have you rewritten the script to include the rest of your family and all their friends?"

Sebastian smiled down at her, too cool to react to her peculiar manner. "*Au contraire,* Madame. I've come to offer you help in these hectic last days. I've persuaded Miss Barwick to help you with the Shakespeares' fittings."

Noisette's dark eyes flashed. "I don't need another apprentice."

"Ha!" Peg barked. "More like the other way around. I wouldn't take orders from you if the house was on fire and you was telling me to run for my life."

"I'm the mistress here," Noisette said. "All work is done according to my exacting standards. My wardrobe, my rules."

Peg crossed her arms. "I'm helping out because we're in a jam, but I work for Mr. Archer, see, not you. In my own room and in my own way."

"Never!" Noisette cried. "I will never allow you to replace me, you fat-fingered —"

"— colorblind —"

"— foul-smelling —"

"— midget!" Peg finished.

Noisette's pale cheeks turned red. She began chanting in her weird, raspy drone, "I've been mistress of the Galaxy for fifteen years. I'll kill you before I let —"

The two dressers had leaned ever closer to one another, now standing almost nose to nose, their work-hardened hands balled into fists. Sebastian wedged between them, pressing them apart with outstretched hands. "Calm down, now, both of you. We'll work out a fair —"

Piercing screams rose from the floor below, one after the other in a shrill cascade.

"What the devil?" Angelina said, but Sebastian had already started running toward the stairs, bounding down two steps at a time. The women followed as quickly as they could. They reached the first floor to find the Delaney sisters fluttering about the hall, flapping their hands in distress.

"What's happened?" Sebastian said. "Is the house on fire?"

"The ghost! The ghost!" they chorused. Amy, the oldest, pointed toward their dressing room with a trembling finger.

Sebastian ran to their room, next door to Angelina's. He dashed inside and came right out again. "No fire." He spoke loudly enough for the other people poking heads out of doors and spilling out of the stairwell to hear. Most of them went back to whatever they'd been doing.

Angelina exhaled the breath she'd been holding. "Come into my room, darlings, and tell us what happened." She and Peg ushered them in and got three of them seated on her fainting couch. The older two stood behind their sisters. Each of them clasped at least one sister's hand. "Would anyone like a tot of brandy?"

Peg shook her head. "We don't have any brandy. I can offer tea?"

They all declined the tea. "We can't stand it anymore, Sebastian," Amy said. "The ghost has been tormenting us for weeks. We can't stay here waiting for it to kill one of us." She met the eyes of each sister in turn, collecting grim nods. Then she faced Sebastian again. "We quit."

"No, Amy, no!" Sebastian stood in front of them with his hands clasped to his chest. He wasn't acting this time. The Delaney sisters were one of the best *corps de ballet* in London. They'd been dancing since they first learned to walk, taught by their parents, who still performed with the four boys as the Delaney Troupe, doing acrobatic routines, including a wildly popular bicycle act. The sisters had been rehearsing *Beanstalk* for weeks. And where else would they ever find five nearly identical girls?

"Tell us what happened," Angelina said. "We'll find a way to sort this out."

Five heads shook in disbelief. "We won't stay," Clarinda said. Or maybe it was Dorinda. "This theater's cursed."

"I can protect you," Sebastian promised. "But only if I know what's happened."

"The ghost tried to strangle Edith," Belinda said. "We'd just come up from rehearsing and were making tea and changing. Dorinda set a glass of water on a little table."

"I wanted a headache powder," Dorinda said. "I went to get some out of my box and heard the glass smash to the floor."

"It fell over all by itself," Belinda said. "No one was anywhere near it."

"Then I felt a cold gust of wind," Edith said. "I cried, 'Ooh!' and ran across to get my scarf from the top of the screen."

"But the ghost lifted it straight up into the air!" Clarinda cried.

"It draped it over my shoulders," Edith said, shivering. "I was petrified!"

"None of us could move," Dorinda said. "It froze us with its spirit breath."

"It tried to wrap the end around Edith's neck," Clarinda said. "It didn't have the strength to pull it tight or it would have strangled her right there in front of us."

Amy finished the story. "We screamed and grabbed Edith's hands and pulled her out into the hall. I'll never go back into that room. Never!"

"Never! Never!" the others echoed. "We can't go back!"

Sebastian had been listening with a solemn expression, hearing each girl in turn, not interrupting with so much as a hum or a cluck of the tongue. Now he stood silent for a moment, thinking. His first words were for Angelina. "Send someone for James, would you?

And don't let anyone into that room. Could you and Peg give us a few minutes here?"

"Of course." She bet he meant to offer himself as a sacrifice to one of them. Belinda, probably; she'd been making eyes at him from the start. She was a beautiful woman — a dream come true for a man who didn't already have a long-term boyfriend.

Angelina and Peg went out into the hall, closing the door. Angelina addressed the small crowd that had gathered. "It's all right, everyone. A spider fell on Edith's head and caused a fright. No harm done." She spotted a familiar face — the lighting man who'd discovered Mr. Fowler's body. "Mr. Williams?" She beckoned him over. "Would you be a dear and pop down to the manager's office to fetch my husband? Professor Moriarty has a special interest in, ah, spiders. We'll watch the door here to make sure it doesn't escape."

The man tipped his cap to her and scurried off.

While she was speaking, Peg sidled behind her to stand in front of the Delaneys' dressing room door. Angelina joined her, leaning against the jamb as if settling in for a spot of gossip. "Before I met James," she murmured, "I would have believed in the ghost."

"Not sure I don't," Peg said. "A scarf rising into the air all by itself?" She shuddered.

"James's disbelief is stronger than my belief. Or maybe it's that I believe in him now more than other things. I only hope he can figure out who's doing this and make it stop."

Peg cast a wary eye at a group of second-tier dancers still gossiping near the stairs. She crossed her arms and turned her back on them, lowering her voice almost to a whisper. "I don't know about these drafts and scarves, but I have my own ideas about who set the trap for *that odious John Fowler.*" She spoke the last phrase in a raspy imitation of Noisette.

"No," Angelina said. "Really? Why would she do such a horrible thing?"

"She hated him; she made that clear enough. And didn't you hear her threaten me? And she spends all day up there, two floors beneath that storeroom, stewing and fuming."

"How would she know how to set off that smoke powder?"

"Pah! How hard can it be? You find the jar labeled *smoke powder*, pour some in a pan, and set a match to it."

"There was a fuse."

Peg gave her a weary look. "How many times have we seen that done, Lina? I could do it. What's more, she's tiny. She could easily hide in the smoke at the end of the corridor. You can barely see her when she's standing right in front of you."

"She did seem to hate Mr. Fowler," Angelina said. "I wonder why?"

"Money, what else?"

"Hmm. I'll tell James, but you know, she couldn't have done the scarf just now. We were with her when the screaming started."

"Then she's got a henchman." Peg's jaw set. She wouldn't give up this pet theory.

Their dressing room door opened, and the five Delaneys trailed out. The last one, Belinda, was holding Sebastian's hand. He gave her a tender smile and said, "I'll have your new dressing room painted, shall I? What's your favorite color?"

She leaned toward him with her pink lips slightly parted. "Blue," she crooned. "The color of your eyes."

Angelina and Peg traded smirks. Belinda detached herself from her new beau and pattered after her sisters. "Half a tick," Sebastian said, nipping past them to lock the Delaneys' dressing room door. Then they went back into Angelina's room.

"What did you have to promise her?" Angelina asked, taking the stool at her dressing table.

"A late-night supper for the two of us," Sebastian said with a rueful grimace. He set the key on her table.

"You're in the soup now, ducky!" Peg settled into her sewing chair. "What'll Hugh say about it?"

"He'll cope." Sebastian stretched out on the fainting couch, balancing the prompt book on his chest so he could fold his hands behind his head. "It's time for him to take a wife anyway. Best to act before his father does the choosing. Viola's helping us sort through the possibles."

"I suppose there's no other way," Angelina said. "That's the great disadvantage of a title: they have to be passed on to somebody."

"We couldn't live together even if he were a chimney sweep." Sebastian had never been one to rail against life's realities. "She has to have money, of course. And we're hoping for one of the horsey kind."

"Now, now," Peg chided. "Don't be cruel."

"Hmm?" Sebastian turned a questioning face toward her. "Oh! No. I didn't mean her face. We don't mind how she looks. But we want one of those women who care more about horses than people. Then she'll be content out there on the family estate while Hugh spends most of his time in London."

Hugh Flexmere's father was a Somebody in the foreign office. He employed his son as a confidential secretary, hoping the scion would one day follow in his footsteps. After a period of resistance during which he'd met Sebastian, Hugh submitted to the inevitable. It was easier for everyone if he did what was expected in public, leaving him to spend private time with Sebastian.

"Still, you'll see less of each other," Angelina said with a sympathetic smile. She wished she could change things for them; they were such a lovely couple. Made for each other in so many ways. Sebastian was the steady one, surprisingly enough. Or perhaps not so surprising since he lived almost entirely inside the compass of the theater world, where the prejudice and prudery of society at large had little power. The aristocracy didn't mind much either, provided everyone observed all the correct forms. But things would change for them once Hugh married and had a child or two. "Here's hoping Belinda is a nice girl who won't expect too much from you," she said, getting a cackling laugh from Peg.

"You don't buy pearl earrings on a dancer's wages, ducky."

"Well, she won't be getting any pearls from me." Sebastian stretched and yawned hugely, then closed his eyes and fell silent.

Angelina caught Peg's gaze and put a finger to her lips. She started sorting through her makeup, wondering if she shouldn't replace the lot and start fresh.

"I thought it was over," Sebastian said, his eyes still closed.

"What was over, darling?"

"The accidents. The ghost. Whatever it is." Sebastian opened his eyes to stare at the ceiling, studying it as if searching for something.

"I thought Fowler's death ended it. You know, that the pound of flesh had been paid."

"More like twelve stone," Peg said dryly.

"Peg!" Angelina scolded.

"Sorry, it just popped out."

"You make it sound like some kind of sacrifice," Angelina said to her brother.

Sebastian shrugged. "Or it was a malicious prankster, like James thinks, scared off by that unintended consequence. Whatever it was, I thought that when I came in, the Galaxy would recognize a new beginning. But now it's happening again."

"James will sort it out. Our job is to put on a bang-up panto and leave him to it."

Sebastian smiled, closing his eyes again. "Have I ever told you how glad I am you married a maths professor?"

She chuckled. James did provide a much-needed balance to their family. She thanked her lucky stars for him every morning and every night.

Then Sebastian opened his eyes, clutched his book, and leapt to his feet in one sudden motion. "I promised those girls I'd paint their new dressing room!"

"Oh, make some excuse," Angelina said. "Belinda will believe anything you tell her."

"Amy won't," Sebastian said. "Besides, a promise is a promise. Apparently, Fowler had a habit of not keeping his, which is partly why everyone hated him." He ran a hand over his head in a futile attempt to smooth his hair.

Angelina picked up a comb and waved him over with it. He bent obediently to let her repair his ruffled locks. "You can't mean to paint that room yourself, Sebby. You've never painted anything in your life, apart from your own sweet face."

He straightened and looked in the mirror, adjusting his tie with his free hand. "I've seen it done. I could play a painter, with real paint, if I had the time, which I don't. But there must someone on the painting crew who wants something I can beg, borrow, or barter from someone else. As long as it doesn't come due before opening night . . ."

He flashed a huge smile and waved at himself in the mirror, then he kissed his sister on the cheek, blew a kiss to Peg, and left.

ELEVEN

Moriarty knocked on the door with a gold star painted over the letter *A*, hoping it was Angelina's. He'd visited Sebastian in his dressing room once, but the neighboring rooms held only other men, so there was no risk of encountering a young woman in a state of undress. This corridor even smelled feminine, with mingled perfumes instead of cigar smoke.

"Come in!" his wife sang.

He opened the door to peek inside, found her fully clothed, and breathed a sigh of relief. Entering, he crossed to give her a kiss, which made everything better for one important moment. "I gather there's been another incident?"

"The ghost frightened the ballet dancers," Angelina said. "So badly they nearly quit."

"I don't suppose we can afford to lose them?" He smiled a greeting at Peg and sat down on a purple sofa he'd never seen before. He'd never seen that ornate teak screen either or any of these old photographs. A picture of his wife in a harem costume almost made his eyes pop.

"They're essential." Angelina told him about a floating scarf, a broken glass, and some cold drafts.

"Is there a window in that room?" He rose to inspect the one here, pulling aside a pair of green drapes. He pounded on the jambs to loosen them but still strained to raise the lower sash so much as an inch. Both women cried out at the inrush of cold air, and he shoved it down again. "That could explain the drafts anyway. I'd like to examine the room, if it hasn't been thoroughly trampled."

"Peg and I guarded it for you," Angelina said, "while Sebastian bartered himself to the Delaneys in exchange for continuing to do their jobs."

Moriarty winced in sympathy. Somehow they'd have to find a way to make this up to him — but not today. "Do I need a key?"

"Right here." She handed him a small iron key, then added, "Don't worry, they're gone."

"Not too far, I hope. I would like to hear the story from one of them *in situ*."

"I'll find one. Belinda, I think, if I can peel her away from Sebastian." Angelina hopped up and they went out together.

"Which way?" he asked.

She pointed to the door next down from hers. "I'll send Belinda in. Then I'll be right here if you need me."

She went off down the hall while he entered the dancers' dressing room. Angelina's was a model of orderliness compared to this chaos. Gauzy garments in a range of pastels appeared to have been flung about the room by a furious whirlwind. The scent of lavender overwhelmed the theater's general smells of gas lighting and what he feared might actually be urine. Evidently one single water closet, inconveniently located beneath the stage, served the entire cast and crew. Its odors subtly permeated the whole backstage area.

The lights were only half-up, although there were many of them. Three dressing tables had been packed into this room, the same size as Angelina's. About twelve foot by eleven, he reckoned, measuring with the six-foot span of his outstretched arms. Each table had a large mirror with three light fixtures — one above and one on either side. Gas pipes ran up the wall and across the ceiling through small holes into the rooms on either side.

A rack laden with coats and hats stood near the door. At one end of the room stood a narrow bed with a small table at its foot. A three-part screen with panels painted in an Oriental scene spanned the farthest corner, with more filmy clothing draped across the top.

That must be where the silk scarf had risen into the air. As he moved toward it, something crunched underfoot. A piece of broken glass; a hazard for women wearing thin slippers. That would have to be cleared up before they were allowed back into this room. More shards glinted in a trail of water beneath the table.

The door opened to admit his wife, towing one of the fair young women by the hand. "It's only for a minute, dear," she was saying. "And you'll be able to collect your coats."

"Ah, good." Moriarty spoke in a bluff voice intended to put the girl at ease. Instead, it made her jump back a step. "I'm James Moriarty, Mrs. — ah, Miss Lovington's husband. I'm going to see if I can't sort this business out for you. Lay the ghost to rest, so to speak." He smiled, but she gaped at him in fresh horror.

Angelina pushed the girl into the room. "I'll be right next door, Belinda. The professor just wants to know who was where at the critical moment." She left the door open.

Moriarty gave up the attempt at geniality. "Well, Miss Delaney, let's start with the cold draft, shall we? Where was that experienced?"

"Dorinda felt it. Cold as ice, she said. She was sitting at her table, right there." She pointed at the dressing table nearest the window.

Just as he had expected. "Did the lights at that table flicker when she felt the draft, by any chance?"

Her lips formed a perfect O of astonishment. "How did you ever guess that? Ghosts fear the light, you know. It must have tried to blow them out."

"Did any of the other lights flicker?"

"No," she breathed, as if it were further proof of a spectral presence rather than a gap somewhere around that window.

"I see." Moriarty went to the window and parted the thick drapes, flooding the room with pale gray light. "Why do you keep these closed?"

"The light's wrong for doing our makeup. The lights onstage are yellow."

"Of course." He inspected the panes, finding no cracks, then moved his hands along the jambs, seeking a trickle of cold air. He found none.

Belinda asked, "Have you known Sebastian Archer for very long?"

"About a year and a half."

"Don't you think he's simply *marvelous*?"

"He's a very capable young man." Moriarty pounded the jambs with his fist, working up as far as he could reach. Nothing shook loose; they were tightly fitted.

"Don't you think he's the handsomest man you've ever seen in your life?"

A panorama of men's faces scrolled unbidden past Moriarty's mind's eye, from recent acquaintances all the way back to his Cambridge rowing crew. Some were clearly unhandsome, but the rest were simply men. "I don't know how to answer that question."

Belinda didn't seem to mind. "I think he's the absolute jammiest bit of jam."

Ah. The inquiry had been purely rhetorical. He gave up on the windows, fairly certain the draft had not derived from that source. Besides, there was no draft now, though the weather outside the window was as wintry as before. "Now, then. Where was your sister standing when the glass fell over?"

"It didn't *fall,* Professor Lovington. The ghost pushed it. Clarinda saw it happen. The glass wobbled a bit and then crashed to the floor and broke."

"Wobbled, eh?" Moriarty went back to study the broken shards and the top of the small table, where a faint circle marked the original location. He could see nothing impinging on the tabletop, such as a cloth that might be tugged out of place when someone sat on the bed. "Was anyone sitting on this bed?"

"No, we were all at our tables, except Edith, who was getting dressed. She's last." Moriarty understood that to mean they dressed in order of age and the others had therefore been ready to go out.

He knelt to look under the bed, but couldn't see much. He wished he had his portable Davy lamp — very handy for searching dark places. "Could you turn the lights up for me, please?"

When she obliged, he folded back the coverlet of the bed, revealing nothing but coils of dust and stray hairpins. No one could have hidden under here without leaving traces.

He turned his attention upward. A pair of pipes ran from the hall straight across the ceiling, turning up at the painted brick wall to run to the floor above. Another pair ran from hall to wall on the other side of the room. The pipes serving the dressing table lights branched off from one of those. The pipes crossing the ceiling were painted a creamy white, while those running down the wall were the pea green used throughout the building. The exposed fixtures thus faded into the background, easily forgotten.

Their changing screen stood under an intersection of pipes, in line with the ones above the bed and the table. An idea began to form. Moriarty pointed at it. "Is this where the scarf began its journey upward?"

Belinda nodded, eyes wide.

"Do you mind if I look behind it?"

She shook her head. Then she took one large sideways step toward the door.

Moriarty peered behind the screen, finding nothing of particular interest. A small stool, a pair of stockings, more dust. Then he looked up, leaning back to study the ceiling along the line of pipes. There he detected a gap of about a quarter inch, invisible from the rest of the room. He backed out from behind the screen. Yes, the gap ran all the way past the small table.

"Is it the ghost?" Belinda whispered.

"I believe so." He turned toward her with a smile. "You and your sisters will have no more trouble from the ghost in this room, Miss Delaney. I can guarantee that." He heaped the coats onto her outstretched arms and ushered her into the hall. He locked the door, pocketing the key. "I have one more test to conduct and then it's all yours again."

"We'll wait until Mr. Archer says it's all right," Belinda said primly. She waddled toward the stairs where her sisters waited.

Moriarty rapped on Angelina's door, waited for the response, and entered. "I think I know what happened."

"Darling! I knew you'd sort things out!" She lay upon the purple couch, studying her lines.

"I'll have a fuller answer after I examine the room above. Do you know what's up there?"

"Another dressing room, I suppose." She swung her legs to the floor. "Shall I pop down and ask Old Sampson for the key?" She suited action to words, returning in little more than a minute.

"You're conveniently located," Moriarty observed.

"Yes, I am." She gave him that extra-sweet smile that meant his observation had been especially simple-minded.

Peg said, "Theaters have a very strict pecking order, Professor. The lower you are, the higher you climb."

"Stars are nearest the stage," Angelina explained. "The room across the hall will be used by the highest-ranking visiting actress. The Delaneys are nearly as important as the Principal Boy in a panto, so they're on this floor too. They could have two rooms if they wanted, but they like to be together. Upstairs will be women's chorus, I imagine, although quite a bit of the second floor is given over to wardrobe."

"Wardrobe again," Peg intoned.

Moriarty frowned at her thoughtfully. "Who's your counterpart on the men's side?"

"Mr. Tweedy, I suppose," Angelina said, turning to Peg for confirmation.

"He has to share with Mr. Sparrow," she answered. "Always more men in a panto. The Giant shares with the Cow. Sebastian's office is on that side too, first floor."

"I see," Moriarty said, wishing again for a plan of the building. "Could I borrow you for a moment, my dear?"

"I'm all yours."

He brought her back to the Delaneys' dressing room and showed her the narrow gap in the ceiling. He allowed himself a brief bask in the glow of her admiration, then said, "I suspect there's another on the other side, where the draft was felt. I hope you'll be able to hear me from upstairs. We'll see if we can put my hypothesis to the test."

He jogged upstairs to knock on the door labeled *G*. No one answered, so he unlocked it and went in. This room was arranged identically to the one below, except that a row of trunks stood in place of the bed. He pulled two of them out of the way, exposing a gap between the floorboards precisely where he expected it. The light from the room below shone through it.

He knelt beside the gap to speak into it. "I'm going to try the draft now, Angelina. Go stand by the table nearest the window."

He opened the door to admit light from the hall, then went to the dressing table in the corresponding corner and probed about its base. He spotted scrapes on the floor showing it had been pulled out from the wall where the pipes came through. There he found a small hole. He got down on hands and knees and blew into it, realizing at once the futility of that gesture. He fished in his pockets and found a copy of an insurance document he'd been studying. He rolled it into a long cone and put one end into the hole, blowing as hard as he could into the other.

He removed his makeshift pipe and called down to his wife. "Did you feel that?"

"Feel what?"

He grunted and sat back on his heels, finding himself looking straight at the curtained window. "Fool!" he chided himself.

"What's that, darling?"

He got up and pulled back the curtains, blinking at the light. The sash rose easily, admitting a gust of chilly air.

Seconds later, his wife shrieked, "James!"

Proof positive. He closed the window and went back to the hole. "I opened a window up here. There's a hole. Can you see it? Right next to the pipes on the back wall there."

She gasped as she found it. "Oh, you clever man!"

"So much for the ghost. I'll scout around here a bit more, but you've done your part, my dear, if you want to go back to your lines. Go ahead and turn the lights down, but let's keep that room locked a little while longer."

With the extra light from the window, the hole in the corner and gap between the boards were easy to see, but if he hadn't known they were there, he doubted he would have noticed them. He went back to the gap and felt the edges gingerly, not wanting to get a splinter in his fingers. They were quite smooth. This gap had been cut deliberately with a fine-toothed saw.

Creating the cold draft was simple enough. But how did the prankster manage the trick with the scarf? He probably used a hook and line — ordinary fishing tackle. Moriarty performed a cursory search of the dressing table drawers, checking behind each table as well as inside the kneeholes. He didn't find anything, but didn't really expect to. The hook and line could easily be coiled up and tucked into a pocket.

Anyone could use a plumb bob to knock the glass over, but it would take skill to catch a scarf, raise it up, and drape it around a woman's shoulders. He'd have to try it out at home. You'd think the Delaney girl would've noticed a wire dangling over her head, but the corner behind the screen was fairly dark. If the hook and line had been painted the same color as the walls, they'd be nearly invisible.

How many of the hundreds of people employed in this vast building had experience fishing? Someone had told him many of the crewmen were former sailors; presumably, every one of them could hook a line and draw up a scarf. Even women enjoyed fishing as a pastime nowadays. That datum would only be useful as a supporting element after he identified the prankster through other means.

He closed the curtains and left the room, locking it behind him. He stood for a moment contemplating the key, which looked exactly like the other one, apart from the label. How many copies existed of each key? And a corollary question: How many keys opened more than one door? That small economy would not be surprising in an institution of this size, especially one with parallel wings for men and women. He made himself a small bet that the room corresponding to this one on the men's side could be opened with this key.

If only he could go straight across. There must be another staircase at the back. He turned in that direction and came face-to-face — or rather chest-to-face — with a very small woman wearing a black dress and a suspicious expression.

"I heard screaming," she said in a high-pitched, constricted voice. "Has there been another death?" Her black eyes shone as if hoping for an affirmative response.

"Just a bit of a fright in one of the women's dressing rooms downstairs," Moriarty said. This must be the Madame Noisette Angelina had mentioned. Interesting that her domain should lie so near the prankster's altered room.

"Are you a policeman?"

He shook his head. "I'm Professor Moriarty. Miss Lovington's husband."

She gave him a long, skeptical look, but said nothing. Odd creature!

He asked, "Did you happen to see anyone going into room *G* before the screams began?"

"I don't stand in the hallways gossiping. I have responsibilities, always too much to do, and yet I do it, whether I receive thanks or not."

"I'm sure your work is very much appreciated. It does seem quiet up here. Who uses these dressing rooms?"

"The chorus. They're not here today. They're villagers this year. Shades of green, red, and yellow. I have a lovely stock of villager costumes in every size."

"Then you saw no one going in or out today?"

She shook her head, whose pile of stiff curls was barely affected by the motion. "I heard screaming. Lots of screaming." She turned to go back into her lair.

Moriarty watched her disappear behind a door labeled *Wardrobe,* leaving him alone in the long hall lined with closed white doors. How many women made up the chorus? Dozens, perhaps. When they were here, this hallway would be abuzz with activity. During a performance or a full rehearsal, there must also be assistants running up and down from other floors to fetch things from the wardrobe.

The prankster had a judicious sense of timing. Today he — or she — had chosen another crucial set of victims. Without the Delaney sisters, the pantomime might have to be canceled. The prankster had almost succeeded in stopping the production once again.

And once again, he or she had been foiled by Sebastian Archer.

Moriarty knocked on his wife's door one last time to let her know he'd be out for an hour or so, meeting Lionel Hatcliff at the bank, but back again for lunch in the office if she'd care to join them. Then he collected his outerwear and strode three blocks down to Risley and Company on Pall Mall East. He only had to spend a few minutes watching passersby loaded with packages before Hatcliff emerged from a hackney and joined him inside the marble lobby.

The portly theater manager exuded success in his fur-trimmed cloak and cashmere scarf. "You're embarking on the greatest adventure of your life today, my dear Moriarty! There's nothing like the theater to keep a man young and vigorous." He clapped his gloved hands together, rubbing them briskly. "You're doing a good deed here as well, for your wife, your brother-in-law, and all the other people at the Galaxy. We might even say a good turn for the very culture of London itself!"

Moriarty would be happier with less hyperbole. He'd made the decision to join Hatcliff as a business partner and was about to transfer nine thousand pounds — almost his whole net worth — into Hatcliff's business account. He agreed with Charles Cudlow's advice: "If you're going in, go all in." He had no intention of changing his mind, but the sooner they got it done, with the least amount of fuss, the better.

A gentleman emerged from the mahogany depths of the bank, introducing himself as Mr. Sheridan. He led them to small office, where he accepted Moriarty's cheque from the Bank of England, written out in advance. He smiled with genuine pleasure at the amount and assured them the funds would be available within a week. They shook hands all around.

Moriarty and Hatcliff walked back to the Galaxy, where Hatcliff poked his head into his assistant's door to ask him to send round to the public house for a bottle of champagne and to summon the stage manager and leading actress. Then they went into his office and shed their coats and hats. Hatcliff went straight to his chair while Moriarty took one of the armchairs in front of the desk meant for visitors.

Hatcliff frowned at the awkward arrangement. "I work at home as often as not. You're more than welcome to take the desk when I'm out."

"I'm sure we'll manage." Moriarty doubted he'd be spending much time here once things got into a routine. "Shall we take care of that partnership agreement now?"

"Indeed, we shall!" Hatcliff drew out a short document he'd had his solicitor prepare. Moriarty read it through and signed at the bottom. Hatcliff added his signature, waved the page to dry the ink, then folded it lengthwise and tucked into his inner jacket pocket. "Bartleby will see that this is all duly registered and then, my friend, we'll be in business together."

The deed was done. They beamed at one another. Moriarty sat back in his chair and looked around the office with fresh interest, noting with approval the glowing embers in the grate and the colorful advertisements for Galaxy productions on the walls. The desk was a good big one with two banks of drawers. These visitor chairs were quite comfortable yet light enough to move around as needed. An upholstered chair with a footstool sat in a corner by a table equipped with a good reading lamp. A long window high on the wall behind the desk admitted natural light without admitting prying eyes. All in all, a well-designed room, both aesthetically pleasing and fitted for work. And now half his.

"How about that quarterly rent, then?" he asked. "Shall we get that cheque off today?"

"Not till next week, Professor. I wangled a reprieve when I realized how behind I'd fallen." Hatcliff frowned, his moustache twitching. "Those scoundrels, whoever they are, will get their money the day it's due and not one day sooner."

"It's a syndicate, I believe you said."

"They call themselves the House of Theatrical Investments. Feh! They could be anybody. I went to the address they gave me once, a set of chambers off Chancery Lane. All I found was one sorry-looking chappie reading a newspaper. He couldn't — or wouldn't — tell me anything."

"Sounds like what they call a convenience address. They clearly don't want to be known." Moriarty could think of a number of reasons a man might want to keep his investments private. "Do they ever interfere with your choice of plays or demand an accounting of receipts?"

"Certainly not! That's none of their business. We've got fifteen years left on a thirty-year lease, plenty of time to recover from my little run of bad luck. Set your mind at rest on that score, Professor. The only way to break that lease is for me to die, and I'm fit as a fiddle!" He thumped his well-padded belly and chuckled. "Perhaps a bass fiddle."

Moriarty smiled and refrained from pointing out that the stage manager had died in that building less than a week ago. "How are we on fire insurance?"

"Up to date, never fear. I never lag on that score."

"How much coverage do you carry?"

"Enough to replace the whole jingbang. The owner insures the building, you know, so I only have to cover the contents. I say 'only,' but you may be surprised to learn that we've got a good twenty-two thousand pounds' worth of properties under this roof." He grinned at Moriarty as if expecting him to be shocked, but it was nearly the same amount Cudlow had predicted.

"Do you conduct an annual inventory?" Moriarty asked. "For insurance purposes?"

Hatcliff's grin faded. "I know what I've got. And Fowler and I give everything a good look-through when we're considering a script. Everything gets re-used, one way or another. I've got a beautiful town-to-country panorama, for example, so we always try to work that in. These things pay for themselves over time. You'll see."

Sebastian appeared in the open doorway with a bottle in one hand and four flutes threaded through the fingers of the other, the prompt book tucked awkwardly under one arm. "Knock, knock! Did someone send for champagne?" He grinned happily and seemed as energetic as ever, but there were dark shadows under his eyes and his jacket looked as if it had been bundled up and sat on. The new job was already taking its toll.

"Come in, my boy! Come in!" Hatcliff lifted a stack of newspapers and dropped them on the floor to clear space on the desktop.

Moriarty rose to help unburden Sebastian, who tossed the book onto the reading chair and lifted the bottle to start removing the foil. "I take it we're celebrating. Dare I guess it's the partnership?"

"Signed and sealed," Hatcliff said, patting his breast pocket.

"Not quite yet delivered," Moriarty added. "We've done our part, at any rate. Another week for the solicitor and the banks to do theirs, and then it's done."

"Shall I pop the cork, or is Lina coming?" Sebastian asked. "I'm truly delighted, but I can't linger too long. We're testing the lighting effects today."

"How is Mr. MacDonald getting along?" Moriarty asked.

"Fully recovered," Sebastian said. "That bottle of twenty-year-old scotch you sent him worked wonders."

"Along with your persuasive powers." Hatcliff winked at Moriarty. "This lad could charm fish from a hungry seagull."

"Speaking of fish," Moriarty said, "I've learned more about our ghost." He told them about the holes cut into the floor above the dancers' dressing room.

"That's diabolical," Sebastian said.

"It isn't nice," Moriarty agreed. "Someone brought a bag of tools into that room and spent an hour or so working away with the specific intention of frightening the women below. It must have been late at night because the wardrobe is only a short distance away. The mistress seems a very odd person, although that doesn't necessarily imply that she's involved."

"Madame Noisette," Sebastian said. "Though that can't be her real name."

"It's Annie Draper," Hatcliff said. "She's an odd one, all right, but very good at her job. The only good thing Nora Verney left me." He frowned deeply, looking for a moment precisely like a very sad walrus. "I've been a very foolish old man."

"Nonsense," Moriarty said, not meaning it. Miss Verney sounded like the most obvious sort of mantrap.

"We all have our weaknesses." Sebastian smiled as if he spoke from experience. He pulled out his watch and flipped it open just as Angelina arrived.

"I hope you haven't started without me!" She paused on the threshold.

"We knew you'd be late," Sebastian said. His tone was mild, but his words caused Angelina's eyes to narrow. He smiled slightly, as if having won a small victory, and set to work on the cork.

Some conflict had already arisen between the two key components in this spectacularly expensive enterprise. Moriarty hoped he wouldn't be expected to arbitrate. But Hatcliff merely blinked at them with a benign smile on his lips, a model of wise non-engagement.

The cork came free with a satisfying pop and they cheered, the way people do. Angelina perched on the arm of Moriarty's chair. Sebastian poured while Hatcliff passed the glasses around. "Here's to old friends and new beginnings," he said, holding his glass high.

"Old friends!" they echoed.

"Never in my wildest dreams," Angelina said, beaming at the three men, "did I ever imagine this most wonderful of possibilities. My dear old friend, my beloved husband, and my darling baby brother, all together in one soon-to-be very happy house."

Sebastian's smile showed teeth for moment at that "baby," but they all raised their glasses to say, "Hear, hear!"

"My troubles will soon be past," Hatcliff said, "thanks to you all. The professor was just telling us about the progress he's making in catching our ghost."

"One small step," Moriarty said. "Unfortunately, it doesn't tell us anything about who the prankster is. It must be someone with a grudge. I can't think of any other reason to do pointless things like destroying hats. I know you're all busy, but try to keep an eye and an ear out for grumblings of any kind."

"Oh, not any kind, darling," Angelina said. "The closer we get to opening night, the more grumbling there'll be."

"We can expect more accidents too," Sebastian said. "The pressure builds up and people get nervous. But there's a vast difference between knocking over a can of paint and sawing a hole in a dressing room ceiling. I'll warn the crew chiefs to keep their eyes peeled."

"Most people seem happy with the new changes," Angelina said. "I'm hearing nothing but good things about Sebastian —"

"And you," Sebastian put in.

"And me," she acknowledged, never one to hide her light under a bushel. "Neither Nora Verney nor John Fowler were favorites, to put it mildly."

"People didn't like Fowler," Sebastian said. "Apart from the scenery crew, who are a fairly independent lot."

"He changed," Hatcliff said. "We built this place together, him and me, from the beginning, but in the past year, his heart didn't seem to be in it anymore. I don't know why."

"But he's gone," Moriarty said, "and I can't see grudges against him as a reason for playing tricks on the dancers. What purpose could that serve?"

"We'd be in a pickle without the Delaneys," Sebastian said. "They're in almost as many scenes as the Dame since they play the fairies whose magic creates all the transformations. We could find other dancers, but it'd be like losing a leg. We'd be limping through the first several weeks at least."

They sipped their wine and pondered that calamity for a few moments. Then Angelina said, "Peg thinks the wardrobe mistress trapped Fowler in that storeroom. She certainly hated him; she made that clear the first time we met."

"I can't see it," Sebastian said, nearly talking right over her. "She's an artist and she seems thoroughly attached to her job. She wouldn't benefit from hurting the show; on the contrary."

"That could be said of anyone in *Beanstalk*," Angelina said. "But in fairness, Peg has a history with the little nut. Ancient history, but you know Peg."

Moriarty nodded. She could hold a grudge — speaking of grudges. But surely Peg was one person they could rule out with confidence, since she'd been nowhere near the Galaxy when Mr. Fowler met his untimely death.

"And there's something going on between the little nut —"

"Madame Noisette," Sebastian corrected. "Let's call her by the name she's chosen, shall we? She's a vital member of our crew and deserves our respect."

"You're right, darling," Angelina said with genuine contrition. "She's an odd little bird, but we shouldn't make fun of her for that. But there is something between her and Mr. Tweedy. And he, as far as I know, is the only person at the Galaxy actively going about complaining about money."

"Gad!" Hatcliff cried. "Every time he sees me. I don't know what's gotten into the man. He was happy enough with the contract in September when we cast the show. He's getting sixty-five a week, which is better than average for a Dame. My Principal Boy's only getting eighty, and he's in nearly every scene." Hatcliff winked at Angelina, who wrinkled her nose at him affectionately.

"It's a fair wage," Sebastian said. "But he is definitely not happy about it now."

"What's changed?" Moriarty asked.

No one seemed to know. "He lost his wife last year around this time," Hatcliff said. "Weak heart or something of that sort. There's a son who lives with an aunt, I believe."

"Sparrow might know more. They share a dressing room." Angelina sighed. "I'll see if I can tease out a reason."

"Might we give him a bit of a rise?" Moriarty asked. "Complaints tend to beget more complaints. Best nip it in the bud, if possible. How much would it take to placate him?"

Sebastian shook his head. "That would have to be kept a very dark secret, James, which is not easily done. I've been telling everyone we won't reconsider salaries until Lady Day." He shrugged. "Just guessing there."

Hatcliff said, "I have no intention of renegotiating any salaries at this late date, new partner or no. Contracts have been signed. Mr. Tweedy will just have to live with it."

"If that's the custom, it should be respected." Moriarty scratched his beard with one finger, catching his wife's gaze. "But in the interests of maintaining the peace, we do have one small pocket that could be safely picked. Angelina doesn't really need a salary. I maintain her, of course, and she'll profit indirectly from the success of the production as a whole." He smiled at her fondly, getting a stony glare in return.

"Why should I be the one to make the sacrifice?" She sat straight up, every line of her figure expressing outrage. "I don't get a penny more than Nora got, even though I have to work twice as hard, coming in late. What would people think if the principal actress worked for nothing? That I'm *worth* nothing!"

"What do you care what people think?" Moriarty asked, recognizing the stupidity of his question as both Sebastian and Hatcliff started chuckling.

"I am an actress, James," his wife explained, pronouncing each word with care. "My career depends on what people think."

"I understand that. But couldn't you give part of your salary to placate Tweedy? Surely you want what's best for the show."

"There are traditions to be respected here. Principles are at stake. It isn't the money, darling. It's the *amount*."

"I don't follow you."

She raised exasperated eyes to heaven, then tried again. "Imagine we were being paid in beans. Magic beans, if you like. I don't care a fig for beans as *beans.* But if the comedians get ten beans, I, as the star, must get twelve. If they get fifteen, I must have eighteen. It doesn't matter exactly how many beans I have, as long as my little sack contains more than theirs."

Moriarty frowned at her, stroking his short beard, puzzling through her absurd analogy.

Sebastian refilled his glass, laughing in his warm, infectious way. "It's theater math, Professor. All the numbers are topsy-turvy. Didn't they teach you that at Cambridge?"

TWELVE

Angelina forced herself to sip her mushroom soup one graceful spoonful at a time instead of tilting back her head and pouring it down her throat. She felt ravenous, although she'd spent most of the afternoon setting a good example by serving as prompter for other actors and letting Peg use her as a mannequin.

"Are you going back tonight?" James asked, breaking apart a chunk of bread so fresh she could smell its yeasty goodness from across the table.

"I thought I'd spend the evening at the piano, if it won't disturb you."

"Not at all."

Rolly removed their soup plates and served the main course: beef and kidney pie for James, grilled chicken with green beans for her.

"It doesn't seem fair," James said. "I ought to be eating what you eat."

"Nonsense." Angelina pulled her questing nose back over her own plate. "I'm the one who's been lolling doing nothing for the past year. You row six miles up and down the Thames every other day to keep yourself in trim. My hips, my penalty."

"Once again and for the record, I like your hips the way they are." He shot a glance at the door and spooned up a portion of his pie, plopping it onto her plate.

She gobbled it up gratefully, licking her lips.

"I don't see what the problem is," James said. "Surely Peg can let your trousers out a little. You could wear a longish jacket, the old-fashioned sort. Jack Trott's meant to be a poor boy, isn't he? He'd wear his father's hand-me-downs."

That suggestion was so thoroughly James — practical, obvious, and woefully out of touch — that she was stumped for a reply. Actresses liked to play boys so they could show off their legs. And audiences liked to see 'em.

She decided to change the subject. "Shall I circulate your discovery that the Delaneys' fright was definitely not the work of a ghost?"

"Would anyone believe you? They seem to relish that idea."

She shrugged. "Better a ghost than looking askance at the person next to you, wondering if they're the one playing these nasty tricks."

"I suppose you're right. And there's no reason to put our prankster on guard by revealing the techniques." James ate a few bites of his delicious pie, then said, "There is one thing you could do, my dear, if you're delicate about it."

"I'm always delicate."

He grinned. "Then you might try to find out what the cast thinks of Lionel Hatcliff. We know there are complaints about John Fowler, but decisions about which play to do and who gets which part rest in Hatcliff's hands, don't they?"

"They do."

"Perhaps there's some lingering resentment from that cause. I have nothing to go on so far that couldn't apply to practically anyone. We might get farther along if we approach the matter from the direction of motive. These pranks seem to be aimed at causing the show to be canceled or to perform poorly. Either could result in Hatcliff's bankruptcy, even with my support." He gave her a dire look. "We'd lose our savings as well, you know."

"More whist for you, then." She reached over to pat his hand. "I've been poor, darling. It doesn't frighten me. As long as we're together, we'll manage."

"Brave woman. But, as you observe, we have resources. At any rate, it seems that someone in that theater — someone who is there now, during rehearsals — wants this show to fail. Why? Who benefits? He or she is clearly undaunted by Fowler's death, which suggests that he or she has a powerful reason for achieving their goal."

"You're so scrupulous in saying 'he or she.' Do you really think these things could be done by a woman?"

James shrugged. "No reason why not. It doesn't take any strength to fish up a thin scarf or light a fuse. A smaller person might have some advantage." His eyes lost their focus for a moment as a new thought captured his attention. "Have all the incidents occurred on the women's side?"

"I think so . . . No, wait! The hats. And the Giant's ruined makeup."

"Hmm."

They ate in silence for a minute or so, then James picked up the thread again. "The odds favor a man since there are so many more of them than women in the theater on a daily basis. A woman would be more noticeable on the men's side than the other way around because the crew is entirely male and they seem to go everywhere."

"Not entirely," Angelina said. "Wardrobe is staffed by women. Madame Noisette goes everywhere too."

"I thought we dismissed her." James used his last piece of bread to mop up the last of his gravy but stopped with the tantalizing morsel in his hand. "However, just because Peg wants her to be guilty doesn't mean she isn't." He shook his head. "That could be phrased more elegantly, but you grasp my meaning. Noisette does seem to be harboring some sort of resentment, unless that's just her nature. She couldn't have done the Delaney tricks though. You were all with her when the screaming started."

"I said the same thing. She could have an accomplice, couldn't she?"

James frowned. "I don't like theories that depend on a proliferation of causes."

"And yet people do conspire, darling. Just as sometimes the person you want to be guilty turns out to be the one who done it."

* * *

At nine o'clock the next morning, Angelina entered the large rehearsal room in the cellar with a mixture of eagerness and trepidation. The Giant, Henry Easton, had offered to teach her enough sword-fighting to do a credible job in their battle scene. The man was six foot six and twice her weight and had the booming baritone voice to match. He was always cast as a giant or king or someone terrible. Luckily, he was as gentle as a kitten with no need to assert himself at the expense of another actor. Who could replace him?

The room was large and bare, with unpainted brick walls and natural light from a row of high windows across the back. Angelina grinned nervously as she accepted her cork-tipped rapier from Mr. Easton. She held it out full length, her arm trembling from the weight. "It's heavier than it looks."

"Lighter than a real one, Miss Lovington. You'll get used to it. We'll take the corks off for the show, but don't worry. We don't really strike each other. We mainly leap about flourishing grandly." He demonstrated with surprising grace.

For the next half hour, he patiently taught her a routine that made the most of the difference in their sizes. Angelina's fears evaporated as she lunged and twirled about the room, brandishing her sword over her head or swishing it fiercely in front. It felt more like dancing than fighting, with the sword like a deadly sort of fairy wand.

She'd worn her old rehearsal tights — off-color and baggy at the knees — and a long-sleeved tunic belted at the waist over her most comfortable corset. She had complete freedom of movement and loved taking advantage of it. She especially adored the little sideways hop-step maneuver done with her sword extended tauntingly at her foe. No wonder so many actresses wanted to play boys. Boys had more fun!

"Good work!" the Giant said after she'd slain him for the fifth time. "Let's take a break." He hopped to his feet as lightly as if he'd been sitting in an armchair resting instead of bounding about the big room playing her part as well as his.

Angelina walked over to where she'd dropped her cloak and slung it around her shoulders, mopping her forehead with the hem. The room had felt cold when she first walked in, but they'd worked up quite a sweat. "I can't thank you enough for helping me, Mr. Easton."

"My pleasure, Miss Lovington." He'd brought a big towel for himself, which he draped over his shoulders. "You're a fast learner. Another session or two and I think we'll have it."

"You're a marvelous teacher. You must be a master of the art of sword-fighting."

His booming laugh echoed through the cavernous space. "I've been doing this for years. But you're quite good for a woman your age — I mean, for an actress who's been out of —" He stopped, swallowed, and tried again. "You're quite good. Better than Miss Verney."

"Am I?" Angelina vowed to spend every spare minute practicing. She could push the drawing room furniture against the walls and borrow a broom from the housemaids. "She had more time to rehearse, of course."

Mr. Easton nodded. "She had a sword-fight in the *Travestie* as well."

"Didn't she play the Scottish lady?"

He chuckled. "Our version bore only the slightest resemblance to the original."

"It must have been very funny, from what I've heard." People kept mentioning that failed burlesque: *The Travestie of MacBreath, or Me Wife Made Me Do It.* It seemed to be when the Galaxy's troubles had begun. "I can't imagine how it failed."

"One problem after another," Easton said. "I've never seen anything like it."

Angelina let that thought settle for a moment, then asked thoughtfully, "What do you think is causing the trouble in this theater, Mr. Easton?"

"The curse," he answered, then shot her a wry grin. "I don't mean spirits, Miss Lovington. But there's a sour mood flowing through this house like a dark fog. I'm hoping you and Mr. Archer will bring us a nice fresh breeze."

"When did it start? With the *Travestie*?"

Easton gave her a measuring look. "The truth? When Miss Verney set her cap for Old Hattie. Can't blame the man. He was awfully lonely after his wife died and Nora's a pretty one. She can be sweet when it suits her too, but she's not what you'd call fair-minded.

Not like Old Hattie. Nora had favorites, like Madame Noisette and Frank Sparrow, who got the little extras — better hours, extra tips. You know the sort of thing I mean."

"I do. Favorites are the very plague. They cause resentment, which grows into grudges . . ." Angelina shook her head. Could that really be what this was about? The usual sorts of petty jealousies grown out of bounds, like a neglected garden? "I appreciate your candor."

"Maybe I'll be in the inner circle this time." Easton gave her a crooked grin.

Better scotch that notion before it got any bigger. "Oh, Sebastian and I have been in this game far too long for that kind of nonsense! It gets in the way of the work."

She was saved from further protestations by one of the message boys, who trotted across to meet them. "Miss Lovington? They've got the beanstalk up. They said you wanted to know."

"Thank you."

Mr. Easton left her at stage level, going up to his dressing room. She walked on through the wings and nearly fell over backward in awe as she confronted her true co-star — the beanstalk. The thing was a marvel of stage carpentry, ten feet wide at the base and towering twenty-five feet up. From the front, it looked like a massive green stalk liberally spiked with fluttering leaves. From behind, it looked like six wide ladders connected with horizontal bars, covered with a painted net supporting a jungle of papier-mâché greenery.

Woven in among the artificial leaves were loops of ropes, painted green, to grasp while climbing. Ladders had been created on each side with flat rungs wide enough to put a whole foot on. The thing looked fairly safe, as monster beanstalks went.

She wasn't expected to climb all the way up into the fly tower, thank goodness. But it would be marvelous — an unforgettable achievement — if she could bring herself to do it. The higher the better, as long as she could still be seen from the galleries. Maybe if they wired her up like a fairy with a couple of strong men in the flies to catch her if she slipped? Though poor James would suffer a shock either way.

She waved at the men high overhead, who were leaning on the railings to watch her reaction. "It's magnificent!" she shouted to them. "Let's give it a try, shall we?"

"Up you come, Lina!" they cheered, waving their caps.

She studied the rungs within easy reach, passing her bare hand lightly over each one, testing for any traces of grease or oil. Not so much as a smudge, not even in the joins. She bent forward to give the rung at nose-level a sniff. Paint and glue, but not soap. Could you wash away grease and leave dust behind? Unlikely.

She grabbed the lowest handhold and hopped onto the first rung, bouncing up and down a bit to test the structure. Nothing shifted. She advanced up several more rungs, placing each foot with deliberation. She'd climbed ladders onstage before, short ones, to perch at the top and sing. This wasn't so very different.

Gaining confidence, she climbed many rungs farther up, moving briskly, feeling quite as agile as a monkey. She stopped again to get her bearings at her new altitude. Looking straight up, she saw the grinning faces of two flymen, who gave her two thumbs-up. Encouraged, she wrapped her left arm around a supporting beam, made sure her feet were firmly planted, and twisted sideways to look out into the hall.

She gasped in delight. "Oh my stars!" She could look right down into the stalls, row after row of plush red seats. She twisted farther around and found herself looking into the first box, so close she could almost leap right inside. James should take that box. He could lean out and she could plant a kiss on his cheek. Then he'd die of mortification and leave her a widow. Perhaps best not to try that particular trick . . .

She stretched out one arm and sang, "La," on middle C. She didn't fall, so she ran some scales, finishing on a good loud note, hearing it echo back to her from the corners of the hall. She could reach everyone from here, even the benches at the very top of the uppermost gallery.

The patrons in the stalls and the boxes in their glittering evening gowns and cutaway coats might pay the bills, but her heart belonged to the folks at the back in the tuppenny seats. They'd been with her from the start, and besides, they were the ones who worked the hardest, every day and every week. They needed an evening in Cloudland more than anyone else. But if they couldn't hear her, what was the point?

Then she made the mistake of looking down. She grabbed the nearest handhold and froze. "How far up am I?" she called out, hoping someone big and strong down below would answer.

"Far enough to break your neck, darling," Nora Verney's girlish voice sang out.

Angelina thrust her whole left arm through one of the security ropes, made sure her feet were firmly planted, and dared to look straight down. Her old rival stood right below her, clutching Lionel's arm, her bandaged foot sticking ostentatiously out from under a pink-chequered walking dress. She wore pale pink gloves and an angled hat plumed with soft pink feathers. Frank Sparrow waited a few respectful feet away with her fur coat.

Angelina contemplated her sweaty tunic and baggy tights. She'd done her hair in flat braids pinned on top of her head to keep it out of her way, but many strands had come loose in the course of her strenuous morning. Under the circumstances, perhaps she should stay put.

But Nora would just wait her out, purring cattish remarks. She could see the dirty tunic — she could see straight *up* the dirty tunic, come to think of it. With that thought, Angelina steeled herself and made her way back down with as much *sangfroid* as she could muster.

"They must have reinforced those ladders a great deal," Nora said, "to bear the extra weight."

Angelina mirrored her sweet smile. "Not a trace of grease, Lionel. Clean and dry and safe as houses. You must have put a foot wrong, Nora dear. It does demand a certain degree of agility."

"Now, ladies," Hatcliff rumbled.

They ignored him. Nora painted a sympathetic frown on her face." You must be terrified to face a London audience again after so much time sitting at home growing, er, rusty."

"Rusty? Me?" Angelina laughed airily. "I couldn't be shinier. Everyone's saying how well prepared I am, compared to — well, in comparison."

Nora drew in a long breath. "I *do* admire your courage, Hattie, taking on a has-been for the most important show of the year. But then you've always been *such* a generous old soul!" She tilted her face up to bat her false lashes at him.

Angelina wondered that she could bat them so rapidly for so long without falling over. Maybe that's how the little minx fell off the beanstalk.

Lionel chuckled, ignoring the undercurrents. "Not at all, my dears! You should hear the excitement at the Garrick. It's Lina Lovington this and Lina Lovington that. London can't wait to reclaim its long-lost sweetheart!" He shot a wink at Angelina.

Nora's cupid lips twisted. Lionel had gotten a little of his own back that time. Then she schooled the lips into a pout. "I only wanted to come say hello to my old friends at the Galaxy. I miss you all."

"We miss you too," Sparrow said. "Especially Mr. Beanstalk here." He imitated Nora's pout in mock communion. His lips had a touch of the bow about them as well, though his features were rarely still.

"Oh, that horrid thing!" She shrank away from it.

"Now, now," Lionel said. "That's the finest beanstalk London's ever seen. Say, you should come back tomorrow! We're rehearsing the transition from act one to act two. You know I like to be the first to ride down in the clouds." He grinned at Angelina. "We've made a bit of a tradition out of it over the years."

"I'll be here."

Nora said, "I'm afraid I'll be busy tomorrow. My life no longer revolves around the Galaxy, you know."

Angelina laughed, though Nora didn't seem to see the humor. But then she remembered an outstanding grievance. "Where's my book, Nora?"

"What book?"

"The principal actor's copy of the complete script. Sebastian said he thought one had been made."

"Oh yes," Lionel said. "It's customary, as you're in so many scenes. Didn't you leave that in the dressing room, Nora, dear?"

"I don't know. I must have." She shot a frowning glance at Sparrow. Why would he have it? He played the Old Farmer who sold

Jack the beans as well as the Giant's Wife. He was in the dream dance with the fairies and the Cow and would do a couple of the variety turns between acts, but he didn't need a full script and wouldn't expect one.

"It is most definitely not in the dressing room," Angelina said.

"I suppose it might have been swept into a trunk by mistake," Nora said, but anyone could see she'd taken it on purpose; out of spite, presumably. What earthly use could she have for it?

"That's the property of the show," Lionel said, his geniality fading. "Copies are expensive, and we don't have time to make another one now. Why don't you send that back as soon as you get home, eh?"

"There you are!" Timothy Tweedy's rich voice boomed from the wings. He strode onto the stage, his broad face creased into angry lines. "You've been avoiding me, Mr. Hatcliff."

"Nonsense!" Lionel patted Nora's arm and handed her over to Sparrow along with her cane. "I'm a busy man, Mr. Tweedy, and you've had your answer in any event."

Tweedy glowered at him, his lips pressed together and his bushy eyebrows furled. His expression shouted anger, but Angelina detected a hint of something else in the depths of his dark eyes. A shimmer of tears, perhaps. Fear? Sorrow?

"I can't accept that answer," he said.

Lionel said. "Let it rest, Mr. Tweedy. You were happy enough when you signed your contract. And I expect you to fulfill the terms. We've all suffered this past year, one way or another. Now we must all pull together."

The comedian raised his arm, striking a pose with a finger raised to heaven. "Never let it be said that Timothy Tweedy failed to give his best performance, from the first night to the last!" The bulky man spun gracefully on his heel and stalked off the stage.

"Shall I go after him?" Angelina offered.

"I'll go," Lionel said. "Try to smooth the ruffled feathers." He tipped his hat to Nora, then plodded after the disgruntled actor.

"I've got feathers too," Sparrow said in his yokel voice, pumping his elbows at his sides.

Angelina shook her head at him. Mockery wouldn't help. Then she asked Nora, "What brings you here today, really? You didn't leave so much as a hat pin behind."

Nora tossed her head. "I wanted to see how you were getting along without me. And say hello to my friends, especially my darling Noisette." She batted her lashes at Sparrow for no apparent reason. He batted his back, giving his elbows another flap.

"I'll walk up with you," Angelina said. "I'm on my way back up to my dressing room." She gave Nora's bandaged foot a worried frown. "Do you need to be carried upstairs? The Giant is around somewhere. He *might* be able to manage it."

Nora gave her a sour look. "Mr. Sparrow will help me." She lifted her cane to point into the left wing. "Sneeze on, MacSnuff!"

Sparrow's mobile face began to twitch and crumple. He sniffed, stuck his finger under his nose, and sighed. Then the process began again with greater exaggeration until he leaned away from Nora, his whole body convulsing into an enormous "Aaaachoooo!"

Angelina laughed in spite of Nora. It really was wonderfully funny. "Up we go, then!" She skipped gaily past her hobbling rival, swinging her arms like a boy and showing off her two good legs. She stopped at the stairs to wait for the others, bowing from the waist to let them go first. Then she paced slowly behind them, speaking now in a conversational tone. "I can't understand how your *Travestie* could fail, to be honest, especially with Mr. Sparrow doing bits like that. The audience must have howled!"

"The sneeze worked," Sparrow said, "but the tree that was supposed to blow down only tilted about half a foot and then got stuck. The cellar men kept pulling on the rope, making it creak down slowly, inch by agonizing inch. It finally made it to the ground, but by then the joke was buried."

"Ugh!" Angelina sympathized. "It must have been a nightmare for you. What went wrong?"

Sparrow shrugged, using both long arms to make the most of the gesture. "Fowler let us down. That wasn't the only disaster with the set."

"People actually left, the second act change took so long," Nora said.

"What was wrong with him?" Angelina asked. "I never knew Mr. Fowler, but he'd been with Lionel for years. He must have been quite good at his job."

Sparrow traded looks with Nora. "We're not privy to management decisions, are we?"

"Hattie didn't really want to do the *Travestie*," Nora said. "We had to talk him into it. But you pinch the wrong penny at the wrong time and the whole thing falls apart."

"Frustrating," Angelina murmured. She didn't believe it. Hatcliff would have been flush with funds from last year's panto at that point and he wasn't small-minded enough to undermine his own show out of peevishness.

They reached the first floor. "This is where I get off," Angelina said. "Ta-ta, darlings!" She waggled her fingers at them and walked to her dressing room door. She kept half an eye on the pair continuing up the stairs as she opened it, then popped her head in to say, "Back in a tick," to Peg and closed it again.

She ran back to the stairs on her toes and peered up as Sparrow's long legs passed out of sight onto the floor above. She jogged silently up and peeked down the corridor in time to see Nora walking normally on both feet, her ebony cane slung over her arm. "Faker," Angelina whispered. She waited until they vanished through the wardrobe doors to tiptoe down the hall.

They'd left the door partly open. She listened, heard their voices moving toward the workshop at the back, and slipped inside, crouching low to hide between the racks of costumes.

Noisette was speaking in her raspy voice. "Miss Nora has come to visit Noisette in spite of her terrible injury. She hasn't forgotten her old friend after all."

"I could never forget you, darling Noisette! I climbed all the way up the stairs to see you."

Angelina knelt on the floor to peer under the racks. Nora lifted her bandaged foot to show her former dresser. Noisette made sympathetic cooing sounds over the counterfeit injury.

That scheming little minx had faked her fall. Why? To break her contract, perhaps. But why would she want to do that? True, she'd get out of several months of hard work, but she also gave up eighty pounds a week for that same length of time. Was Nora rich enough to tide herself over that large a gap? Surely Lionel wasn't supporting her after all she'd done — that would be too bad. She must have another patron lurking in the wings.

Noisette said, "I had hoped you might return to us, Miss Nora, now the odious John Fowler is gone, putting an end to his —" She stopped abruptly.

"Poor John Fowler, something of a growler, guilty of a howler," Sparrow sang to a made-up tune. Nora clucked her tongue at him.

"I've moved beyond playing Principal Boy," Nora said. "I'm considering other options."

"Miss Nora is an artiste," Noisette said. "She should play important roles. Queens and sorceresses. Shakespeare."

"In exquisite costumes made by you, dearest Noisette," Nora said. "No one has your taste, not the finest designers in Paris, nor your sensitivity to an actress's individual sense of style and movement."

"Miss Nora is always so graceful, sweeping the stage in my beautiful gowns."

"That's why I've come," Nora said, finally getting to the point. "I want to wear Lady MacBreath's gown to a party next week. You don't need it for the panto, and you know I'll take good care of it."

"Take one of my gowns out of the Galaxy?" Noisette squeaked. "No, you mustn't ask me that, not again. My dresses belong to the theater. I made them in the theater, for the theater. They must remain in the theater."

"I would only be borrowing it. Mr. Fowler used to borrow costumes sometimes."

"Borrow," Noisette echoed in her throaty rasp. "That odious John Fowler hired Noisette fifteen years ago. He could turn her out into the street at any —"

"No one's turning you out into the street, Annie!" Nora snapped. "And I'm certain I saw Mr. Tweedy —"

"Mr. Tweedy is a gentleman, always courteous, always so considerate. His need is great, and no one would help him except faithful Noisette, always a friend —"

"Tweedy is needy, but Verney is yearney," Sparrow quipped. "A gown for the town brings a frown to —"

"Give it a rest, Frank," Nora snapped. "I'm simply devastated, Madame, that after all our years together, you can't bring yourself to do this one teensy little favor for me."

A long silence followed. Then Noisette began muttering a litany of grief and betrayal, moving into the racks, thus forcing Angelina to scurry back a few yards. "No friends, Noisette is alone, always alone, Archers everywhere, threatening her with replacements, no one to trust . . ."

A rack of clothes shuddered as something was removed, then Nora said, "Lovely! Be a lamb and wrap that inside my coat for now. Thank you *so* much, darling Annie, and do give my love to your sister at Christmas!"

Angelina pressed into a row of animal costumes to hide, but the visitors' footsteps pattered straight to the door, which opened and closed as they left. Nora hadn't even bothered to limp on the way out. Unfortunately, they'd really closed the door this time, making a quiet escape more problematical.

"I know you're in there," Noisette squeaked. Escape impossible, then.

"Here I am!" Angelina sang, popping her head above the racks. "I came in to look for something gypsy-ish and didn't want to interrupt."

Noisette met that excuse with narrowed eyes but allowed herself to be distracted from the shabby treatment Nora had dished out. Angelina sympathized, but what could she say? She followed the little woman around as she selected an adorable dress with a green bolero and a hem trimmed with red bobbles. Noisette really was good at her job.

Angelina thanked her, layering in lots of praise, and left. She'd gained two victories just then. The lovely costume, of course, but even better, an absolute stunner of a motive for some sort of skullduggery.

Peg had valued some of these costumes at upwards of a hundred pounds. Now it would seem that both the odious John Fowler and the troubled Mr. Tweedy had been helping themselves to the Galaxy's bounty.

THIRTEEN

Moriarty unwrapped the sandwich delivered from the Bear and Staff around the corner. Cheddar and chutney — one of his favorites. He uncorked a bottle of beer and poured himself a glass. He waved the bottle at Sebastian. They were lunching in the manager's office today. Sebastian could no longer be persuaded to leave the theater, and Angelina had insisted on being present to ensure that he ate.

"Thanks," Sebastian said, getting up to accept a glass. He'd settled himself in the reading chair, using the footstool as a makeshift table. He'd tucked the prompt book behind him, as if anyone in this room would dare to lay a finger on the sacred object.

"Tea for me," Angelina said with more virtue than she deserved. She didn't much care for beer. She sat beside him at the desk, reaching across to help herself to a thick sandwich of pâté and pickles. Evidently the slimming program had gone by the wayside.

She had her hair in braids crossed over her head like a country girl and wore an unfussy gingham dress Moriarty hadn't known she possessed. It must have been in her theater trunks all this time. He liked the simple style and hoped her Jack costume would run along similar lines. It made her look fresh and youthful.

"You know, darlings," she said, lowering her voice, "I've just learned the most —"

"Put that beer away!" Lionel Hatcliff sauntered into the room waving a champagne bottle. "We're having champagne today."

Again? Was this a daily habit for him?

"With liverwurst sandwiches?" Angelina asked, grinning. "What's the occasion?"

"No occasion," Hatcliff answered, although a twinkle in his eyes belied that claim. "Apart from the cloud coming down today." He popped the cork and looked about for glasses. There weren't any, so he filled four teacups and passed them around. "To a full house and a long run!"

The others echoed his toast. Hatcliff drained his cup, refilled it, and sat in one of the visitor's chairs, beaming at them contentedly. "What were we discussing?"

"Angelina was about to tell us something she's learned," Moriarty said.

"Was I? I've forgotten." She used her sandwich to shield her face from Hatcliff while giving her husband a slight shake of her head. Not a topic for Hatcliff's ears, evidently.

Sebastian jumped in. "The cloud gondola should be ready for your test-run by the time we finish lunch."

Hatcliff nodded. "My signature effect. You should join me this year, my boy."

"You don't have to ask me twice!" Sebastian drained his cup of champagne.

"What's this about a cloud?" Moriarty asked.

Sebastian dusted crumbs from his hands. "The cloud descends in the dream scene dividing the first act, which takes place in the real world, from the second act, which takes place in Cloudland, where the Giant lives. Someone magical has come down in a cloud in every pantomime since Lionel took over this theater."

"I didn't invent the idea," Hatcliff said, though he seemed proud of it. "It's an old standard. The *deus ex machina,* you know the stuff. I try to put a fresh twist on it every year."

Sebastian nodded eagerly. "This year the twist is a slow descent from up left through a mist lit from behind with a pink filter. The music will be ethereal. The figure in the clouds appears at first to be an angel coming down from heaven to speak to Jack" — he gestured with an open palm at his sister — "who's lying on a bed of straw down right. But when the gondola reaches the bottom, the figure steps out, and it's Timothy Tweedy with a halo on his head!"

The other three laughed with delight, so Moriarty followed suit with a chuckle, but he didn't understand the joke. Apparently, Mr.

Tweedy was humor made flesh, his mere appearance enough to convulse an audience.

"You know," Hatcliff said, his eyes watery, "that ghost might have been trying to do me harm, but instead it's done me the greatest favor. Fowler was a good man in his day, but he changed, don't ask me why. The truth is, I'd been thinking about letting him go. And now I've got you instead, my dear boy. You're ten times the theater man Fowler was at his best."

Sebastian grinned, seeming surprised by the praise. Angelina smiled and nodded. She'd known it all along.

"I can't wait to see how everything works," Moriarty said. "I had no idea theaters employed such advanced machinery."

"Once things settle into a routine," Sebastian said, rapping the wooden arm of his chair with his knuckles for luck, "I'll show you around the departments. I'll tell you, James, you've never met such a clever bunch of craftsmen — and women. They can do just about anything and gladly, if you ask nicely and pay a fair wage. Building Rome in a day would be nothing for these clever people."

"That's music to my ears, my boy." Hatcliff rose to add champagne to everyone's cups. "I'm hearing good reports from all quarters about my new stage manager. They say you're quite the clever chappie yourself. If you'd be interested in staying on after *Beanstalk*'s run its course, we could put together quite a program for '87."

"There's nothing I'd like better, Lionel," Sebastian said, his fair face alight. "This is what I've been wanting, even though I didn't know it."

A knock sounded on the door and the clerk poked his head in to say, "The cloud's ready, Mr. Hatcliff."

"Hurrah!" Sebastian stuffed the last of his sandwich into his mouth and leapt to his feet, grabbing his book. Hatcliff set his cup on the mantel and followed him out. Angelina said, "We'd better go too, darling. It must be a Galaxy ritual."

Sebastian bounded across the stage into the wings on the women's side. Hatcliff strode after him. Angelina took Moriarty by the hand and led him toward a towering, vine-covered monstrosity that had sprung up on the left side of the stage.

"Great Scott! Is that your beanstalk?" He leaned back to look all the way to the top. "It must be thirty feet tall."

"Twenty-five, I'm told." She stroked the fake leaves as if caressing a pet.

"You don't mean to climb all the way up there."

"I only have to climb about ten feet, which I did this morning without incident. It's as sturdy as can be, James."

"Hmm." Moriarty walked around the construction, noting the two climbing routes laid out on opposite sides. He grabbed a rung with both hands and gave it a good hard shake. Nothing moved. He looked down and saw that the thing was bolted securely to the floor. He stepped onto the lowest rung and peered inside. It had been raised in sections, which were also securely bolted together. With enough men, the thing could be built or unbuilt in a quarter hour.

He looked up, shrugged, and climbed about halfway up. Then he turned, dangling from one handhold and one foot, and looked down on his wife. "Halloo, below!"

"James!" she cried. "Do be careful!"

"Shoe's on the other foot now, eh, my dear?" He felt quite as rambunctious as a schoolboy up here. It must be the effect of drinking both beer and champagne at lunch. He was beginning to see the appeal of this theater venture. Cudlow had it all wrong. It wasn't the girls or the gambling, it was the clever constructions and the machinery!

He turned halfway around and gazed out into the vast auditorium. Many of the seats were filled by people in work clothes or the informal garments actors wore for rehearsing, come to watch the cloud ceremony. Moriarty found himself near enough to the lowest box to carry on a quiet conversation, if anyone had been in it. Perhaps he would reserve that box for himself and his guests.

He swung back around to look at the cloud gondola hanging overhead. From here, he could clearly see how it was made. The base consisted of a narrow wooden platform with a railing around the sides. Each end of the railing was supported by a rope, which passed over a huge roller set into a sort of gear mechanism, controlled by another rope held by a man on one of the catwalks. A counterweight hung off the opposite side of the gear. The rope had been painted blue, the color of the backdrop. Frothy pink-and-white gauze had been stapled all around the front and side railings, hanging down a foot or two to hide the platform from the audience. Ingenious!

At the moment, the thing was snugged up against the bridge like a dinghy at a pier. Sebastian appeared and opened a section of the railing, then turned to look back the way he'd come, waiting for Hatcliff to catch up.

Moriarty wanted to watch the descent from the stage with his wife, so he climbed down, stomping heavily on each rung as he descended for a final test. Then he leapt the last five or so feet, landing smartly on the stage.

Angelina twitched her lips at him. "You're far more reckless than I ever am."

"Good! I'd be happier if I could test all the contraptions before you use them."

"You just want to play with the props. Wait and see; before the end of this show, you'll be sword-fighting with Sebastian and swinging overhead on a trapeze."

He gave her a dry look. "They offer fencing lessons at the London Athletic Club, you know. I may not be quite as ignorant of that skill as you think."

"Oh really? We'll have to explore that question one of these days."

He took her hand and folded it into the crook of his arm. "In my estimation, my dear, climbing that beanstalk is safer than crossing the Strand on a Saturday afternoon. Frankly, I'm not sure how your Miss Verney managed to fall in such a way as to sprain her ankle."

"I don't think she did. I think she's faking it. That's one of the things I wanted to tell you about."

"We're ready!" Sebastian shouted, waving with one hand. The other still clutched the prompt book.

"We're watching!" Angelina shouted back.

They strolled to the edge of the stage and looked up. "From this perspective, the thing looks completely insubstantial," Moriarty said.

"That's the idea, darling."

Hatcliff stood beside the gondola and spread his arms wide. "Friends, Romans, countrymen," he boomed, his voice carrying into the hall.

"Lend us your ears!" the people in the stalls responded.

"What fun!" Angelina's eyes sparkled. Moriarty had to agree. It all felt very festive.

Hatcliff stepped onto the gondola, which wobbled a little as he moved toward the center. The far end sagged a few inches. Moriarty frowned, but he supposed there could be a bit of give in the rope. Hatcliff must weigh more than the average actor.

Sebastian stepped on and closed the railing. Two crew men pushed the thing away from the bridge while the man on the catwalk let out his rope. The gondola sank a few inches, swaying gently. Then the rope nearest the bridge snapped, ends flying apart. The gondola tilted steeply down, flinging Hatcliff into the gauze around its edge. Sebastian's book landed on the wooden stage with a thump.

Angelina screamed, her shrill voice filling the hall. Moriarty's first instinct was to grab her and pull her protectively into his chest. He looked past her at Sebastian, clinging to the rope at the top of the upended gondola with both hands while Hatcliff swung upside down from the bottom, his feet tangled in the gauze.

Everyone started shouting and wailing. Men ran onto the bridge with hooks on ropes and tossed them at the gondola, trying to catch it and drag it back. A sharp ripping sound split the air and everyone stopped, holding their breaths, while the swatch of fabric holding Hatcliff tore free. He plummeted thirty feet to the stage and lay crumpled on one side, not moving.

"Sebastian!" Angelina cried, standing beneath her brother, her face contorted with terror.

"Get the book!" Sebastian shouted.

Moriarty scooped up the precious object and knelt beside Hatcliff, probing for a pulse. "He's alive," he called into the chaos. No one answered. He watched while the flymen succeeded in catching the gondola, drawing Sebastian to safety.

A shuddering sob escaped Angelina as she turned toward Hatcliff. "Alive?" She knelt beside him and placed a hand on his cheek. "Lionel? Can you hear me?"

Hatcliff groaned.

"Thank God," Angelina whispered.

Moriarty ran his hands along the man's limbs, pressing lightly, not sure what he expected to find or what he would do if he found it. He shouted out to the audience, "Call a doctor! Get an ambulance!"

"Home," Hatcliff groaned. "Home."

"He's probably better off there," Angelina said. She hated hospitals, with good reason.

Hatcliff's clerk ran onto the stage and stood beside them, wringing his hands with tears streaming down his face. Moriarty told him to do two things as quickly as he could: get some kind of conveyance — a wagon, a large coach, anything — and send for Hatcliff's doctor to meet them at his house. The clerk dashed off.

"You'll soon be tucked into your own bed, Lionel dear," Angelina told the fallen man. She clasped his limp hand in both of hers.

"I'll be right back." Moriarty got to his feet and went to stand under the dangling remains of the gondola. Once Sebastian had climbed off, it had risen to the top of the gear-and-pulley mechanism, where it now dangled, spinning slowly. He couldn't see the broken end of the rope well enough to tell if it had been cut or had simply frayed and broken.

Sebastian was standing on the bridge performing a similar inspection. He called down, just loud enough to be heard, "Don't worry, Professor. I'll see that nothing's touched and the area is closed off."

Moriarty showed him the book, receiving a thumbs-up. He went back to kneel beside his wife, who had folded up some scraps of gauze to pillow Hatcliff's head.

"Was it an accident?" she whispered.

He could offer her only a shrug and a shake of the head. "I doubt it."

FOURTEEN

Angelina knelt by Lionel's head, stroking his brow. James stood beside her with his hand on her shoulder. Lionel muttered something she couldn't understand. She could only murmur, "You're going to be all right, darling. We'll take care of you."

Then Sebastian appeared and knelt on the other side. "Anything broken?"

"I don't think so," James said.

"That's a mercy," Sebastian said. "Has he spoken? Is he awake?"

"He said 'home,'" Angelina said, "and he's been muttering, but he could be asleep, for all I can tell."

Lionel opened his eyes and rolled them first toward her and then toward Sebastian. He closed them again, smiled, and said, "Angels."

"He knows us," Sebastian said. "That's a good sign, isn't it?"

"Us from twenty years ago." Angelina shook her head. "His mind may be wandering."

Other people gathered onto the stage, whispering together, but kept their distance, for which she was grateful. It could only trouble Lionel to sense a crowd looming around him. After a few minutes, the clerk rushed out to say, "I've found a coach. Can we get him up?" He had Lionel's coat and hat.

Mr. Easton came over to help. "Someone get his feet."

Sebastian obeyed. Lionel groaned as they raised him up, the giant man grappling Lionel's whole round torso against his mighty chest. The others formed a circle around them, clearing a path through the wings and out the stage door to a large coach waiting in the alley. James opened the door and jumped in, tossing the book on the bench, then squatting to help Easton maneuver Lionel inside as gently as possible. He seated himself behind the unconscious man to serve as a cushion. Angelina climbed in and took the opposite seat. The clerk and Sebastian tried to enter at the same time, jamming at the door.

"You should stay," Sebastian said. "People will want to know what's happened. Outsiders too." He looked at Lionel, slumped unconscious against James's chest, and sent a questioning glance toward Angelina.

"The last thing we want is a general panic," she said.

Sebastian nodded. "Tell everyone Mr. Hatcliff is going to be fine. You might write a notice for the press minimizing the accident."

"We'll let you know what the doctor says," Angelina added.

"I'll do my best." The clerk passed the hat and coat to Sebastian. "I hope it turns out to be true."

They rolled through the city in silence, too worried to talk, to Lionel's house in Regent's Park. The clerk had thought to telegram ahead, so the manservant flung open the door as soon as the coach pulled up to the stoop. He and James got Lionel upstairs to his bedroom, where a fire had been lit, laying him gently onto his bed. The front bell rang, and soon the doctor came bustling in with his bag, sending everyone but the servant downstairs.

The housekeeper showed them into the library. "I lit the fire in here too, thinking someone might be wanting to wait."

Angelina stood as close to the flames as she could, hugging herself and rubbing her arms. Sebastian put the book where he could see it and joined her, turning his back to the fire, his hands behind his back. James found a shawl and wrapped it around her. He flung himself into an armchair, crossed his legs, and pressed his palm against his forehead.

And so they waited, each thinking their own thoughts. Angelina's memory kept replaying those horrible moments when the rope snapped, nearly sending her brother hurtling to the floor along with poor dear Lionel. She distracted herself by letting her gaze rove around the handsome library. Bookshelves filled with leather-bound volumes ran from floor to ceiling on two walls. Wide books bound with cheap pasteboard lay in stacks on top of their expensive cousins; scripts, no doubt, sent to him by hopeful writers. Papers were strewn across the surface of a broad desk in front of the curtained windows, looking as though Lionel had just gotten up from a morning's work. The walls not given up to shelves were covered with framed posters from the Galaxy's pantomimes, including last year's *Cinderella* with Nora Verney in the title role.

"What will we do now?" James asked.

"I don't know." She and Sebastian traded sorrowful looks. He'd come to the same conclusion. "I suppose we'll have to close the show."

"What?" James's high forehead creased in confusion. "I can't have heard you correctly. Do you mean to give up?"

Sebastian blew out a weary breath. "I hate to say it, but what else can we do? First John Fowler, now Lionel . . ." He rubbed his stubbled chin. "He doesn't look good, James. That chalky color . . . Even if he lives, he won't be able to work. And this'll be the last straw for the cast and crew. The curse has taken another victim."

"It's too horrible, darling," Angelina said. "Who's next? We can't risk another accident like this one. There'll be another play another day. We have to know when to fold up our tents."

James had started frowning as Sebastian spoke. Before Angelina finished, he was shaking his head. Now he uncrossed his legs and set his fists on his thighs, glaring at each of them in turn. "We will not fold up our tents. We will not close the show. We will not be driven out with our tails between our legs! I will catch this murdering bastard — pardon my language — and you two will put on the most thrilling pantomime anyone has ever seen. They'll be lining up all the way around Leicester Square to see you climb that beanstalk, and I'll be the one clapping the loudest."

Angelina's heart swelled with love and pride for her gallant husband, but they couldn't possibly continue. "James, I appreciate your —"

"No, my dear, I won't hear it." He shook his finger at her. "I rarely put my foot down, but this time I must insist. You want this more than anything; Sebastian too. I'm new at this game, though I'm beginning to understand the appeal. But we aren't the only ones to consider here. There are over a hundred people in that theater counting on this show to keep the wolf from their doors this winter. Are we going to let them down? Lionel Hatcliff wouldn't. As his partner, it's my job to speak for him. And apart from all that, I'll be damned to the lowest circle of hell before I'll allow some reckless, malicious, murdering prankster to shut down *my theater*!" He slapped his hand on his thigh and jutted out his chin, daring them to refute his arguments.

The slap rang into silence. Then Angelina laughed and swooped in to plant a kiss on his forehead. "I knew I married you for a reason," she murmured into his ear.

"Put it that way," Sebastian said, "and I'm with you. Although I must say I'm surprised. I had the feeling you weren't all that keen, especially after Fowler's death."

"I'll admit I had my doubts," James said, "but that was before I discovered what a complex undertaking a Christmas pantomime is. Hundreds of skilled craftsmen and women — and actors, of course — devoting countless hours to fabricating the most inventive structures and devices. I'm impressed and eager to see it all come together."

"I knew it," Angelina said. "You can't bear to see good machinery being misused."

James gave her a knowing look. "That's a factor — a small one. More importantly, you both seem to have forgotten that Lionel Hatcliff came to me only two short weeks ago to put a stop to the pranks at the Galaxy. What kind of a consulting detective would I be if I allowed my opponent to defeat me by attacking my client?"

The door opened and the doctor entered, holding his bag in one hand. He recognized Sebastian with a blink and a smile, looked at Angelina with a hint of wonder, then turned a professional smile toward James, who rose to receive the report. "I'm James Moriarty. This is my wife and my brother-in-law —"

"Of course I recognize Mr. Archer." The doctor chuckled, transferring his bag to his left hand so he could shake hands. He beamed at Angelina. "I recognize you as well, Miss Lovington. Good to see you back."

"How is Mr. Hatcliff, Doctor?" Angelina asked.

"He woke up while we were undressing him and seemed relieved to be in his own room. No broken bones, though I suspect he has sustained internal injuries. I couldn't find any bleeding, but there's tenderness in the abdomen, which is a bit worrisome, and a nasty lump on the head that needs watching. The best thing for him now is sleep. I've given him morphine to help with that."

"Thank you," James said. "What can we do?"

"Nothing, except try not to worry too much. These things can go either way. Give him a chance to rest and mend. I'll send a nurse over to stay with him and come back in the morning."

"Very good," James said. He glanced at the other two and added, "There is one small thing. We're only a week or so from opening night at the Galaxy."

The doctor nodded. "I know about the panto. I've been Mr. Hatcliff's doctor for many years."

"Then you'll understand how important it is that this accident not stir up negative publicity."

"Never fear, Mr. Moriarty. Most of my patients are theater people. You can rely on my discretion, as well as that of my nurse. I'll have a word with the servants on the way out."

"That's a load off our minds," James said.

The doctor turned to go, but paused on the threshold to shoot them a wink. "My wife and I love the pantos at the Galaxy. We always take a box. And we wouldn't miss Lina Lovington's return to the London stage for all the world."

The housekeeper entered as the doctor left. "Will you be wanting tea?"

Angelina traded questioning looks with the others. James said, "We do need to talk." Angelina said to the housekeeper, "Tea would be lovely. Thank you, Mrs. . . . ?"

"Lind, ma'am. Mr. Lind's my husband." She folded her hands in front of her spotless apron. "We've been with Mr. Hatcliff for years now. We were both actors in our day, Mr. Lind and me. We know what rumors can do to a show. You can trust us not to breathe a word to anyone, not even the milkman. Resting and mending, that's our story. We'll stick to it."

Angelina thanked her again and introduced the three of them. "One or the other of us will be coming by every day to see how

Lionel is doing. If his condition changes for better or worse, please send to us at once."

"Very well, Miss Lovington." Mrs. Lind bowed her head and left.

Lind came in to set the tea table beside a couple of chairs, drawing up another one for Angelina. Sebastian sat down, but James remained standing. "I'd like to send a telegram to our clerk at the Galaxy."

Lind guided him to the desk and located the form. He waited while James wrote his message and then took charge of it. James had barely seated himself when Lind returned, saying, "The nurse is here. Did you want to speak with her?"

"Yes." James got up again and went out. Mrs. Lind brought in a large tray holding a brilliantly polished silver tea service. She set it on the table, and Angelina poured three cups of tea, adding sugar and milk according to preferences she knew as well as her own. James came back in and closed the door firmly. He rubbed his hands together and said, "Ah, tea!" He sat down, took a large swallow from his cup, and then surveyed the offerings. "What are these, cheese and pickle?" He helped himself to a sandwich.

Mrs. Lind had brought a plate heaped with sandwiches, another with slices of ginger nut cake and lemon tarts. Angelina waited until the men had fortified themselves, then she refilled their cups and repeated James's original question. "What will we do now?"

James smiled at her. "I thought my little speech made that fairly clear. The show must go on."

"Yes, darling, you were marvelous. I meant, what must we do? Go back and pick up where we left off?"

Sebastian glanced at the clock on the mantelpiece. "I should get back right away. I'll reassure people as best I can. 'Resting and mending nicely' — I suppose those are our watchwords until further notice." His eyes still held a shadow of concern, but otherwise he seemed eager to get back to work.

This job had transformed him. Gone was the fastidious, aloof, languid man about town, replaced by this purposeful, hardworking stage manager. His tie bulged out of his waistcoat and his shirt had come untucked in back. True, he'd just narrowly escaped death, but that didn't explain the stubble on his cheeks or the scuffed shoes and wrinkled trousers. Angelina had never seen her brother so disheveled. Had he really changed though, or just adopted a new role?

James said, "We will go back and carry on, but we must also put our heads together and stop these — Well, we can't call them accidents anymore, can we?"

"That rope didn't break by itself," Sebastian said. "I haven't seen it, but my crew would never use a frayed rope for such a purpose. They know their jobs."

James nodded. "I believe it was a deliberate attempt to maim or murder Lionel Hatcliff."

"Oh, horrible!" Angelina cried. She believed him, but she couldn't bear it. "Who would do such a thing?"

"That's what we must find out," James said, "and soon. We don't even know what these villains want. Who's next on their list?"

"Me or Lina," Sebastian said. "If their goal is to stop *Beanstalk* from opening. We should all be on our guards from here out."

"That's such a vile thought." Angelina shuddered. Then she remembered the conversation in the wardrobe earlier. "Oh! I almost forgot. I learned two things this morning that might help. First, there is nothing wrong with Nora Verney's ankle. She faked that accident, probably to get out of her contract. Now I don't know why she wanted to do that."

"To close the show," Sebastian said. "That's what all these things are aiming at. Disable the stage manager, lose the leading actress, scare off the *corps de ballet.* Any one of those things might have worked if Hatcliff hadn't come to you."

"And if you hadn't been there to leap into the gap." Angelina gave his hand a warm squeeze.

"Our involvement could not have been predicted," James said. "Which explains the boldness of this last attempt. We've made them more desperate. But why? That's the question that baffles me. Who would benefit from the cancellation of this pantomime?"

"No one," Angelina said. "Many people lose. The cast, the crew, the front office people. The advertisement people, the company that supplies the refreshments. The list goes on and on."

"All I can think of is a rival theater manager," Sebastian said. "But I've never heard of anything like this happening before."

Angelina lifted the large teapot and gave it a little shake. Enough for another round. She gestured for their cups and refilled them.

"What was the second thing?" James asked her as he accepted his full cup.

"Something rather serious, though I don't know how it relates to these accidents." Angelina told them about following Nora up to the wardrobe and listening while she persuaded the mistress to give her a gown. "Noisette didn't like it, though she eventually gave in. She knows that gown will never come back. She more or less accused John Fowler of stealing costumes. Some of them are worth hundreds, darling," she added for James's benefit.

He frowned at the sum.

Sebastian said, "That explains why the property chief is so testy with me. He hates to show me anything that isn't already in use. He must think I'm scouting out more booty."

"We should conduct a thorough inventory," James said.

"After," Sebastian said, meaning after the panto settled into a routine. "And I want amnesty for any of my people who may have been dragged in unwittingly or unwillingly."

Angelina loved the way he said "my people." They simply had to catch this wicked person and his — or her — accomplices. She'd been longing to get back on the stage, but she never dreamed of anything as perfect as having James in the front office and Sebastian in charge backstage.

"Don't forget about Nora," she said. "She's at the center of all this somehow. Oh, and Timothy Tweedy took a costume too; just one, I think. Noisette made an excuse for him. 'His need was great,' she said, or something like that."

"His money problem," Sebastian said. "I'd like to get to the bottom of that. He'd be as hard to replace as you or me." He pointed at Angelina. "You'll draw a lot of curious folks in the first few weeks, but a long run depends on Sparrow and Tweedy too. They're madly popular."

"We should put them on their guard too," Angelina said.

"Unless Tweedy's money problem could be solved by stopping the show," James said. "How can we find out what that's about?"

"Peg will know," Angelina said. "They seem to have rekindled an old flame. She's always finding excuses to run out for this or that and stays gone for an hour. I caught them together once, sitting in a corner at the Bear and Staff."

Sebastian grinned. "That explains her new style. I've never seen her looking so spiffy."

"She takes as long to get dressed these days as I do," Angelina said. "I'm so happy for her." Then another view of that supposed romance sprang into her mind. "Unless he's using her to put us off, in which case I'll hang the man myself."

"Peg has better sense than that," James said, not sounding convinced. He'd seen the roses blooming in her cheeks too.

Angelina frowned at him. "I hope you're right. And I do think she knows something about his troubles. She gets this mulish look whenever I ask."

"Peg Barwick is the worst liar on this green earth," Sebastian said. "You'd think she'd be better at it after so many years with us. Get her in a corner and press hard. She'll crack like an egg." He said it with a smile. "Or let me do it."

"She can be stubborn when she wants to be," Angelina said. "But I'll work on her. And I'll have a chat with Mr. Sparrow. He's known Tweedy for ages and he's been at the Galaxy longer than Nora, I think. The troubles seem to have started last spring, with that disastrous *Travestie of MacBreath*. He'll know what was going on at that time."

Sebastian wrinkled his nose. "If you can get any sense out of him. He works hard, I'll give him that, but he's always in character."

Pot calling the kettle black there. Sebastian lived whatever role he was playing. Little angel, dashing flâneur, featherbrained toff . . . dedicated stage manager.

"Be careful when you talk to people," James said. "We don't know who's behind all this."

"It's Nora," Angelina said. "I don't know how and I don't know why, but I can feel it. She may not be cutting ropes or shoving wedges under doors, but she's a greedy little witch and doesn't much care who gets hurt, as long as she gets her way."

"This ghostly stuff is too imaginative for Nora," Sebastian said. "Borrowing gowns and not returning them is one thing. She thinks they're hers anyway. And wheedling Lionel into advancing her career is her standard mode of operation. That's how she caught old What's-His-Name, that music hall owner who left her the two small halls in Southwark."

"Maybe she thought Hatcliff would give her the Galaxy," Angelina said.

James shook his head. "It isn't his to give. He has a thirty-year lease with some fifteen years left to go."

"She wanted to rule at his side, then," Sebastian said. "Choosing plays, casting, sashaying about in a fur stole on opening night."

"Which she can't do if there's no play," Angelina said. "If she wanted to be the great actress-manager, like Marie Wilton, she'd hang on to *Beanstalk* with both hands and feet."

She and Sebastian traded stories about actors who had gotten out of contracts and why and when and where. James listened, stroking his bearded cheek with his index finger and gazing at Hatcliff's cluttered desk. He waited for their talk to wind down and said, "I'd like to go through that desk, but it doesn't seem right. I can start at the theater. Maybe there's something in the accounts that suggests a motive. It must be about money somehow. What other reason could there be?"

"Envy," Sebastian suggested. "Or ambition."

"Spite," Angelina said. "But breaking that rope is too serious for that."

"I'm not so sure," James said. "Our prankster has a rather nasty sense of humor."

Mean jokes, thwarted ambitions. Favorites and the trouble they caused. Money troubles, resentment, secret thieving with pressure to aid and abet. If they wanted motives, they had plenty to choose from in that theater of grudges.

FIFTEEN

On Saturday night, Moriarty indulged himself by draining a few gallons of lukewarm bathwater and replacing it with fresh, reveling in the modern plumbing that could deliver piping-hot water from a boiler three stories below with the simple turn of a tap. He shook in a few drops of the rose-scented oil his wife had given him for his birthday, feeling a bit like a Turkish sultan. That foolish notion came from the name on the label: "Hammam," from Penhaligon's. A bit lush for a former maths professor, but Angelina liked it, and it did smell nice.

He draped a washcloth over his bald scalp to hold in the heat and lay back against the smooth porcelain. He'd been advised to take his time since they daren't appear at the Beerbohms' a single minute before half past eleven.

He could fall asleep if he wished, secure in the knowledge that he would not be disturbed. The other men in the house — Rolly and Antoine — bathed in a copper tub in the scullery. The women preferred warm sponge baths by the fire in their respective bedrooms. For all her cultural sophistication, Angelina still clung to old-fashioned ideas about drains, suspecting them of harboring all manner of vague miasmas. Peg had a Cockney disdain for anything newfangled. And the one time he'd suggested the housemaids might enjoy a bath, they'd gaped at him in abject horror. Angelina had rescued them from a house in which the master had done worse than merely suggest a bath — far worse. Moriarty thought they'd learned to trust him, but some old wounds never fully healed. He'd refrained from mentioning anything related to bathing in their presence again.

This party they were attending, a *soirée* or *conversazione* — why social events couldn't have plain English names, he could not begin to fathom — would take place in the home of Sir Herbert Beerbohm Tree, another theater manager. Angelina insisted they go in spite of Lionel's condition; because of it, in fact. Rumors of the accident would already be circulating. Their job was to sally forth and counteract them with a unified front of optimism and good cheer.

They had bigger problems than gossip, however. That quarterly rent check was due in four days, along with the Christmas pay for the entire cast and crew. Hatcliff hadn't said anything on Friday about the solicitor registering their partnership agreement. Had it been done? How long did it take? Moriarty's money was somewhere en route from his bank to Hatcliff's. Would he be able to get at it when it arrived without a legal business relationship to support his signature?

That worry nagged at him like a bit of nutshell between the teeth. But it was too soon to worry Angelina about it. She should enjoy herself tonight.

Moriarty wrapped himself in his long dressing gown and strode swiftly across the hall to the bedroom. He wouldn't want his bare feet to alarm the mouse maids. Angelina was fully gowned and doodling about at her dressing table. He hastened to catch up, donning his low-fronted waistcoat and the tailcoat with the satin collar. He stood behind his wife to use her mirror to tie his white tie.

"Rolly's ordered the coach," Angelina said, smiling her approval at his appearance. She was faultless, as always, in a confection of dark purple silk and lavender lace that made her eyes glow like burnished copper. The neckline could be higher to suit him better — at least for public display — but in private, he could admire the effect without reservation.

"It seems silly to take a coach to travel a mere eighth of a mile. These people live barely six blocks away."

"James." Angelina put down the ivory comb with which she'd been shaping tiny curls around her face and rose from her cushioned bench. She strode to a clearing between the bed and the front windows and turned so that the train of her gown pooled gracefully at her feet. The bustle on this gown extended a full foot from her natural form and was augmented by great swoopings of vivid cloth.

"You cannot seriously expect me to walk an eighth of a mile in this dress."

He laughed. "I suppose not. You are magnificent, my dear."

She accepted the compliment with a lift of her chin. "And don't even think about sneaking home to spend an hour reading in your own chair and then sneaking back to collect me. Their house isn't any bigger than ours. I'll know if you go missing."

Moriarty snapped his fingers, only half joking. The thought had crossed his mind, but he'd ruled it out on his own. His conscience could only bear so many challenges in one day. "It seems extravagant, that's all."

She returned to her bench to choose a pair of earrings. She met his gaze in the mirror and asked, "Are you that worried about money?"

"I'm not worried about *us*. Our rent is paid through this time next year. I've kept enough in our account to keep food on the table for several months. And our servants will never leave us, whether we pay them or not, for fear of imminent arrest." They shared a chuckle over the benefits of Angelina's unorthodox hiring practices. He added, "And there's always another wealthy whist player looking for a set-down."

"But the theater?"

He busied himself flattening the fringe of hair around his bald dome, avoiding her eyes. He didn't like lying to her, but now was not the time. "Let's get through a week without further incident. Once we open and the show is a roaring success, we should have —"

"Shush!" She reached up and put a finger across his lips. "The gods of luck are envious of their prerogatives. Don't tempt their wrath by presuming to know what they will do!"

He kissed the finger before it was withdrawn. "That makes no sense, my dear. How can anyone manage a business without making forecasts about expected revenues?"

"Hmm, I see your point. At least try not to forecast without saying things like, 'We're certain to have the absolute scorchingest box office in history!'"

"You may assure yourself and any relevant gods that I will never use the word 'scorchingest.' But I can't guarantee the continuation of *Beanstalk*, not without Hatcliff to guide me. I feel as if I'm sailing into uncharted waters."

"All plays are like that, darling. It's part of the fun."

"If you say so."

"I do say so." She rose again and straightened his tie. "Now. We're going to a lovely party filled with lovely theater people and we're going to have a lovely time. We're going to tell everyone that Lionel is mending nicely, that *Beanstalk* is shaping up beautifully, and that we're confident the show will be a roaring success."

Now Moriarty was completely confused. "Won't that offend your gods of luck?"

"Not at all, darling." She smiled complacently. "Because everyone will know we're lying."

* * *

It took longer to get Angelina and her sea of velvet into the coach and out again than it did to clop around a few corners to Rosary Gardens. A uniformed maidservant took their outer garments as a tall man with a full head of red hair emerged from the dining room to welcome them. Or what ought to be the dining room — they'd removed the table to make room for more guests.

Herbert Beerbohm Tree, their host, kissed Angelina's hand. "Such a pleasure to meet you at last! I saw you in *La Perichole,* of course. It made a lasting impression." He winked at Moriarty, who must have been the only man in England not to see her in that role. "Your brother, Sebastian, and I worked together in *The Private Secretary* a few years ago. I'm all athirst to hear about his new role as stage manager. I invited him tonight, but he claims to be busy."

"He hasn't left the Galaxy since he took that job," Angelina said, smiling to make the truth seem like a joke.

"People underestimate him," Tree said as he turned to shake Moriarty's hand.

"I don't. He seems to know how everything in that great barn of a building works and who should be doing what and when. I'd be lost without him."

"You'll soon learn the ropes," Tree said. "And of course you've got a fine mentor in Lionel Hatcliff. How is he, by the way? Helen and I would love to call and pay our respects."

"Resting comfortably and mending nicely," Angelina said. "The best thing for him now is peace and quiet. We'll let you know when he's ready for visitors — or rather, he will! He's as eager as anyone for opening night."

They repeated that message over and over, with minor variations to keep it fresh, as they worked their way through the press of stylish people milling about the house. Angelina presented him to everyone they met, then drifted toward the piano at the back of the drawing room, where a group had already gathered. Moriarty drifted unobtrusively the other way. He could listen to his wife sing at home and didn't care about the others. Worse, on another occasion some cheerful wag had tried to drag him into the mix, saying, "Come on now, Professor, it's your turn!"

He'd barely escaped with his dignity intact.

He guessed Tree's library would occupy the rear portion of the ground floor and be the designated cigar-and-brandy preserve for gentlemen like himself. He was right on both counts. He found a masculine enclave replete with leather upholstery and a collection of portraits of the Trees arrayed in the costumes of their many theatrical roles. Three men sat in the alcove talking in low voices. A small fire glowed in the hearth.

Charles Cudlow leaned against the mahogany mantelpiece, smoking a cigar. He grinned with pleasure as Moriarty entered, closing the door on the noise of the party. "Why, it's Professor Moriarty! I hadn't expected to see you here."

"Nor I you." They shook hands like old friends. Cudlow offered him one of their host's excellent cigars and directed him to the drinks table to pour himself a brandy. Thus supplied, Moriarty took up a position a few feet from the fire, leaning a hip on the back of an unoccupied chair. "I'm surprised to see you as well, Cudlow. This crowd seems to be mostly actors and actresses."

"I'm here with an actress, as it happens. You know my little penchant in that direction."

Moriarty smiled as if he didn't find the sport of actress-chasing repugnant. "We're bound to bump into each other more frequently, I suppose, now that I've gone into partnership with Lionel Hatcliff."

"So you made the leap. Very thrilling!"

"Perhaps a bit too much." Moriarty offered him a wry grimace. "There's a lot to learn before we open on Boxing Day."

"Well, you've got a good teacher. How is old Hatcliff anyway? Everyone here says he's mending nicely. Can that be true? I heard it was the devil of a fall."

"He's resting comfortably," Moriarty said. Then he caught the dry look in Cudlow's eyes and realized the line had grown stale. Cudlow prided himself on being in the know. He must have informants inside the Galaxy, and he was no fool. He'd know that a man of Hatcliff's age couldn't fall thirty feet without suffering serious injury.

Moriarty decided to give up a strategic morsel of truth. "He took quite a blow to the head and was out cold for a while. But the doctor is optimistic and says there's no reason we shouldn't be as well."

"Lucky man." Cudlow tapped the ash of his cigar vaguely toward the fire. "And lucky to have such devoted friends looking out for him."

"He and the Archers were quite close many years ago. She's been delighted to renew that old friendship."

"I should imagine so," Cudlow said, "especially since it brought her a plum role in which to make her London *debut redux*, if I may so term it."

Moriarty chuckled, ignoring the edge under the smooth words. "It does seem like a fun role. Very playful."

"That is rather the point of a panto, isn't it? The Galaxy is renowned for its spectaculars. Good old Hattie spares no expense. You know, I'd love to visit the old fellow, if he's up to it."

"Ah," Moriarty said. "He's not quite up to visitors yet."

"Apart from you, your wife, and your brother-in-law, you mean."

"Well, we're practically family now that we've —"

"Taken over the theater?" Cudlow's genial smile grew teeth.

"Gone into partnership. Mr. Hatcliff is well-tended by a nurse and his two devoted servants. Mrs. Moriarty and I check with them once or twice a day to make sure they have everything they need, but they have his care well in hand."

"Glad to hear it," Cudlow said. "Still, I'd love to pay a brief call with the traditional basket of fruit. Let the dear chap know the gang at the Garrick hasn't forgotten him."

"That's thoughtful of you. I'll let you know when he's ready."

Cudlow regarded him with a cool gaze. Moriarty had the distinct feeling he knew Hatcliff was worse off than they were pretending.

"Are you going forward with the production, then?" Cudlow asked. "In spite of Hatcliff's diminished capacity?"

"Physically diminished," Moriarty said. He hated being forced into an outright lie. Not only because it offended his moral core, but because lies had a way of coming out and making the situation worse. "We rely on his advice, naturally. Though my brother-in-law is turning out to be a thoroughly capable manager, and at this point things are very much in train."

"You're taking over the front office, I assume."

"Not so much *taking over* as filling in."

"Complex business, a Christmas pantomime. Most people don't realize how complex. I must say, Archer's stepping in was a surprise. We all assumed he was what he appeared to be — the light-brained, easygoing star of light-brained, easygoing comedies. Who knew he had such hidden depths?"

"Oh, some of us knew." Moriarty drew on his cigar and dismissed Cudlow's characterization with a puff of smoke. "Lionel Hatcliff, for one."

"You make quite the indomitable team, don't you? Office manager, leading actress, and stage manager, all in one convenient family package. Carrying on in the face of adversity, overcoming one obstacle after the other."

Moriarty chuckled. "I suppose you could see it that way. But things just happened, one step after the other, responding to each new crisis as it arose."

"Crises that began after you three came on board. Curious, that, don't you think?"

"I don't follow you. Hatcliff only came to us after Miss Verney's accident put the show in jeopardy."

Cudlow dismissed that with a shake of the head. "She has a perfectly competent understudy. No, I meant John Fowler's death, which opened the door for your brother-in-law to seize control backstage. Now Hatcliff's near-fatal accident leaves you in sole possession of the front office. Once your wife brings in the successful run she inevitably will, your family will find themselves in possession of one of the West End's largest venues. That's the coincidence I find so curious."

Moriarty grunted, taken aback. He shook his head as if bemused by Cudlow's wild imagination and took a slow drink of brandy. He'd reached the conclusion himself that someone was causing accidents at the Galaxy for unknown reasons. Cudlow had apparently reached the same conclusion, but assigned the blame to the most obvious benefactors — Moriarty and his family.

SIXTEEN

On Monday morning, Angelina left her dressing room to go down to the small rehearsal room, but as she reached stage level, someone screamed. She raced out of the wings to see Sebastian throwing a bucket of sand over a small fire. The lighting crew was testing the footlights this morning, and somehow one of the colored silks had been set too close to the gas flame.

"Warn't me," a crewman said, setting his jaw.

"I believe you," Sebastian answered. "But let's check, double-check, and check again, shall we? And make sure the fire buckets are full. Stage level sand, upper floors water. Hop to it!"

"Are you all right?" Angelina patted his shoulder.

He gave her a peck on the cheek. "I've been putting out fires all morning, though this is the first literal one." He lowered his voice, tilting his head toward the extinguished footlight. "This is why I'm sure the prankster is one of us — someone who's here all day, every day. The easiest way to stop *Beanstalk* would be to set the house on fire, but then they might be trapped along with the rest of us."

"So, better to hope there's a murderer among us?" Angelina shuddered. "Or maybe they just don't want to burn up a fortune in costumes and properties."

"My little ray of sunshine. Don't you have work to do?"

"I'm meeting Mr. Sparrow to work on our scene in the Giant's kitchen. I'm not used to that rapid patter and I feel like I'm making the scene drag."

"You're doing fine, Lina. Better than Nora, by all accounts."

"Bless you for that! At this point, I'll be happy to get through the whole show without falling on my face."

"I thought you fell on your face in act three."

She swatted him on the shoulder. "Don't you have work to do?"

They walked off in opposite directions. Angelina had barely reached the stairs when another cry arose from the stage. "My head! Where the devil is my head?"

She turned right around. The actor who played Jack's Cow had caught Sebastian by the arm. "I can't practice my dance without that head. I left it in my dressing room last night, as usual, and now it's gone!"

"We'll find it," Sebastian said. He walked him through his movements the night before, getting nowhere. Then someone on the bridge shouted, "Here it is!" The man pointed at the top of the beanstalk, where someone had hung the big brown cow's head. It seemed to be looking down at them, ears drooping sadly.

"I'll get it," Sebastian said. He handed Angelina the prompt book. "Guard this with your life."

"Be careful, Sebby. It could be a trap to lure someone up to a broken step."

"I know." Sebastian studied the ladder leading directly to the cow's head, then went around to one on the other side. He climbed up, testing each step and handhold as he went. He reached the top, which was many feet narrower than the base, and worked his way around the back where the scaffolding wasn't covered with fake foliage. He grabbed the head and shouted, "Here it comes," then tossed it down to the grateful actor.

Then he started down the other side with even greater care. About fifteen feet from the stage, he cried, "Aha!" Gripping one rope handhold securely, he displayed the cut end of another one. He stretched a foot past one rung to the next and made it the rest of the way down without incident.

"The rung by the cut rope has been tampered with too," he told the carpenter chief, who came out to watch the acrobatics. "Let's check every step and handhold morning and evening, shall we?"

"And again every time we set it up for act two," the chief said, nodding. "We'll make extra steps and holds so we can change them out in a jiffy."

"Good plan." Sebastian walked off with him. The Cow put on his head and started working on his dance steps. Other people who had gathered to watch drifted away. Angelina remained fixed in place, staring up at the beanstalk, her heart still pounding at the risk her brother had taken.

If the villain's aim was to stop *Beanstalk* from opening, his best targets were now the people she loved most: Sebastian and James. And her as well. Jack's understudy was a complete nonentity — Nora's choice, no doubt. If Angelina fell off the beanstalk or into an open trap door or even down the stairs, the show would fail as surely as if the money stopped flowing or Sebastian stopped being six places at once to find lost costumes and put out fires.

She needed a cup of tea. She walked off right and nearly bumped into Frank Sparrow. "There you are," he said. "Sorry I was late."

"It's been a madhouse up here. I'm desperate for some tea. Care to join me? Peg keeps the kettle on."

"Lead on, Mac — Oh, never mind." Sparrow grinned, bowing her toward the stairs.

They found Peg in her sewing chair with a lap full of green organdy. She tucked a stray lock of hair behind her ear when she saw Sparrow nudging in behind Angelina, but didn't get up. "Too many pins," she said by way of an excuse.

Angelina directed Sparrow to the sofa, asking Peg, "Is there tea?" There was not, but she soon remedied that with hot water from Peg's cherished samovar, a gift from a fellow dresser with whom she'd had a torrid affair in Austria during a long winter opera season. She added milk and sugar as requested and handed Sparrow his cup, then refilled Peg's before settling with her own much-desired cup at her dressing table.

"I thought I heard screaming," Peg said, "but I'm getting so used to it, I didn't even bother to go look."

Angelina told them both about the small fire and the cow's head stuck on top of the beanstalk. "I miss all the excitement," Sparrow said. "Luckily, your brother seems to be everywhere at once these days."

"He's charmed," Peg said. "I've always said so."

Sparrow smiled at her as if they'd only just met. "Then it must be true, according to my partner. I rarely see you, but hear your praises sung daily."

"Go on!" Peg's cheeks flared.

"All right, I will," Sparrow said with a wink at Angelina. "First, I'll say thank you. Mr. Tweedy's temper is much sweeter since you came along."

"I never thought of him as bad-tempered," Angelina said.

"He has his ups and downs," Sparrow said, tracing a rising and falling line in the air. "We've been partners twelve years, so I'm used to it."

Peg smirked. "He's a right little lamb once you get under the gruff."

"A largish lamb with a few extra chins," Sparrow said. He was lean where Tweedy was stout.

"You'd never know it from the way he badgers Mr. Hatcliff about his salary," Angelina said. "What's that all about, Mr. Sparrow?"

He shrugged. "I don't know. I work with the man; I don't live in his pocket. He's stopped rattling on about it in our dressing room, for which I'm grateful. We were happy enough with the contract when we renewed it in September."

"It's his business, isn't it?" Peg snapped. "A man's got a right to mind his own business, don't he?" Her expression turned mulish again. She knew what the trouble was, sure enough.

Sparrow regarded her with a wry look. "Don't we all want more than we have, when you think about it? I want a villa in Spain, for instance. But I won't get one by harassing Old Hattie, now will I?"

Peg pursed her lips at him but made no reply.

Angelina changed the subject. "Twelve years, didn't you say? When you and Mr. Tweedy joined forces? Let's see, that would be about 1874, wouldn't it?"

Sparrow nodded. "We kept bowing each other on and off the stage that spring and decided it would save bending if we put our acts together."

"Sparrow and Tweedy, I remember," Peg said. "Though I only saw you the once. That was right before we left for Rome, ducky."

"I must have missed you," Angelina said. "I didn't get to see other acts much back then. I'm looking forward to watching from the wings this time."

"No, ma'am, not during *Beanstalk*," Sparrow said. "Have you never done a panto?"

Angelina shook her head.

"Well, you're in nearly every scene, leaping and jumping, climbing up and down. You'll be spending every break right here on this purple sofa with your feet up."

"Heavens, I've forgotten the art of the twenty-minute nap." She sighed as if dismayed, but she actually felt inspired. She loved the exhilaration and the exhaustion both.

Peg snapped her fingers toward Sparrow. "Now I remember! I saw you once before you teamed up with Mr. Tweedy. You had a dummy act, a whatchacallum —"

"Ventriloquist," Sparrow said, chuckling. "You've got quite a memory, Miss Barwick."

"Fair laughed my head off," Peg said. "Artful Joe, that was the dummy's name. What an impudent little scamp!"

"My worser half," Sparrow told Angelina.

"I missed that one too," she said with a mock pout. "Too busy working."

Sparrow pouted back, then grinned. "Beats the bottle factory."

"Don't it though?" Peg mirrored his grin.

A comfortable sense of camaraderie fell around the three old music hall veterans. Angelina realized this was the perfect opportunity to dig into another of her questions. "When did you and Mr. Tweedy become regulars at the Galaxy, Mr. Sparrow? Did you come in with Mr. Hatcliff? He took over the lease in '78, I think."

"Not that far back." Sparrow set his empty cup on the floor and crossed his long legs, leaning against the wall behind the sofa. "We did variety turns between acts here for a couple of years. Old Hattie learned he could count on us to fill in at short notice, even if it meant a mad dash across town, so when he started doing a burlesque every spring, he made us an offer and we jumped at the chance."

"Regular work," Angelina said, understanding the logic. "No more spending half your week going around trying to book dates for the other half."

"Not to mention being able to keep your stuff in one place," Sparrow said. He pointed his chin at the big trunk occupying one corner of the small room. "Tweedy and I have been in good old AA for, hmm . . . By Jove! Six years. That's longer than I lived with my father." He laughed so heartily, Angelina wasn't sure if the last part was a joke or not. "No wonder we're getting so fat and grumpy." He hunched his shoulders and puffed out his cheeks, though nothing could make his string-bean figure look fat.

Angelina laughed at the effort, then adopted a thoughtful tone. "The Galaxy was a roaring success during most of those years, from what I hear. What changed, Mr. Sparrow? Some people blame the curse of the Scottish play, but other theaters have similar things without calling down the wrath of the gods."

"Someone wasn't happy," Sparrow said. "Whether it was gods, ghosts, or just John Fowler, I couldn't tell you."

"Why would Mr. Fowler sabotage his own production?"

"He wasn't happy about the way things were going."

"What things?" Angelina asked.

Sparrow waggled his eyebrows suggestively. "Managerial things, trending in the direction of matrimonial things."

"Oh. You mean Nora. Now I understand." Angelina gave Sparrow a knowing look. "Hattie let her help make decisions, didn't he? Casting and whatnot. So Mr. Fowler felt left out?"

"He lost his voice." Sparrow drew a finger across his neck, then startled. "Sorry. Not funny under the circumstances. But you've got the right end of the stick. I didn't see him do anything out of the ordinary myself, but the accidents started the night the *Travestie* opened. Then people started talking about curses, and everything went sour."

"Such a shame! It doesn't sound like dear old Lionel, does it, Peg?"

Peg shrugged. "Men of a certain age, ducky. When did he lose his wife?"

"I don't know." Both women turned expectant faces toward the guest.

"Not long after he took over the Galaxy, I think," Sparrow said. "That's when he threw himself into his work. He was here day and night when we started."

"That makes sense," Angelina said. "Then along comes Adorable Nora with her girlish voice and her cupid lips — and her taste for old men with large theaters." She clapped a hand to her mouth as if she'd spoken out of turn. She wanted to heat up the gossip a bit. You couldn't learn anything when everyone was being polite.

Peg caught on and laughed. "Younger men are harder to catch."

"Poor old Hattie never got off the mark," Sparrow said. "Nora started out with a few variety turns, like we did, but in next to no time she'd wheedled her way into the regular cast. She played the ingenue, which is where she belongs, if you ask me. Alas, her grasp exceeded her reach. To be honest, I put the start of the Galaxy's troubles at last year's panto, *Cinderella*. Nora's a cutie and she can be swell to work with, but she wasn't up to the role."

"How so?" Angelina leaned forward, clasping her hands. "I need all the hints I can get."

Sparrow chuckled. "You'll be fine. Adorable Nora doesn't really like to work. She had her routines, at which she was very good — the parasol, the flower-draped swing . . ."

"Songs like "Seaside Girls," Angelina said. "We both grew up doing that sort of thing. I could stand downstage and sing all night long. It's tiring, but not like playing Jack. I love it, don't mistake me. But Cinderella didn't have to climb up and down a beanstalk!"

"No, but she had to duel the Queen of the Hornets," Sparrow said. "Hattie does love to embellish the classics. But the Giant tells me you're quite good, Miss Lovington."

"He does? All he tells me is, 'Move your feet!'"

"And move them you do. No, Nora is always and only Adorable Nora — never Cinderella or Lady MacBreath."

"Mmm," Angelina said. "I can see that. You can't play the ingenue forever. Eventually, you have to put down the parasol and stretch your wings."

"That's another advantage of being part of the house," Sparrow said. "We're in everything, Tweedy and me, with a new burlesque every spring and a new melodrama every autumn."

"I suppose Nora found that burdensome," Angelina said.

"To put it mildly! She wanted to be the Queen of the Galaxy, saying 'Yes, this; no, that,' and going to lots of parties." Sparrow shrugged. "Which would have been fine by most of us. We'd have gotten a sprightlier leading actress, and things would've gone on as they had been."

"Except for Mr. Fowler," Angelina said. "Although I don't see how ruining the shows would get Nora out of his hair."

"Don't you?" Sparrow waggled his black brows again.

She shook her head.

"Those accidents have caused terrific losses this year. That's after a weak panto, mind you. Nobody liked Nora's Cinderella, I'm afraid. We only ran for a month and the provinces weren't terribly keen."

"Oh dear, that is bad." Then Angelina caught his meaning. "Oh! I see! Nora wouldn't be so interested in an old man with a bankrupt theater."

"Not so much." Sparrow pursed his lips and rolled his eyes. "Mr. Fowler achieved his goal. Alas, he didn't live to enjoy it."

Angelina let a moment of silence go by, then said softly, "My husband's certain his death wasn't an accident. The door was wedged shut, did you know that?"

"I heard a rumor."

Angelina nodded. "But however much they disliked one another, Nora couldn't have put that wedge there. She was gone by then."

"Gone, but not forgotten." Sparrow wagged a long finger. "She comes and goes as she pleases, does our Nora. Young Sampson is besotted with her."

"I didn't know that," Angelina said, nodding at Peg as if noting a new fact of importance. "But you can't seriously think she had anything to do with Fowler's death!"

"I don't think anything," Sparrow said. "Not my department. I'm paid to sing and dance and make jokes. But if one were the noticing sort, which you seem to be, one might notice that Fowler's pranks never hurt anyone. The accidents didn't turn deadly till after you lot came along."

That ugly interpretation struck Angelina mute. Peg leapt to the defense. "Lina never did harm to anyone! Even if she wanted to, which she never would, how is she meant to know there's a room full of deadly gas way up there under the roof?" She jabbed her threaded needle at Sparrow as if she could poke him with it from across the room.

He held up both hands to plead for mercy. "I didn't mean anything. I don't think, remember? But Mr. Archer seems to know everything, including where the gas is stored. It's just a coincidence — *I* know it's just a coincidence — but anyone can see it's rather a striking coincidence that our stage manager should die the week after we get a new leading lady with a brother who's looking to stretch his wings. And nothing short of a miracle that this agile and surprisingly capable brother should catch hold of a rope and save himself while poor old Hattie plunges to his doom."

"Not his doom, darling," Angelina said weakly, stunned by the accusation. "Not yet."

SEVENTEEN

"Mr. Moriarty?" A man in a flat tweed cap poked his head around the door of the theater manager's office, where Moriarty sat at what he still considered another man's desk.

"Professor," he replied automatically.

"Sorry?" The man stepped inside. He was on the short side, like so many of the crew who worked in the upper reaches of the theater, but looked strong, with broad shoulders.

"Never mind." The old title bore little relevance in this environment. "What can I do for you, Mr. . . . ?"

"Gibbs. Elmer Gibbs. I'm the scenery chief. Mr. Archer told me not to change out the broken rope until you had a look at it. Well, the new gondola's about ready to fly, and we're on a tight schedule."

"Of course. Thank you for waiting." Moriarty stuck his pen into the holder and grabbed his hat, following the man out the door. He'd been digging into the salary figures, dismayed by the sheer number of persons whose livelihoods depended on a successful play. Last year, he'd taken a wife — a woman with expensive tastes, granted, but not so great a burden at first. They'd spent their early months together traveling around the Continent. They'd treated themselves well, but hadn't owned more than could be packed into half a dozen trunks.

When they'd returned to London, Angelina swiftly added a house with a complement of servants to his list of dependents. Now, by the calamity of one cut rope, he'd inherited the responsibility for several hundred hardworking English men and women.

He hoped he was up to it.

He followed Gibbs to the top floor on the men's side backstage. The theater people called it "off right," having their own way of reckoning directions. A whitewashed corridor extended before them to a metal winding stair that continued on up.

"What's in these rooms?" Moriarty asked as they walked down the hall.

"Supplies," Gibbs answered over his shoulder. "Ropes, tackle, tools. That sort of thing."

"Do you keep them locked?" Moriarty asked as they climbed the winding stair, thinking about the light crew's closets on the other side with their stores of deadly chemicals.

"Wouldn't be very handy, would it?" Gibbs's tone had cooled. He clearly didn't like being questioned any more than the testy Scotsman had.

Well, they'd have to get used to it. Moriarty didn't come backstage often, always seeming to be in someone's way when he did, but he'd spotted many questionable practices. He'd observe the protocols and work through Sebastian, but things were going to change at the Galaxy if he had anything to say about it.

They reached another landing, which opened onto a four-foot-wide wood-and-metal pathway with railings on both sides. The left side ran along the brick wall of the building.

"Welcome to the fly gallery," Gibbs said, pausing to give his guest time to acclimate.

"How high up are we?"

"About thirty-five feet." A light in his eyes betrayed his expectation that Moriarty would feel discomfited by the height.

No joy for him there. Moriarty had climbed mountains in Switzerland and had no fear of heights whatsoever. He set both hands on the sturdy railing and peered straight down into a conical construction made of wooden spars wrapped in green netting. "Why, that's the beanstalk!" He grinned at his guide.

"We get a different view of things from up here."

"Marvelous craftsmanship."

Gibbs merely flicked his eyebrows. Not his department. "We work the cloud gondola from the bridge." He moved on to a suspension bridge spanning the rear of the fly tower.

"Ah," Moriarty said. "So there are three ways to get from one side of the stage to the other. Up here, across the stage, or down in the cellar."

"You don't walk across the stage while the play's on," Gibbs said with a touch of disdain. "You walk behind the black curtain. See?" He pointed down from the far side of the bridge.

Moriarty turned around to look down onto a broad utilitarian passageway running between the brick wall of the building and a huge frame filled with black canvas. "Gads, this is marvelous! I had no idea how interesting the inner workings of a theater could be." He pointed at a pair of big metal doors. "You could even bring things in and out during a play, couldn't you, without the audience being any the wiser."

Gibbs's face expressed the tedium of being told the obvious by a rank amateur.

Back on the stage side, Moriarty saw a team of carpenters tapping away at the cloud gondola. That odd little woman from wardrobe and an assistant bustled around them, tacking up puffs of gauze. From this perspective, the gondola looked like the sort of platform men used to wash windows on tall office buildings in the city.

"I'm surprised you've decided to go ahead with that cloud contraption," he said. "I can't imagine anyone being brave enough to ride in it now."

Gibbs regarded him with a cold eye. "Actors will do whatever the scene demands. That's not the first accident to happen in a theater, and it won't be the last."

"No, I suppose not." Moriarty gave up trying to appease the surly fellow. "Well, let's have a look at the evidence, shall we? I know you're keen to get on with your work."

Gibbs nodded shortly. "We had to remove the rope from the pulley so we could replace it. I kept the pieces, like Mr. Archer said. They're on the other side over there, with a couple of other items I found. But first let me explain to you how it works."

He pointed overhead at a pair of huge iron spindles connected by means of an axle. The larger one was toothed like a gear. Two long ropes had been threaded around and over them, painted blue to match the scene painting that hung behind the clouds. A weight, like a giant plumb bob, dangled from the far end of one rope. The other ends were tied to the railing with tidy knots.

Gibbs laid his hand on one of the knots. "How we did it before was we snugged the gondola up to the railing here, lashing it tight, so it'd be handy when the time came for the actors to climb aboard. The way we've got it weighted and balanced, one man can raise and lower it with this third rope here."

"Ingenious," Moriarty murmured, winning his first glimmer of friendly spirit. "That's how it was when the vandal came up, then?"

"Must've been. But we're changing that now. Mr. Archer wants us to leave the gondola hanging out there" — Gibbs pointed into the air beneath the pulleys — "whenever it's not in use. We'll throw out a hook to haul it in when we need it."

"Like that man did when he rescued Mr. Archer. That's one quick-thinking fellow. I'd like to thank him."

Gibbs didn't say, but something in the set of his mouth suggested that quick-thinker had been him. "Got to be quick on your feet up here in the flies, Professor. Lives depend on us. I tested those ropes myself that very morning. Can't think how I could have missed one of 'em being cut half-through." He seemed angry, justifiably so.

"How do you test them?" Moriarty asked. "Do you step onto the cloud platform?"

"No, I just reach out and give 'em a tug, like this." He stretched his arm out and grasped one of the ropes at about the level of his head, a good two feet above the knot. Gibbs's gaze tracked Moriarty's from fist to knot. "Well, I'll be damned." The rope right above the knot hadn't so much as twitched. The support held firm from fist to spindle, the part that would normally be of greatest concern, but his tug hadn't tested the short stretch from fist to knot at all.

"I would've done the same thing. Where was the cut, do you remember?"

"Right about here." Gibbs pointed about four inches above the knot.

"Easy to reach. Does that tell us anything about the height of the vandal?"

"Huh." Gibbs scratched his unshaven jaw. He pulled out a pocket knife, grabbed the rope, and pretended to saw at it. The unopened knife struck the rope about four inches from the knot.

"Let me try." Moriarty took the knife and did the same thing, trying to behave naturally. This time the knife struck a few inches higher. "Not as tall as me, then."

"Unless he was faking it," Gibbs said. "I wouldn't put it past him. Whoever this fellow is, he's pretty clever."

"Agreed." They traded tight smiles. "What are these items you found?"

"This way." Gibbs led him on across the bridge to another railed gallery and down another set of winding stairs to another whitewashed corridor. He pulled a large set of keys out of his baggy jacket pocket and unlocked the first door with a sly glance at his guest. "Didn't want the villain coming up to steal back what he forgot."

"A wise precaution." They entered a workroom, also lit by a skylight and as neatly organized as the lighting crew's, but with different stores — spools of rope in various widths, racks of weights in different sizes, and an assortment of tools.

"These were at the corner of the bridge in a bit of shadow." Gibbs pointed at the table, where he'd assembled two pieces of coiled rope, a small pot of glue with a brush stuck in it, and a pair of long-bladed scissors.

"Scissors," Moriarty said, surprised. "Do you usually cut your ropes with scissors?"

"No, sir. We have a rope-cutter. Out there, I'd use this." He pulled out his pocket knife and opened it up to display a blunt-ended straight blade, a long sharp spike, and a curved blade with a serrated edge. "Scissors like that are for cutting cloth."

"They must be Madame Noisette's. I saw her down on the stage just now, tacking that puffy stuff to the gondola. Would she work on that up here?"

"Not unless she can fly," Gibbs said. "It's the backside of the gondola that got lashed to the railing. Clouds go on the front. Can't remember her ever leaving a tool anywhere either. Those must have cost a pretty penny."

Moriarty nodded. A pound or two, he would guess. "They weren't left behind by accident. They're meant to point the finger at Madame Noisette. Is she tall enough to make a cut in the right place?"

"She'd be working about shoulder height, which isn't comfortable. But don't underestimate her, Professor. That little woman can outwork us all. And I'd guess her hands are plenty strong enough to do the deed. Why she'd want to, I couldn't guess."

"Nor could I," Moriarty said, although both Angelina and Peg had their doubts about her. She'd been a party to the costume-thieving scheme, for one thing. And she was bitter about something; she made that clear on first meeting.

But no one would leave such a vital clue on the scene by accident. Either they'd been left to implicate her or she left them herself to lead him around in this exonerating circle.

* * *

Moriarty took both pieces of rope with him after thanking the scenery chief for delaying his work to satisfy his curiosity. He knocked on Angelina's dressing room door on the way down, but Peg told him she was rehearsing and wouldn't be back for another hour. He told her he was going home for the day, then suited actions to words.

He wanted to put his hypotheses to empirical tests to see what practice could add to theory. He stopped off at an ironmonger's on the way home to purchase a pair of shears and a pocket knife the clerk avowed to be much in use among theater crews. He also bought a quantity of fishing line and an assortment of hooks.

As he entered his home and handed his packages to Rolly, he noted the footman was much the same height as the Galaxy's wardrobe mistress — five feet or so. He sent the boy down to ask Antoine for a tray of tea and sandwiches, to be brought up to the aerie. "Get enough for both of us, Rolly. I'll need your assistance this afternoon."

"You ain't going ter 'ypnotize me again, are you, Perfessor?" Rolly asked, eyes wide.

"Not today. We're going to cut ropes and dangle fish hooks."

He changed into a more comfortable jacket on his way up the stairs to his study-cum-laboratory at the top of the house. His wife had created this space for him, hiring a crew to raise the roof and install skylights and fitted bookcases. They'd even built a platform on the roof itself from which he could view the stars on clear nights. She'd thought of everything, including a long table down the center of the room.

He laid out his purchases and the pieces of rope, then stood for a moment considering how best to replicate the circumstances of the sabotaged gondola. Sherlock Holmes had probably written a monograph on manila rope in standard thicknesses and cuts made thereupon with various instruments. Very useful, if one could lay one's hands on it. Moriarty had searched for monographs by a Mr. S. Holmes in the library at Burlington House one rainy afternoon without success. Holmes wasn't a member of the Royal Society. He probably published the things at his own expense and had Watson spend his evenings tucking them into envelopes and affixing the proper postage, addressing one copy to every metropolitan police department in England. If they actually existed.

But a comprehensive study wasn't needed here, nor did he need to suspend a platform from the ceiling. He merely wanted a vertical stretch of rope on which to employ his different cutting tools. He could achieve that by removing that lamp from its bracket and tying one end of the rope there, then securing the other to the back of that chair. A stack of books loaded onto the seat of the chair grounded it sufficiently for present purposes.

He was uncoiling the long pieces of rope when Rolly and the mouse maids arrived, puffing slightly, with well-laden trays. "Ah, tea!" Moriarty directed them to put the trays at one end of the table, then shooed the maids out. "I'm quite capable of pouring a cup of tea."

He filled two cups from the large silver pot, pushing one toward Rolly to amend to his own taste. Then he chose one of Antoine's inimitable ham sandwiches and munched on it while he explained the plan, perching on a tall stool. All formalities were banished from this den of scientific inquiry.

"First," he said, "we must examine the base case: the cut made by the fly crew."

The manila rope, three-quarters of an inch thick, felt rough to the hand and stiff, rather like bendable wood. One piece, about three feet long, was kinked and twisted at one end. "This must have been tied to the bridge railing." He took his magnifying glass and examined one end. "Nearly straight across. I expect this was done with the rope-cutter in the workshop. Here, have a look."

Rolly hopped up from the stool where he'd been scarfing cheese-and-jelly sandwiches and came over to peer through the glass. "Ho! That's big! And neat as ever you please."

Moriarty smiled. "Now let's look at the other end." He positioned the piece under the glass, though he could see the difference well enough with the naked eye. "What do you see, Rolly?"

"It's got stuff on it, like sticky bits."

"That's paste. Meant to obscure the cuts from a casual inspection, one assumes."

"This one's got two cuts, like 'e done one side first and then t'other. Wif a big sprouty part right in the middle, all straggy and stretched-out like."

"Precisely so. I believe our vandal left just enough rope in the center to maintain the illusion that all was well, but not enough to support the gondola with a grown man in it."

"'E's a fat one, Mr. 'Atcliff. No disrespect."

"An observable fact, Rolly. Now let's conduct our experiment. See if you can cut this with these scissors." He pointed at a section of his vertical rope installation about four feet from the ground.

The boy set to work. "It's tough! Kind of slippery too, Perfessor."

"Keep at it. Your goal is to work around the outer circumference, leaving the core uncut."

Rolly screwed up his lips and grunted with the effort, but he managed to make two good cuts, front and back, by twisting the rope with his other hand to get access to the outer surface. It wasn't easy, but he got it done.

Moriarty took the scissors and tried it himself, higher up. His hands were undoubtedly much stronger than Madame Noisette's, but hers were probably stronger than Rolly's, given the nature of her work. He got the magnifying glass and examined the edges, using the flat side of a blade on the pocket knife to tease open the cuts. Rolly verified his observations. Then they tried the same experiment on different spots with both the straight edge and the serrated edge of the pocket knife. The serrated edge, like the one the scenery chief had shown him, made much shorter work of it, but also a much coarser cut, readily distinguished under the glass.

Moriarty folded the blades back into the knife and returned the tools to the table. Then he leaned against the bookcase behind him and folded his arms. "I'm satisfied on two counts. First, those cuts were made with scissors, not a knife. Second, a person as small as the wardrobe mistress could have made them."

"That's why you needed me." Rolly leaned against the doorjamb and folded his arms, mirroring Moriarty's pose.

"I value your insights as well." Moriarty reached for another sandwich, devouring it thoughtfully. That made him want more tea, which he poured. "Unfortunately, this experiment tells us how, but not who."

"The wardrobe lady!"

"That's what we're meant to think. But someone intelligent enough to manage the costumes for a theater as large as the Galaxy would be clever enough to remove that clue from the scene of her crime."

"Lose the scissors too, wouldn't she? Hantoine wouldn't leave 'is knives lying about."

"He would not," Moriarty said. "He won't let anyone so much as touch them. From my single encounter with Madame Noisette, I would expect her to resemble Antoine in that respect. I think we might rule her out on that basis alone."

Rolly nodded his assent. "What about that scenery cove? 'E's up there all day long. That fing took time to cut, didn't it?"

"Many minutes, by our test. Whoever did it would have been in full view of the stage and in danger of being spotted by one of the other crewmen. He must have done it at night. They leave the gas on low, I'm told, and I've noticed lanterns here and there." He picked up his cup and took a large swallow of tea. "But a single light would have made him more visible, if there were anyone to see."

They each ate another sandwich. Then Rolly asked, "What's next, Perfessor?"

"Now we're going fishing."

"What, in this weather?" Rolly scowled at the dark clouds visible through the skylights.

"No, right here in this room." Moriarty explained the trick he'd uncovered of moving objects in one room through a gap in the floor of the room above it.

"Like a medium!"

"A what?"

"A medium. You know, the ladies what talks to spirits. Like Mistress King, what I used to work for." Rolly shrugged. "She didn't keep me long. She wanted someone 'oo could fake voices. You know, to sound like the dearly departed."

"You're talking about a séance," Moriarty said. "I've read about them. How do they involve fish hooks?"

"Like you said wif them dancers. Move fings about and twitch the curtains, like the spirit's comin' in through the winder."

"Is it difficult? I mean, does it require special training or skill?"

Rolly shrugged. "Girls can do it."

Moriarty took that as evidence for the fundamental simplicity of the craft. "What sort of a person was your Mistress King?"

Another shrug. "I slept in the attic. Not as cold as you fink. And she gave me breakfast, as well as my tea."

Not the right question for this informant. Angelina and Peg might know more about mediums and the sorts of persons they employed to perform their séances. That thought was accompanied by the simultaneous realization that he had never characterized any part of his youth in terms of the bed and board provided, not even Rugby, his public school. Vowing never again to complain about his wife's eccentric hiring practices, he pushed the plate of sandwiches under Rolly's hand.

"Do you suppose there could be other people with experience like yours at the Galaxy? Men or women who have worked for mediums or other sorts of magicians?"

Rolly stopped still, his jelly sandwich halfway to his mouth, which hung open in sheer disbelief. "In an 'ouse full of hactors?"

EIGHTEEN

Angelina walked slowly down the steps at Lionel Hatcliff's house and climbed into the hackney cab she'd kept waiting at the curb while she popped in to take a peek at her old friend. This was Tuesday morning, three days and four nights since the accident. She hoped to see some improvement, but no, he seemed to have gotten worse — barely breathing, with that dreadful waxy pallor. The nurse was not optimistic. She didn't actually speak the words, "It won't be long now," but they'd been lurking behind the professional sympathy in her eyes.

Dear old Lionel! Angelina had so many warm memories of him. She'd hoped to make many more, working together under the same big roof. And what would become of the theater without him? He was the heart of the Galaxy, and its memory as well. No one could replace him.

She pushed those thoughts away. Where there was life, there was hope. And Christmas was right around the corner, with opening night hard on its heels.

"Where to, Miss?" the cabbie asked.

"The Galaxy Theater." But as they drove past Regent's Park, she remembered that Nora Verney lived nearby and the little minx had two things she wanted: her copy of the complete playbook and the spare key to her dressing room. She knocked on the trap and gave the driver that address instead.

She snuggled her gloved hands into her fur muff and gazed out the window at the well-tended terraces lining Park Road. Many houses already had holly draped around their iron railings, held up with bright red bows. *Already?* Christmas was only four days away!

She'd barely given it a moment's thought, she'd been so busy learning her part and coping with the daily disasters.

Christmas Day had never been as important in her theatrical family as Boxing Day, when pantomimes traditionally opened. Rehearsals on Christmas Eve with a theater full of theater folk, struggling to get everything to work — Exhausting! So the next day was spent resting with the feet up and a stack of magazines beside the uncollected trays of dishes supplied by whatever hotel they were living in at the time. Not that there was anything to do on the one day of the year when London rolled up the sidewalks and went home. They might as well have been at the Moriartys' frosty vicarage in Miswell, Gloucestershire, for all the fun that could be had. Then came Boxing Day, with everyone refreshed and ready to jump back into the bustle of life.

Last year, she and James had spent Christmas on the Riviera enjoying the sunshine and casinos. They'd be there now if Lionel hadn't come along with his extraordinary plea. James had no fond memories to recreate, but for some reason their servants had gone all sentimental about holiday traditions. Some observance must be made.

Angelina didn't have to do anything about Christmas dinner, thank goodness. Viola would play hostess at the Mayfair home of her protector, Lord Brockaway. Lady Brockaway had been banished to southern France for *very* bad behavior the year before, so Viola more or less ruled that roost, though she had a house of her own a few streets away.

Angelina intended to sleep as late as possible and enjoy a leisurely breakfast in bed with her husband. Then she would dress for comfort *en famille* and stuff herself silly at dinner. Lord Brockaway was sending an extra coach to convey the Moriartys' servants to join his staff for their holiday feast, so no one at Bellenden Crescent would be obliged to do any work at all.

The only thing missing was a present for James on Christmas morning. She had nothing. She'd meant to buy him another mathematical instrument from Elliott Brothers — scientific men were *so* easy to shop for — but there was no time for that now. He wouldn't appreciate the extravagance anyway, given his current money worries. He'd just have to settle for extra kisses this year. Those she had in abundance.

The cab halted in front of Nora's house. "Shall I wait again, Miss?"

"Please. I won't be long." She trotted up the stairs to Nora's landing and rapped on the door. The maidservant opened it a few inches, recognized Angelina, and sniffed. "Miss Verney isn't receiving visitors this morning."

Angelina had no intention of giving Nora a chance to throw that book away. "I won't be a minute." She pushed past the maid, through the foyer and into the drawing room.

She found Nora lounging on the same sofa she'd occupied last time, wearing a flowered wrapper with pink silk stockings on two unbandaged ankles. A gentleman in shirtsleeves and waistcoat stood by the window smoking a cigarette. He set the cigarette on a silver dish and pulled on his jacket as Angelina came in, smiling as if anticipating a show.

"What do you mean, barging in like this?" Nora demanded, thrusting her sharp little chin forward.

"Forgive the intrusion, darling, but I was passing by and remembered you have something that belongs to me."

"I do not!"

"You must. You said you packed it up when you left the Galaxy."

"I never said any such thing, whatever it is you're talking about."

"You have my prompt book, Nora, and I want it."

"Your dressing room was such chaos," the man said in an amused tone, "I doubt you know what you had in there." He stubbed out his cigarette and walked toward the two women. He and Angelina smiled at each other in that vague, tight way people who don't know one another do when caught in an awkward situation.

The man gave Nora a chance to do the honors, then rolled his eyes for Angelina's benefit. He held out a hand. "Allow me to introduce myself. I'm Charles Cudlow. Of course I recognize you, Miss Lovington, or rather Mrs. Moriarty. I've met your husband recently."

"Of course!" Angelina shook the proffered hand limply. "James found your advice *tremendously* helpful in making up his mind.

Investment that and insurance this." She trilled a laugh. "The part of the theater world I'm happy to know *nothing* about."

She played the featherbrain as a protective cover while her mind whirled. Charles Cudlow, the playboy-turned-investor, in Nora's flat at this hour of the morning? He'd told James he had a liking for actresses. When had this little *affaire* begun? Before or after the fake ankle-spraining incident?

Angelina beamed at him while he burbled on about some past performance of hers that had meant something to him once upon a time. Tall, blond, well-formed, and beautifully dressed — she could see the appeal. Far younger and handsomer than Lionel, in addition to being the eldest son of a Baron Somebody. The ideal man for an actress with ambitions beyond the stage. But Nora wouldn't get much more than a steak dinner and a pretty bracelet from this cool cove.

"Tell us," Cudlow said, his expression somber, "how is dear old Hattie? I understand from your husband that you two are looking after him. Nora and I would be glad to help with that burden in any way we can."

"Oh, heavens! It's no burden. He has the loveliest couple waiting on him hand and foot. They're so attentive, he may never get out of bed!" Angelina laughed, then she realized she was laughing alone. "In all seriousness, he's stable. He's comfortable. He's resting. The best thing any of us can do is to give him the peace and quiet he needs right now."

"Hmm." Cudlow's eyes glittered with the same open disbelief James had described. "Well, do keep us posted."

"Of course! *So* kind of you. And now, Nora darling, if I could get that book and my spare key, I'll leave you to enjoy your morning." She held out her two hands as if expecting to be given the items at once.

Nora glared at her, plainly discomfited by being the only person seated, as well as the only one *en dishabille,* then snapped her tongue irritably. She swung her feet to the carpet and swept away, returning in a moment with the book and the key on a bit of pink ribbon. She handed them to Angelina, saying, "I'll see you out. You must be *frightfully* busy, managing everyone and everything."

"Just an ordinary, working actress, darling. Like you used to be." Angelina nodded at Cudlow and let Nora lead her to the front door. Then her better nature made her pause on the threshold to offer a bit of unsolicited advice. She lowered her voice. "A word to the wise, Nora. Don't count on your Mr. Cudlow. He'll never marry you."

"Little you know about it! The Honorable Frederick Arthur Wellesley married Kate Vaughan, didn't he?"

"Yes, but, darling — he loved her."

Nora's blue eyes turned to slits as she shoved Angelina out and closed the door.

* * *

"Here at last!" Angelina sang, as she entered her dressing room. Peg stuffed something into a workbasket and picked up a mound of organdy, smiling a greeting, all innocence.

"What was that?" Angelina pointed her chin at the basket.

"Titania's gown. I showed it to you yesterday."

"No, the other. It looked like Tweedy's Dame Trott costume."

Peg's jaw stiffened. "What if it was?"

"I was only asking." Angelina hung her hat and coat on the rack by the door and put her book on the dressing table. Then she went behind the screen to change into her rehearsal clothes. Speaking over the top of the carved teak, she said, "I'm glad you two have found each other again, you and Mr. Tweedy. He's a lovely man. But what *can* be making him act like such a bear, Peg? He's plainly disgruntled, and you know we think a disgruntled person may be causing all these accidents."

"Timothy Tweedy would never harm so much as a fly!" Peg's cheeks flared pink with indignation. "You can't know him at all if you can think such a wicked thing."

"I don't *think* it, I'm only worried about —"

"If you only knew what that poor man is suffering!"

"I want to know. Why can't you tell me?" Angelina pulled her tunic over her head. "You've never kept secrets from me before."

"Ha! 'Course I have. You wouldn't know, would you, being secrets. Besides, this one isn't mine to tell."

Angelina sat on the stool to pull her tights over her goose-pimpled legs. She added an extra pair of long socks and then stuffed her feet into a pair of flexible slippers. She came out from behind the screen and wrapped a shawl around her shoulders before sitting down at her dressing table. She'd done her hair in flat braids at home, but would've worn a more fashionable style to visit Nora, if she'd thought ahead. Oh well. Her hat had covered the worst of it. But no wonder Mr. Cudlow had kept grinning at her in that familiar way.

"How's Lionel?" Peg asked.

Angelina shook her head. "Not long for this world, I'm afraid."

"What will happen when he goes?"

"I don't know. James will think of something." They traded worried looks, the moment of opposition past. "I dropped in on Nora Verney on the way here."

"Oh?"

Angelina gave Peg the full report.

"That bloke might marry her, for all you know," Peg said, being contrary. "Stranger things have happened."

"Not this bloke. He barely likes her, if you ask me. But don't you think it's curious how this Charles Cudlow keeps cropping up?"

Peg shrugged. "Why shouldn't he crop if he wants to? Nothing strange about Nora Verney having a fling with a toff. That's Nora all over."

"But he's so suspicious. He acts like he thinks we're deliberately keeping people away from Lionel."

"Which you are."

"Well, yes, we are. Of course we are. But for a perfectly good reason. There's nothing *nefarious* about it."

Peg shrugged again, still contrary. "It's a bit rich, Lina, to fuss about someone suspecting you of doing exactly what you really are doing."

Angelina couldn't argue with that. "Let's just hope Nora keeps her nose out until Lionel gets better."

Peg pressed her lips together in the way that meant she could say more on that subject, but what would be the point? They both knew Lionel wasn't going to get better.

Angelina left Peg to her sewing and went down to the stage, where throngs of people bustled about as if it were a public square — only half of them would be arrested for indecency. Sebastian wanted her to rehearse the scene in which Jack runs through an obstacle course in the Giant's kitchen to grab the golden goose before climbing down the beanstalk. Things would pop up from the cellar through trap doors to frighten her as she zigged and zagged across the stage.

A path had been cleared downstage. She joined Sebastian where he stood watching a workman talking through an open trap door to someone in the cellar. "How long should it take me to get from one side to the other?" she asked. They discussed the pace and her reactions. The general goal was to take as long as possible, for maximum impact on the audience, without her ever seeming to simply stand and wait for the next thing to happen.

"We're ready!" someone called, and the test began. Sebastian went to the prompt corner off left and opened the book on its stand, ready to make notes.

Angelina took a few steps downstage and said her lines to the empty stalls. "If only I could catch that golden goose! Then me old Mum would never have to worry about money again!" She started slow-jogging across the stage, aiming for the square patch of boards that marked the first trap. About a foot away, the trap dropped down and flung up a great cloud of smoke. During the performance, the orchestra would supply the sounds. Since they weren't here, Sebastian shouted, "Boom!"

Angelina laughed and leapt into the air, pumping her legs. The next obstacle was a star trap, which flew open to reveal a workman crouched on the platform, filling in for an actor in a dog suit. "Grr! Woof!" Sebastian barked. Angelina shrieked at the workman, jumping downstage and landing in a terror posture, facing the audience with her legs wide, her mouth open, and both hands pulling imaginary hair straight up from her head. This was fun!

Two more clouds of purple smoke with Sebastian's ridiculous sound effects and she had the hang of it. The great trick was to shrill a high-pitched shriek and launch herself as high into the air as she could manage so the people at the back of the uppermost gallery could see and hear. She jogged toward the last trap, ready for another workman to spring up. But when this trap fell, a real explosion boomed, knocking her backward onto the hard stage.

Sparks flew amid the billowing smoke. A patch of something burning landed on the skirt of her tunic and flared. Angelina screamed. Two men leapt toward her and rolled her over, pounding at her tunic with their flat hands.

"You're all right," one said, "it's out. You're all right."

She rolled back over and sat up, patting herself on the chest to slow her heartbeat, tears springing into her eyes from the smoke and the fright. "I'm all right," she echoed as Sebastian skidded onto his knees beside her and began patting her legs and pressing her arms, as if expecting some part of her to crumble into ash.

"Are you sure?" His blue eyes were dark with worry.

"A nasty fright and a toasted tunic, but otherwise, no harm done." She caught his gaze. "Don't tell James."

* * *

Peg clucked and grumbled while she inspected Angelina's singed tunic. "I don't like it, ducky. It could have been a lot worse."

"I'm not so sure it could."

Sebastian had roundly scolded the cellar chief, but apparently someone had thrown an extra handful of explosive powder into the pan along with a few shreds of something like gun cotton. The chief swore up and down that no one on his crew would do such a thing. They'd lose their jobs, for starters, and right before Christmas. But now they'd have to throw out the powder they'd mixed for today, so the rehearsal was over.

Time for lunch.

She splashed cool water on her face and washed her hands, then changed into the plain dress James thought was her regular rehearsal garb. Peg shook her head at her with pursed lips. "It's a mite cruel, ducky, to let the poor man see you in your Jack suit for the first time in front of a thousand other people."

Angelina sat down at her dressing table and met her own eyes in the mirror. They told her the same thing. She started unpinning her frayed braids. "He's got enough to worry about at the moment," she told herself. The face in the mirror did not look convinced.

Tidy enough for the front of the house, she joined her husband in the manager's office. James had already laid out the sandwiches and bottles of beer. "Mr. Tidwell can bring tea, if you'd rather."

"I'm in the mood for something a trifle stronger today." Angelina had long since stopped worrying about her waistline. She chose the largest cheese-and-pickle sandwich too.

Sebastian came in before she'd had more than a bite, made his selections, and settled in his usual chair with the book tucked in behind him.

"Any accidents today?" James asked, his now-standard greeting.

"Only one suspicious one." Sebastian scrupulously avoided looking at Angelina. "Several others that are probably the ordinary sort."

"Everyone's worried about Lionel too," Angelina said. She told them about the nurse's pessimistic manner. They frowned into their beers.

"I learned another interesting thing this morning," she said. "And I got my prompt book back." She told them about her surprise visit to Nora and the gentleman she'd discovered smoking by the window.

"I don't like it," James said. "If he's that intimate with Miss Verney, why did he never mention it? That smacks of something underhanded."

"Not necessarily," Sebastian said. "Most people keep their love affairs secret. Take me and Hugh, for example."

"That's different, darling," Angelina said. "Nora has nothing to lose."

"Cudlow might," Sebastian countered. "For all we know, he's got a stuffy little heiress on a string somewhere. And I'm afraid I can't see anything too alarming about an actress angling for a lord."

"She'll never catch him," Angelina said.

"I don't know what to make of Charles Cudlow," James said. "He was affability itself that night at the club. Then at the party, he practically accused me, along with the two of you, of engineering

Fowler's death and Hatcliff's accident in order to take control of the Galaxy."

"He *what?*" Sebastian nearly choked on his sandwich. "You didn't tell me that."

"When have we had the chance?" Angelina rolled her eyes. "Frank Sparrow said much the same thing. Although he loves to be outrageous, so I don't know how general a rumor it might really be. He could have made it up on the spot just to tweak my nose."

Sebastian groaned and ran a hand through his hair, which already looked as if he'd been styling it with the wind machine. "It'll be all over the theater by now. It can't be doing much harm. Worse is the ugly rumor going around nobody will be paid tomorrow since Hatcliff's on the brink of death."

"Nobody will," James said. "There's barely enough cash to pay for this lunch, much less meet a payroll of this size."

Angelina and Sebastian traded looks of alarm. "But, darling," Angelina said, "people must be paid. It's Christmas on Saturday."

"I know," James said, "but we have no money. No cash, no pay. Not until the show starts earning or Hatcliff wakes up and signs a nice fat check — which he doesn't seem likely to do, poor wretch."

"I thought you transferred a whacking great sum into Hattie's Galaxy account last week," Sebastian said.

"I did," James said. "That's the problem. If I still had possession of it, we'd be fine. Or if I could lay my hands on that damned partnership agreement to show the bank. Payroll's only half the problem. The quarterly rent is due tomorrow without fail. Hatcliff's already had one week's forgiveness. That's a cool thousand pounds locked up at Risley and Company. It might as well be in South America." He looked so bleak and woebegone that Angelina's heart melted. "I'm sorry, my dear. I've made a mess of things."

"Not you." She grasped his hand, filling the touch with love and admiration for his courage and resourcefulness. "You've kept us going this far. We'll find a way."

"What happened to that agreement?" Sebastian asked. "Didn't you sign it that day we had champagne? I mean the first time. Last Wednesday, I think it was."

"Yes," James said. "Hatcliff was going to bring it straight over to his solicitor, but I haven't heard a word since, and I've watching for a letter here or at his house. I should have insisted on going to see the man together right then."

He fell silent, defeated by this final obstacle. Sebastian looked at Angelina with raised eyebrows, asking what was so dashed final about it. Once again she found herself straddling the broad gap between the Archer ways and James's ways.

She took a swig of beer and laid down the first plank of the bridge. "If Lionel can't write the cheque, you'll just have to do it for him, James. It is your money, after all, whether it's in his bank or yours."

"I can't sign another man's name!" James looked aghast, as she'd expected.

She nodded as if she fully understood the moral dilemma. "No, that would be asking too much, wouldn't it?"

"Isn't there a register for business agreements?" Sebastian asked. He gave her a slight nod to show he understood. They had to work James around to committing a smallish crime, but gently, gently. He should feel that he'd reached the necessary conclusion himself.

"I stopped in at Company House, but couldn't find any record. I've written twice to Hatcliff's lawyer, with no response. He must have it; if not, I can only assume it was stolen."

Angelina had not expected that twist. "Who would steal such a thing?"

"Whoever it is that's trying to stop us from putting on this pantomime. I admit, it's a leap from cut ropes to stolen papers, but it ties our hands just as effectively. If we can't pay people, they may leave. And if we don't pay the rent, we'll be evicted."

"We have to pay our people," Sebastian said. "They're depending on us. It's nearly Christmas and most of them have families. Little children eager for their treats. We'd be turning their favorite holiday into a day of mourning."

Poor James! He had the stoniest face, but one of the softest hearts. "I know. Perhaps we could sell some things?" He turned pleading eyes toward her.

"At this late date?"

"You know," Sebastian said, as if the thought had just occurred to him, "I'll bet Antoine could do a bang-up job of copying Lionel's signature."

James flicked that idea away. "I could never allow Antoine to commit a crime in this country. It's too dangerous for him. It would give the London police a reason to communicate with the French Sûreté. He'd be exposed."

"There was that detective's identity card last year," Angelina murmured.

"Well, yes, but I only used it once, and it was to save a young woman's life."

"That's true," Angelina said. "This is a quite different situation, isn't it? No one will die from going without their Christmas goose."

"What would Lionel want us to do, I wonder?" Sebastian mused.

James met his gaze with a sigh. "I know it seems finicky to you — my scruples. It is my money in truth, and yes, Lionel intended it to go to the rent and the payroll. The only obstacle is a bit of a hiccup between the banks, the solicitor, and the Company House registry. I've been thinking about this since Friday, you know. Apart from our people and their families, I would consider it a greater moral violation to allow the villain to succeed by means of violence. But forgery is a very serious crime, my friends. It was a hanging matter only fifty years ago."

"So much has changed in the last fifty years," Angelina observed. Almost there.

"Perhaps Antoine could teach you how to sign the name," Sebastian suggested. "Then you wouldn't have to implicate anyone but yourself."

Great Scott, Sebastian was good at this game! Only James could be persuaded to commit a crime by the assurance that only he could be convicted of it if caught.

That argument turned the trick. James nodded, his lips pressed so tightly together they almost disappeared. "All right. We'll work on it tonight after supper." He began shuffling through the papers on top of the desk. "I'll need a few good examples . . . and Lionel's chequebook, of course." Once he'd made up his mind, he wouldn't continue to quibble. Another thing she loved about him.

Angelina met Sebastian's eyes. They allowed themselves a mutual twinkle, but kept their faces straight. Although she knew James's battle wasn't over yet. He would commit this crime because it had to be done and he couldn't in good conscience allow anyone else to do it. Then it would be her job to help him live with it.

NINETEEN

Moriarty spent his evening sitting at the table in the kitchen, practicing Lionel Hatcliff's signature under Antoine's exacting tutelage. *"Non, non, monsieur! Comme ça!"* He finally managed to produce a facsimile judged acceptable by the Committee of Three: Antoine, Rolly, and Peg. Angelina declared herself too partisan to render a fair verdict.

He wrote out a cheque for one thousand pounds, payable to the House of Theatrical Investments, and sent Rolly out to drop it in the nearest postbox. It would be collected at half past seven in the morning and delivered by noon at the latest. That was cutting it a bit too fine for Moriarty's taste, even given the reliability of the Royal Mail. Next quarter he'd get the payment off well in advance.

He wrote a second cheque for a thousand pounds, payable to one James Moriarty. That should be enough to cover tomorrow's payroll and the next one two weeks later, along with any incidental expenses that might arise before the show started turning a profit. He would present this cheque at Hatcliff's bank, where the manager who had taken his request to transfer funds last week ought to remember him.

He tucked the evidence of his descent into criminality into his notecase, thanked the committee, and took his wife up to bed, where he passed an anxious night.

The next morning he decided to make two last attempts to secure a legitimate solution to the present crisis. He would stop in at Company House to see if, by miracle of bureaucratic efficiency, his partnership with Hatcliff had been registered. If not, he would beard Hatcliff's solicitor in his chambers at Gray's Inn.

Fortune granted him a swift start to his morning's quests. A hansom cab trotted up behind him before he'd walked ten feet from his stoop. The cabman, swathed in layers of coats and scarves against the December drizzle, called "Where to, Guv'nor?" in a thick East End accent. Moriarty climbed in, setting his small valise in his lap, and directed him to Serjeant's Inn on Chancery Lane.

He should have had the man wait. It only took ten minutes to learn that no companies or partnerships bearing the names Hatcliff or Moriarty had been registered in the past week. The clerk showed him the relevant pages in the great book, holding it close enough to read, but not touch. The clerk further vowed that on receipt of the proper documents, registration took next to no time — in any season other than this. "It's almost Christmas, sir!"

Moriarty wished him a merry one and buttoned his coat to his chin, deciding to stretch his legs for the short distance from Serjeant's to Gray's. Five brisk minutes later, his cheeks were numb, but he was fully awake. He found the right building, climbed to the fourth story, and knocked on the door labeled *Rufus Bartleby, Counselor at Law.*

No one answered. He knocked again, pressing his ear to the aged oak door. No sounds could be detected within. Then he noticed a corner of an envelope sticking out from beneath the door. He hesitated, his conscience balking at tampering with another's man mail until he remembered he'd spent hours the night before forging another man's signature. He stooped and teased out the envelope, reading it where it lay on the coir mat.

Nothing to do with him. He pushed it back, farther this time, so he wouldn't be tempted again. It was a good thing he hadn't brought Rolly or they'd be picking the lock to slip inside and rifle through the man's desk.

Moriarty took out his notebook and fountain pen and jotted a request for immediate communication, leaving addresses for both himself and Hatcliff, adding the Galaxy office for good measure. He folded the paper once and wrote "URGENT" across the front, then stuffed it into the crack between door and jamb at eye level.

Then he turned toward the stairs with a sigh of resignation. Back on the street, a cab responded immediately to his raised arm.

Moriarty noticed the cabman's plaid Inverness cape. "We meet again," he said, climbing inside.

"Sorry?" the cabman growled through the trap in a thick West Country burr.

"My mistake," Moriarty said. "Pall Mall East, please. Opposite the National Gallery."

"Very good, sir."

The moment of truth had come. The heavy doors at Risley and Company opened into a marble lobby thronged with people. Men and women in bulky winter coats milled around and between long queues stretched before each teller window. It would appear that everyone needed extra cash for the holiday weekend.

Before he met Angelina, Moriarty never bothered much about Christmas; in fact, he'd rather prided himself on escaping the endless queues and insipid carols. Now, observing the garlands of green stuff draped under the windows and the red bows tied around every possible object, he found himself oddly wishing it would snow. He hadn't seen many white Christmases growing up in Gloucestershire. Snow wouldn't have excused any deviation from Vicar Moriarty's strict holiday protocols in any event. No snowmen or sing-alongs for young James and younger Jeremy. The birth of our Lord was a solemn occasion, commemorated by the exchange of worthy books and an extra-long sermon.

Imagining the vicar's reaction to news that his son had committed forgery to fund a pantomime cheered Moriarty immensely, giving him that final boost of courage. He'd committed smaller crimes, after all, including presenting that detective's identity card to gain admittance to Newgate Prison — not to mention sneaking into the Exhibition Hall one night to add an indicator to his rival's steam engine. Minor, compared to forging a cheque, but his father always taught that sin was a progressive disease.

He finally made it to the front of his queue, grateful not to be in the next one over, where a fussy old man with too many pockets obstructed the flow. Moriarty exchanged routine greetings with his teller and drew his artistic effort out of his notecase, placing it squarely under the grill.

The teller examined his cheque. "Oh my, this is rather a large sum, Mr. Moriarty."

"Professor."

"I beg your pardon, Professor. Allow me a moment to call my supervisor, if you don't mind."

"Not at all." Moriarty racked his brain for the name of the man he'd met with Hatcliff last week. Ah! There it was. "Ask for Mr. Sheridan. He should remember me."

The teller walked away and returned a moment later with another gentleman in a better suit and a taller hat. His gaze fell on Moriarty's face as he approached. He smiled with recognition as he wished his client a good morning. He picked up the cheque and examined it, then gave Moriarty a rueful smile. "You haven't given us much time to invest your funds, have you, Professor?"

"I'm afraid we rather underestimated our immediate needs. I hope you can honor it. I didn't realize you'd be so busy today." He glanced at the obstructed queue to his right, where the old man was turning pages in a grubby account book, licking his finger for each new page.

"Yes, it's always like this the week before Christmas. But you've got your cast and crew to pay, as I recall." Sheridan smiled blandly. "I wish Mr. Hatcliff had come with you. I wanted to wish him good luck with his show."

"I'll pass that along." Moriarty felt beads of sweat forming on his brow and hoped they weren't noticeable. He disliked small talk in the best of times, and this was surely the worst. "More efficient to have the new man run the simpler errands. So much to learn, you know."

"I should imagine so!" Sheridan chuckled like a man with nothing better to do. Then he tapped the edge of the cheque on the counter and said, "Well, we mustn't keep you. Go ahead and cash this, Underwood. Good to see you, Professor." Sheridan touched the brim of his hat and left.

Moriarty suppressed a sigh of relief while the teller scribbled something on the back of the cheque and entered the transaction details in his log. "How would you like to take this, Professor?"

"Let's have half in large denominations. The rest should be in notes no larger than five pounds." They worked out a reasonable distribution of coins and small bills, given Moriarty's requirements and the teller's available resources. The teller packed the money into Moriarty's valise and bade him a good day.

And that was that. Moriarty stopped to set his valise on an oval counter near the front doors, pretending to adjust its contents while he recovered his equilibrium. He made sure the latch was fully engaged, then rewrapped his scarf, tucking the ends inside his coat.

As he stepped out onto the pavement, elation replaced his anxiety, as if he'd downed a glass of champagne in one draught. He'd done it! It had been touch and go there when the teller insisted on calling his supervisor, but in the end, that worked in his favor. If anyone discovered any irregularity in the future, Mr. Sheridan's judgment would be called into question as well.

Moriarty allowed himself a small chuckle. It wouldn't do to lose all sense of caution, however; not with a thousand pounds in cash in his hand. He tightened his grip on the valise and turned toward the street to look for a cab. His eyes met the watchful gaze of the cabman in the plaid Inverness cape, who stood leaning against a lamppost with his arms crossed, his horse waiting patiently behind him. He'd pulled the scarves from the lower half of his face, revealing an amused half-smile and a large hawk-like nose.

Holmes!

Moriarty's first thought was one of exasperation. John Watson must be out of town, forcing the ever-restless Holmes to seek another playmate. The second thought sent a shiver up his spine having nothing to do with the bitter east wind. Why should Sherlock Holmes appear at the very moment Moriarty committed his first real criminal act?

No — before that moment. Holmes had brazenly picked him up when he left his house that morning, relying on the many-layered garb of the London cabbie and the average man's lack of attention to protect his identity. He carried him from Gray's to Pall Mall too, without being recognized. Yet now here he stood, openly showing himself. What game was he playing?

"You were the old man in the next queue," Moriarty said, skipping past the usual civilities. Holmes disdained them, so why bother? "How did you manage to reach the head of your queue at the same time as I did mine?"

"The main requirement is a complete lack of shame. I had to keep up that act for a good six minutes, by the clock on the wall. I thought the man behind me might start kicking at my shins. Once I saw you would succeed in your, ah, venture, I made a quick exit."

Moriarty knew better than to respond to that ploy. Holmes had a gift for teasing out the truth with shrewd guesses. "Why are you following me?"

"I have a client who's interested in the goings-on at the Galaxy Theater of Varieties."

"Who?"

"I never reveal a client's name."

"Then why reveal yourself to me now? You had me quite fooled, as I'm sure you know."

Holmes raised a single dark eyebrow. "It's more fun this way."

That would be sufficient reason for this thoroughly self-governed individual. "I suppose you need the practice. I'll do my best to give you a good drill."

"I look forward to it. You're getting better at lying, I noticed."

"When? In there? I uttered no lies, apart from the conventionalities." Had the man heard every word? Moriarty had taken pains to say nothing implying anything whatsoever about Hatcliff's present condition. Stick to platitudes, commonplaces, and truisms — just as Angelina had taught him.

"That's what I mean. Your words were nearly devoid of content. It's a form of art, speaking fluently while saying nothing. Takes practice."

"If you say so. Now if you'll forgive me, I must be off. I have a theater to manage, as you appear to know."

"A new direction for you, Professor."

"I'm only helping out a friend of my wife's."

"Helping out a friend, or helping a friend *out*?" Holmes smiled thinly.

Moriarty made a dismissive noise. "I don't have time for your riddles today. But pop round the office sometime. I'll give you a pair of tickets to *Beanstalk*. Box seats."

"I'm sure Watson would enjoy it. But do allow me to give you a lift." Holmes waved a hand at his empty cab.

"I'd rather walk. It's only a few blocks."

"Don't be absurd, Professor. You can't struggle through this bustling district clutching a valise stuffed with money. Hop in!"

Moriarty regarded the man before him with a level gaze. Holmes had been a pursuer and a collaborator, on different occasions. They'd broken bread in each other's homes and taken each other's measure in more ways than one, but he would never make the mistake of considering the eccentric detective a friend. On the other hand, he was carrying a great deal of cash.

"I won't pay you this time," he warned.

Holmes laughed heartily, showing a full set of excellent teeth. Then he opened the half-door on the front of cab so that Moriarty could climb inside.

* * *

Moriarty stopped at the Galaxy only long enough to lock the five hundred pounds in small bills and coins in the safe in Hatcliff's office. He wasn't quite ready to think of it as his. He tucked ten fifty-pound notes into the slim leather case he carried next to his breast, to be deposited in the safe in his study at home. He'd break them into smaller bills when the next payday rolled around, if receipts from the box office couldn't cover expenses by then.

He sent a note to Sebastian saying all was well, not wanting to hike through the building to deliver the news in person. Then he went out again. He should pay a call on Hatcliff's servants to warn them about Sherlock Holmes.

This time he waited for a coach and subjected the driver to careful scrutiny before accepting his services. On entering Hatcliff's house, he could tell at once that the patient's condition had declined since yesterday. The place had the hushed and somber atmosphere of a house of mourning.

"The doctor's here," Lind said, helping Moriarty off with his coat and hat.

"Any improvement?"

Lind shook his head. "Worse, I'm afraid." Moriarty followed him to the study and accepted the offer of tea. He started to sit in the armchair before the unlit fire, but Lind motioned him toward the desk. "What should I do with Mr. Hatcliff's mail, Professor?" He indicated a small stack of envelopes.

"Oh dear." Moriarty looked at the desk with dismay. This additional burden somehow made the whole load harder to bear. He sighed. "I'd better have a look. There might be something from the solicitor." He seated himself behind the desk, feeling even more like an imposter than he had at the bank. He picked up the ivory-handled letter opener and began reading another's man mail.

He quickly sorted out the advertising handbills, astonished so many businesses thought it worth the price of a stamp to supply London's housemaids with screws of paper for lighting the morning fire. The two largest envelopes contained Christmas cards from Hatcliff's relations; none local, thank goodness. The rest were bills from local tradesmen — the tailor, the butcher, the coal merchant, etcetera. They ought to be paid at once.

Moriarty frowned, realizing that the Linds had probably not been paid their half-month's wages either. Their Christmas would be sad enough without that additional worry. He took one of the fifty-pound notes out of his case. When Lind returned to light the fire, Moriarty handed it to him along with the bills. "Would you be so kind as to make sure these are paid at your earliest convenience? And please subtract whatever's owing to you and Mrs. Lind."

"That's very kind of you, sir. I'll take care of it." The man knelt to light the ready-laid fire. He rose and paused. "What's going to happen to us, Professor?"

"I don't know. Mr. Hatcliff's solicitor appears to be away at the moment. We may have to wait until he returns to learn how Mr. Hatcliff intended to dispose of things." Observing the crease in Lind's forehead, he added, "Allow me to offer my personal assurance that you and Mrs. Lind will be able to remain in this house until satisfactory arrangements can be made."

"Thank you, sir."

Moriarty waited until the door had closed to search the desk again for the partnership agreement or, now that he'd thought of it,

Hatcliff's will. That was probably filed neatly away in Bartleby's chambers as well. Damn the man! What possessed him to go off on holiday with unfinished business on his desk?

Mrs. Lind brought in tea and a plate of almond biscuits. "Will that be all?"

"Not quite. Something occurred this morning which made me aware that other persons are taking an interest in Mr. Hatcliff's condition."

She looked offended. "It's no one's business what's going on in this house. We've made sure no prying busybodies can poke their noses in where they're not wanted."

"I expected no less. But have you noticed anyone hanging about? Asking questions at the shops, for example. It might be someone very plausible. A tall person with a large nose?"

"I haven't noticed such a thing. Do you mean a man or a woman?"

"Could be either. This individual is very good at disguises."

"An actor?"

"Of sorts," Moriarty said. "He calls himself a consulting detective. His name is Sherlock Holmes, but he won't present himself in that guise. He'll pretend to be a delivery man or some such and nose about trying to find some irregularity in the household situation. Stopping the milk, for example, or ordering less bread."

"We thought of that," Mrs. Lind said. "We've kept up the same orders as usual. I've even cooked Mr. Hatcliff's regular meals, though most of it goes to waste." Her face brightened. "Perhaps I could send you home with a nice couple of meat pies, Professor?"

"Oh yes, thank you." Moriarty could pass them on to the clerks at the theater. He shuddered to think of Antoine's reaction to the importation of another cook's pie. "And thank you for your precautions. I would ask you to go one step further for at least a few more days. I believe someone may be watching the house. We're telling people Mr. Hatcliff is able to keep up with theater business at home. Let Mr. Lind light the fire in here for a few hours every day. If it isn't too much to ask, perhaps he could even wrap himself in a shawl and sit at this desk for half an hour or so with the drapes open."

"I understand," the former actress said. "We'll light lamps in here as well, on the schedule Mr. Hatcliff used to keep. That one by his favorite reading chair in the evening, for example."

"Excellent," Moriarty said, hoping they wouldn't have to maintain the charade much longer, one way or another.

Mrs. Lind left him to his worries and his tea. He was about to get up and start searching for a hidden safe when the doctor came in. "How is he?" Moriarty asked.

The doctor shook his head. "He may not last the night. He must have sustained some grave internal injury."

"I am sorry. My wife will be very sad to hear it." Moriarty hesitated. "Should I go up to see him?"

"He wouldn't know you were there. I've given him another dose of morphine, so he isn't suffering. There's nothing to do now but wait for the end."

Moriarty nodded. One more question had to be asked. "What happens then, Doctor? We're in a rather delicate situation here, as you know."

"Ah yes, I remember. You've got a troubled show on your hands, haven't you?"

"If Mr. Hatcliff should die before I can locate his solicitor, the whole production could fail tomorrow. I don't know the terms of his lease or who takes over on his death, and there are problems with the flow of funds . . ."

"I see your difficulty." The doctor studied Moriarty's features, as if assessing his character from the cut of his moustache and the bald dome of his forehead. Then he nodded, apparently satisfied with what he saw. "I've been Lionel Hatcliff's doctor for a good long while, Professor. After Mrs. Hatcliff passed away, the Galaxy became all in all to him. They never had children, you know. He regarded that theater as his legacy. He didn't like the new owners, I know that too. He meant to buy the building himself when he built up the funds. He believed he had something of value to contribute to the cultural life of the city, you see. He would be deeply grieved if the mere accident of his death at the wrong moment brought all that to naught."

"But what can we do?"

The doctor smiled. "Why don't you leave that to me? The undertaker I work with is a man of infinite discretion. We'll adjust the date of death by a few days if necessary. Only a few, mind you. There are natural limits. I'd get on to that solicitor as quickly as I could, if I were you."

"I'll do that, Doctor. Thank you."

The doctor left. Moriarty returned to the desk and poured himself another cup of tea, adding extra sugar to the cup. That was a major relief. They'd at least be able to get through opening night before the news of Lionel Hatcliff's imminent demise spread through the theater world. But what then?

Moriarty felt like he was patching holes on a foundering ship; fill one and another burst open. He must lay his hands on that partnership agreement. He wanted the lease, and he wanted a copy of Hatcliff's will. He was learning another fundamental truth about the theater: the whole great spectacle of a Christmas pantomime, with its fairies, giants, flying clouds, and smoke-filled explosions, depended on three joyless legal documents — which he did not possess.

TWENTY

Angelina paid one last call on Lionel Wednesday morning, in spite of James's warning that he might already have given up the ghost. But no, he still breathed, if raggedly. His hand was so cold when she clasped it in both of her own.

"We'll take care of your theater for you, Lionel, darling. I promise you that. All your people, front, back, and on the stage, all your beautiful sets and costumes. Everything you've worked so hard to create. James, Sebastian, and I will take good care of it all."

She tucked his cold hand beneath the coverlet and bent to place a kiss on his pale forehead. Then she thanked the nurse for her vigilance and left.

The contrast between that house of near-mourning and the vibrant Galaxy Theater could not have been greater. The building swarmed with people dashing purposefully in all directions. Only four days left before Boxing Day and opening night!

Today they would conduct the dress parade, in which everyone who appeared in the panto would walk across the stage in his or her costume under the critical view of the stage manager and the wardrobe mistress, along with anyone else who wanted a peek — which included everyone who could escape from their work for a few minutes.

Angelina changed into her Jack suit, including the short boy's wig that went on under his feathered cap. One of these days she'd cut her hair — but not today. She pulled on her short boots and took a few turns in front of the mirror.

"Won't you do your full makeup?" Peg asked.

"Oh no. I'm only walking across the stage and turning around a few times. Hardly worth the bother to —"

Screams echoed in the corridor, punctuated by the pounding of many feet. Angelina flung open the dressing room door to see a flock of winged fairies bouncing up and down crying, "A rat! A rat!"

Peg joined Angelina in the doorway. "A lifetime in the theater and they've never seen a rat?" Angelina shrugged. She wasn't terrified of the little beasts, but she wasn't fond enough to chase after one either.

The panicking fairies created a jam in the corridor, blocking people coming down from wardrobe via the back stairs. Frank Sparrow, dressed as the Old Farmer with straw poking through his hat, pushed through to the front of the jam. "What's happened? Another ghost?"

On learning this was only an ordinary, earthly rat, he laughed and beckoned to another man in the crowd. "Let's catch the rascal and feed him to the cats in the alley." They went into the dressing room.

Sebastian pushed his way through the crowd on the other side, got the gist of the situation from Amy, made soothing noises at the other sisters, and then caught Belinda by both hands. She tittered a little but calmed as Sebastian held her gaze with the warm attention he used to employ while Viola sneaked around behind the besotted victim to relieve her of her valuables. Vice versa, if the mark were male.

"Everything's fine; you're perfectly safe," he crooned. "Why don't you tell me what happened?"

"We keep our room clean," Belinda said. "No food. Mother taught us that. We've never had trouble with vermin. Never! But today Dorinda used up her blue paint and went to open her case for another stick. Out leapt the most hideous, the most horrible —" She shuddered.

Sebastian drew her into his arms, patting her on the back, winking at Angelina over her shoulder. She shook her head at him. He was digging an awfully deep hole for himself there.

The two men emerged from the dancers' dressing room, Sparrow dangling the offending creature by its tail. He held it up as he passed the eldest Delaney sister, jiggling it a bit as the rat seemed to ask in a high, squeaky voice, "Don't you love you me anymore, Amy?"

Amy shrank back in disgust. "Oh, stop it, Frank! Enough is enough."

Sparrow clapped his free hand to his breast. "*I* didn't say anything. 'Twas the rat what spoke." Several people laughed as they parted to let him pass through with his prize. Good humor prevailed, in spite of the incident, since everyone had been paid that morning in full. Christmas would be merry for the Galaxy cast and crew come Saturday.

Sebastian released Belinda and spoke to the crowd. "Excitement's over, everyone. Let's go down for the dress parade."

Angelina watched the younger Delaneys prance past and fell in beside Amy, the eldest. "What was that about? With Mr. Sparrow and the rat?"

"I guess he's still miffed because I found someone better, but it's been months. He should get over it."

"You and Frank Sparrow were courting?"

Amy gave a one-shouldered shrug. "He's quite nice-looking when he's not acting up. And he can be awfully good fun. But where's he going?"

"Out to the alley," Angelina said, puzzled. "Didn't you hear him?"

"I mean in life. Will he still be jigging and joking when he's forty? My new beau, Mr. Yancy, is first assistant to the scenery chief. He has a workshop in his back garden where he makes props to sell to other theaters. In time, he'll become the scenery chief here or somewhere else. And he has the sweetest smile and the broadest chest . . ." Amy gave a little wriggle of pleasure.

Sparrow's physique ran long rather than broad. He couldn't compete in that department. But a good comedian could work till he dropped. Still, Angelina wouldn't want a boyfriend who dangled rats in her face either.

Angelina fell behind Amy to go down the stairs single file, but moved up beside her again as they joined the queue leading onto the stage. Amy was about twenty-one now, and apparently considering her marital prospects. Naturally, she would seek a mate inside the theater. Who else would understand the life she led? Her parents and grandparents had all been performers of one kind or another, like

Angelina's. Half the people in this dress parade descended from theater families, although few were as numerous or as prominent as the Delaney clan. They must be connected to everyone somehow.

Which reminded her of one of her pending questions about the theater's ghost. "Do you happen to know any mediums, Amy?"

"Spiritualists, you mean?" The young woman shook her head. Then her eyes widened. "Why? Do you have someone you wish to speak with?"

"Don't we all?"

"It isn't Lionel Hatcliff, is it?" Amy whispered.

"No, no, no." Angelina laughed as if the idea were absurd, hoping the poor man still breathed. "He's resting comfortably. I'm just curious. You must know everyone in the theater world; the Delaneys have been such a central part of it for so long."

"We're dancers and acrobats," Amy said. "We don't do magic tricks. Mediums don't perform on the stage anyway, do they? But you should ask Nora Verney. Wasn't her mother a spiritualist? I remember she used to hold séances at a house in Bethnal Green."

"Did she?" Nora Verney's mother, a medium? Could Adorable Nora have been upstairs pulling the strings while Mummy communicated with the dearly departed? Learning a skill that would come in handy again when she decided to drive poor Lionel out of his theater.

They finally reached the edge of the stage, where Angelina could get a better view of the parade. Sebastian had returned to his seat in the center of the stalls next to Madame Noisette. He had the prompt book open in his lap. They didn't seem to care about the order of presentation. Each performer walked to center stage and turned full around twice, slowly, then did a bit of whatever they would do during the performance: limp, leap, dance a jig. Sebastian and Noisette watched each one critically. As each actor exited stage right, Sebastian bent his blond head toward Noisette's dark one to hear her comments, sometimes jotting a note on the loose sheets of paper tucked into his book.

Most performers went down the apron steps and found a seat in the stalls to watch the rest of the parade. Some, like Mr. Tweedy and

Mr. Sparrow, who played different characters in different scenes, disappeared into the wings to change costumes for a second review.

The Delaney sisters went out in a group, where they turned in unison, fluttering prettily. Then Belinda stepped forward and introduced them, explaining to the audience that they were the five fairies who executed the magic contained in the five beans Jack gets in trade for his cow. Everyone knew that already, but Angelina had not known Belinda possessed such a clear, pleasant, carrying voice. That must have been the purpose of her breaking the tradition.

Sebastian smiled at her, nodding. Message received: she wanted a speaking part. That explained the batting lashes and the tittering as well. Perhaps he'd be let off from that promised tête-à-tête; more likely it would turn into a business meeting, with new roles to be arranged for both parties. The fairy sisters danced off the stage.

Angelina strode out to center stage, taking long steps like a confident boy. She stood for a moment with fists on hips, then stomped around in a circle twice. Then she turned a cartwheel, winning a spatter of applause. She'd practiced that over and over yesterday.

Sebastian bent his head toward Noisette, nodded, and called, "Let's have Jack and the Giant side by side, if you please."

Mr. Easton worked his way forward. He wore a one-shouldered tunic covered with green leaves over a flesh-colored body suit. He also wore big black boots, which added a good three inches to his frame. He positively towered over Angelina. If she hadn't spent so many hours learning to fight with him, she would find him quite alarming. They lunged and parried with invisible swords for a few seconds, then waited for Sebastian's nod of approval. Then they shook hands and made their way down to the stalls.

Peg had saved Angelina a seat on the aisle about six rows from the stage. They enjoyed the show in silence for a while, watching the five pairs of Shakespeare characters strut the boards in their evocative costumes. After Oberon and Titania had performed their stately turns, Peg muttered, "Well, I have to hand it to the little nut. Those costumes are pure magic."

Angelina chuckled. High praise indeed! Too bad Noisette would never hear it. Peg would sooner be racked in the bloody Tower.

Mr. Tweedy appeared in his Dame Trott costume, swinging his hips in the flat-footed, waddling walk that brought audiences to tears of laughter. Peg sighed like a schoolgirl watching a young cavalry officer. Angelina started to ask her how the budding romance was coming along when Madame Noisette's shrill voice broke through the general hubbub.

"What is that trash around your neck, Mr. Tweedy? I never put that there!"

Tweedy fingered the triangle of lace draped across his shoulders. "Um, er . . ." He shot a frown toward Peg, who called out, "I added that touch. You need a bit of something to mark Jack's dream scene off from the everyday."

"Mother Trott can't afford lace!" Noisette shouted. "She's desperately poor! So poor she has to sell her cow. If she possessed such a great swath of lace, don't you think she would sell that first?" The wardrobe mistress hopped to her feet and struggled over the other people in her row to reach the aisle. She jogged up the steps and crossed the apron, jumping up to catch the end of the lace, trying to yank it off.

Peg leapt from her seat and bounded up to the stage. "You leave that right where it is. Those are my stitches. You'll tear the whole dress apart before you get it loose."

"Now, ladies," Tweedy said, waving his hands, plainly unable to decide which woman to defend — or avoid.

"It's an affront to the eye!" Noisette cried. "Off it comes, this very minute!"

Peg grabbed Noisette's arm to stop her. The little woman swatted at her with her free hand. "Get away from him, you great lumbering cow!"

"Me, a cow! You gormless moppet!" Peg put some muscle into it and succeeded in tearing both Noisette and the lace away from the man.

Noisette screamed. She shook her arm free from Peg's grasp, then took a few steps back, lowered her head, and charged at her like a bull, catching her in the stomach and knocking her off her feet. Peg clutched at Noisette's dress as she went down, pulling her down too. Soon they were rolling around on the wooden floor of the stage, pulling at each other's hair and cursing Cockney blue streaks. "Barmy slag!" "Manky minger!"

Tweedy recklessly moved toward them rather than away, reaching out both hands in an attempt to grasp whoever was on top. One of the women sent out a kick in his direction, catching him sharply on the shin. "Ow!" he cried, hopping on the other leg right over the edge of the stage, crashing down into the orchestra pit.

That calamity broke up the fight between the two seamstresses, who shimmied forward on their bellies to peer down at him. "Mr. Tweedy!" they cried — in unison, but not united.

Several men reached into the pit to haul the comedian out, but when they tried to set him on his feet, he yelped in pain. "Look what you've done!" he scolded the two combatants, who were being hauled to their feet by actors from the disrupted queue. "I've sprained me bleedin' ankle."

Frank Sparrow came up to put an arm around Tweedy's shoulder, his rubbery features shifting between sympathy and laughter. "You can't write this stuff," he said. "No one would believe it."

Angelina had followed Peg up to the stage, but hadn't been bold enough to step into the fray. "Oh, Mr. Tweedy," she said. "Are you in terrible pain? Shall we call for your understudy?" She traded worried looks with Sebastian, who finally made it through the gawkers onto the stage. She guessed they were thinking the same thing: losing Timothy Tweedy would be a major blow. Enough to be sure the show would fail? But who could have predicted this sequence of events?

"Who's your understudy?" Sebastian asked. "I don't believe I've ever seen him at any of your rehearsals."

"Not to worry," Sparrow said. "You'd have to cut off both Tim's legs to keep him out of the show. Though I'm not sure that would work, come to think of it."

"I don't need that worthless scrounger lurking around me like a bloody vulture," Tweedy grumbled. "Pardon my French. Just wrap my leg up in a bandage, I'll be fine. Dame Trott with a crutch will be twice as funny, watch and see."

"Oh, Mr. Tweedy," Noisette gushed. "You are so brave."

He frowned at her. "Annie, I never meant to imply —"

Peg cut him off. "Don't you call him brave, you harpy! He doesn't care what you think!" The two seamstresses strained toward one another, snarling with bared teeth, restrained by members of the men's chorus, fittingly costumed as guardsmen.

Angelina moved between the two women, holding her hands out wide. "No more fighting, you two. It's undignified! You've ruined the parade."

"She destroyed my costume!" Noisette fumed.

"I'm sure it can be mended," Sebastian said, entering the safety zone. "It doesn't look too badly torn."

Tweedy probed at the disputed area. "There's a nasty little rip here, but patches won't matter. Dame Trott is a thrifty soul. I could just drape the lace over for the dream sequence."

"I've got another piece of that lace," Peg said.

"No lace!" Noisette glared at Peg, then turned her baleful glare on Angelina and Sebastian. "I should have known you Archers would take her side. You're all against me. You're plotting to turn me out and put *her* in my place!"

"No, we're not," Sebastian said. "No one's replacing anyone, especially not you, Madame Noisette."

"You want to force me out and give her my job." She pointed an accusing finger at Peg.

"No," Sebastian said. "I do not. I need you. Your creations are extraordinary, Madame. I've been looking at the sketches in Mr. Fowler's notebooks, and I'm in awe of your talent. I hope you'll stay on long after *Beanstalk* is done and help me make the Galaxy the pre-eminent theater of varieties in London."

The anger leached out of the tiny woman's reddened cheeks as she met his gaze and held it, probing for deception. She didn't seem to find any, but then her eyes narrowed. "What about that lace?"

"No lace," Sebastian said. "I agree with you. Mother Trott can't afford it." He turned to Peg. "In future, all costume changes will be approved by Madame Noisette. Apart from Lina's variety turns, of course. You have full discretion there."

Peg tossed her head, dislodging the last of the pins holding her brown hair together. "I never wanted to be wardrobe mistress in the first place. I just won't be bossed by her, that's all."

Sebastian shook his head, then extended a hand to Noisette. "Are we in agreement, Madame Noisette?"

"We are, Mr. Archer." She shook his hand solemnly, but her black eyes shone. He'd won an ally there. Would that put a stop to the rats and the cold drafts? Angelina wondered.

Noisette turned to Tweedy with a markedly cooler gaze. "Bring me that dress when you get out of it, Mr. Tweedy. Or send someone if you can't manage the stairs." She turned on her heel and swept away with as much dignity as a woman scarcely five feet tall could muster, going back down to the stalls to watch the rest of the dress parade.

Sebastian, however, wasn't finished. "I didn't hear an answer to my question, Mr. Tweedy. Where's your understudy?"

"How the devil should I know?" He made a clown face at Sparrow, who responded in kind. Part of their old act, the lean face mirroring the fat one.

Sebastian was not amused. "And where is yours, Mr. Sparrow? And yours, Miss Lovington? I haven't seen understudies shadowing any of your rehearsals."

Angelina rolled her eyes. "We don't really need understudies, Sebastian. None of us would let a little thing like a sprained ankle or a cold in the head stop us from doing our jobs. We're old warhorses, we three." The three principals grinned at one another like the best of pals.

"What about a fall from the cloud gondola? Would that stop you?" Sebastian set his fists on his hips, his blue eyes blazing. "If you'd been six inches closer to that exploding powder, you'd be in bandages from head to toe, Lina — if you survived it."

"But I wasn't hurt," Angelina said. "Not even a scratch. Really, Sebastian! You're a fine one to scold us on this count. What was the name of your last understudy?"

"I don't know. I admit it. I've never missed a performance either. But I was wrong, and you're wrong now." He was as angry as she'd ever seen him — she hadn't known he had it in him to be so insistent.

"Don't you get it yet? Someone is trying to stop *Beanstalk*. If it were me, I'd be going after the three of you with everything I've got. But if you have understudies who are fully prepared to step in and take your parts, it wouldn't do me any good, would it?"

He turned to face the collected cast scattered about the stalls. "Did everyone hear that? I want the understudies for these three" — he pointed at Angelina, Tweedy, and Sparrow in turn — "to sit in that box right there every night until you're word perfect and know all their moves." He pointed at the closest box on the left. "Then once we pass the hundredth — no, the fiftieth — no, the *fortieth* night, you'll perform every Tuesday and alternate Sunday afternoons."

Tweedy started spluttering and Sebastian spun around to stab a finger at him. "Yes, Mr. Tweedy, for the same pay as already agreed." He pointed that finger at Sparrow and Angelina in turn, holding the pose until each one nodded in submission. A light spatter of applause rose up from the stalls at his performance — or perhaps it was the understudies cheering their new status.

Sebastian grinned at the people, then raised his face to the empty galleries. "Do you hear that, Mr. Ghost? You won't close this show by taking out one of our principals. We're ready for you! *Beanstalk* will go on!"

That won a full round of applause from everyone in the stalls and the actors still standing around the stage, including the three chastened stars.

Angelina had had enough of the costume parade. Too much excitement! She wandered back to her dressing room, where she found Peg muttering at the teapot. The dresser handed her a cup as she pulled off her Jack wig and flopped onto the bench at her dressing table.

"I knew you'd be up as soon as Sebastian started in on that rant," Peg said.

"I didn't know he had any ranting in him," Angelina said. "What's become of our cool, unflappable idler?" She sipped the sweet, hot, life-restoring tea.

"Never idle, ducky, not really." Peg took her own cup over to her sewing chair. "I suppose he's been waiting for the right thing to come along and wake him up."

"Well, he's awake now. I have to cooperate with my understudy! The pinch-faced little vixen. I suppose I'll have to be nice to her, get to know her, have her round for tea on holidays."

Peg chuckled. "Don't get carried away now."

Angelina regarded her old friend over the rim of her cup. "It's very naughty of Mr. Tweedy to lead Madame Noisette on, don't you think?"

"He never did! She's barmy, is what she is."

"I don't know, Peg. She acted as though she and Mr. Tweedy had some sort of understanding."

"Yes. The understanding that she's a looney." Peg set down her cup and picked up some work, then put it down it again. "He never gave her any such idea, Lina. She made that up herself. He got into a spot of trouble last summer and confided in her during a fitting. You know how that happens. He didn't have anyone else. She stitched up the rest of it out of whole cloth."

"Hmm." Angelina drank some tea, then swung around on her bench to start pulling pins out of her braids. She shot Peg a sideways glance. "He's still in that spot of trouble, isn't he?"

Peg shrugged. "He might be."

Angelina let a small silence develop while she worked on her hair. Then she set down her comb and turned to face her friend, clasping her hands between her legs. "He must tell us, Peg. We can't have any serious secrets here. Not now. Lionel won't live out the week, you know."

"You said he was resting comfortably!"

Angelina didn't bother to answer that.

Peg frowned and picked up the blouse or skirt or whatever it was she held in her lap. She turned it around a few times as if looking for a seam, then scrunched it up with both hands. "Mr. Tweedy never cut that rope, nor any of the other business."

"I believe you. But there's something going on with him." Angelina tried and failed to catch Peg's eyes. "What is it, Peg? Don't you trust me anymore?"

"'Course I trust you! What a thing to say!"

"Then who? You don't trust James?"

"How could anyone not trust James Moriarty? He's the honestest man that ever walked." Peg tapped her foot. "It's not my secret."

"But you know it," Angelina pressed. "And you know we need to know. Can't you go find Mr. Tweedy right now and ask him to come have a quiet cup of tea and tell me what it is? We might be able to help him, you know. James is very resourceful."

Peg's foot tapped faster, then stopped abruptly. She stuffed the wad of cloth into her work basket and got to her feet. "Someone has to help him. All he's doing is digging a deeper hole." She walked out without another word, leaving Angelina with arguments yet to plead.

She took advantage of the moment to change out of her Jack suit and back into street clothes. She ought to seek out her understudy and do something with her, but she didn't want to fall into line too readily with Sebastian's demands. If being the stage manager's sister gave her no advantage, she'd just have to pull rank. She was the leading actress at the Galaxy, after all. She had the dignity of her position to uphold.

The door opened to the sound of Peg's voice, saying, "Here we are, Mr. Tweedy. A few more steps and we'll get you a nice cup of tea. We've got a tin of lemon squares made by a real French chef. You'll like that, I'll wager."

Tweedy had changed into his street clothes too, and had acquired a handsome ebony walking stick from somewhere. He hobbled in, greeted Angelina, and sat down on the purple sofa. Peg bustled about in a wifely fashion, serving him tea with a plate of lemon squares and freshening her and Angelina's cups. Angelina and Tweedy shared grumbles about the understudy business, two old pros with a common grievance against an oppressive manager. That and the tea and the cozy room created an atmosphere of comfortable congeniality.

Angelina smiled at Peg. "Why don't you get us started?"

Tweedy pressed his lips together in a tight smile, nodded at Peg, then turned to Angelina. "No need. Miss Barwick has persuaded me to make a clean breast. I can't pay any more anyway. I'm tapped out.

And God knows I don't want to be suspected of causing harm to Old Hattie."

His story began fifteen years ago, shortly after Peg and Angelina left for Italy. Tweedy claimed his tender heart had been broken, but soon he met a woman named Gladys, whom he married not long after. That turned out to be a disastrous mistake. They bickered and battled for a year or so, until one night he came home from the theater to find her clothes missing, along with his small store of valuables. No note, no indication of where she'd gone or with whom. Time passed without a word. He convinced himself she'd died somewhere out there. He married again, a quiet, sweet-tempered woman named Linda. She bore him a son, whom they named Timothy, and they all lived contentedly in their little house in Islington for many years.

Those years came to a tragic end last June when Linda succumbed to a fever. Tweedy struggled along for a month trying to care for his young son on his own but finally gave in to necessity and sent him to Hampshire to live with his sister and her family. Music halls and theater dressing rooms were no place to raise a child!

Angelina and Peg traded wry looks at that observation but let it pass.

Tweedy threw himself into his work in spite of the growing ill humor at the Galaxy. Then, late one night toward the end of September, a knock came on his door. He opened it to find Gladys, looking much older and worn out, as if the intervening years had been hard ones. She'd been in America and had fallen on bad times but finally made it back to her native shores. There she chanced upon an obituary mentioning the bereaved widower Timothy Tweedy, resident of Islington. Seemed as though he'd come up while she went down, and she meant to even the score. She'd held on to their marriage certificate and now threatened to expose him as a bigamist, making a bastard of innocent little Timmy. She wanted money: fifty pounds to start, then sixty, now a hundred. Tweedy had been forced to sell the house Linda had brought to their marriage and move into cheap rooms in Whitechapel. She'd started biting into his biweekly pay, and he could see no end to it.

"Oh, Mr. Tweedy," Angelina said. "You should never pay a blackmailer. That's one of life's basic rules." The kind of life she'd led anyway. "They always come back for more. You have to get the thing away from them — the letters or the marriage certificate or whatever it is."

"Marriage is a matter of public record," Tweedy said. "It wouldn't do me any good to get that scrap of paper. I could've taken it from her on the spot that first night."

Angelina frowned in sympathy. Trying to steal back compromising letters hadn't worked that well for her either. "Then we must find something worse about her and turn the tables. Blackmail the blackmailer. I can recommend that strategy from experience."

Tweedy screwed up his face, thinking, then shook his head. "She's bound to have done something awful somewhere, but damned if I can find it out. She's been abroad all these years."

"Well then, you just have to tell the truth yourself before she can do it her way. Stand up and take the consequences." Angelina looked directly into his eyes. "We'll stand by you, Mr. Tweedy. The professor, Sebastian, Peg, and me. In fact, I think you could safely count every man and woman in the Galaxy as your friend in such dire straits as these."

Tears shimmered in his brown eyes. "I thank you for that, Miss — er, Mrs. Moriarty. From the bottom of my heart. But it's my audience I'm worried about. What'll they think of me?"

"They won't care a fig," Peg said. "Who's that composer who was tried for bigamy? It didn't even slow him down."

"Edward Solomon," Angelina said. "You're right. He's utterly unrepentant, and no one cares a single jot. And what about William Horace Lingard, Captain Jinks of the Horse Marines? An extra wife or two didn't do him any harm either."

That last one struck home. "I forgot about Captain Jinks, with his quirks and his kinks. Maybe you're right."

"The people love you," Peg said. Her tone made it clear that they weren't the only ones. "You should trust them to stick by you, thick or thin."

"I'm thick; Sparrow's thin," Tweedy said absently. Then he shook his head. "But no. She'll make my son a bastard, the poor wee sprite! He's done nothing to deserve such a stain."

"You can adopt him," Angelina said. "Do it quickly and quietly, before the scandal hits the newspapers, if it ever does."

"Oh no," Tweedy said. "That takes lawyers and such. I wouldn't know where to start."

"James will," Angelina said. "Leave it to us. In fact, next time that loathsome Gladys tries to meet with you, bring her here, to James's office. He'll glower at her in that reptilian, mathematical way he has."

Peg laughed. "She'll run screaming all the way back to whatever hole she crawled out from."

Tweedy grinned from ear to ear. "I'd like to see that glower — from a safe distance." He looked five years younger, as if a great weight had been pressing on his head and had now been removed.

Peg got up to fix more tea and pass it around. Angelina munched a lemon square. After a few minutes, she said conversationally, "Do you have any idea who's been doing these horrible things at the Galaxy, Mr. Tweedy?"

"Unless it's a ghost, I haven't a clue."

Angelina believed him. He'd been too busy with his own problems to pay attention to pranksters sneaking about with stolen scissors and handfuls of explosive powder. She'd ruled him out the minute he fell off the stage and refused to call his understudy. Why bother to hurt himself if his goal was to stop the pantomime? Mr. Sparrow had been right: no one could predict a fight breaking out between two rival seamstresses. It simply never happened.

"Have you known Nora Verney for a long time?" she asked him.

"Long enough." He gave her a curious look. "Do you think she's involved in all this?"

"She must be. It started with those burlesques she forced poor Lionel to put on."

"She didn't *force* him so much as wheedle him into it." Tweedy winked at Peg, as if she were quite the wheedler herself.

"That's what I meant." Angelina decided to change tacks. "Did you know her mother was once a spiritualist?"

"Sally Sparrow? Oh yes, I remember her. Before your time. She had her day in the sun though, or rather, her evenings in the dark. Her séances were quite the vogue for a while. That was before Frank's father died. Now *there* was a bitter man. They were both better off without him. Then Sally married Dr. Verney and gradually gave up her own work. You remember him, I'll wager. Dr. Verney, the great mesmerist? He played the Paramount several times."

"I remember him," Peg said. "His eyes bugged out like a demon. He terrified me! I was afraid he'd turn me into a frog."

Tweedy teased her about mixing up mesmerists and magicians, while Angelina's mind whirled around the words "Sally Sparrow" and "Frank's father." That must mean Frank was Nora's half brother. No wonder she took him for granted, shoving her coat at him like a manservant — or a brother. And he'd called her "Nora" too instead of "Miss Verney." She'd thought at the time it was because she'd used the familiar name for her old rival herself.

So Frank Sparrow had been the child in the spiritualist's house, upstairs twitching hooks on dark lines while Mummy communed with the great beyond. What a useful set of skills for haunting a theater!

Frank Sparrow, who spent the better part of every day inside the Galaxy, going wherever he liked, making people laugh and thus welcomed wherever he went. Frank Sparrow, who had been jilted by Amy Delaney, now getting his revenge by playing tricks in the dancers' dressing room. Frank Sparrow, ventriloquist, sending whispers down corridors and ominous voices through walls.

Angelina could easily see him making doors blow shut or even smashing the hats of men who'd annoyed him in some petty way. He liked a little sting in his jokes. But what good would it do him to shut down *Beanstalk* and bankrupt Lionel Hatcliff? He'd be out of the best job he'd ever had, according to his own words, out on the street with his hat in his hand, just like everyone else.

TWENTY-ONE

"Another theater fire. No injuries, thank goodness." Moriarty lowered *The Times* to share that bit of news with his wife. He sat in his armchair at the designated head of their octagonal dining table — the side with its back to the windows. He preferred natural light in the morning, even on a gray day like this one, and had no interest in the comings and goings of the neighbors.

"Oh dear! Which one?"

"Howard's Music Hall. In Southwark. Do you know it?"

"Not well. An older one, isn't it?"

Rolly entered with their eggs and toast on a tray. Moriarty folded his paper into precise quarters so he could continue to read while he ate. Angelina had assured him she didn't mind his reading at breakfast. She liked to gaze through the lace curtains, contemplating the weather and planning her day. She also liked noting which neighbor left at what hour in what sort of clothes.

This morning they had more serious concerns. She had brought home a surprising bit of news last night, which they'd been too tired to discuss thoroughly. "What do you think about Frank Sparrow?" she asked. "As the ghost, I mean?"

"I don't remember Sparrow. Isn't he one of the principals?" Moriarty slathered Antoine's succulent orange marmalade on a piece of toast, wondering how he'd ever tolerated the bottled stuff. That was the problem with money: once you had it, you had to keep getting more of it to sustain the flow of luxuries you could no longer live without.

"He's the tall, thin one with the long face. Very funny, I used to think, though I'm not sure I could laugh at him now." Angelina tucked into her boiled egg as if she would never get another meal.

Her appetite had grown by leaps with the advent of daily rehearsals. She'd never been anything but stunningly beautiful, but now her color was even fresher and she moved with an extra grace born of increased vigor. "You may not have met him."

"There are always so many people when I go backstage, and they all have something unusual about their appearance."

"Once you've seen a few shows, you'll be better able to sort them out."

Moriarty chewed a bite of toast while he reviewed the list of ghostly infractions the Galaxy had suffered in recent months, thinking about how each one might have been performed. "If Sparrow's mother was a spiritualist, I think we can assume the skills to play all the standard tricks are within his scope: floating scarves, chilly drafts, doors blowing shut, skirts being lifted, etcetera."

"He was a ventriloquist too, before he joined Mr. Tweedy."

"Then add the moaning voices and the whispering in corridors to his bill. Yes, I believe it. He's more likely than Nora Verney. From what you've told me, she doesn't seem the sort to slip in and out of a place unnoticed. Mr. Sparrow is in the Galaxy every day as a matter of course. But why, Angelina? What purpose does this ghost nonsense serve him?"

"It makes people anxious and unhappy. That's never good. Bad feeling among the cast can sink a show as fast as a hostile critic."

"Failure does seem to be the major theme. We keep coming back to that motive, but it feels like an end to me, not the beginning." Moriarty polished off his first piece of toast while he chewed on that idea, washing it down with a gulp of tea. "First Miss Verney pushed Hatcliff into expensive productions, then she, or Mr. Fowler, ensured those plays would fail before expenses could be recouped. What good did that do anyone?"

"It produced more valuable properties for them to steal. If they weren't being used, they wouldn't be missed."

Moriarty frowned, his spoon suspended over his egg. "That's a bit thin, my dear. Miss Verney seems to have contradictory objectives. On the one hand, she wanted Hatcliff to marry her so she could gain control of the Galaxy, along with its full complement of valuable properties. On the other hand, she seems to have made a concerted effort to drive her matrimonial prospect into bankruptcy."

Angelina peered into the cavity of her empty egg shell, clearly wondering if she should ask for another one. Then she set her spoon down with a decisive clink. "I wonder if the bankruptcy ploy began before or after she met Charles Cudlow."

"Now there's an interesting addition to the mix. Someone at the theater must know when Verney switched horses, so to speak. Perhaps one of your Delaney sisters, who seem to know everything. But what's Cudlow's interest?

"I don't know. An investment strategy? That's something you could look into, isn't it, darling?"

"I would like to know the names behind the syndicate that owns our theater," Moriarty said, noting the flash of pleasure in his wife's eyes at his choice of pronoun. "But what could Sparrow gain by destroying Hatcliff? He'd lose his job. He and Mr. Tweedy could undoubtedly find other bookings, but from what you've told me, it's better to be part of the regular cast."

"Far better. Steady pay, your own personal dressing room, and no more going door to door every Thursday afternoon begging for work on Saturday night."

"I suppose his sister might share the proceeds of her thefts with him, but then why play all the nasty tricks? They only put people on the alert. One should think that would make the thefts more difficult."

"He could be doing the haunting purely for fun. He has a bit of mean streak, you know. Clowns often do. They enjoy splashing mud on people and making fools of them. It's funny for everyone else."

"Not once John Fowler died." Moriarty tilted his chin at the teapot, and his wife obligingly refilled his cup. He added a splash of milk and stirred in a lump of sugar. "An honest clown would have stopped his pranks at that point; instead, they've gotten worse. You and Sebastian don't tell me everything, but we're not completely isolated at the front of the house. I've heard reports of small fires, stuck doors, loose ropes, vermin in unexpected places. Even the odd explosion on the stage." He gave Angelina a pointed look, who granted him a sheepish grin.

"I can imagine Nora wanting *Beanstalk* to fail out of spite," she said, "though I can't imagine her going to so much effort to achieve it. Perhaps she's paying her brother. Maybe he owes her money." Her eyes flashed. "Maybe she's blackmailing him!"

"It does seem to be going around." Moriarty glanced at his folded paper with its notice of the fire in Southwark, and something started niggling at the back of his mind. "We're missing a piece of this puzzle. A big one."

Moriarty unfolded the paper hoping for more details, but found none. *The Stage* might have a longer article. Hatcliff kept stacks of back issues in his office at the Galaxy. It might be worth seeing what he could find out about other theater fires in the past year while he was about it. He would like to know who owned them and how much money they'd collected from their insurance companies.

"In a way," he said, "I find the idea of a grown man performing such reckless pranks to amuse himself more disturbing than a ring of thieves working inside the theater. Please be extra careful, my dear, especially in your dealings with Mr. Sparrow."

"He won't notice any difference."

Moriarty smiled at the confection in green-and-red plaid she wore this morning, which had more flounces than he'd seen in recent weeks. "Aren't you rehearsing today?"

"No," she said, her tone taking the sharp upturn that meant dissatisfaction. "Today I am going to sit with my hands in my lap watching my understudy rehearse with Mr. Tweedy and Mr. Sparrow's understudies. Then I am going to take Miss Grouper, or whatever her name is, out to lunch to prove that I can be gracious and cooperative."

Moriarty chuckled. "Sebastian's idea, one supposes. I agree with him. If your understudies are prepared to step into your roles, the malefactor can't stop the show by hurting you. And I like the idea of forcing Mr. Sparrow to sit and watch that possibility evaporate before his eyes."

"That might make it slightly less tedious." She drank some tea and changed the subject. "Can we help Mr. Tweedy, do you think?"

"We can try." Moriarty shook his head. "But one should never pay a blackmailer. We've learned that the hard way ourselves. We'll never get any of his money back."

"Couldn't we at least engage Lionel's lawyer to manage the adoption process?"

"Certainly, if the man ever reappears. I have the strongest feeling my partnership agreement is lying on the carpet inside his chamber door. I'm on the brink of taking Rolly over to Gray's Inn to pick that lock." Moriarty held up a finger to forestall her imminent approval of that rash plan. "Purest wishful thinking. I can hardly go about breaking into offices with Sherlock Holmes hot on my trail."

"Have you seen him lately?"

"A hundred times — or none. Cabmen have a way of casting their eyes at men standing on the pavement that seems to be nearly universal, now that I'm noticing. In this season, they're all wrapped up in scarves with their hats pulled low. He could be any one of them. Or he might have changed tactics and camped out in Leicester Square. I spotted an unusually tall woman feeding pigeons over there yesterday."

"I don't like it, James. We don't know what he's up to. He just chooses whichever side amuses him the most. The man has no moral compass."

Moriarty thought that a bit rich coming from a woman who'd supported herself partly through confidence trickery until she'd married him. She and Sherlock Holmes had more in common than either of them cared to admit.

Angelina sniffed. "I wish he would leave Lionel's servants alone. It's ghoulish to lurk around outside the house of a dying man."

"That's what he was hired to do, I suspect. His client wants to catch us covering up Hatcliff's incapacitation." Why anyone would care enough to hire a consulting detective was another question that needed answering.

"Poor Lionel. It won't be long now." Angelina polished off her last morsel of toast and wiped her fingers with her napkin. "What will happen? After he goes?"

"I don't know. A reasonable building owner would be eager to renew the lease in my name, I should think. A bird in the hand, a play ready to go on. No delay, no loss of revenue. But a syndicate doesn't necessarily think like a man. And we have these malefactors working against us, whoever they are and whatever they're hoping to gain." Moriarty frowned into his china cup, then downed the last of his tea. "They might as well be ghosts, their actions are so disconnected and their motives so indeterminate."

Angelina turned wide eyes toward him and asked in a hushed voice, "Do you think it really could be ghosts, James?"

Moriarty leveled an admonitory look at her, and she laughed.

Then she sobered with a sigh. "I wish it were ghosts. Better some long-dead actor with an ancient grudge than someone we know and work with every day."

* * *

Moriarty resisted the urge to study the faces of everyone he passed on the way from Bellenden Crescent to Leicester Square. If Sherlock Holmes wanted to waste his time following him from his home to his office, let him.

As he passed down the long corridor to Hatcliff's office, he saw that Mr. Tidwell's door was partly open. After a nicely judged interval — time for Moriarty to doff his outer garments, hang them on the rack, sit at his desk, and scan the slew of notes left for him — Tidwell rapped on the door and entered. "Good morning, Professor. Anything I can do for you?"

"Yes, as a matter of fact. I believe I've seen back issues of *The Stage* stacked somewhere around here."

"I keep them in my office and have them bound at the start of each year. Mr. Hatcliff likes to see what's been done at other theaters when he's working out our annual program."

"A sensible policy. Could you scout out last year's issues for me? I'd like to do a little research of my own."

"Back in a tick."

Tidwell was true to his word. Moriarty barely had time to jot down the questions he meant to pursue before the assistant returned with an armload of newspapers. Moriarty jumped up to clear a corner of his desk. Tidwell set them down and said, "I may have scrambled the order a bit taking them off the shelf. Shall I sort them again? I could lay them out on the floor."

"Good thought. It's always best to begin at the beginning." Moriarty moved a chair and a footstool to make room on the Turkey carpet. "But I can do this myself, Tidwell. You must have more important work to do."

The young man shrugged. "It is Christmas Eve. We're closed all day tomorrow and whatever needed doing before we open again on Boxing Day is done. We've got advertisements in all the popular papers and placards in every shop window in the West End. Jostling with all the other pantos, of course, but no one else has a drawing of Lina Lovington climbing a giant beanstalk." He crossed his fingers and grinned.

Moriarty hadn't noticed those advertisements. He didn't look in shop windows. When he wanted something, he went directly to the place where the best of such somethings were sold and bought one. "I keep forgetting about the holiday, just counting the days until we open. Does everyone take the whole weekend off?"

"Yes, sir. We turn off the gas and lock the whole place up, front and back. If it hasn't been done by now, it will just have to be sorted during the first week. That's always a shaking-out period, you know, even after a normal month of preparation. Which we have not had this year." Tidwell's face showed the strain of the past weeks in the dark hollows under his brown eyes. He gazed at the stack of newspapers sadly, perhaps thinking of the man who had read them in this office and would now probably never return.

Moriarty considered the young man standing before him, his conservative suit made festive with a seasonal red tie that clashed with his fiery red hair. Tidwell had proved himself to be a capable and devoted assistant. Moriarty would need his guidance in the months to come. He decided to trust him now.

"I could use your help with this, Tidwell, as a matter of fact. I had an idea this morning — the beginnings of one anyway — that might explain everything that's been going on at the Galaxy in the past year."

"I'm all ears, Professor."

Moriarty gestured for him to sit down and took his own chair behind the desk. "First, everyone keeps telling me how valuable theatrical properties are. Painted scenery worthy of museums, historically accurate costumes, etcetera, etcetera. Mr. Hatcliff said the Galaxy's properties were valued at something like twenty-three thousand pounds."

"That sounds about right."

"That seems to me a staggering sum, but apparently it isn't unusual."

"The Galaxy's at the large end of the spectrum, but no, I expect Drury Lane and the Alhambra have at least that much in their cellars." Tidwell seemed unimpressed by the figures under discussion.

Moriarty moved on. "That establishes the foundation of my theory, so to speak. Then I have read more than one article in the news lately about fires in theaters in which thousands of pounds of properties were destroyed. Insurance companies were obliged to reimburse the owners."

"I should think they would be! That's the whole purpose of insurance."

"That's the second observation. The third is that properties have apparently been stolen from the Galaxy. Costumes, certainly, but possibly also scenery and props. I believe John Fowler coordinated these thefts."

"Fowler?" Tidwell looked shocked. "He was with Mr. Hatcliff for years!" His hurt and surprise faded, replaced by a knowing gleam. He nodded his head slowly. "On the other hand, it does explain the rash of accidents under his watch. And we heard grumblings from the crew about it too. We haven't had any fires though."

"Not yet," Moriarty said. "But I suspect the conspiracy runs deeper. This building is owned by a syndicate that owns several other theaters, I believe. I want to know if any of those are among these recent disasters. It strikes me that the syndicate could make a fortune by removing the valuable properties, burning down the house, and then claiming the properties as lost."

"Good gad, Professor! You're talking about insurance fraud on a city-wide scale!" Tidwell grinned, not at all the expected response.

"Are you fond of fraud, Mr. Tidwell?"

"Not of the actual deed, Professor; not at all. But as a dramatic device." The young man shrugged, grinning from ear to oversized ear. "I've been reading up on the subject, you see. Dickens, Trollope — it's a popular theme. I'm writing a play, as it happens. A melodrama based on the Black Widows of Liverpool."

Moriarty blinked at him and shook his head. "Who?"

"Two women who committed murder in order to collect on life insurance policies. It's a terrible thing." Tidwell's eyes shone with pleasure. "I hadn't thought of fire insurance, but of course that's even easier, isn't it? Wouldn't make such a good play, of course, not having any murders in it, but you'd make a great deal of money from the actual fraud. And you'd get to modernize your theater at the insurance company's expense to boot."

"I hadn't thought of that." It would seem Tidwell had an active imagination in addition to more conventional skills. The single word "fraud"' had caused all the pieces to fall together in Moriarty's mind.

He tapped his finger on the desk while walking through the hypothetical scheme. "Let's say the owner of this building — that syndicate — wants to modernize and change directions. But here's Lionel Hatcliff with fifteen years left on his lease. They want to drive him out by driving him into bankruptcy. They can do that by forcing cancellation of the pantomime, which helpfully rids the theater of its cast and crew. Then they steal the properties before Hatcliff can sell them to cover his debts, burn the place down, and start fresh."

"They wouldn't be able to claim Mr. Hatcliff's properties themselves though," Tidwell pointed out.

"No, they wouldn't. But they'd be in possession of them." Moriarty didn't add that Hatcliff's death might leave the ownership of those properties up in the air. If Miss Verney had succeeded in marrying him, she would have been the most likely beneficiary. She must have abandoned that plan before the decision was taken to cut the rope on the cloud gondola. That suggested that this conspiracy, if it really existed, wasn't perfectly well coordinated. "Is it difficult to sell such things?"

"Not at all," Tidwell said. "Scenery gets touched up fairly often. Little changes here and there for each new show. Add a Swiss flavor to your village or paint the Swiss flavor out. There's a market for used scenery as well. Provincial theaters, for example. New theaters spring up and fail all the time. It's a volatile business, seen from the larger view."

"So they could make a tidy sum from the Galaxy's properties even without defrauding another insurance company." Moriarty clapped his hands together. "Let's dig into these newspapers, Mr. Tidwell. We're looking for any notice relating to theater fires in the past year. Let's list the owners and managers of any such, along with valuations of lost properties and the companies against whom the claims are being filed."

They divided the papers between them and set to work, Moriarty at his desk and Tidwell in the reading chair. They worked in companionable silence, apart from the rustling of pages. Each man had a pad of paper on which to scribble his notes.

They made quick work of it, scanning each weekly paper for the words "fire" and "loss," getting through their respective stacks in about half an hour. "Very interesting," Moriarty said as he folded up his last paper and set it on the discard stack. "Are you ready to trade notes?"

Tidwell nodded. "Shall I fetch us some tea?" He went out, returning in a few minutes with a well-stocked tray. "Mrs. Bankside brought raisin buns this morning." He served them both and returned to his chair.

Moriarty welcomed the refreshments, needing fuel for his whirling mind. "I found two excellent cases in my stack. The music hall in Southwark that caught fire yesterday and a medium-sized theater in Islington that was nearly gutted in June. Both are owned by our syndicate, the House of Theatrical Investments."

"They do seem to be having a bad year, don't they?" Tidwell chuckled. "I found one in Whitechapel — the Royal Brunswick — and another in the St. James district. The same house owns them both. The distribution is suggestive, isn't it?"

"North, south, east, and west. I suppose it prevents anyone from discerning a pattern."

"And stops the crews from noticing as well," Tidwell said. "Theaters tend to draw staff from the surrounding district to some extent. They'll gather in public houses around their place of work, at any rate. The distance would keep crews from gossiping with one another or seeing their work show up on the stage of another hall."

Moriarty tore a bun in half and dunked it in his tea. "It's a good thing you're here, Mr. Tidwell. I couldn't solve this puzzle without your help." He consulted his notes. "My two fires report a combined total of eleven thousand pounds in losses. The Southwark hall was insured by Vulcan Assurance and the Islington one by Haliburton's."

"Mine were both insured by Middlesex Fire and Life. They reported losses of, let's see — Great Scott! Fifteen thousand pounds!"

"That gives us a total of twenty-six thousand in one year." Moriarty shook his head, still coming to terms with the immense value of a collection of painted flats, papier-mâché castles, and sequined costumes.

"They wouldn't have to sell a single ticket to count themselves among the wealthiest men in London," Tidwell said. "Depending on how that house is structured. Do you know if it's a limited corporation? Do they sell shares?"

"I don't believe so. I couldn't find the name in the books at Company House." Moriarty shrugged. "A group of gentlemen acting privately can call themselves whatever they like. They use a solicitor as a convenience address."

Tidwell shook his head. "Glad I'm not one of these insurance agents. They've had their pockets picked, right and proper!"

"How would you manage it, Mr. Tidwell? Those painted sets are huge. Assuming you could get them out of the theater without alarming your crew, where could you hide them?"

"Getting them out isn't necessarily such a great trick. They go out now and then, you know, to be touched up or cleaned. Most of the painting is done in a studio nowadays. They take it off the frame and roll up the canvas. The frames are only wood — cheap enough to replace. The ones with the fancy three-dimensional effects are trickier, but you could take them out when the house is closed, like at the end of a run. It's not an accident that two of these fires happened in the early summer. We send a successful pantomime out to the provinces around May or June, the whole works: lock, stock, and barrel."

"Could you store things in a goods van or railway wagon?"

"Not for long, I shouldn't think. But they'd fit in a barn. If we can trace this syndicate, I'll wager we'll find a nice big warehouse down in the Limehouse district."

"I won't take that bet," Moriarty said. He wasn't prepared to utter Charles Cudlow's name out loud — if he was wrong, that would constitute a vile slander — but he strongly suspected him of being the head of the House of Theatrical Investments and the creative mind behind the whole elaborate system of frauds. No doubt he sought out insurance men keen to impress a member of the aristocracy, and thus easy to deceive. "The Galaxy's considerably larger than the other four theaters on our list. I suppose he — or rather, they — overstretched themselves here."

"They didn't reckon on you, did they, Professor? Mr. Hatcliff had an ace up his sleeve."

A poor advantage since he'd been unable to save the man. Moriarty would pursue Cudlow to the very gates of hell for that. "If we found that warehouse and gained entry to it, how could we prove a given canvas came from our stock?"

"Well, the first thing we'd do is scout out the purchase record. I make a note of every item ever bought for the Galaxy, from paper tickets to paste for costumes. We tend to work with the same suppliers, like Hobson and Sons in Croydon. They'll have their records too. Then there's the man who did the actual painting. Find the painter, show him the canvas. He'll say, yes, that's mine, and I sold it to the Galaxy in May of '85. That'd be proof enough for anyone."

"I should think so." Moriarty tapped his pencil on his short page of notes, wondering how to proceed. It would take a lot of footwork, snooping about the byways of Limehouse, an unfamiliar district with a dangerous reputation. "I'm not sure what my next step should be, assuming we really have uncovered a conspiracy to commit fraud and not just a provocative coincidence."

"Four fires at theaters owned by the same outfit in one year is too much of a coincidence for me, Professor. Apart from the fraud, fires are dangerous. They can never be certain those buildings are completely empty. They risk setting the buildings on either side ablaze too."

"That's true," Moriarty said. "If they're responsible for the accidents at the Galaxy, they've shown a shocking degree of recklessness. A man has died. One of the conspirators, we believe, but even so. And Mr. Hatcliff was deliberately —" He stopped himself from uttering the word "murdered."

Tears shimmered in Tidwell's eyes. "Will he be coming back soon, do you think?"

"I doubt it." Moriarty hated lying to this loyal young man. "The doctor says it could be any day now."

Tidwell nodded. "He looked so broken when we put him into that coach. If it has to be soon, I hope it isn't Christmas Day. That would be too sad. Tonight would be best, wouldn't it?"

"How so?"

"Well, we tell ghost stories on Christmas Eve, don't we? Gathered round the fire with our wassail cups. He'd have company, wouldn't he? Other ghosts to walk him home."

* * *

Moriarty left Tidwell to clarify their notes, adding references to the relevant articles. He hated newspaper clippings; they made the rest of the paper impossible to fold. He thought about popping up to Angelina's dressing room to invite her out for lunch but remembered she was being gracious today, entertaining her understudy.

He might as well go home, or rather, to his club for a few hours of quiet reading. Angelina had warned him not to arrive at Bellenden Crescent before five o'clock that evening, to give the servants a chance to decorate. They were united in a desire to produce all the traditional trimmings since this would be their first Christmas together as a household.

But first he wanted to warn Sebastian about Frank Sparrow and apprise him of the new working theory. After making a circuit backstage, he went up to the stage manager's office on the first floor of the men's side. Moriarty knocked and heard a voice within call, "Hold on!" A long moment later, the door opened a crack to reveal a sliver of Sebastian's face. "James! Ha! Come in!" He stood back to open the door just enough to admit the visitor, then closed it again.

The office was the same size as Angelina's dressing room, with long curtains on one wall implying a window. This room had neither dressing table nor mirror, although it did boast a small bed and an upholstered chair. The dominant piece of furniture was a battered desk with an armchair on casters and a huge bookcase looming behind it, both barely visible under a maelstrom of open books, unrolled plans and sketches, stray articles of clothing, pieces of props, and a veritable rat's nest of pillows and blankets screwed up on the bed.

"Great Scott, Sebastian! This place looks like a rubbish tip. Do you live this way at home?"

The once dapper young man flapped a hand at the mess. "Don't be silly. I have a valet and a weekly char. Hermes is off on his annual holiday and the char is . . . wherever chars go."

The airy disregard for the woman who cleaned his home reassured Moriarty that his brother-in-law hadn't suffered any fundamental change of character. Although judging by the fusty aroma, he could definitely use a bath. "How long have you been living in here?"

"Since my third day. I have so much to learn, and then with the pranks and the normal run of accidents, I'm happier being on the spot around the clock." Sebastian ran a hand through the bird's nest on his head. "Don't tell Lina."

Moriarty shook his head. "Mum's the word." He'd been a graduate student for many long years. Sometimes a man simply needed to focus his attention on his work.

Sebastian looked vaguely around the chaos. "There should be a chair in here somewhere . . ."

"No need. I won't be long. But don't you meet your staff in here?"

"I don't let anyone in here." He smiled grimly. "The day I took possession, a bookcase fell on me."

"What?"

"I dodged it easily enough. It's my job to be light on my feet. But it had been rigged to fall forward at the least touch. As long as we don't know who's involved in these deadly pranks, I mean to be wary. That doesn't apply to you, of course."

"Or your sister, I presume, though she'd be horrified by this squalor."

Sebastian laughed. "Never happen, old chum. She's the star; I go to her. She's gracious about it, from long practice, but make no mistake. She'll insist on every scrap of privilege." He shrugged. "She'll earn it. She works her tail off and makes the audience love her."

Moriarty nodded. He pointed at a Davy lamp hanging from a hook beside the door — his birthday gift from last January. The devices were lit by striking a spark inside the enclosing glass, obviating the need for matches and making them safe even under conditions of leaking gas. "I have one in my office as well."

"I wouldn't mind having a couple more. One by the stage door and one at the prompt corner at least. There's nothing darker than a theater with the lights off."

"They'll turn them all off tonight, I suppose."

"Not all. We always leave at least one light on over the stage — to let the ghosts know we're coming back." Sebastian grinned. "It may sound funny, but I can't wait for this pesky holiday to be over and done with. I've never been so eager for an opening night in my life."

"I'm looking forward to it myself. But speaking of ghosts, I believe I can put a name to ours at last. That's the main reason I came up here. I wanted to warn you to be especially wary of Frank Sparrow."

Sebastian's jaw dropped at the name. "Sparrow! How?"

Moriarty related Angelina's discovery of the relationship between Sparrow and Nora Verney and their mother's early career as a spiritualist. While he spoke, Sebastian nodded, as if putting things together in his mind.

"This explains a number of things, doesn't it? For one, I run into him all over the place. My job naturally takes me into every corner, but his doesn't. He claims to be restless and out stretching his legs, which is plausible enough, especially in this weather. But I don't see anyone else doing it. And the man enjoys playing tricks on people. Switching choristers' hats, for instance, so two men try to put on the wrong size and have to sort it out. It's funny in a small way, but it wastes that little bit of time and makes the victims that little bit unhappy."

"Angelina says all clowns have a cruel streak."

Sebastian nodded. "Usually they turn it on themselves. But Sparrow enjoys getting a laugh at someone else's expense. Hanging the cow's head from the top of the beanstalk is right up his alley, but sawing the rungs nearly in half is another kettle of fish, isn't it?"

"To say nothing of cutting the gondola rope," Moriarty said. "I'm not certain we'll ever find direct evidence against him for that, but we might be able to apply pressure on his co-conspirators."

That happy thought had just occurred to him. He explained his new theory of motive: a syndicate organized to commit insurance fraud. He listed the theaters they knew about so far with the total claims of over twenty thousand pounds. "Mr. Tidwell had several good suggestions for collecting proofs."

"You know, I'll bet I can add to them. I didn't know what to make of this before, but now . . ." Sebastian scrabbled through the mess on his desk and unearthed a large book, like the prompt book he carried everywhere. "I've been studying the books from past productions, getting a sense of how things work here. I'm considering giving those Shakespeare burlesques another try, for instance. With me in the lead and Lina as the lady. I think the *Travestie of MacBreath* — but that's beside the point. Let's see . . ." He opened the book on his desk and flipped through the pages. "Fowler made notes here and there about touching up the paintings on 'the Brunswick flats.' I thought that was the painter's name, but now I'll bet he meant scenery taken from the Royal Brunswick before the fire."

Moriarty got up to peer over Sebastian's shoulder at a verso page densely annotated in a neat script. "This suggests Fowler was in on the scheme from the start. He didn't get the idea from Miss Verney. She probably got it from him, catching him in the act somehow."

"Sparrow caught him, I'll bet, roaming around plotting some prank." Sebastian scratched at his scruffy beard. "Fowler had to be in on it. You can't bring scenery into a theater without the stage manager's knowledge."

"Or the scenery chief," Moriarty said, "and at least a couple of men on that crew, I should think."

"Mr. Gibbs. I wondered why he's always so cantankerous." Sebastian drummed his fingers on his desk, frowning. Then he shook himself. "Too late to do anything about him now, but he'll have to be replaced."

"We haven't any proof yet, remember." Moriarty frowned in turn. How soon could they rid themselves of these dubious employees? "What turned Fowler into a thief, I wonder? He'd been here for years before the trouble started."

"He played the ponies," Sebastian said. "I found a drawer full of clippings about jockeys and racing stables. Now there's a money sink if there ever was one. I picked pockets at the track when I was a kid, but never had the urge to place a bet."

"I've built my fortune on that urge, I'm sorry to say." Moriarty grinned ruefully.

"Your sheep come to you with shears in their hands, begging to be fleeced. And your skill at the card table will benefit a great many people this Christmas." Sebastian closed the prompt book and placed both hands on top of it, a speculative gleam in his eyes. "Gibbs has an able assistant, but Frank Sparrow is another matter altogether. He and Tweedy work as a team, you know, and they're a major draw. We can't easily replace him."

"If he's the one who cut the rope on that gondola, then he's an appallingly ruthless man. Far too dangerous to leave at large in a place as crowded and filled with hazards as this theater."

"No, you're right. Of course you're right." Sebastian flung himself into his chair. "But it will take you a good while to collect your evidence, won't it? We'll have time to get the show off the ground."

Moriarty bit back a chiding remark. He knew better than to expect the Archers to share the depth of his moral outrage on any score. Besides, it wouldn't do to put the syndicate on their guard before he had something concrete to show the insurance companies. "Just be careful, I beg you."

"I'm always careful."

"And feel free to drop by the house anytime you like. I've a first-rate bathtub that no one uses but me." Moriarty gave his rather ripe brother-in-law a meaningful look.

Sebastian chuckled. "Point taken. But Vi's closer, and she has everything I need. Hugh's hosting some sort of do tonight."

"We'll see you at dinner tomorrow, then." Moriarty made his way out of the theater. His earlier elation at putting the pieces of this complicated puzzle together had faded, replaced by a grudging admission that Cudlow and his co-conspirators had gotten the best of him — so far.

He could hire private investigators to scour the alleys of Limehouse and Canary Wharf in search of those missing properties, but that could take weeks — or even months. Moriarty wished he could come up with a swifter, more certain form of justice. But what?

TWENTY-TWO

Sebastian had no intention of leaving the Galaxy for even a minute; not tonight and not tomorrow either. He'd slip out and clean up on Monday when the crews came back to get ready for opening night. He'd miss Christmas dinner at Lord Brockaway's, but Viola would understand and she'd keep everyone else out of his hair.

He'd intended to go, right up to the moment James had made the connection between theater fires and insurance fraud. He'd been looking forward to getting out of this building for a little while and taking a long, hot bath at Wilton House. But since Christmas fell on a Saturday this year, Boxing Day had to be shoved back to Monday so as not to fall on a Sunday. He'd never quite understood the system, but there it was.

The important point was that counting Christmas Eve — tonight — it added up to three nights and two days of holiday. Plenty of time to steal properties from a theater on Leicester Square. The thieves would need a monster van, big enough to block traffic and attract attention during a normal week. If Cudlow's syndicate wanted to shut down *Beanstalk*, this weekend was their last chance.

First things first. Sebastian wrote up a list of supplies and sent a boy down to the Bear and Staff to collect them. No reason to starve during his vigil. Then he spent the afternoon re-reading Fowler's prompt books, marking every page that might pertain to the frauds. He had to admire the syndicate's cleverness, whoever they were. Theaters caught fire all the time from natural causes, and unless the insurance company made them its specialty, the agents wouldn't know how to evaluate the claims.

Sebastian opened one of the bottles of beer in his box of goodies and raised it toward the bust of Shakespeare stuck on top of a cabinet. "And now half those unburnt properties are right here in my theater, where you'll never get them back. You may be clever, Mr. Syndicate, but my brother-in-law is cleverer by half."

At five o'clock, he went out to help the Sampson clan — father, son, and two brothers who pitched in when extra security was required — walk through the whole theater to make sure everyone was out. Sebastian used his master key to open every dressing room door. Some of them were as messy as his office and a few of them smelled even worse, making him wonder if he oughtn't to institute some sort of hygiene regulations. James wanted to electrify the building. Maybe they could replace some of the miles of gas pipes with water pipes and install a WC and a sink on every floor.

A massive undertaking. Sebastian shook his head as he locked Lina's door, the last one on his tour. He had to respect the ruthless logic in burning up the whole interior, getting the money from some poor sod of an insurance agent, and rebuilding to modern standards. Move your props back in and start selling tickets again.

But there was no logic in sending Lionel Hatcliff crashing to the stage. Nor could it be excused as an accident gone wrong. Someone had cut that rope on that day on purpose.

He told Old Sampson he had one last thing to do and then he would lock the stage door himself. He waved them out with a "Merry Christmas," made sure the door was locked, and walked to stand at center stage under the single light left burning.

Its yellow glow barely reached the stalls and the gilt fretwork around the boxes. The stage was set for the first scene on Monday night, with Jack's hovel on the left and the village on the right. The magnificent painted scene of farmland dotted with trees seemed real under the soft light. This was all the countryside Sebastian had ever needed.

Facing the cavernous darkness, he spoke to the empty galleries. "It's just you and me now, Spirits. I'm counting on you to help me guard."

He went to sit on the edge of the stage where he could stare into the blackness and revel in the sensation of being utterly alone in his private kingdom. And of successfully evading all the people who wanted him to be somewhere else. He'd told Viola he planned to spend the evening dropping in and out of parties, ending up in his own flat for a few hours of sleep. He'd told James and Lina he was spending the evening with Hugh. But Hugh had galloped off to Hampshire to pay court to the daughter of a reasonably well-off baron. As they weren't going to Greece, he'd jolly well better get busy and find that wife his father kept nagging him about.

Sebastian wasn't jealous — much. He prided himself on his ability to look reality square in the eye. Let Hugh have his baroness. Sebastian had finally won his first and only true love: a theater to call his own. He might marry Belinda Delaney and establish another great actor-manager partnership, like Squire Bancroft and Marie Wilton. He'd had a short fling with one of her brothers back before he met Hugh. He didn't know if Belinda knew about that, but doubted she would turn a hair at the idea. They could work out a very companionable arrangement if they put their minds to it.

Hugh had been miffed when Sebastian took this job, calling it a whim, even though they'd had many arguments about how bored he was playing the wise-cracking chum and the featherbrained husband. He wanted something bigger, but not Shakespeare or an American tour. His singing voice was good enough for musical comedy, but he hadn't Lina's vocal power, and he didn't much like opera anyway. Furthermore, he was a Londoner born and bred and never wanted to live anywhere else.

Managing the Galaxy was a dream come true. He'd be twice damned if he'd let some faceless syndicate snatch it away before he'd fairly gotten started. He could keep up with Frank Sparrow too, now that he knew who to watch.

He got to his feet and went to the prompt corner where he'd stashed his Davy lamp. Lighting it, he made another tour to check every entrance, starting with the loading bay behind the stage. The thieves would have to use these doors to carry out the properties. Some of the scene paintings were thirty feet tall; even removed from their frames and rolled up, it would take several men to carry one. Gibbs would pretty well have to bring in a crew, three or four men at the least, not counting the driver.

He followed the beam of his lamp up the aisle along the darkened stalls and through the swinging doors to the lobby. He toured the front of the house, pausing to appreciate the pale yellow rectangles cast by street lamps on the square shining through the glass front doors. The rain had started up again. Last-minute shoppers scurried down the pavement with their shoulders hunched and their hats pulled low, ignored by the loaded cabs clopping past. It'd be best for the show if it rained all weekend, clearing up on Boxing Day. Everyone would be absolutely panting to get out of the house.

He pulled out his pocket watch — nearly six o'clock. The shops would be closing soon, and then the shopkeepers would go home too. In a few hours, partygoers would be out and about in cabs and coaches, mostly in the more fashionable districts. Leicester Square, normally alive with theatergoers on a Friday night, would be nearly deserted. Even the lightskirts would find somewhere warmer to ply their trade.

Nothing would happen until midnight at the earliest. He might as well go up to his office and have a little supper. He had cold duck and an assortment of side dishes, not to mention a lovely toffee cake for pudding. But as he entered the stalls again, he thought he saw a glimmer beneath the stage, behind the orchestra pit.

He shuttered his lamp. The light above the stage was enough to get into the wings, and the railing would guide him downstairs to the cellar. He reached the bottom in pitch darkness. He must have imagined the winking light. Then he heard the gurgle of the water closet and knew he had company. He set the lamp at the foot of the stairs where he could find it again and took a few silent steps in the direction of the WC.

"Let it be Frank Sparrow," he whispered soundlessly, crossing his fingers. He had the advantage of surprise, not to mention being younger and faster. He owed the man a punch in the beak at least. He'd be funnier with a bandaged nose anyway.

The door opened on a sliver of light. Sebastian held his breath and moved closer, keeping the door between him and his target until it opened enough for a figure to emerge. Then he leapt, crying, "Gotcher!" grappling the figure around the middle — or what he'd thought would be the middle of a taller than average man.

He caught an armful of hair while his ears rang with a high-pitched scream. The candle dropped to the floor and went out. Small arms batted at him furiously as he struggled to regain his balance.

"Who the bloody hell —"

"Let go of me!" a shrill voice demanded.

"Noisette?" Sebastian managed to catch one of the flailing arms. "It's me — Sebastian. Calm down. Stop hitting me!"

"Mr. Archer?" Her other hand found his and traveled up to his shoulder, patting as if she could recognize him by his clothes. Maybe she could. "What are you doing here?"

"I should ask you that." He took her hand and led her back to the stairs with short, shuffling steps. His toes struck a riser and he let her go to pick up his lamp. He opened the cover a slit, aiming it to one side so as not to blind either of them. "Come on, let's go up to my office." Whatever she was doing here tonight, he wasn't afraid of her.

She made him wait while she collected her candle and holder, then pattered up the stairs behind him in silence, holding the lamp while he dug his keys out of his pocket and unlocked the door. She made a sour face as he invited her inside. "My workshop is much cleaner."

"This'll do." He bade her keep the lamp while he lit another since they'd turned off the gas in the dressing rooms. Then he unearthed a chair, tossing the armload of whatnot onto the bed. He hung the Davy lamp on its hook by the door and waved to her to sit down. "Beer or sherry?"

"Sherry, if the glass is clean."

"Clean as a whistle. They sent two of everything." He served drinks and fixed plates of cheese and crackers, doling out olives and pickled gherkins. Then he plopped down behind his desk and put his feet up on an overturned wastebasket. "First, tell me how you managed to escape me and the Sampson clan. I thought we were pretty thorough."

"I hid beneath my worktable," she said in her raspy, childlike voice. "I keep a trundle bed concealed behind lengths of cloth. It's very cozy."

"No doubt." He studied the little woman, perched among the flotsam of this crowded room like another prop in need of repair. His intuitions, honed over a lifetime of confidence tricks, told him she could be trusted. But he'd been wrong once or twice. She might have stayed behind to open those bay doors at the appointed hour. "Second question: Why are you here? Don't you spend Christmas with your family, like everyone else?"

"Not if I can help it. I live with my sister. My brother-in-law comes home for the holidays, and he's very unpleasant when he's been drinking."

"Sorry to hear that." Poor wretch. She'd probably spent her whole life on the fringes of someone else's, never quite belonging. "Couldn't you spend the weekend with Nora Verney? I understand you were her dresser for many years." Peg would be in the thick of it at Lina's house tonight, telling tall tales of the old days, no doubt, and getting tipsy on mulled wine.

"You should be at a party," Noisette countered. "A glittering gala with a glittering actress on each arm."

Sebastian grinned. "I could do without the actresses, but you're right. I ought to be at my sister Viola's soirée at Wilton House in Mayfair."

"Your twin. You used to dance together. I saw you do "Deck the Halls" one year. You were very pretty." She spoke that last word almost like a term of scorn.

"She'll understand. My place is here. But surely Adorable Nora's having a dazzling do tonight. More fun than a dark theater, I should imagine."

Noisette leveled her black eyes at him over the rim of her glass, as if weighing him on some inner scale. He waited. Finally, she drew a long breath through her narrow nose and said, "Miss Verney has betrayed me."

"How so?" he asked softly. Willing to listen, but not prying; that was the right note.

"She left the Galaxy. She left *me.* And everything changed."

"Things had changed before she left though, hadn't they?" He gave her a sympathetic nod. "I think you knew. About the thefts, I mean."

Another long silence. Sebastian liked the way she simply held her peace rather than filling the void with distracting chatter. He placed cheese on a cracker and popped it into his mouth. Being comfortable with such silences was one of his gifts. People would tell you everything, if you waited for it.

Noisette sipped her sherry, licked her lips, and said, "That odious Mr. Fowler took whatever he liked. But after the first time, I wouldn't let him have any of my costumes."

"You're an honest woman, Madame Noisette. I suspected as much."

"I'm a loyal woman, Mr. Archer. Those are two very different things."

Sebastian chuckled. "Honest enough not to claim an undeserved title. But you're right, they are different." He cocked his head. "Who are you loyal to now that Miss Verney has lost your allegiance?"

"Not you." Was that a smile? "I'll be loyal to the Galaxy for as long as I have my job."

"Good answer." He pointed his beer bottle at her. "You'll have that job for as long as I'm here, I can promise you that much."

He'd expected another shadow of a smile, but her expression sobered again. She ate a cracker in tiny nibbles, taking her time about it. Then she said in an ominous tone, "You must leave, Mr. Archer. Leave now. Do not stay in this theater tonight."

She knew. Nora had probably blabbed the whole scheme to her old dresser, unable to conceive of her as a real person with a mind of her own. "What time are they coming?"

"You know."

"I do. James is cleverer than your Mr. Gibbs."

"Not *mine.*" Her mouth twisted in a bitter grimace. Then she blinked. "Who's James?"

"Professor Moriarty. Mr. Hatcliff's new partner."

"I thought his name was Mr. Lovington."

Sebastian laughed. "Please don't call him that. He understands, but he doesn't like it. Hatcliff hired him to stop the accidents. We've known someone was trying to stop *Beanstalk* from opening. Now we know who it is."

"That odious Frank Sparrow."

"So you knew that too. He tried to implicate you, you know."

"He stole my scissors. I didn't know why." She gave him another measuring look. "You didn't suspect me?"

"James thought it too obvious. He thinks you're too intelligent to leave an expensive pair of dressmaker's shears lying under the cut rope."

This time she smiled, eyes included. "Thank him for me."

"Thank him yourself, on opening night. What time are they coming?"

"One o'clock."

Sebastian pulled out his watch: half past six. "Good. We have time for supper." He bounced up to clear a space on the desktop and began laying out the feast: cold roast duck, ham salad, deviled eggs, preserved fruits, and all sorts of lovely pickled things. Noisette rose to help him unwrap the treats. He poured small glasses of wine and heaped their plates with food.

Once they had taken the edge off their hunger, he said, "I've been wanting to talk to you about those two burlesques, *The Travestie of MacBreath* and *Queer Old King Leer*. I'm thinking of trying again this spring with me and Lina in the leads. You'll find she's much funnier than Nora."

"A rocking chair would be funnier than Nora."

That startled a laugh from him. "Agreed. But your costumes are too good to waste. Most people don't recognize what a difficult art a good burlesque is. Yet you found that perfect, delicate balance between homage and satire."

"Those, Mr. Archer, are two very different things."

* * *

Sebastian had seldom enjoyed such stimulating conversation about theatrical productions in his life. Noisette was a veritable fountain of insights, which didn't surprise him so much when he thought about it. She was as used to being ignored as he was to being watched. Oddly, those opposite circumstances had trained them to the same habitual state of skeptical observation.

They enjoyed a merry feast, though the duck was too dry and they couldn't drink much, needing to stay alert. They decided to go downstairs well before the appointed hour to wait in Jack's hovel, where they could hear both the stage door and the bay doors at the back. The thieves would not attempt to enter through the front. Even in the wee hours of Christmas morning, an occasional constable would cross the square on his rounds.

Sebastian brought the prompt book so they could continue their debate about the second act. He refilled the Davy lamp and handed it to Noisette, extinguishing the other lights and locking the door behind them. They moved silently down the stairs and through the wings, respectful of the hush inside the vacant theater.

They climbed under the papier-mâché table jutting out from the angled wall of Jack's cottage. Noisette sat cross-legged, her black skirts forming a pool around her straight figure. Sebastian sprawled on his stomach and opened the book, setting his watch beside it to keep an eye on the time. They spoke in near-whispers.

"Mr. Gibbs must have a key to the stage door," Sebastian said. "Otherwise, how will he get the bay doors open? They're padlocked on the inside."

"Someone is here with us already," Noisette said.

"Not possible," he said, though her words gave him the shivers. "We looked everywhere. I checked every dressing room myself."

"What about the storage lockers behind the fly galleries?"

"The Sampsons did the fly tower," Sebastian answered, realizing with dread that a group of men might be playing cards in the rope locker at this very moment. He sighed. Nothing they could do about it now.

"What will we do, Mr. Archer? We can't stop them by ourselves."

"My plan was to slip out the front as soon as they entered the back and run for help. Although I didn't fully believe they were coming before I caught you. Now I think I should stay and watch while you go for help. I can see what they take and who's with them. Or perhaps it would be safer —"

"I'll go. I'll blow my police whistle on the square." She pulled a bright silver whistle on a silver chain out of her bodice.

"Madame Noisette! You continue to amaze me." Sebastian grinned at her. "You'll need a key to get out the front." He rolled over and fished a large chain from his trouser pocket, then rolled back to thumb through them to find the right one. He unhooked it and handed it to her with a soft chuckle. "I went about for a whole year with nothing in my pockets, not even a card case. Everyone who mattered knew who I was, and someone was always willing to give me a fag or buy me a drink or whatever it was I wanted. Funny how things change, eh?"

She didn't answer. Things had never been funny in that way for her.

"Can you get through the hall in the dark?" he asked.

She gave him a weary look. "It's never dark in the lobby. The lamps are always lit on Leicester Square."

"That's us with a plan, then. Good." They still had half an hour to wait. Sebastian turned back to the book. "The thing that worries me most is how to replace Mr. Sparrow."

"He isn't a nice man. If he thought you suspected him . . ." She shook her head.

"But he's so funny. We need him."

"No, we don't. Mr. Tweedy found him. Mr. Tweedy trained him. Mr. Tweedy can train another one. Mr. Tweedy is a genius."

A genius at wooing the right supporters anyway. "I'll take your word for it." Sebastian propped himself up on one elbow to look into her pale face. Her dark eyebrows and false pile of curls seemed even thicker and blacker in the dim light. "He's not the right man for you, Madame. You know that, I think. He's too self-important."

"But you think he's good enough for Peg Barwick."

"Peg can handle him. She's lived with Lina almost all her life, remember. She can hold her own. But you're a more sensitive person. Creative. You can do better."

Her black eyes shone wetly. He'd gone too far, but he meant every word. He'd put Lina onto finding a suitable man for Noisette when things settled down. She'd relish the challenge to her matchmaking skills. One of the fly crew, perhaps. They tended to be on the short side. Someone who could appreciate a craftswoman of

Noisette's caliber. They'd hold a cast party onstage sometime soon and Lina could —

"Shhhh!" Noisette hissed, her slight frame going rigid.

He heard the slap of feet coming down the stairs by the stage door. One man, not trying to be quiet. That meant he didn't know they were in the building. Keys jangled as the feet passed behind the canvas flat that sheltered them from view.

A voice high overhead called, "Hoist her up!"

Sebastian got to his hands and knees and poked his head cautiously out from under the table. He saw men on the bridge, hauling up the black canvas backdrop. Raising it would give them more room to maneuver and more light from the lamp above center.

Mr. Gibbs, the scenery chief, strode over to the bay doors and unlocked the padlock, hooking it on the staple before swinging the great doors wide to reveal the back of an enormous goods van wedged into the alleyway. Cold air rushed into the theater.

Sebastian wished he'd thought to put his jacket on over his knitted waistcoat. Too late now. "You'll be cold out there," he whispered to Noisette.

"I'll run very fast."

Sebastian crawled to the other side of the cottage and peered into the wings. Empty. The thieves were focused on lowering scenery flats from the tower. He twisted around and whispered, "Go!"

Noisette gathered her skirts into a ball and scuttled out from under the table and down into the stalls. Sebastian watched her small form glide up the aisle toward the lobby doors. Then a muffled grunt caught his ear. His head whipped toward the edge of the wings, where Frank Sparrow stood with a sequined gown over one arm, staring after her.

Had he heard her going down the wooden steps? Or did the man have some preternatural sense of other presences in his haunting ground?

Sparrow walked toward the apron, his long legs making short work of the distance. Noisette would have to feel her way through the inky black of the foyer before gaining the faint light from the street in the front lobby. It wouldn't be easy to fit a key into the lock under that weak illumination. Sparrow would catch her, easily, and wouldn't hesitate to hurt her.

"Hey!" Sebastian jumped up, moving upstage, away from the stalls. He clutched the prompt book to his chest to keep Sparrow from stealing it just to hinder him.

"Archer!" Sparrow wheeled around and strode back to the stage. "Why are you so confounded hard to get rid of?"

Sebastian decided to play the fool to buy time for Noisette to escape. "What luck finding you here, Sparrow! I have a question about some of your lines in Act Three. I don't think it's plausible for the Giant's wife —"

Sparrow drew a pistol from his pocket and shot him. The bullet hit him square in the chest, punching into the prompt book and knocking him backward off his feet. The gun boomed again and Sebastian screamed as hot lead tore through his leg.

He must have fainted because he felt his mind swimming back to consciousness. Sparrow seemed to be gone. No more bullets anyway. Someone off away behind him shouted, "Leave that there, ya bleedin' idiot! Let's get out the hell out of here!"

Did they mean the scenery? He must be the bleeding idiot. He seemed to be bleeding and he certainly had been an idiot. Sebastian sprawled, helpless, on the wooden boards of his stage, staring up at the one lonely light as the blood trickling from his leg grew cold beneath him.

TWENTY-THREE

Angelina slept as late as she could on Boxing Day. Easier said than done, given James's propensity to whistle while he dressed and the mouse maids creeping in every half hour to see if she was ready for her tea. But they'd been awakened in the wee hours on Christmas morning with such harrowing news she hadn't gotten a wink of sleep afterward and not much more on Sunday either.

Christmas Eve had been lovely. They sang carols and told stories around the fire, drinking many cups of Antoine's mulled wine, the mere perfume of which made you tipsy. She and James set aside their week of troubles and exchanged their presents in bed, along with deeper expressions of conjugal attachment. They'd fallen asleep in each other's arms.

Then at three o'clock, their dreams of sugar plums had been shattered by a violent pounding on the door. One of Lord Brockaway's footmen insisted they come with him at once, claiming Sebastian had been shot at the Galaxy while foiling a gang of thieves. Madness!

They rushed upstairs to throw on some clothes and clambered with Peg into the waiting coach. By the time they reached the Mayfair mansion, the doctor had come and gone. He'd bound up Sebastian's wound and given him a hefty dose of morphine. The bullet was preserved in a jar of alcohol. It had missed the femoral artery, thank God, though Sebastian had lost a fair amount of blood. Another bullet had been stopped half an inch from his heart by that ridiculous, wonderfully thick prompt book.

Boundless thanks were due to that quick-thinking, unflappable wardrobe mistress. She told them the whole story when the worst was past and Viola gathered everyone into Brockaway's library, making sure they each had a good stiff drink.

Noisette had dashed out of the Galaxy into the cold night and planted herself in the middle of Leicester Square, where she blew on her police whistle until three constables turned up. She led them back to the theater, where they apprehended the scenery chief and the van driver. The rest of the thieves had scarpered. They found Sebastian bleeding in the center of the stage. No one knew who had shot him. Everyone assumed it was Mr. Gibbs, however stoutly he denied it.

Noisette made one of the constables convey her to Wilton House in Mayfair, where she gained entrance to the exclusive party by sheer force of personality. Viola took over from there, but Noisette had earned the eternal gratitude of the entire extended Archer clan. A footman escorted her back to the theater to collect a few belongings, then Brockaway's housekeeper installed her in the second-best guest room. Sebastian had the best one, naturally.

Lord Brockaway summoned the Metropolitan Police while James rousted out the Sampson men, sending them to guard the theater in shifts until Monday at triple pay.

They finally got home as dawn was breaking, a little after eight o'clock, to find Mr. Lind waiting in the drawing room with a cold cup of tea on the table beside him. Lionel Hatcliff had slipped away during the night. Sad news, if not unexpected, but the reminder of their uncertain financial state drew the worry lines back across James's forehead.

Sebastian and Noisette had foiled the scenery thieves. Mr. Gibbs was in jail, never to leave that place as a free man. Nothing had been lost, and the stage was still set for tonight's performance. *Jack and the Beanstalk* would open on time.

* * *

"That's the last word." Angelina handed a square envelope to Rolly, addressed to Sebastian at Wilton House in Mayfair. "No more letters today, I promise."

"'Oo won the battle?" the boy asked.

"The professor, of course. By an unfair application of reason."

She and Sebastian had been arguing by means of the Royal Mail since she found his first salvo on her breakfast tray. He felt fine, he claimed, and meant to go to the Galaxy at four o'clock as he would have done had he not been nearly murdered there on Friday night. She had dashed off her first response before even getting out of bed, forbidding him in the strongest terms from doing anything of the sort. The doctor had prescribed rest, and rest he would.

Once she'd gotten up and wrapped herself in her quilted dressing gown, she'd transferred her battle station to the dining room, where Peg had joined the fray, vigorously supporting the "Rest In Bed" platform. Viola contributed her usual sardonic remarks, pointing out that they had plenty of morphine and could send two footmen to prop Sebastian up. He usually crumbled under the force of his twin's sarcasm, but this time he held his ground.

The battle raged through three rounds of postal deliveries until James happened to notice the most recent volley on the tray. "Has Sebastian taken a turn for the worse?"

Angelina reassured him that, on the contrary, her fool of a baby brother was insisting on going to work. James failed to leap to her support. He observed in a neutral tone that he'd been told by all and sundry, repeatedly and without caveat, that the production of a Christmas pantomime was a vast and complex undertaking. He delivered the decisive blow by asking one simple question: "Who would take his place?"

No one. Sebastian, the great supporter of understudies, had trained no one else to do his job. Worse, he said he had the prompt book in bed beside him and vowed never to surrender it.

She gave up. James hammered in the final nail by noting that without Sebastian to ensure the show's success, Frank Sparrow would win, even if he hadn't managed to murder his intended victim.

That was the other exciting piece of news. When Sebastian had finally awoken from his healing slumber, he told them Frank Sparrow was the one who shot him. Lord Brockaway summoned the police again to put out a warrant for the man's immediate arrest. No one knew where he was, but once they found him, he would go to jail and stay there until the day he hanged.

Peg had been dispatched to Mr. Tweedy's lodgings to tell him the whole sordid story and ask him to prepare to work with a novice that night. More letters had flown between Mayfair and South Kensington while Angelina and Sebastian bickered over the schedule of *entr'actes*. They had to replace both Sparrow and Sebastian, who had planned to do a couple of song-and-dance numbers himself. Angelina gallantly offered to fill in a few of the empty spots, but Sebastian had flatly refused her, insisting she get as much rest as she could between scenes.

That was rich, considering the source.

Now she lounged on the sofa in the drawing room, wondering if she should take James's advice and spend half an hour dozing in his bathtub. It was only three o'clock. The curtain rose at six. She planned to arrive in her dressing room at about twenty past five. It wouldn't do to set a bad precedent by getting there early.

She yawned, stretching out one leg and winning an admiring glance from James. She decided not to risk a bath on this day of days, but had the maids bring hot water up to her room, where she freshened up and changed into something a bit more suitable for the middle of the afternoon.

She was pinning up her hair in a loose chignon when Dolly knocked and entered. "There's a visitor, Missus. A *man*. He's in the drawing room with the professor!" The silly girl whisked herself away, pattering upstairs to hide in her room without mentioning the visitor's name. It wasn't always quite the thing to have maids who were terrified of strangers.

Angelina descended to find James standing by the windows in the front drawing room with a sheet of paper in one hand, running the other over his bald pate in the way that told her he'd just received some sort of shock. Before him stood a well-dressed man of middle years, balder than James, with a thin blond moustache. He had his thumbs tucked into his waistcoat pockets and smiled with an air of personal satisfaction. The room rang with an unspoken tension that raised the hairs on the back of her neck.

"What's happened?" she cried, flying in to grasp James by the arm. "Has someone else been hurt?"

"No, no. Nothing of the kind. It's good news." He patted her hand and nodded toward the visitor. "This is Mr. Bartleby, Lionel Hatcliff's solicitor. He's been visiting his wife's family in Manchester and only got back last night. He's brought my partnership agreement, duly stamped and registered, giving me full legal rights to manage the theater business."

He handed her the paper with a slight tremble, betraying the depth of his relief. No one else would ever appreciate the severity of the strain he'd been under, struggling to keep the money flowing by fair means or foul. She would show her gratitude the minute the solicitor left.

"I'm sorry if I've caused you any inconvenience," Bartleby said. He had a genial manner, but she sensed a shrewd mind underneath. "I found the professor's letters when I unlocked the door to my chambers. We go to Manchester every Christmas. My wife's family lives there, you see. Never occurred to me there'd be urgent matters to deal with at this time of year."

"Inconvenience," Angelina echoed, resisting the urge to box the man's ears. Why couldn't he leave a forwarding address with his clients, for pity's sake? Or send a Christmas card? The Royal Mail penetrated all the way to Manchester, one assumed.

"That's not all, my dear." James set the paper on the table to take both her hands in both of his, grinning broadly. "Remember the day Lionel brought champagne to the office for lunch?"

Angelina nodded. "He never said what we were celebrating."

"Now we know. He had made out a new will, leaving everything to Sebastian. His house, his savings, and his share of the partnership — all. Everything in the Galaxy now belongs to us: the props, the costumes, and all that blasted scenery."

"Oh, James!" She gazed into his warm brown eyes, which glistened with an uncharacteristic sheen. Or perhaps it was an illusion created by her own brimming eyes. Then she startled and dropped James's hands, turning toward the solicitor. "Do excuse me, Mr. Bartleby. It would appear I have another raft of letters to write."

Obviously, she thought as she jogged downstairs to the dining table, James should be regarded as the senior partner, particularly in matters concerning casting and the selection of plays. That should be made clear from the start. And if Sebastian were going to occupy Lionel's house, he ought to consider another sort of strategic alliance. Belinda Delaney must be aware of his preferences by this time — they'd known each other nearly all their lives. She clearly had ambitions of her own. Viola should sound her out . . .

TWENTY-FOUR

"Are you sure you don't want to ride over there with me? I can wait while you finish dressing, if you don't dally." Moriarty perched on the edge of a chair in his bedroom watching his wife pull on her stockings, a daily ritual that never failed to command his attention. He hadn't seen many bare female legs in his life, but he'd wager Angelina's were among the shapeliest.

"It won't do for the star to arrive early, darling, especially with Sebastian playing it all high and mighty."

Moriarty knew better than to follow in that suit. The war between manager and leading lady had scarcely begun. He would stick to the front office, where he belonged, writing cheques and saying, "Hmm, I see your point," when pressed for an opinion.

"You don't need go early either, James. You won't have anything to do but sit at your desk and twiddle your thumbs until curtain time."

"Better to twiddle there than here. I'll confess I'm as anxious as a bridegroom about tonight after all the trouble we've been through."

"Oh, there'll be plenty of bumps ahead, never fear! Someone vital will go missing, costumes won't fit after all those Christmas dinners, and five of the children in the procession will throw up in the wings." Angelina clipped the supporters to the top of her stockings and turned to the mirror to look at her hair. Her gaze shifted toward Moriarty, and she saw something that made her swing full around on her little bench. "You're not worried about the play! You just want to watch money pouring into the box office. Really, James! I never thought you to be so mercenary."

Moriarty rose and collected his hat and gloves. Then he gave his wife a sly smile. "It isn't the *money,* my dear, as you once instructed me. It's the *amount.* I'd be glad to see the balance moving up for a change."

* * *

He had to fight his way through the crowd outside the Galaxy. The line for tickets stretched clear around the corner and dozens of people thronged around the front doors, laughing and chattering, shivering in the evening gloom. The doorman failed to recognize him, so he had to wait while Tidwell was fetched to verify his identity. He would have been more impressed by the security measures if he hadn't seen two urchins slip past the other doorman while he waited.

"We're sold out," Tidwell confided as they walked down the hall. "Standing room only!"

"What about all those people queuing in front?"

"They'll have to settle for another night. Although we're sold out for the whole week." Tidwell laughed happily as he reached to open the office door. "News of the foiled thievery plot has gotten out, and people want a look at the scenery that's worth stealing. We're not in the black yet, Professor, but it's a promising start."

"That's good news indeed."

Tidwell closed the door before going back to his own office. Moriarty shed his hat and coat and sat down at his desk, placing both palms on the surface and gazing at the framed posters on the walls. He must remind Tidwell to add one of *Beanstalk*'s to the collection as soon as possible.

The door opened and he started to say, "Ah, Tidwell," before recognizing the visitor — or rather, the intruder. Charles Cudlow, wearing stylish checked trousers and a fur-lined overcoat, sauntered in with the air of a tourist visiting the local sights.

"How did you get in?" Moriarty demanded.

Cudlow smiled as if in response to a more conventional greeting. "You'd be surprised how many doors can be opened with a five-pound note."

Moriarty sat back in his chair, his palms still flat on the table. "What do you want?"

"Such a chilly welcome! I only wanted to see for myself a man foolhardy or ignorant enough to open a panto without a stage manager."

"Oh, you've come to gloat." Moriarty smiled. "I'm afraid your information is inaccurate. Sebastian was only slightly injured. I've no doubt he's backstage whipping everything into shape even as we speak."

Cudlow's lip curled. "That man has more lives than a cat."

"You'll find we're all fairly tenacious. I'm surprised to see *you,* however. I should think you'd be on your way to Casablanca or some such place by now."

"I'm not going anywhere. You may have some sort of theory—"

"More than a theory, Cudlow. We have Elmer Gibbs in jail, eager to share everything he knows about scenery paintings that amazingly survived a whole series of fires." That was an assumption, but not an implausible one.

Cudlow's expression soured, but he made a game attempt at a defense. "He's delusional, of course. This wild plot you've concocted will be harder to prove than you think, especially now that your ring of nefarious conspirators has been warned."

"You have no idea what I'm capable of." Moriarty spoke with more confidence than he felt. He suffered no illusions about the difficulty of bringing Cudlow's crimes home to him. He'd have to move fast, and he'd have to find help.

"I perceive that your gloating is also premature, Professor. Those golden eggs haven't hatched yet. Opening nights are full of hazards, you know, especially big Christmas pantos. And I fear Frank Sparrow isn't the sort to give up so easily. He really *hates* Sebastian Archer. And now you too. He wants this show to fail; all the more, since he's no longer in it. And you know how much he loves his pranks. How much fun do you think he'll have with a thousand people to enjoy his effects?" Cudlow tipped his silk hat and swept out of the office.

Moriarty bared his teeth at the mute oak door. He would be thrice damned if he'd let that man walk away from his crimes scot-free. The police would apprehend Sparrow soon enough and arrest him for attempted murder. They wouldn't be able to prove Hatcliff's murder against him, but he'd spend the rest of his life in jail. Good enough.

Cudlow, however . . . Moriarty drummed his fingers on the desktop, then jumped up and shrugged on his coat. Fast, reliable help, able to investigate independently, with an expert knowledge of London's seamiest dockside neighborhoods? He knew exactly where to find it.

He clapped on his hat and made a brief stop in Tidwell's office, then shouldered back out to the crowded pavement, jogging across the street to the corner where he'd spotted the peculiar tall woman doggedly feeding pigeons even as night began to fall. The hawk-nosed harridan grinned as he approached. "Here to make a full confession, Moriarty?"

"I've nothing to confess to you, Holmes. I've come to advise you that your client isn't worthy of your services."

"Ah, that middle-class snobbery! You'll want to rid yourself of it if you intend to make your way in the theater world. Broad-minded is the view you want."

The ragged layers of drab skirts and shawls did nothing to mitigate the man's arrogance. Good; Moriarty was counting on it. "I don't have time for banter this evening. The curtain's rising in half an hour." He proceeded to explain Cudlow's scheme to defraud insurance companies while the detective listened with his characteristic intensity of attention. At the end, Moriarty pretended to swallow his pride before adding, "I'm afraid it's too much for me. I simply don't have the manpower — or the expertise, to be honest. And now Cudlow knows I'm on to him . . ."

"The clock is ticking. Yes, I see your problem." Holmes's dark eyes glittered with interest. "The investigation of this kind of fraud requires a talent for deception, not to mention an intimate knowledge of London's warehouse districts."

Moriarty pursed his lips and shook his head. "Angelina thinks we should turn everything over to the Middlesex Fire and Life —"

"Tush, tush!" Holmes chuckled. "The same blind, incompetent fools who let this happen in the first place? No, my good Moriarty, they're not up to it either. This sort of thing requires finesse. And, as you sagaciously noted, time is of the essence. Evidence must be gathered swiftly yet subtly, so as to present the definitive *coup de grâce* before the villain can collect his profits and flee the country."

Moriarty nodded as if absorbing a valuable lesson. "That sounds right up your street, Holmes, now that I think of it."

Holmes regarded him with a level gaze. He knew he was being played and had decided to allow it. "I know you forged that cheque."

"The point is moot now." Moriarty shrugged. "Hatcliff's lawyer finally turned up with all the documents we need, properly executed. Hatcliff left everything to Sebastian Archer."

"That seems fitting." Holmes didn't seem to mind losing that brief contest, if that was what it had been. "But now I know which lines you're willing to cross."

Moriarty shrugged again. "I assume you know Lionel Hatcliff died in his sleep on Christmas Eve. You can lay that death at your client's door as well."

"My client?" Holmes asked with an arched eyebrow. "You mean my quarry." He found the edge of a tattered shawl and flung it over his shoulder in a flamboyant gesture. "The game's afoot, Moriarty. No time to waste gossiping in the square." He began to walk away.

"One last thing, Holmes," Moriarty called. He waited for him to turn back, impatience writ clear across his aquiline features. "Merry Christmas!"

The detective turned on his heel and stalked away, his hearty laughter ringing in his wake.

* * *

Moriarty checked the clock on the wall in his office: thirty-five minutes to curtain time. The doors would open at half past five. He planned to go up to his box around that time to enjoy watching the hall fill with patrons. Five minutes to go.

He began straightening the papers on his desk as a way of clearing his mind and found a single sheet of the Galaxy's stationery placed under the hand-carved bust of Shakespeare that served as a paperweight. "What's this?"

Writing in an unfamiliar hand covered the page. The writer appeared to have borrowed his ink as well as his paper, probably sitting in this very chair. Moriarty's eyes dropped to the signature, and a chill raised the fine hairs on his neck.

Dear Mr. Lovington,

You've cost me a comfortable early retirement on the coast of Spain. I hope I've repaid you by removing your stage manager, but that damned Archer has a way of popping back up. Beanstalk will fall flat without me, but to make sure its crushing failure is seared into the public's memory, I've left a few surprises here and there. Nothing like a few fatal injuries to give a theater a deadly reputation! It's on your shoulders now. Solve the riddles and save the show; fail just once and blood will flow.

Here are some hints to help you get started. I'm sure I'll think of more as I'm walking out the door.

1. Who gives the golden harp its strings will scream before it sings.

2. Fee fi fo foom, when Giant grows he might go boom!

3. Here's another little joke: Jack's goose lays eggs of golden smoke.

4. The guardian of the gods will fail, however loudly they might rail.

From the villain of the piece,

Frank Sparrow.

Moriarty pressed a hand to his forehead as he read the letter again. What kind of deranged mind could conceive of such things? It was one thing to target him and his family; they were standing in the way of Cudlow's scheme. But to put innocent people at risk?

He must assume the threats were real. Sebastian knew the program better than anyone; he might be able to decipher these riddles. They'd find the traps and spring them before anyone could be hurt.

He raced out of his office, clutching the letter, ignoring the throng of well-dressed people outside the front doors as he hastened across the lobby and through the hall. All the lamps were turned up full. The brightness dazzled his eyes, making the blood-red plush seats and the golden fretwork on the front of the galleries more vivid.

No time to admire the effect. He charged up the steps and fought his way through the thick red curtains hanging across the proscenium to the prompt corner in the wings, where Sebastian sat in a well-cushioned wheelchair. He'd been restored to his former self, his hair cut and combed, all traces of the scruffy beard removed. He wore a dapper gray suit with a cashmere blanket covering his legs.

"James! It's about time for you to be going up to your box, isn't it? You don't want to get stuck in the crowds streaming into the foyers."

"We have to hold them back." Moriarty handed him the letter.

Sebastian's face turned ashen. He laid a hand on his leg as if to calm a sudden pang. "He's here, I can feel it! By gad, James! He's been in here all weekend. God knows what's he's done!"

"We'll find it all. We'll fix it." Moriarty gripped Sebastian's shoulders and held his gaze, willing courage into both their hearts. "I will not allow this madman to win. Not after all we've been through. Gather the crew chiefs. Have them check every screw and thread, every pan of flash powder. Every trap, every rope . . ."

Sebastian crumpled the letter in his fist. "You're right. We'll do it." He turned to the boy waiting at his side, looking alarmed by what he'd overheard, and bade him to summon the crew chiefs to the stage. He should send another boy to the front offices to tell Mr. Tidwell to bar the doors until further notice. Another should ask the dancing master to assemble the cast in the large rehearsal room and then come up to the prompt corner for further instructions. "Run!"

The boy dashed away. Moriarty said, "I'm hoping you can solve these riddles."

Sebastian smoothed the letter out atop the prompt book in his lap. "Let's see. 'Who gives the golden harp its strings will scream before it sings?' Does he mean the prop? That's in a storeroom off the fly galleries. It first appears in Cloudland."

The sound of violins being tuned rose beyond the red curtain. Moriarty and Sebastian met each other's eyes. "I'll go," Moriarty said, moving as he spoke. He pushed through the curtain and leapt into the orchestra pit to a round of curses from the clarinetist. The harpist stood at the back, drawing the cover from her golden instrument.

"Don't touch that harp!" he bellowed.

She raised her hands like a criminal caught in the act. "Why not?"

He pushed past the other musicians and bent to inspect the harp strings. Sure enough, a silver wire, the kind used to cut cheese, winked brightly among the dull catgut strings. It would have sliced open her finger when she plucked it. Moriarty pointed at it. "Can you replace that without hurting yourself?"

She nodded mutely, eyes wide.

Moriarty paused to tell the conductor in a low voice about Sparrow's sabotage. "Have everyone double-check everything that's been in the theater overnight. Carefully!" He hauled himself back up onto the stage, returning to Sebastian for the next challenge.

"The second clue is obvious," Sebastian said. "The giant's boots. They have lifts inside to make him taller. Sparrow must have loaded them with flash powder. I've sent a cellar man to take the boots out to the alley and explode them there. Mr. Easton is an old hand; he'll adapt."

"Two down!" Moriarty rubbed his hands together. "What's next?"

"The golden eggs," Sebastian said. "They're hollow — papier-mâché painted gold. He's probably filled them with flash powder too."

"Where will I find them?"

"That's my department." A burly man in a work jacket and tweed cap came out of the wings, followed by half a dozen others. "What's going on? The boy says Frank Sparrow's gone mad and is running amok in the theater."

"That's about the size of it." Sebastian beckoned the men into a half-circle around his chair. "He's got a grudge against me and the professor here. We'll tell you about that later. For now, we've got to get this show ready to open. He may have been in here since he shot me on Christmas Eve, setting all kinds of little traps."

Everyone had already heard the news about the scenery thieves, but Sparrow's collusion came as a surprise. The men's faces darkened with anger.

"That bleedin' bastard!" MacDonald, the lighting chief said, his fists clenched. "I'll wring his bloody neck if I catch him up in my turf."

"Do it," Sebastian said with a grim smile. "But more importantly, don't let him cause any more harm."

Yancy, the newly elevated scenery chief, said, "We've had enough tricks to last us a good long while, Mr. Archer. You can count on us."

Sebastian instructed them to set their crews to work checking every last item that would be used in the pantomime. The property chief should carry the golden eggs carefully outside and give them the same treatment as the giant's boots. Noisette volunteered to fashion replacements from wads of shiny gold cloth for tonight.

"We won't start the play until I hear from each of you," Sebastian said, "so be quick — but be thorough."

The men strode off in different directions. The dancing master presented himself and received instructions to hold the cast downstairs, explaining the situation but emphasizing the fact that the stage manager and crew chiefs had everything well in hand. "Ask Lina to come up," Sebastian finished. "She can sing something that works with her Jack costume." He grinned at James. "It's a bitter night out there. We'll have to start letting people in soon, or we'll lose them. If anyone can hold the audience until we're ready, she can."

Moriarty spared a moment to marvel at this view of his versatile wife. Seeing her perform for the first time filled him with anticipation mingled with a dread nearly as great as his present fear of Frank Sparrow.

The dancing master sprang away. Sebastian sent another boy to tell the ushers to check every seat and bench in the hall by hand and to do it quickly.

"What can this last clue mean?" Moriarty pointed at the letter. "Who are the gods and why do they rail?"

"The gods are the audience in the topmost —"

The lights went out. Moriarty felt almost dizzy with the sudden disorientation of total blackness. Then screams split the dark.

Sebastian broke the spell, shouting, "He's in the cellar! Gas panel!" His stage voice projected through the whole backstage area, hopefully penetrating to the lowest level, which housed the panel controlling every gas line in the theater.

"Half a tick," he said in his normal voice. His wheelchair squeaked, followed by a few metallic clicks. Then light welled in the Davy lamp now resting on the arm of his wheelchair.

"Good man!" Moriarty clapped him on the shoulder. He let out a rush of breath, relieved to have his sight restored.

Another light moved toward them, borne by Old Sampson. "I keep a spare by my desk in case the one outside the stage door goes out."

"Excellent," Moriarty said. "Bring that one in too and lock that door. No one goes in or out." He paused to consider what ought to be done next and remembered he wasn't the one in charge back here. He shrugged an apology at his brother-in-law. "Sorry. Didn't mean to usurp your authority."

"Not at all." Sebastian smiled. "But my crew chiefs know what to do. We'll have light again in a few minutes. I'm not worried about the folks back here — they know to sit tight — but it sounds like a lot of people are stranded in the dark out front."

"They must've slipped in before Tidwell could bar the doors. I'll go speak to them." Moriarty passed through the red curtains, holding a fold back to allow a glimmer of light from the lamp. He could see a few seats past the orchestra pit, but not much farther.

He turned his face toward the inky depths at the back of the hall. "Do not be alarmed," he called in his professorial voice. He'd never lectured in an auditorium this large, of course, but some of the halls at university were fairly sizeable. "You should not have been allowed to take your seats so early. We're just giving the lighting system its final check. Stay right where you are. Do not attempt to move about. The lamps will soon be — Ah, here they come!"

Two men appeared in an upper gallery. One held a lamp while the other had a long pole with a flame at the tip. They lit the chandelier in the center of the high ceiling, raising a chorus of sighs as light bloomed through the hall. How the devil did so many people get in here already?

Then a woman screamed and someone shouted, "Oh, horrible!"

Frank Sparrow loomed out of the flickering shadows in a box on the second tier near the stage, holding a small girl by the arm, dangling her little body over the edge. She mewled piteously, her face frozen in a mask of terror. She wore a frilly dress with her hair arranged in long curls — all dressed up for the family Christmas treat. Two women clung to one another at the rear of the box weeping, their fearful gazes shifting from Sparrow to something on the floor at their feet.

Sparrow cocked his head at Moriarty. "What can you be thinking, letting all these innocent folks in here tonight? Didn't you get my letter? Any sensible person would have closed the doors as a precaution. But no, no. You Archers must squeeze out every last penny, regardless of whom you put in peril."

"It's Moriarty, you imbecile. Professor James Moriarty. At least get my name right." If he could engage the man's attention, keep him talking, perhaps he'd set the girl back inside the box. He strolled across the stage to stand as close as he could to the dangling child. "Let her go, Sparrow. It's all over. We've found most of your little traps already, and the chiefs will soon have the rest. I've set Sherlock Holmes on your master's trail. That means he'll be in jail in a matter of days, where he'll gladly throw you over to save his own skin. Give it up, man. It's finished. You can't hurt us anymore."

Sparrow looked down on him, his expressive features twisted in disdain. "Maybe not. But I can hurt her."

"No!" Moriarty lunged as Sparrow let go of the girl, diving out over the orchestra pit with his arms outstretched. He caught her and was caught in turn by the men who played the kettle drums. He handed the girl off to someone and regained his feet, craning his neck to spot his opponent, but Sparrow had vanished into the shadows at the back of the box.

Moriarty measured the distance up the aisle with his eyes and summoned a vision of the lobby, stairs, and foyers leading to the boxes. The fastest way after his quarry would be to go straight up the front.

"Give me a boost," he said to the drummers. They clambered onto the stage, where one drummer made a sling with his hands. Moriarty stepped into it and was propelled up to the first box. From there he climbed across the fronts to the second tier, where the child now risked being smothered in the embrace of her anxious family. He cut off their outpouring of gratitude with a wave of his hand and opened the door at the rear of the box. The foyer was empty. All the doors were closed.

Then Sparrow's voice echoed inside the hall. "I'm out here, Professor! Catch me if you can!" Moriarty whirled back to the front of the box in time to see something fly through the air and land on the stage, exploding into an orange smoke stinking of sulfur. More screams rose up, this time accompanied by a smattering of applause. *Good gad!* People must have thought he was part of the show, entertainment for the early arrivals.

Moriarty leaned out of his box to take a quick survey. Several dozen people — perhaps as many as a hundred — had managed to get in. A dozen or so youths had gained the uppermost gallery while a band of fashionable young men in cutaway coats occupied the center of the stalls. Couples stood at the edge of several boxes, eagerly watching as Sparrow climbed up the supporting pillar into a box on the third tier.

"What are you doing up there, Frank Sparrow?" one of the swells in the stalls shouted. "Are you going to fly?"

"I might," Sparrow called back. "But first I'll lay another egg." He threw another fist-sized ball down to explode, filling an aisle with sulfurous smoke. This time a flame shot up.

Moriarty shouted, "Ushers! Put out that fire!" Two men in navy blue Galaxy uniforms ran toward the smoke, pulling off their jackets. Sparrow disappeared.

Moriarty raced out to the foyer and up the stairs, bounding up two at a time to the third floor. He dove into the first box — mercifully empty — and grabbed the supporting pillar to lean way out.

"Here I am!" Sparrow waved from the level above. He seemed to be working diagonally, climbing across the fronts of the boxes as agile as a monkey.

One of the ushers cupped his hands to shout up at Moriarty. "He's heading for the gods!"

"Where?"

"Up here, Professor!" Rolly appeared in the uppermost gallery, waving his arms and grinning. "We're ready for him!"

"Stay away from him, do you hear me! He's dangerous!"

Fear lit a fire in Moriarty's breast, propelling him up onto the box-front. He couldn't allow Sparrow to reach those youngsters forty feet above the stalls. No one could survive such a fall.

He schooled himself to ignore the sheer drop at his back and shimmied up the pillar to grab hold of an iron lamp bracket. He pulled himself up to stand on the thing, giving silent thanks to the skilled craftsman who made it. That put him high enough to reach the top of the box-front above him. He gained the safety of that new level and swung easily around the supporting pillar into the next one over.

The climb was arduous, requiring every bit of muscle he possessed, but faster than winding up through the stairs and foyers. He kept his eyes on the painted fretwork and iron brackets under his hands and feet, ignoring Sparrow's taunts and the cries of alarm as more smoke bombs landed in the stalls. Finally, he gained the top gallery and gave himself a moment to catch his breath.

He'd never been up here. The stage seemed miles away, but he had a striking view inside some of the boxes. The long, curving gallery was filled with rows of benches, rising gradually toward the wall. Most were empty, apart from a gang of boys that included his own footman, dressed up to the nines in striped pants and top hat. "Welcome to 'eaven, Perfessor. The 'ome of the gods." Rolly grinned as if heartily enjoying the play so far.

Sparrow stood in the center aisle near the front with his hands on his hips and an insolent grin on his face. "Bit slow, aren't you, Professor?"

"It's over, Sparrow," Moriarty said, rolling up his sleeves. "There's nowhere left to run. The police will be here any minute."

"They won't be able to catch me either. Not when I can do this." He grabbed a boy by the arm and flung him toward the railing. Moriarty's heart stopped for a second, but luckily the sturdy barrier held. The boy rolled onto his knees and scuttled away from the edge.

"Rolly, clear these benches. Get the boys well out of the way." Moriarty removed his jacket, handing it to his footman and rolling up his sleeves. "I'm going to give this varlet the sound thrashing he deserves."

"You're in for a treat now, old chums!" Rolly told his mates, shooing them back.

Sparrow beckoned Moriarty forward with both hands. "That's more like it. Why waste time on these paltry substitutes when you're the one I really —"

His head snapped back as Moriarty punched him smack in that ever-gabbling mouth. The time for talk was long past. He danced back, bouncing on his toes, and neatly dodged Sparrow's wild swing. The man's arms were longer, but Moriarty took weekly boxing lessons at the London Athletic Club as part of his regular round of physical exercises. He sank another blow into the center of the tall man's body, pushing him away from the half-circle of cheering boys.

"Get 'im, Perfessor," Rolly said. "Show him what for." The other boys echoed, "Get 'im, Perfessor, get 'im."

They distracted him for a critical moment, allowing Sparrow to strike a glancing blow on the side of Moriarty's head, knocking him sideways. But he recovered quickly and came back fast, stepping inside his opponent's reach to hammer home a series of short, hard blows to the body, throwing him off balance. Then he took a big step back, drew his right fist over his shoulder, and drove it straight into Sparrow's sneering face.

His head snapped back, pulling him off his feet. He stumbled backward against the railing, which broke behind him with a loud crack, the whole section separating from the rest. Sparrow screamed as man and barrier flew into space, falling forty feet to the floor below.

"Stand back," Moriarty commanded the boys, spanning the gap with his outstretched arms. Then he stepped gingerly to the brink and peered down into the stalls. Sparrow lay sprawled across a row of seats, his head twisted at a most unnatural angle. Dead. Two of the ushers moved toward him. Moriarty called to them, "Get him out of here."

He turned his attention to the broken barrier. Now he could see where the boards on either side of the four-foot opening had been sawed nearly through. Sparrow had used the same trick with the ropes on the gondola, leaving just enough material to hold the piece in place until someone trusted it to support their weight.

Moriarty instructed Rolly to block the gap with benches and keep everyone clear. He put his jacket on and ran down the many flights of stairs to the lobby. He searched out Mr. Tidwell and said, "It's over. Sparrow's dead, caught in his own trap. As soon as they carry him out, we can get started."

He didn't linger to answer questions, but sped on through the swinging doors. The two ushers had lifted Sparrow's broken body and laid him out in the aisle. Now they were clearing up the debris from the section of broken railing. Moriarty conferred with them about the seats of death, as one of them put it. They agreed that a black cloth would be found and fitted snugly over the four affected seats. If anyone objected to being shut out of their favorite spot, they could be brought up to Moriarty's box. It had an inferior view of the stage, but greater status.

People started coming in behind him, bringing gusts of cool air and wafts of perfume. He moved on down the aisle, past the questions from the young swells in the cutaway coats, and up the stairs at the side of the apron. Backstage once again, he strode over to Sebastian in the prompt corner. "I'm happy to report that Mr. Sparrow solved the fourth riddle himself, ending the game. He lost."

Sebastian chuckled. "I heard. Good work, James! I won't grieve for that slippery bastard."

"Nor I. An ugly business." Moriarty shook the image out of his mind and pulled out his pocket watch. "Great Scott, it's half past six! How long before we're ready?"

"Another half an hour, I'm afraid. We've been finding all sorts of little traps. Nothing terribly dangerous, mostly nuisances like glue inside shoes and gloves. Enough to embarrass an actor and cause delays on stage. But add up enough of that sort of thing and the show is spoiled."

Someone across the stage called, "The hall is filling up fast. It's like a dam has broken out there!"

"Oh dear," Moriarty said. "They'll just have to be patient. I'll go make another announcement." He turned around to go out one more time, barely hearing Sebastian's suggestion that he let one of the actors take over. He waded through the two layers of red velvet and stood again in the center of the stage.

As he emerged, one of the young swells called, "There he is! That's the fellow who did for Mad Frank Sparrow!"

"Perfessor Moriarty!" Rolly shouted from way up at the top of the hall. "Hip hip hooray!" His chums repeated the cheer, along with a fresh crowd of folks in the gallery who rose to their feet and joined in.

The swells started clapping their hands together loudly. In a matter of seconds, everyone between the gods and the orchestra pit was clapping as well, two thousand hands thundering like a tidal wave swelling through the vast hall. Everywhere he looked he saw faces — men, women, children, thousands of them — beaming at him with with broad smiles and glowing eyes.

Moriarty was stunned, stricken speechless, pinned to the strip of stage between the pit and the velvet wall. He stood with his mouth half-open, mesmerized, for some uncountable span of time.

Then music penetrated the numbness of his mind. Some heavenly voice was singing "Beautiful Dreamer," moving toward him on this narrow precipice. Then the orchestra started playing the same tune, and the swells in the front rows started crying, "Lina! Lina! It's Lina Lovington!" Her name echoed up the tiers to the top.

A hand touched his shoulder and he turned to see his wife singing, apparently, to him. The thousand faces disappeared, replaced by the one he knew and loved the best. He smiled at her and she smiled back, stroking his cheek, taking his hand, and turning slightly away to include the audience as she continued her song. Her voice soared into the hall, filling it, pushing back the sea of noise as the audience fell into a rapt silence.

The house lights went down, and a circle of limelight fell around the two of them. Angelina took a step away, still holding his hand, and finished her song on an arching note whose echoes rang for a long moment before the hall erupted into another round of thunderous applause.

But this time he wasn't alone. Moriarty laughed as his wife coaxed him into taking a bow — the first, and hopefully last, of his life. "My husband, ladies and gentlemen!" she called. She threw kisses to the crowd with her free hand, then led him into another bow. She stood smiling, waiting until the applause tapered off, then leaned toward him with a wink. "I think that's enough for your debut, don't you, darling?"

"More than enough." He drew in a deep breath and blew it out in a rush of pure exhilaration. Then he noticed, for the first time, that she'd rushed out to rescue him without getting properly dressed. She had nothing on but a filmy blouse and puffy pants shorter than her chemise, with a pair of pink tights exposing every curve of her long, shapely legs. The woman was practically naked, in full view of a thousand people!

"My dear, what are you wearing!" Moriarty pulled off his coat and wrapped it around her waist, tying its arms firmly behind her while laughter rang out and flowers pelted the stage.

HISTORICAL NOTES

I fashioned everyone in this book out of whole cloth, except for Sir Arthur Conan Doyle's immortals: Sherlock Holmes and James Moriarty. I reshaped them for my own narrative purposes. This is one of the risks of fame — that your works will outlive you and become the playthings of lesser minds.

This one's set in a theater, because Angelina hinted about getting back on the stage so often in book two, *Moriarty Takes His Medicine.* I made up the Galaxy Theatre of Varieties on Leicester Square, though of course the square is real. I mention the Alhambra Theatre, once a very real, very popular theater and music hall on the east side of Leicester Square. I made up another place called the Paramount, but the Royal Brunswick in Islington was real. There's a wonderful website -- www.Arthur Lloyd.co.uk/LondonsLostTheatres.htm — which provides histories of many delightful houses of entertainment in the Victorian period, often with old photographs to go with the descriptions. I shop around in there when I'm looking for a real one. The Paramount Theater inspiration came from right here in River City — Austin, Texas.

Sir Herbert Beerbohm Tree makes a brief appearance, hosting a party in his home in South Kensington. I would have dragged in more historical persons of the acting persuasion, because they were all interesting people, but they have their own histories, which had nothing whatsoever to do with my plot! Short-sighted of them, when you think about it. Sir Herbert was about Angelina's age and one of the versatile, hard-working actor-managers of the day. The most famous of those was Henry Irving. Women did it too, like Marie Wilton and Sarah Bernhardt.

Edward Solomon and William Horace Lindgard are mentioned as examples of bigamists. Real men and really bigamists, whom Angelina very likely read about in *The Stage* or similar. That newspaper is real too, and still going.

I borrowed bits and pieces from pantomimes produced in the late Victorian era from Jeffrey Richards' *The Golden Age of Pantomime: Slapstick, Spectacle and Subversion in Victorian England* (2015; London: I.B. Tauris.) My whole setting came out of that book and Michael R. Booth's *Theatre in the Victorian Age* (1991; Cambridge: Cambridge University Press.) Although my theater was safer and saner, apart from the murderer running loose, than the real ones.

ABOUT THE AUTHOR

Anna Castle holds an eclectic set of degrees: BA in the Classics, MS in Computer Science, and a Ph.D. in Linguistics. She has had a correspondingly eclectic series of careers: waitressing, software engineering, grammar-writing, a short stint as an associate professor, and managing a digital archive. Historical fiction combines her lifelong love of stories and learning. She physically resides in Austin, Texas, but mentally counts herself a queen of infinite space.

BOOKS BY ANNA CASTLE

Keep up with all my books and short stories with my newsletter. Sign up at www.annacastle.com

The Francis Bacon Series

Book 1, Murder by Misrule

Francis Bacon is charged with investigating the murder of a fellow barrister at Gray's Inn. He recruits his unwanted protégé Thomas Clarady to do the tiresome legwork. The son of a privateer, Clarady will do anything to climb the Elizabethan social ladder. Bacon's powerful uncle Lord Burghley suspects Catholic conspirators of the crime, but other motives quickly emerge. Rival barristers contend for the murdered man's legal honors and wealthy clients. Highly-placed courtiers are implicated as the investigation reaches from Whitehall to the London streets. Bacon does the thinking; Clarady does the fencing. Everyone has something up his pinked and padded sleeve. Even the brilliant Francis Bacon is at a loss — and in danger — until he sees through the disguises of the season of Misrule.

Book 2, Death by Disputation

Thomas Clarady is recruited to spy on the increasingly rebellious Puritans at Cambridge University. Francis Bacon is his spymaster; his tutor in both tradecraft and religious politics. Their commission gets off to a deadly start when Tom finds his chief informant hanging from the roof beams. Now he must catch a murderer as well as a seditioner. His first suspect is volatile poet Christopher Marlowe, who keeps turning up in the wrong places.

Dogged by unreliable assistants, chased by three lusty women, and harangued daily by the exacting Bacon, Tom risks his very soul to catch the villains and win his reward.

Book 3, The Widows Guild

London, 1588: Someone is turning Catholics into widows, taking advantage of armada fever to mask the crimes. Francis Bacon is charged with identifying the murderer by the Andromache Society, a widows' guild led by his formidable aunt. He must free his friends from the Tower, track an exotic poison, and untangle multiple crimes to determine if the motive is patriotism, greed, lunacy — or all three.

Book 4, Publish and Perish.

It's 1589 and England is embroiled in a furious pamphlet war between an impudent Puritan calling himself Martin Marprelate and London's wittiest writers. The archbishop wants Martin to hang. The Privy Council wants the tumult to end. But nobody knows who Martin is or where he's hiding his illegal press.

Then two writers are strangled, mistaken for Thomas Nashe, the pamphleteer who is hot on Martin's trail. Francis Bacon is tasked with stopping the murders — and catching Martin, while he's about it. But the more he learns, the more he fears Martin may be someone dangerously close to home.

Can Bacon and his band of intelligencers stop the strangler before another writer dies, without stepping on Martin's possibly very important toes?

Book 5, Let Slip the Dogs

It's Midsummer, 1591, at Richmond Palace, and love is in the air. Gallant courtiers sport with great ladies while Tom and Trumpet bring their long-laid plans to fruition at last. Everybody's doing it — even Francis Bacon enjoys a private liaison with the secretary to the new French ambassador. But the Queen loathes scandal and will punish anyone rash enough to get caught.

Still, it's all in a summer day until a young man is found dead. He had few talents beyond a keen nose for gossip and was doubtless murdered to keep a secret. But what sort — romantic, or political?

They carried different penalties: banishment from court or a traitor's death. Either way, worth killing to protect.

Bacon wants nothing more than to leave things alone. He has no position and no patron; in fact, he's being discouraged from investigating. But can he live with himself if another innocent person dies?

The Professor & Mrs. Moriarty Series

Book 1, Moriarty Meets His Match

Professor James Moriarty has but one desire left in his shattered life: to prevent the man who ruined him from harming anyone else. Then he meets amber-eyed Angelina Gould and his world turns upside down.

At an exhibition of new inventions, an exploding steam engine kills a man. When Moriarty tries to figure out what happened, he comes up against Sherlock Holmes, sent to investigate by Moriarty's old enemy. Holmes collects evidence that points at Moriarty, who realizes he must either solve the crime or swing it for it himself. He soon uncovers trouble among the board members of the engine company and its unscrupulous promoter. Moriarty tries to untangle those relationships, but everywhere he turns, he meets the alluring Angelina. She's playing some game, but what's her goal? And whose side is she on?

Between them, Holmes and Angelina push Moriarty to his limits -- and beyond. He'll have to lose himself to save his life and win the woman he loves.

Book 2, Moriarty Takes His Medicine

James and Angelina Moriarty are settling into their new marriage and their fashionable new home — or trying to. But James has too little to occupy his mind and Angelina has too many secrets pressing on her heart. They fear they'll never learn to live together. Then Sherlock Holmes comes to call with a challenging case. He suspects a prominent Harley Street specialist of committing murders for hire, sending patients home from his private hospital with deadly doses or fatal conditions. Holmes intends to investigate, but the doctor's clientele is exclusively female. He needs Angelina's help.

While Moriarty, Holmes, and Watson explore the alarming number of ways a doctor can murder his patients with impunity, Angelina enters into treatment with their primary suspect, posing as a nervous woman who fears her husband wants to be rid of her. Then a hasty conclusion and an ill-considered word drive James and Angelina apart, sending her deep into danger. Now they must find the courage to trust each other as they race the clock to win justice for the murdered women before they become victims themselves.

Book 3, Moriarty Brings Down the House

An old friend brings a strange problem to Professor and Mrs. Moriarty: either his theater is being haunted by an angry ghost or someone is trying to drive him into bankruptcy. He wants the Moriartys to make it stop; more, he wants Angelina to play the lead in his Christmas pantomime and James to contribute a large infusion of much-needed cash.

The Moriartys gladly accept the fresh challenges, but the day they arrive at the theater, the stage manager dies. It isn't an accident, and it is most definitely not a ghost. While Angelina works backstage turning up secrets and old grudges, James follows the money in search of a motive. The pranks grow deadlier and more frequent. Then someone sets Sherlock Holmes on the trail, trying to catch our sleuths crossing the line into crime. How far will the Moriartys have to go to keep the show afloat? And will they all make it to opening night in one piece?

Printed in Great Britain
by Amazon

74318940R00161